Oh God...
Where s...

Claire knew the pepper spray would buy
her five seconds, ten at most, since she'd
missed hitting his eyes directly. She kicked
off her low business pumps and hit her full
running speed within a few strides. When
she risked one more glance back, she saw
the killer running after her.

Her bare feet slapped on the slick pavement as fast as she could make them move.
She could feel the force of the man's will
reaching out to her. It was almost a physical
touch. She was terrified that she would feel
his hand grab her shoulder or hair at any
second.

Then she heard the sawing breath of the
man behind her. And she knew if he caught
her, she would die. . . .

"Heather Lowell is going to set the gold
standard for modern romantic suspense.
Her writing is fresh, hot, romantic, and
scary. I can't wait for her next book."
Jayne Ann Krentz

HEATHER LOWELL

WHEN THE STORM BREAKS

HarperTorch
An Imprint of HarperCollinsPublishers

HARPERTORCH
An Imprint of HarperCollins*Publishers*
10 East 53rd Street
New York, New York 10022-5299

Copyright © 2003 by Two of a Kind, Inc.
ISBN: 0-06-054212-8

First HarperTorch paperback printing: August 2003

HarperCollins ®, HarperTorch™, and ❦™ are trademarks of Harper-Collins Publishers Inc.

Printed in the United States of America

Visit HarperTorch on the World Wide Web at www.harpercollins.com

10 9 8 7 6 5 4 3 2 1

*To my parents,
for knowing when to catch me,
and when to let me fly.
And always believing
that the latter was possible.*

Chapter 1

Washington, D.C.
July
Friday evening

*"Southern Belle, thirty, seeks prince to carry
her off to his castle and take care of her forever."*

"What do you think, dear?" Peggy Gallagher looked over the table at her new client.

Claire Lambert shifted in her chair, struggling for a response that wouldn't offend Peggy. She turned to her friend Afton for assistance, since she had been the one to talk her into joining a dating service in the first place.

"Doesn't that caption sound like something to grab a man's attention, Marie Claire?" Peggy pressed.

Deciding Afton wasn't going to help, Claire thought about her options. She might have been tired after a long day—a long week, really—but not tired enough to let that gem get by her untouched. Joining the Gallaghers' dating service was humiliating enough, but having a blurb like the one Peggy had suggested appear next to her picture would be pathetic.

Besides, she hated being called Marie Claire.

Claire worked hard to look serious. "I was thinking more along the lines of '*Businesswoman, thirty, has castle, seeks prince to help with upkeep and provide occasional foot massage.*'"

Claire's deadpan expression was angelic. She had spent her formative years tormenting the nuns at Our Heavenly Savior Catholic Girls School in New Orleans, so getting Peggy's back up was easy.

Peggy drew herself up straight in her chair, inhaling through her flared nostrils, while across the table, her daughter and business partner covered laughter with a cough. Afton Gallagher truly enjoyed seeing someone make her mother pucker up—it happened so rarely.

"Mom, why don't you make sure the computer is set up for Claire to view the eligible candidates. She and I can work on her bio later," Afton said, careful to not meet Claire's gaze.

Peggy surveyed them both for a long moment. "All right. But really, Marie Claire, you should put more thought into developing the caption to go with your picture in the catalogue. It's the first impression the male candidates will have of you, and you certainly don't want to come across as too flip. Or assertive. Men don't care for that in a young lady."

Peggy pushed back from the table, straightened her skirt with a practiced move, and went out the door of the conference room. Claire looked closely at her departing figure, trying to see if Peggy was, indeed, wearing nylons and a slip in the sweltering heat of a Washington, D.C. summer.

Claire looked up and caught Afton rolling her eyes.

They shared a moment of silent humor over Peggy's stodgy approach to both fashion and romance in the twenty-first century.

Then Claire straightened in her chair, turning dancing black eyes to Afton. "Hey, I left out the part about 'providing foot massages in exchange for the occasional blow job.'"

Afton laughed out loud. It was just like Claire to say something outrageous and make her forget that it was after nine on a Friday evening, and she had been working without a break for the last seven days. She'd had to stay late tonight to accommodate Claire's busy schedule, but she didn't mind doing her friend this favor. Besides, it had been Afton's nagging that had convinced Claire to give the dating service a try in the first place. The least she could do was offer moral support.

"I'm suddenly not sure about signing up for a dating service," Claire said once she'd stopped laughing. "It seems so, I don't know, sad. Needy." That was one word she would never use to describe herself. She hated being in a situation where that particular shoe might fit.

"Don't be ridiculous," Afton said quickly, not wanting Claire to back out now that she had finally dragged her in. "We went over this before. You're paying for a service—special friend's price, I might add—just like getting your carpets cleaned or your car washed. We're providing you with something you don't have time to do yourself. It's as simple as that."

"Maybe, but I never had to fill out my preferences for eyes, hair, and build on the carpet cleaner or car wash guy before." Claire's eyes were serious, yet she gave a half smile. Afton had become a very close friend in the past six months because Claire admired intelligence, guts, and determination. She didn't want to wimp out and waste everyone's time. "Oh, never mind. Let's go look at our selection of eligible studs in the catalogue before I lose my nerve completely."

Chapter 2

Several hours later Claire watched the elevator doors swish closed on the offices of Camelot Dating Services, Inc. Finally, an end to what had to be one of the more humiliating evenings she had endured in her thirty years on the planet.

How had she let Afton talk her into diving back into the dating pool? And with a *dating service*—talk about the deep end. Claire cringed every time she thought about it. After looking at hundreds of pictures of male candidates, and reading hundreds of intros ranging from mildly clever to downright cheesy, she was convinced she'd never find anyone worth dating in a single's catalogue.

Monday she'd call Afton and tell her it had all been a big mistake.

The elevator doors opened into the lobby. Claire passed a heavyset security guard on her way out to the street.

"Want me to call you a cab, miss?" The guard apparently hoped she would answer no, because he barely looked up from the magazine he was flipping through.

"No, thank you. I'm just going to walk to Dupont Circle and catch the bus into Georgetown. There's one coming by just after midnight."

"Gonna get wet. Storm's about to break." This was offered with another indolent flip of the pages, punctuated by a rumble of thunder outside.

"I'm prepared—my umbrella is right here." She was always prepared. Checking the Weather Channel every morning before getting dressed was part of her comfortable daily routine.

On her way out the heavy revolving door, she hesitated a moment too long before stepping through the opening. The door jammed on the full-length umbrella trailing behind her. She set her jaw, pulled the umbrella free, and left before seeing whether the noise had been enough to stir the security guard from his comfortable perch.

As she hurried down the street, Claire tried to open the mangled umbrella decorated with a whimsical depiction of blue skies and sunshine. It stopped opening after no more than a few inches. Leaves rustled as a gust of wind brought a light spatter of raindrops down across her silk blouse.

"Beautiful. Livvie's going to kill me," Claire muttered out loud. The umbrella had been a present from her best friend Olivia, brought back after a visit to the Metropolitan Museum in New York.

Claire checked her watch as another gust of wind ruffled her collar. She'd better hurry if she wanted to catch that bus. Despite the late hour, she chose a shortcut across the grounds of one of the area's numerous schools. She took a canister of pepper spray from her purse and trotted across the poorly lit area. As she hurried across the blacktop playground, she rehearsed what she would tell Afton when she canceled her dating service membership on Monday.

Just tell her you've had terrible luck dating in the past, that it's only ever brought boredom or disaster. Claire ducked her head to keep the rain out of her eyes. *Tell her you've come to your senses and aren't really that desperate for someone to go with to museum exhibitions and quiet dinners.*

She laughed humorlessly at her own pitiful dating aspirations.

Lightning flashed, briefly illuminating the lonely playground with its creaking swings and jungle gym. When thunder crashed directly overhead, Claire paused. Lightning came again. She counted the seconds until the thunder as she struggled to open her umbrella.

No luck.

Raindrops came faster now, driven by the sticky, restless wind. A few dark curls were pulled from the neat twist she wore while at work.

As she pushed hair back out of her face, she began to jog in earnest, thinking of the tiny shelter provided at the bus stop. If the storm got really bad, she could always go into one of the bars off the Circle and call for a cab. Right now the rain was a welcome break from the night's oppressive humidity.

Claire rounded a corner and saw a dark shape about ten feet away. When lightning flashed, she saw the shape was a man. He had his back to her and was leaning over something. Abruptly he bent down and moved his right arm in several precise, controlled motions. As he rose and turned toward her, she saw that he was standing over a woman sprawled on her back, dead eyes open to the rain-filled sky.

Claire's heart stopped. An icy-hot feeling slithered through her belly. Her pulse pounded in her ears, blocking out the sound of wind and thunder.

As lightning flashed again, her stunned eyes shifted

from the body on the ground to the man. He was looking directly at her, holding a long object in his right hand. Slowly his lips turned up into an odd, closed-mouth smile. She stared in shock, focused on his mouth, as the image of a photo flashed in her mind. Her paralyzed lungs filled with a gasp.

She had seen his smile before.

The man lunged toward her.

A knife. He has a knife.

Claire's survival instinct kicked in, along with a dozen years of urban-woman-living-alone advice. She blasted the man with her pepper spray and flung the useless umbrella at him in an awkward left-handed throw.

He made a hoarse sound as the spray hit his forehead and splashed his eyes.

Run, Claire. Run!

Heeding the voice screaming inside her head, she dropped her purse and the now useless canister and ran. When she looked back for a second, she saw that the killer was holding his hands to his eyes as he turned his face up to the steady rain.

She knew the spray would only buy her five seconds, ten at most, since she'd missed hitting his eyes directly. She kicked off her low business pumps and hit her full running speed within a few strides. Soon her breath was rasping in and out of her lungs. When she risked one more glance back, she saw the killer running after her.

Oh, God. Oh, God.

She snapped her head forward and refused to look again.

Where should I go? Back to Camelot and the pudgy security guard?

She paused for a heartbeat, then decided to take her

chances with the Friday night crowds at Dupont Circle's restaurants and clubs.

Feet pounded closer behind her.

She pushed her burning legs into running faster. She was in decent shape from regular workouts, but sprinting wasn't part of her routine. Her bare feet slapped on the slick pavement as fast as she could make them move. Raindrops hit her mouth as she tried to breathe. They tasted sweet, and eased the dryness of her lips.

She could feel the force of the man's will reaching out to her. It was almost a physical touch. She was terrified that she would feel his hand grab her shoulder or hair at any second.

With a tight sound of fear and exertion, she turned left and raced down a dark backstreet filled with Dumpsters and cardboard boxes. She thought there was a bar or something on the corner at the end of the alley.

It never occurred to Claire to call for help. With her body in pure survival mode and her throat paralyzed by fear, she focused on escape. She had to get to a safe place before he caught up with her.

God, how long is this street?

She felt as if she were running flat out yet standing still. The end of the alley seemed no closer than when she'd started. For the first time she wondered if she would get away. Then she heard the sawing breath of the man behind her and knew if he caught her she would die.

Fresh adrenaline shot through her, giving her a rush of strength. She opened the gap between herself and the man chasing her.

When she finally reached the street, Claire's instincts took her to the right. Her heart sank when she saw that the area was empty—no cars, no pedestrians, everyone had been driven inside by the summer rain that continued to pour down in wind-driven waves.

But the faint pulsing beat of music drew her forward. Two doors up the street she saw neon lights coming from windows set at basement level—a nightclub. A set of dark metal stairs was all that separated Claire from safety. She threw herself down the steps as fast as she could force her trembling legs to move.

Risking one more glance behind her, Claire didn't see any sign of the man chasing her, but she knew he could come around the corner at any moment. She paused to look again, and the momentary break in her rhythm caused her bare feet to slip on the metal stairs.

Between one heartbeat and the next, her feet went out from under her. With a defeated cry, she felt herself falling. When she struck the back of her head with brutal force on the metal edge of a stair, the world went briefly white, then black.

Chapter 3

*B*itch.
   The man couldn't believe she had outrun him.

What was she, a fucking gazelle?

He'd planned the evening perfectly—things were supposed to go smoothly, just like the other times. And everything had, until she'd shown up.

Frustrated rage gave him strength. He threw himself around the corner of the alley and into the street. A moment of rational thought slowed him down. He looked around; the woman was gone.

Did she get away?

He paused to calm his breathing. His other senses began to process the surrounding environment—the wet pavement smell and the steam rising lazily off the street. The thunderstorm was moving to the east, leaving behind cooler temperatures.

As his breathing slowed, he heard music nearby, a throbbing undertone of bass that penetrated the sound of the rain. The volume increased. Doors opened, and a rush of voices added to the din. The man slowly approached a stairway that led down to the source of the music. He glanced up at the sign over the entrance.

Suds 'n Studs—Ladies Only.

A strip bar. How very tacky. Cautiously looking around the corner and down the stairway, he saw a mass of women huddled around something on the steps. The gazelle, apparently.

"Is she breathing?"

"God, what happened?"

"Her eyes are twitching, is she having a seizure?"

The questions came rapid fire, directed at no one in particular. Bellowing for someone inside to call 911, a muscled bouncer tried to clear the excited patrons away from the stairs. From just inside the doors, a woman pushed through the crowd, shouting that she was a doctor. The music stopped abruptly.

The killer took in the scene, assessing his options. Too many witnesses. He'd better cut his losses. The injured woman wouldn't be able to clearly identify him—it had been rainy and dark.

Besides, he'd take care of her soon enough.

He turned away from the strip bar and headed down the street towards Dupont Circle. Once he was a few blocks away, he paused under a streetlight to pull the gazelle's small purse from his jacket. He'd stopped to pick up the handbag, which was one of the reasons she'd outrun him.

At least that's what he told himself.

He flipped open the wallet, quickly reading through the information on her driver's license. Marie Claire Lambert, 30, Georgetown address. And keys to let him in.

The man's mouth twisted upward in a cruel smile. "You're dead, Marie Claire."

Chapter 4

Officer Reggie Garfield had responded to calls at the Suds 'n Studs before. When it came over the radio that a woman was down in front of the entrance, he figured this would be a fairly routine incident involving Friday night, alcohol, and a boisterous strip club. Backup was on the way, and the ambulance was a couple of minutes behind him. It should be an open-and-shut report. He figured to be back on the streets before 2 A.M.

Garfield stepped out of his patrol car. He automatically moved to put the nightstick in its belt loop, shifting his love handles briefly when they interfered with this process. He grabbed the shoulder microphone to radio back that he had arrived on the scene. His first job would be to find someone who knew what had happened. He went down the stairs to get a look at the victim and start gathering information.

"Stand back, everybody, coming through." The words came automatically from Garfield's mouth.

He saw a huge, heavily muscled guy in a sea of females. "You the bouncer? Get everyone back in the club and clear the way for the paramedics." He pitched his voice louder. "Ladies, the show is over, please go back inside and let us do our job."

The crowd reluctantly began breaking up. Most of the women stopped just inside the open double doors to the club, milling and chatting about how awful it was, stretching their necks to get one last glimpse of the scene.

"You a nurse?" he asked a woman who had remained crouched next to the unconscious victim, monitoring her pulse.

The woman looked up in brief irritation but kept a hand on the victim's shoulder as if to hold her down. "No, I'm a doctor. Third-year resident." When the officer looked surprised, she rolled her eyes. "They do have female doctors, you know."

He sighed. Great—attitude to go along with his late-night call. He got out his notebook. "She slip down the steps, then?"

"I don't know. Some women came out of the club and said they found her at the bottom of the stairs. Nobody knows her. She took a hell of a blow to the back of her head, but I'm not sure if it was on the stairs."

Garfield raised his eyebrows. "You don't think she just fell in the rain? Maybe had too much to drink?"

"I'll tell you what I do know—the victim has a serious head wound. She was disoriented and incoherent, and kept trying to get up when I first arrived. She's got no ID, no purse. And look here—she's barefoot and there are cuts all over the soles of her feet." The doctor lifted a white bar towel that had been wrapped around the victim's feet. She paused, then spoke softly. "She was also saying some pretty scary stuff."

The cop came to attention. Leaning over to look at the woman's dirty, bloodied feet, he made notes in his book.

"What kinda stuff?"

"They were broken phrases. Like I said, she was disoriented. I did catch a couple of them, though. 'He killed her. I saw them, at the school. Run!' She repeated that last one while struggling to sit up. We had to get the bouncer to hold her down."

"She seems quiet now—think she'll be all right?" Garfield paused in his note-taking.

"I don't know." The young doctor reached again to take the victim's pulse. "I'm not a neurologist. She lost consciousness just before you arrived, but her vital signs are stable. She needs to get to a hospital and have a CT scan done. If the injury is severe enough, she might need surgery."

The doctor gently pushed back wet black curls from the woman's white face, then checked her pupils with the bouncer's flashlight.

Garfield left the steps and went to talk to one of the officers that had arrived as backup. "Start talking to witnesses inside. I'll get the doc's contact info and get the vic on her way to the hospital."

An ambulance siren grew slowly louder, its sound distorted by the humid night air.

Garfield cleared the crowd that had begun to form again by the time the ambulance arrived. The doctor was giving two paramedics instructions as they strapped the victim onto a backboard, and several firemen waited to help carry the unconscious woman up the stairs. As the group reached the ambulance doors, the doctor approached him.

"I'm going to ride to the hospital with her." She stopped, took a deep breath, and then spoke before she lost her nerve. "Look, there's a school a couple of blocks from here. A middle school or something. I don't want to tell you how to do your job, but if you'd seen how scared she was. . . ." The woman's voice trailed off.

"Don't worry, Doc. I'm on my way over there right now. We'll check it out."

Garfield helped the doctor into the ambulance and closed the doors, banging his fist twice on the side in a signal for the driver to take off.

Chapter 5

Detective Sean Richter swore luridly when his pager went off in the darkness, sounding like a crazed hornet as it buzzed on the nightstand. His curses became more creative when he saw the time. 2 A.M. He'd worked until an hour ago on one of the cases he was investigating.

He worked in the cold cases section of the Homicide Division for the DCPD. Along with his partner, Sean handled cases that had no clues, few leads, and no real suspects after six to twelve months of active investigation. He was assigned to these difficult cases full time, but there weren't enough hours in the day to do the job, so he often worked nights as well.

He grabbed his phone and dialed the number in the pager's glowing display.

"Richter. What's up?" he said in a rusty voice.

"Sean, my man, you owe me big for this."

The voice belonged to a cheerful night person. Officer Ambrose "Banjo" Caulley often sat up until dawn listening to his police scanner and monitoring the communications of other D.C. Police Department staff.

"How about I be the judge of that, Banjo? What've you got?"

"A call came through a little while ago. Murder at a school near Dupont Circle. Young female, multiple stab wounds. She was practically still warm." Banjo drew his story out with relish.

"I'm listening," Sean said, rubbing the back of his neck tiredly.

"Seems the victim, a dark-haired female in her midtwenties, was stabbed in the lower abdomen three or four times with a real big knife. No other signs of trauma. No sexual assault, no robbery."

Sean's pulse picked up. The preliminary description was similar to two other murders he was working with the Cold Cases Unit—cases he believed were related. But there wasn't enough evidence to bear out this theory yet. His other cases involved prostitutes who were also drug addicts, women on the seamy edge of society.

"Was the victim a working girl?"

"Not clear yet. But here's what you're really going to like. They've got a witness, someone they think saw the crime."

"You're shitting me." Sean jumped to his feet and reached for the jeans he had left hanging over the back of a chair. "Who? Where is he right now?" He pulled the jeans on over his boxers, then put on and buttoned his shirt one-handed while feeling around blindly with his feet in search of shoes.

"Hang on a second, I'm getting to it. The report is that an unidentified woman fell down the stairs at Suds 'n Studs. That's a male strip club on Dupont Circle. Accord-

ing to people who helped her at the scene, she was incoherent and hysterical, saying something about seeing a
man kill a woman at a school. The first officer on the
scene went to a middle school off the Circle, just to check
things out. He found the murder victim and called it in.
Then I called you."

"Where's the witness now?" Sean asked.

He turned on the light, slipped on his shoulder harness,
checked that the weapon on the nightstand was ready to
go, and put it in the holster.

"She knocked herself silly, probably from falling down
the stairs. She was taken to GWU Hospital, but I don't
think you can see her yet. She was apparently unconscious when they left the club, so she'll probably be tied
up in the ER for a while."

"Damn. Is she going to be all right?"

"Officer on the scene couldn't say. Why don't you head
out to the school first, talk to him if he's still there?
Name's Reggie Garfield. You can swing by the hospital in
the morning."

"I'm on my way. What's the address?" Sean scribbled
the information on a tablet while attaching his pager and
cell phone to his belt. "I owe you big time, buddy."

"I know." Banjo's tone said he would enjoy collecting.
"You want me to call Burke for you?"

"Not yet. His lady friend got back in town last night and
is leaving again tomorrow, so he's probably, ah, engaged
right now. Anyway, I've been working the other two cases
most recently. I'll give him a call when I get a feel for
whether this murder is related to the others. I'll have my
cell phone on if you hear anything more."

Sean hung up and headed out the door. He reached the
scene of the murder within thirty minutes. Despite the fact

that it was nearly 3 A.M., gawkers were gathered around the site, drawn by the flashing lights and predawn activity. They were held back by yellow crime scene tape, with a uniformed officer on the other side.

Sean pushed his way through a knot of milling teenagers. "Jesus, where are your parents? Let me get through, here—and go home!"

Even though he was a head taller and much stronger than the teens, they gave him a lot of attitude. He ignored it, flipped open his ID for the uniform on duty, and asked, "Where's Garfield?"

"Over there," the cop said, pointing toward a heavyset patrolman by the victim's body.

"Officer Garfield?" Sean called out to him.

"Yeah."

Sean approached him, ID in hand. "Detective Sean Richter. I'm with the Homicide Cold Cases Unit. I want to see if there might be some overlap with this murder and a couple of ongoing investigations."

"What makes you think there's any connection? Forensics hasn't even assessed the scene yet."

Obviously Garfield was feeling a little protective of his crime scene. But if the cases were linked, Sean's claim would take precedence.

"Similarities in the victim's physical profile, cause of death, and a hunch," Sean said. "If you'll tell me what you know about this victim, I'll get out of your hair and wait for the report to come out. I just wanted to see the crime scene myself."

Garfield raised his eyebrows. "Victim is in her mid-twenties, dark hair, slender build. No sign of sexual assault, but we'll wait for the medical examiner to confirm. Cause of death looks to be multiple stab wounds to the abdomen. Her purse was found nearby, wallet inside. Credit cards, driver's license, and eighteen dollars in cash. She has gold jewelry as well, so I'm thinking robbery wasn't the motive."

"Do you recognize her from the streets? Does she have any kind of record?"

"Nah, she's not a working girl. The name on the ID comes back as a teacher at this school, Renata Mendes."

Sean processed the information. The victim's physical profile fit with the other cases, all young Hispanic females. But not the teacher bit. The two other murdered women had been drug addicts who had sold their bodies to support crack or meth habits. "What kind of stab wounds?"

"Big ones. Lots of blood."

"Any defensive wounds?"

"Not so you can tell. Looks like the perp was a strong guy, and he probably surprised her."

That fit. "Who reported the murder?"

"Now that's the funny part. Seems there might be a witness. In fact, that's what sent us up here in the first place." He briefed Sean on the incident with the woman injured at the Suds 'n Studs club.

"Were you able to speak to her?" Sean asked over the sudden squawking of Garfield's radio.

"Nah. She was out cold when I got there, but people on the scene confirmed what she said right after she was found." Garfield reached up to silence the radio on his shoulder. "My gut says she saw something that scared her half to death. She's in the ER right now."

"Thanks. I'll take a look around, then get out of your way."

Sean turned away and went to the victim's body, where

evidence technicians were just starting their work. They bustled around, testing equipment and setting up free-standing lights to illuminate the area for the video cameras.

While the techs worked on the lighting, Sean borrowed a flashlight from one of the patrolmen and briefly recon-noitered the area around the victim. He crouched over a bent umbrella and a leather-wrapped canister of pepper spray, or maybe mace. Both objects had paint around them, waiting to be photographed and tagged as evidence.

Sean made a mental note to check if the fingerprint analysis came up with anything that could connect the items to the victim. A little farther away, he found two more objects. Medium-heeled women's shoes, sprawled a couple of feet apart, size 7. Glancing over at the victim, he saw sensible black flats on her feet.

"OK, team, we're ready to start," one of the technicians shouted. The forensics team had the scene lit up like cen-ter stage at a Vegas show.

Stepping closer to the victim, Sean examined the body objectively. He had seen death before, yet still he had to work to distance himself from the victim's humanity and vulnerability.

This one had brown eyes that were wide open. Her mouth was open as well, as if she had died crying out. Sean's lips thinned as he took in the victim's clothing, hairstyle, jewelry. She looked like a kid.

Crouching down, he examined the stab wounds more closely. A decent-sized blade had been used. One stab alone would have been mortal from the look of things, yet there were at least four other wounds. Something to keep in mind about the murderer—he enjoyed his work and be-lieved in overkill.

A technician shifted a piece of equipment, throwing a

stark light across the victim from a different angle. Sean focused immediately on a cloth loop at the woman's slender waist. Shifting around, he saw an identical bit of fabric on the other side. It looked like she had been wearing a belt, but he didn't see it anywhere.

Sean motioned to one of the technicians. "Did one of you guys find a belt or sash? It looks like there was one here—see the loops? She wouldn't wear the dress with these things just hanging off her sides, would she?"

The forensics tech studied the victim and nodded his agreement. He made a note on his tiny laptop and called out questions to his team members.

No one had seen any belt.

All of the victim's other articles were there next to her body. Sean looked over her effects—a straw purse and umbrella, a Mickey Mouse key ring with four keys attached. No belt.

"We'll look for it," the tech assured Sean.

"Good, but I don't think you'll find anything."

"Why not? Looks like maybe this was a robbery attempt or something. Sure, her money and stuff is right here," the tech said, "but word is the killer was interrupted by a witness, which would explain why the valuables got left behind."

Sean's eyes were pale blue and cold in the artificial light. "I think our killer got exactly what he wanted from this victim, and then kept a little something to remember her by."

"You think the guy wanted a trophy? The belt?" The tech sounded excited. "Hey, I bet you're right!"

Sean didn't say anything. Sometimes he hated being right.

Chapter 6

Sean's instincts were screaming all the way to George Washington University Medical Center. Even at this very preliminary stage, he was betting the murder of Renata Mendes was connected to at least one of the cases he and his partner were investigating. *If* the crimes were related, and *if* they could get anything from the eyewitness, it might give them the first real lead in close to a year. And *if* he could pull enough strings with the captain to get assigned to the Mendes case, which wasn't cold at the moment.

Big ifs.

It was time for reinforcements. He hit the speed dial on his cell phone and imagined Aidan Burke's irritation with relish. Waking up his cousin, who was also his partner on the Cold Cases Unit, was always a pleasure.

Moments later his partner's sleepy voice came across the line. "This had better be good, Sean."

"Don't you love caller ID? Hey, did I wake you?" Sean's tone was upbeat and friendly.

"Of course not. It's what, four A.M.? Why would I be asleep?" Aidan's tone wasn't happy.

"Sorry, partner, but I think we might have a break on the Herrera case," Sean said.

"What have you got?" His partner's voice wasn't sleepy anymore.

"I'd rather meet you at GWU Hospital's ER, have you talk to a witness, and let you make your own assessment." Sean trusted his cousin without qualification. If he was jumping at shadows, Aidan would be the first to tell him so. Aidan would also be the first to back Sean if he was right.

His cousin sighed loudly. "I'll be right over."

A murmured feminine protest came clearly across the line.

Sean snickered. Aidan's girlfriend was a consultant whose job kept her constantly on the road. "Apologize to her for me. You'll make it up to her on her next trip through town. In a couple of months or so."

"Blow me. No, not you, darlin'." Aidan yawned. "See you at the hospital in half an hour."

Sean hung up and turned into the hospital driveway. A few minutes later he strode into the ER and flashed his badge at the desk clerk. "I'm looking for a Jane Doe brought in with head injuries a little while ago."

"The doctors are with her in curtain three. I'll page them."

"Never mind. I can find it."

Sean went through the doors into the heart of the ER. He walked toward a curtained area and saw a doctor standing in front of the green drape, giving instructions to a nurse.

"Doctor? I'm Detective Richter. Is this our Jane Doe back here?"

"I'm Dr. Springer. Actually, she's not a Jane Doe any longer. She regained consciousness briefly after her head CT and was able to give us her name and address. That's an excellent sign."

"So she's going to be okay?" Sean asked.

"It looks like she will. Her test results were good—a serious concussion, a nice bump, a couple of stitches, but no skull fracture. She has a very hard head." Dr. Springer smiled briefly at Sean, then continued. "She's still pretty dazed, so we haven't pressed her for much beyond her basic information."

Sean got out his notebook. "What's her name?"

"Claire Lambert. Thirty years of age, lives in Georgetown."

"When can I speak with her?" Sean pocketed the notebook impatiently, already starting toward the curtain.

The doctor held up a hand to stop him. "My patient is resting right now. She's in pain, but we can't give her much to ease it. She'll be admitted to the hospital as soon as they can find a bed for her upstairs. She'll likely be here for a couple of days."

"I don't want to disturb anyone, but it's critical that I speak to her as soon as possible. This woman is a potential eyewitness in a homicide investigation." Sean's intense look overrode the doctor's objections. "What's more, nobody gets into this area without authorization. Post a guard and let your staff know."

Dr. Springer nodded, stifling a yawn. "I'll be back to check her in a while."

Sean walked through the curtain, eager to see his witness. The first thing he noticed was her hair, lying in a halo of black curls around her face. Her skin was very pale, with no freckles or blemishes to detract from its ivory smoothness. Her face was finely chiseled and delicate with well-shaped brows, a small nose, and a full mouth.

Sean immediately thought of the painting of a young courtesan he had seen at a cultural exhibit one of Aidan's girlfriends had dragged them to—Art of the Italian Renaissance, or something like that. He pulled his gaze from the woman's face and moved on to the rest of her, automatically estimating her height at under five and a half feet. He took in her curvy build next. The slow rise and fall of nicely shaped breasts, the indentation at the waist, and the lush flare of hips beneath the light sheet. He stepped back to better absorb the image of the woman lying in the hospital bed.

Well, well. Even laid up in a hospital bed, Claire Lambert was a knockout.

Her hand lifted from the bed and moved toward her face. When she reached to touch the back of her head, he jumped forward to stop her.

"Easy, now. You don't want to be messing with those stitches just yet."

She made a soft sound, trying to pull her hand free. She wanted to rub the painful spot on the back of her head.

"Ms. Lambert, can you hear me?" Sean kept one hand wrapped gently around hers to keep her from disturbing the bandages. "Ms. Lambert? Are you awake?"

As he watched intently, long lashes fluttered, then opened. His insides squeezed at the pain in her dazed black eyes.

"It's all right," he said. "You're in the hospital, but you're okay." He kept his voice gentle and soothing as he stroked her hand. He wanted to erase the shattered look he'd seen in her eyes, to help ease her slowly into full awareness.

"Who are you?" she whispered, as if speaking were painful. "What happened?"

"Don't you remember?" Sean's stomach lurched. Maybe the doctor had been wrong and she was severely injured. "Do you know your name?"

"Claire. Marie Claire Lambert." She blinked once, then again. Long, slow blinks. "Who are you?"

"Detective Richter. Can you tell me what happened to you tonight?"

Claire rested with her eyes closed for a moment, her forehead creased in distress. Sean could practically feel the waves of pain rolling off her. He pressed the call button next to her bed to summon a nurse.

"I don't know. My head hurts." Her voice broke on the last word.

"I'm sure it does. I called for a nurse." Another stroke of his hand over hers. "Do you remember being near Dupont Circle tonight? Did you see anything there?"

Sean knew he was probably pushing too hard, but he was afraid she would drift into sleep again. He needed any information she had and he needed it now.

She met his intense blue gaze "I'm sorry. I can't think right now. It hurts." She winced and looked away, turning her head gingerly on the pillow. She was asleep before taking another breath.

Sean forced back his frustration. Yes, he needed information, but she was clearly exhausted and in pain. He would have to wait for a few hours.

He sat on the edge of the bed to wait, keeping his hold on Claire's warm fingers.

"How's she doing?" Aidan Burke asked. He was standing in the entrance to ER curtain three, filling the empty space with his broad shoulders. Sean had been so absorbed that he hadn't noticed his cousin's arrival.

"She's hurting. She has a concussion, and they're going to keep her for a few days. She'll go upstairs in a couple of minutes," Sean said without looking away from Claire.

Aidan said nothing, observing the way his partner held the woman's hand. Sean was always gentle with the victims and families they dealt with in their investigations, but he wasn't normally this touchy-feely.

Sean looked up, caught Aidan's speculative hazel gaze, and lifted his eyebrow.

"Pretty lady." Aidan's voice was neutral. "Claire, is it?"

Sean nodded. "She's a lucky lady, too. You should have seen the girl that didn't get away."

"I heard—I talked to Banjo on the way down. How did this one escape?" Aidan gestured toward the bed with his chin.

"I don't have any information from her yet. I found a can of pepper spray near the body, plus a bent umbrella and a pair of shoes that didn't belong to the dead girl. When Claire was admitted, her feet were bare, cut and scratched."

"Go on."

"My guess is she surprised our killer in the act. He must have come after her. She hit him with the spray, kicked off her pumps, and ran like hell." Sean's voice was admiring.

Aidan assessed the sleeping woman, taking in her average height and pale, fragile appearance. Looks could be deceptive. From what Sean was saying, this was a woman who didn't play the victim willingly. "That took balls."

"Yeah. We can't confirm yet whether the killer chased her, but I'm betting he did. He just didn't catch her. The club where she was found is several blocks from the school, and no one reported seeing any strange men hanging around. Since it was a female-only club, I'm guessing that a guy would have stood out."

Aidan was quiet for a moment, digesting the information and letting his own analysis fill in the blanks. "You think we have a serial killer here. The Dominguez and Herrera cases, now this."

"Exactly. Three dark-haired, slender women of Hispanic descent, all stabbed in the abdomen with a large blade in the last two years. Other pieces don't seem to fit, but I think it's all there for us to dig up. I can't leave Claire until I take her statement, but I want you to go to the crime scene and have a look around, talk to some of the forensics team, then let me know if you agree."

Aidan heard what wasn't said—Sean wanted him to validate the serial killer theory before they took it to their boss. The unspoken communication between the two men, a result of being raised together, made them a powerful investigative team.

"On my way. You take care of our witness," Aidan said. "Call me when she wakes up."

Chapter 7

An insistent hand briskly shook Claire's shoulder.
"Ms. Lambert? Claire? Wake up."

The ritual had been repeated many times that morning.
Claire was getting used to being shaken awake just as she
was falling deeply asleep. She generally dozed right off
after they left her alone, but she was getting irritated with
the constant interruptions. Sleep was important, and she
wasn't getting any.

She opened her eyes. Looking around, she remembered
that she was in the hospital, in a white-on-white private
room. There was an older man standing next to her who
looked vaguely familiar. She jolted when the man pried
her lids wide open and flashed a penlight across her face.
White coat, fifty-something, receding hairline, tired
brown eyes. His name was . . . yes, Dr. Springer.

"How are you feeling?" The doctor checked her pupils
a second time.

She considered the question for a moment. She no
longer felt like her head was going to explode with each

heartbeat. Every other one, maybe, but that was an improvement. "The headache is still there, but bearable."

"Good, good. Follow my finger." He moved his finger up and down, then side to side. "Very good. You're one lucky young lady. Your responses are excellent, and there is no sign of serious swelling on your brain. We'll need to observe you for about forty-eight hours, but I think you can go home by Monday morning."

"Thank God. I can't wait to get out of here. No offense, but this place isn't exactly a five-star hotel." She wrinkled her nose. "And it smells funny."

"If you can complain about that, you're definitely on the road to recovery."

The doctor surprised Claire by pulling up a chair next to her bed.

"While I am satisfied with your physical condition," he said, "we need to talk a little bit more about your neurological health. With head wounds like yours, it's not uncommon to have some type of memory loss or impact on other cognitive functions."

"I've been thinking about that," Claire admitted. "I tried a couple of times to remember what happened, but there's nothing there."

"What's the last thing you recall before waking up in the hospital?"

She shifted against the pillows and thought for a moment. "I left work late yesterday evening. I had an appointment."

The doctor made an encouraging sound. "What kind of appointment?"

"I was going to meet my friend Afton at her office."

"What were you going to do?"

Claire touched the corner of her mouth with her tongue.

"She, ah, runs a dating service. I was signing up that night."

Dr. Springer raised his eyebrows. "What happened when you got there?"

"I don't know. I don't remember *being* there, I just know that's where I was going."

"What's the next thing you remember?"

"Waking up in this room a couple of hours ago. There was a man here—he had dark hair and light blue eyes. The nurse made him leave so she could help me to the bathroom. I went to sleep afterward."

"Nothing else?" The doctor looked at her intently. "You don't remember the time between these two incidents?"

"Not really. It's hard to explain." Claire sighed and rubbed her forehead absently. "I have some images in my head. Like snapshots. You know when you smell something familiar, like pumpkin pie, and for a second your mind flashes back to Thanksgiving fifteen years ago at Grandma's house? That's what it's like. First an image, then a feeling, then it's gone."

Dr. Springer nodded and stood to make notes on Claire's chart. "I'm not too concerned. It's quite common in a case like yours to remember nothing about the time leading up to the injury. Your memory may come back fully as your brain heals itself. You may only remember bits and pieces, or you may never remember another thing. Especially as the events leading up to injury were . . . traumatic."

Claire looked at the doctor with dark, bleak eyes. "I feel like something terrible happened, but I don't know what it was. Can you tell me?"

"I should probably leave that to Detective Richter."

"Who?"

The doctor smiled. "The man with light blue eyes. He's been with you since you were downstairs in the ER, early this morning. He's out in the hall right now. The police are very eager to take your statement."

"Why? What happened to me? Was I attacked—raped?" She bunched her hands into fists, then immediately straightened her fingers as the IV catheter dug into the back of her left hand.

"There's no evidence you were sexually assaulted. Why would you think you were?"

"I remember thinking that I had to run," Claire said hoarsely. "If I didn't, someone would catch me. I was really scared."

Her head began to throb as she concentrated on the night before. She winced at the pain and wondered if her head would actually explode. She tried to focus on the doctor's words, necktie, nose hairs—anything not to think about her suddenly pounding head.

"The police believe you witnessed a murder, then fled the scene with the killer in pursuit. You were injured when you fell down some stairs outside a club, presumably trying to reach help."

I don't have any idea what he's saying. He's talking about what happened to me, and I don't remember any of it.

There was a surreal, disjointed quality to the moment, a delay between watching Dr. Springer's mouth move, hearing the words, and then understanding them. She fought a spinning, nauseous feeling.

"I don't remember anything about it. God, who would want to? Maybe it's better that way."

"The Homicide Unit and Detective Richter would be quite disappointed if you have traumatic amnesia," Dr.

Springer said, "but maybe that would be best for your safety."

Normally Claire was very quick, but right now she wasn't able to track a simple conversation. "I don't understand."

"You witnessed a murder. It's only logical that your life might be in danger, especially if the killer knows where you are. Why do you think the detective has been with you all morning?"

Claire's murky thoughts abruptly cleared. Surely she would have remembered if there had been an armed man standing over her, but all she recalled was a pair of hypnotic, ice blue eyes. Like glacier water.

"You mean the detective is guarding me?"

"You'll have to ask him that. Look, I don't want to upset you. I want you to rest and recover, and don't be too hard on yourself if the events of last night never come back to you. I'll tell the detective to come back later."

Feeling numb and cold, Claire watched the doctor leave.

Someone tried to kill me.

With stunning clarity that fact burned into her brain. Then came another—that same man had savagely murdered at least one other woman. Worse, the killer could walk through the door to her hospital room right now and she wouldn't know him from the guy who changed bedpans.

She scrubbed her hands over her face, reining in her imagination. The murderer wasn't going to walk in with a policeman on guard. And she would be careful as well. The blow to her head had stolen part of her memory, but she still had the rest of her faculties.

Think, Claire. Don't react, think.

She would be in danger as long as the killer was running around free. If she remembered last night, she could help the police catch him. But how could she remember? The doctor certainly hadn't been any help with his talk of traumatic amnesia.

Maybe all she needed was rest and a little chance to recover. Maybe then she would remember enough to give the police a description. Maybe she would at least recognize the murderer if he stood in line behind her at an ATM.

The thought of a faceless killer approaching her increased her resolve to remember. Until she knew the horrible details of Friday night, and the man responsible for them, she wouldn't have control over her own life.

And that was one thing that Claire Lambert simply would not accept. In the last eight years she'd worked hard to build a safe and comfortable life. She wouldn't let the killer take that away from her, too.

She closed her eyes and almost instantly began to dream of pale eyes, photographs, and cruel smiles.

Chapter 8

Washington, D.C.
Saturday afternoon

Claire emerged from a sleep so deep she hadn't moved in hours. As her mind slowly came awake, she took stock of herself. Her head still hurt, no doubt about it, but she no longer felt as if there were a sharp-toothed demon gnawing her brain from the inside out. She stretched gently, testing the rest of her body. Her thigh and calf muscles were stiff, and her feet were sore, but everything else was in good shape—except her memory.

She opened her eyelids and looked directly into a compelling hazel gaze. Tilting her head she studied the green-blue eyes. They were set in a wide face with strong cheekbones, a square jaw, and nicely shaped lips. As she continued to stare, the lips moved in a smile. A very charming smile. He looked to be in his early thirties, though he sprawled in an armchair with the ease of a teenager. He seemed vaguely familiar, but he wasn't one of the doctors, which meant he had to be the detective.

"I thought your eyes were blue," she said.

"Nope. They're hazel." The room door opened and the

man next to her gestured with his chin. "My cousin's eyes are blue."

She turned to look at the newcomer. Here were the stark blue eyes that had punctuated her dreams. She couldn't believe she hadn't remembered the rest of the package, as well. Dark hair, tall, athletic build with broad shoulders and long legs. And a truly striking face.

He wasn't drop-dead gorgeous, though he was certainly handsome. His power lay in his icy eyes, which weighed the world with tangible intelligence.

"I see you two have met." Blue Eyes approached the bed, holding out a cup of coffee to the other man.

"We were just getting there. Why don't you make the introductions?" Hazel Eyes and Charming Smile took the coffee and sipped from the steaming container.

"This is Aidan Burke, my cousin and partner. I'm Sean Richter, in case you don't remember me. We're both detectives with DCPD's Homicide Division. Aidan, meet Marie Claire Lambert." Though he spoke to the other man, Sean's blue eyes continued to look intently at Claire.

"Please, just Claire," she said. "My Catholic mother mistakenly thought I'd learn grace and humility if she named me after the Blessed Virgin, but it's been years since anyone actually called me Marie Claire."

"And what did you do to the last person who called you that?" Aidan teased.

She smiled and said in her best Louisiana drawl, "Now, *cher*, is that something I'd tell a detective?"

As the words echoed in the room, her smile dimmed. Detectives. These men were here to take her statement about a series of deadly events she couldn't even recall.

"Claire it is," Aidan said. "Is there anyone we can call for you? Family, boyfriend, roommate?"

The last of her smile faded at the question.

No, no family at all.

She pushed aside the old sadness at having outlived all of her close relatives. "I don't have any family, but— Livvie! I have to call her. What time is it? We were supposed to have lunch today. She'll be frantic."

Claire sat up and flung back the sheet to reach for the phone. Instead her hands grabbed her head. "God *damn* it."

"Easy does it." Sean caught Claire's bandaged feet before they touched the floor. "No sense in breaking open these cuts or fainting and hitting your head again. Aidan will call your friend while we talk."

Sean gently swiveled her legs back on the bed and drew the sheet over their pale, distracting length. He had to work very hard to keep his eyes on hers and off the sleekly muscled line of calf and thigh.

Even with the distraction of her pounding head, Claire shivered at the touch of his hands. Considering the fact that she had been handled like a piece of meat by complete strangers ever since entering the hospital, she told herself that her reaction was ridiculous.

But this man didn't feel like a stranger.

She looked away from Sean's face to his hands. They were very nice—large, with long, tapered fingers and neatly trimmed nails. A sprinkling of dark hair dusted the back of each knuckle. She tried to recall what Olivia had said about a man with big hands. Then she remembered, and blushed.

"Do you remember your friend's number?" Aidan asked.

Claire gave him the number and he walked to the far end of the room, dialing his cell phone as he went.

Sean waited until she faced him again. When she simply studied him for a long moment, he raised a questioning eyebrow.

"Sorry, I just feel like—you seem very familiar," she said, embarrassed.

He was surprised she felt the same thing he did, a kind of visceral recognition of the other person. It had been bothering him. So he told her what he had been telling himself. "I've been sitting by your bed for almost twelve hours, and sometimes you'd wake up and look right at me. Naturally I seem familiar."

The idea of him watching her as she slept should have made Claire uncomfortable, but his matter-of-fact words reassured her. "I guess that would do it."

Aidan came back to Claire's bed and sat in the nearby chair. "Your friend is on her way. I didn't tell her much, just that you were injured but would be fine."

"Thank you. She's quite the mother hen, so I know she'll be worried." That was an understatement. Olivia would probably get multiple speeding tickets on the way down Wisconsin Avenue.

Sean put his hand on Claire's arm. "I know you've been through a very difficult time. I spoke to Dr. Springer, and he said you couldn't remember anything after leaving work Friday evening, but that might change as your brain heals itself. Have you been able to remember anything else?"

"I just have some images in my head. Some feelings."

"Like what?"

"I was walking, then I stopped short. A man smiling— a nasty, mean smile. I was afraid, and I remember running. Being chased." Her eyes stared ahead, unfocused. She shivered and blinked, then looked at Sean. "Nothing really makes sense, because there's no context. I don't know when it was, where I was, what I was doing there. It's like looking at pictures in a photo album but not knowing the story behind them." She frowned and tried to hold a thought that was teasing just at the edges of her memory. "Photos."

"What?" Sean asked, leaning toward her.

"I looked at that cruel smile and thought . . . thought I'd seen a photo of the man smiling at me. The idea just popped in my head. It was . . . surreal."

"Good." He took her hands and spoke soothingly. "What did the man look like?"

She tried to remember. After a full minute of silence, all she had was a vicious headache. "I don't know. I had to get away, so I ran. I just ran. That's all."

Sean's hands tightened around hers in an instinctive protest. To come so close, to have an eyewitness to the crime, and yet come away with nothing. *Shit.*

Aidan murmured reassuringly to her as she freed her hands from Sean's.

"I'm so sorry." Claire wiped her clammy forehead with the back of her arm. "I just can't remember anything clearly."

Sean paced toward the door, running his hand through his hair and then letting his fingers rest on the back of his neck. Silently he considered the possibilities, revising his approach to getting information.

"Do you remember anything after thinking you needed to run?" Aidan asked.

"Nothing." Claire's mouth was as flat as her voice. "I woke up here."

Silence filled the room.

She looked at Aidan, then Sean. "Sorry to disappoint you."

"We're not blaming you," Sean said emphatically. "We blame the criminal who's responsible for this whole mess. Sure, it would be nice if you could give us a description, but we've got more now than we did yesterday."

"Like what?" Her voice was skeptical. She wondered if he was patronizing her the way the doctor had.

"We've got a new crime scene with new forensic evidence. We know we're dealing with a man, a man with what you describe as a cruel smile. We know there is a photograph of the man or someone who looks like him—"

"No. A photograph of *him*," she interrupted. "It's the only thing I'm certain of, that flash of recognition."

"Okay," Sean said. "Where did you see this photograph?"

"I—I don't remember."

"Could it have been in a newspaper?"

"I don't subscribe to any papers. I get my news online, text version usually."

"Then what photos, particularly photos with men, have you seen recently?" Aidan asked.

"I may have looked at photos—a lot of photos—during an appointment after work last night. But I can't say for sure. I don't even remember going to the meeting."

Sean tried to imagine why she would review pictures during a business meeting. He came up blank. "What was this appointment about?"

Her cheeks turned a dusky red. God, talk about adding insult to injury. "It was a dating service."

Aidan's jaw dropped. "You're shitting me."

"You went *where*?" Sean's voice rose on the last word. He shook his head in disbelief.

Claire counted to ten and hoped her blush would be mistaken for anger. "All right, gentlemen, I'm only going to say this once, so listen up. I had an appointment with a dating service last night. I'd just joined, so we were going to spend part of the evening reviewing the catalogue and looking at pictures of male clients to see if there were any matches for me."

Sean was too shocked to say anything. Aidan coughed and jumped up from his seat to look out the window, studying the street below with apparent interest. Both men worked hard to look normal.

"It's not funny." Her voice was defensive.

"I'm not laughing," Aidan said, but he didn't turn around.

Sean shook his head. "I can't believe someone like you would have trouble finding a date."

She narrowed her eyes at him. "I didn't say I had trouble *finding* a date. I just have trouble finding someone I *want* to date. Big difference."

"Amen to that," Sean muttered under his breath.

He hadn't been out with a woman in months, since just after the end of his last relationship. He'd quickly grown tired of the casual partner-swapping of D.C.'s singles scene and had buried himself in his caseload with few regrets.

"Look, I don't think we should be focusing on the dating service," she said in a voice that was intended to close the subject. "I could have been picking up my dry cleaning."

Sean almost smiled. Temper made her eyes sparkle and added color to her face. His witness was obviously beginning to feel better.

Aidan, having gained control of his laughter, turned back from the window. "Hang on a sec. Where is this dating service located?"

"It's not far from Dupont Circle—you can walk there

easily from the metro." Claire gave them the address and cross streets.

The men exchanged a quick glance. Sean mentally ran through the various routes a pedestrian could take between the Circle and the address Claire had given. One of the shorter ways went directly through the schoolyard where the murder had occurred.

"Did you plan on walking?" Sean asked.

"Yes. I was going to take the metro to Dupont Circle, walk to the dating service, then take the bus home to Georgetown. We expected the meeting to take several hours, but the bus runs pretty regularly along that route."

"Do you normally walk around the city at night? Alone?" Though Sean's tone was calm, his eyes narrowed at the thought of a solitary woman walking the dark streets of Washington, D.C. As a cop, he knew exactly what happened to some of those women. Claire had been lucky. His case files were full of women whose luck had run out.

Claire's chin shot up at Sean's deliberately neutral tone. "Yes, I do. I'm not stupid, nor am I a child. I just refuse to live in fear. I stick to populated areas and well-lit streets. If I have to leave them for some reason, I carry pepper spray in my purse."

The detectives traded looks again. Sean's theory for why the pepper spray had been at the crime scene had just been confirmed.

Then Sean thought of something. "Were you carrying a purse?"

"Of course."

"Where is it? It wasn't with you at the club where you were found, and we didn't find it at the murder scene. Are you sure you were carrying it Friday night?"

"I must have been. I never go anywhere without it. Maybe I dropped it and someone stole it?"

Sean thought about it but dismissed the notion. If someone had come across her purse on the street, he or she might have stripped the wallet of cash and credit cards, then stuffed everything in a Dumpster somewhere. But Sean didn't think so. He remembered being on the murder scene and the gut feeling he'd had that the killer liked to keep trophies.

"What's usually in your purse?" Aidan asked before Sean could.

"The normal stuff—wallet, compact, checkbook, house keys."

"Did you have a driver's license or other ID in your wallet?" Sean asked.

"Of course."

Sean's eyes narrowed. "Did it have your current address on it?"

Claire nodded. "I've lived there for over five years. Why?"

"We need to get your locks changed," Aidan interrupted. "It's a good idea after you lose your keys."

"You're right," she said, nodding absently as she thought about it. Great, some punk off the street could have her keys and address—another thing to worry about. Then she picked up on the undercurrents of what Sean and Aidan weren't saying. "You guys think the killer has my stuff?"

"We don't know that," Sean tried to reassure her.

Mentally he cursed her quickness. They would have to work fast to stay ahead of her, but he admired the fact that she was picking up his unspoken worries despite her concussion. He'd always found smart women sexy.

Steady, man. You're working, not trolling.

Sean reminded himself that Claire was a witness in a homicide investigation. His job was to work with her to close the case, nothing more. That was the way it had to be, regardless of how attractive she was to him, with her wild raven hair and intelligent black eyes.

And he'd always thought he preferred blondes.

"We don't want to assume anything here," Sean began. He was interrupted by the sound of a commanding voice in the hall.

"I'm here to see Claire Lambert. Which room is hers?"

"Olivia," Claire said to the men.

Aidan walked to the door. "I'll explain to her what's going on." He left it to Sean to reassure Claire.

Sean leaned toward her and waited until she looked at him. "I don't want you to jump to conclusions. I'll have foot patrols at the murder scene search for your purse. We'll need a description of it, plus a list of your credit cards so we can track whether they're being used."

"Okay." She met his reassuring eyes but didn't feel any better. In fact, as she thought about this new threat, her headache came back with increased intensity.

He looked at her closely and thought she seemed less vibrant than she had a few minutes ago. "Is your head hurting?"

Claire nodded once, carefully.

"Then let us worry about the purse. We'll talk later about the description and your credit cards."

She nodded again, looking away from the eyes that saw right through her to read her thoughts. He knew she was deeply disturbed by the idea of the killer having access to her home—knew, too, that her head had started its dull throbbing again. She looked out the window and tried not to think about Sean's ability to read her like a book. It had a disturbing effect on her.

Silence grew in the room.

Sean was tempted to break it, but Claire's body language didn't invite conversation. He settled back in the chair and planned the next steps in the investigation.

Chapter 9

Washington, D. C.
Saturday afternoon

The chunky heels on Olivia Goodhue's loafers clicked loudly in the quiet hospital corridor. She turned the corner and walked as fast as her short legs would allow. Her adrenaline was still racing from the phone call she'd received.

"I'm here to see Claire Lambert. Which room is hers?" Nerves made her tone sharper than usual, though her Southern accent still came through clearly.

A nurse briefly verified Olivia's visitor badge, then pointed to a room on the right. Olivia approached, then paused before opening the door. Claire needed a calm and supportive presence, not fear and nerves. Olivia didn't know what had happened, but if Claire had a head injury severe enough to require hospitalization, then she certainly didn't need an emotional friend.

Olivia had been worried when Claire had missed their lunch date. It wasn't like her at all. The phone call Olivia had received half an hour ago had been a nightmare come true, and it had jolted her to the core.

She reached for the door handle again, only to have it pulled right out of her hand. She found herself staring at a man's chest as he stood in the doorway. She looked up. And up. Lord, he was tall. It wasn't fair that some people towered over six feet, while Olivia had to stand up poker-straight in order to top five foot one at the doctor's office.

"You're going to get a crick in your neck," an amused male voice said.

Olivia narrowed her eyes in annoyance. Did the man read minds, or did he just naturally go for the jugular? She was forced to step back as he gently crowded her into the hall and pulled the door shut behind him.

Aidan looked down at the tiny, redheaded woman in front of him. He could tell that he'd annoyed her with his comment about her height. Or lack thereof.

He smiled as he looked over the rest of her—irritated navy blue eyes set in a triangular face. Her slim, petite frame had just enough curves to be interesting, but her real glory was the thick red hair brushing against her shoulders. The sleeveless tank she wore revealed milky-white skin with a generous sprinkling of freckles on her arms and chest. No freckles on her face, though, which meant she either wore a hat outside or had covered them with makeup.

He imagined she must be Irish, then lost that train of thought when she crossed her arms over her dainty bosom.

"Um, Ms. Goodhue? I'm Aidan Burke. We spoke on the phone earlier."

"Oh, yes. Are you Claire's doctor?" Olivia latched onto the man, hoping for more information about her friend's condition.

"Doctor? Ah, no." Aidan was amused at the idea. "Look, Claire is fine, Ms. Goodhue—"

"Olivia, please. Ms. Goodhue makes me think of my mother." She smiled, and a dimple appeared on her right cheek.

"Olivia." He rolled the name off his tongue, though he was unable to say it as she did, with a slight Southern flavor. "I'm a detective with the DCPD Homicide Division."

"Homicide?" Olivia's face turned gray. She grabbed Aidan's wrist. "You said Claire was going to be fine."

"She is fine—in fact, I was just speaking with her. I'm sorry to have alarmed you, but another woman was murdered last night. We believe Claire was a witness."

"Jesus, you scared me half to death. You'd better give me the whole story, and don't drop any more bombs. My heart can't take it." Olivia let go of Aidan and put a hand to her chest as if to slow the wild pounding there.

He could see the pulse beating in her throat. Olivia obviously cared about her friend a great deal, so he gave her a brief, careful summary of last night's events to put her mind at ease.

"Dear God, you mean she actually saw this man kill a woman?" Olivia's eyes were huge.

"We don't know for sure. Claire can't remember any details of what happened. The doctor says she's probably suffering from traumatic amnesia. He's hopeful that as her brain repairs itself her memory might return."

Olivia said nothing, just looked at Aidan's big body as if trying to see through it to her friend. Her lips trembled as she thought of what could have happened. Her first impulse was to rush into the room and gather Claire up in a tight hug, but she needed to get control before she saw her friend.

"Hey." Aidan gently touched Olivia's arm. "She's going to be fine, really. She was cracking jokes with me not half an hour ago."

Olivia smiled, though it was a bit wobbly. "That's Claire for you. She's as solid as they come."

But Olivia knew that Claire's tough exterior shielded a tender heart.

The two had been friends since their first day of kindergarten, and there was no one alive who knew Claire better. Certainly no one who would understand just how devastating something like this would be to Claire's quiet, predictable life.

Olivia bit her lip as she thought about what would need to be done to help her friend get through the next few days.

"Olivia? I don't think it's a good idea for you to go in there if you're going to fall apart. Claire needs some calm right now." Aidan's tone was bracing. He really hoped the redhead wasn't going to start crying.

"What?"

Olivia pinned Aidan with a glare worthy of Miss Throckmorton, the never-married schoolteacher who had been the bane of his high school years in small-town Wyoming. He opened his mouth to defend himself but never got the chance.

"I am not going to fall apart, Detective Aidan Burke. Nor do I appreciate you telling me what my best friend does or does not need. I know her better than you, and I realize she needs me to be strong and supportive. Especially after having to deal with the police all day."

She snorted and looked him up and down. Her tone left no doubt she was referring to Aidan, and that she felt it would be a real hardship to spend the day in his presence. Part of her understood she was snapping at him because he was right, but right now she wasn't feeling charitable enough to admit that out loud.

Aidan raised his eyebrows, silently stepped aside, and motioned Olivia into the room.

"Livvie! How many red lights did you run getting down here?"

Claire's attempt at humor would have been convincing to someone who didn't know her. Olivia saw right through the casual tone and forced smile. Emotion briefly tightened her throat as she quickly assessed her friend.

"I came as soon as I heard, *chère*." Ignoring the room's other occupants Olivia crossed to the bed and enfolded her friend in a gentle hug.

Claire closed her eyes as she put her own arms around Olivia's delicate frame. Her friend's perfumed embrace had always meant unconditional love, acceptance, and support. Claire hadn't realized just how much she'd needed that until she'd heard Olivia's voice.

Sean stood up to meet Olivia, pleased to see the tension relaxing from Claire's face as she hugged her friend, then released her.

Olivia stepped back and pushed Claire's wild hair from her face, studying what she saw there. She seemed to be satisfied, because she set her huge purse down on the bed and began rummaging inside.

"Livvie, this is Sean, er, Detective Richter. He's working on my case, I guess you could say." Claire gestured toward Sean with a shrug, wondering how else to introduce him.

Olivia looked up briefly from her purse to perform a thorough once-over of Sean. She took in the uncompromising masculine strength and rolled her eyes.

"How long has the testosterone brigade been in here

grilling you, *chère*? Did they at least let you take a break to get something to eat?"

A giggle escaped Claire's lips before she could contain it. Olivia had picked right up on the leashed male energy in the room and wasn't afraid to put her opinion of it into words.

"They're *cousins*, if you can believe it," Claire said.

Olivia's sniff said she had no trouble whatsoever believing the two men were related. She waved a hand to dismiss them and removed a large plastic container from her cavernous bag.

"I've brought gumbo for your supper. For dessert you can have these beignets I picked up this morning. They're a little stale, but I'm sure they'll be better than anything the hospital cafeteria makes."

Claire licked her lips as the spicy scent of gumbo filled the room.

A hopeless scavenger, Aidan perked up as he sniffed the air appreciatively. "Didn't you say earlier that you weren't hungry, Claire? It would be a shame to let that delicious-smelling gumbo go to waste."

He ignored the elbow Sean dug into his ribs and summoned his most charming smile for the women.

Claire shot Aidan a smug look and took a bite of the rich soup. "Livvie, even my sainted *grandmère* didn't make better gumbo." She settled back on the pillows to get comfortable with her dinner.

"After you finish that, we'll get you into a real gown, not one of these tacky numbers with the rear ventilation." Olivia fingered Claire's thin, hospital-issue nightgown, then studied her friend's face. "What did they do to your hair?"

The thought of what her corkscrew curls looked like

when they hadn't been tamed into some kind of style made Claire grimace. "I guess it got wet and I slept on it." She slanted a brief glance at Sean, embarrassed that she looked like a train wreck. *Oh, well. I bet I look better than most of the people he comes across in his line of work.*

Olivia watched while Claire tried to arrange her hair with one hand. Then Olivia dug a brush and a clip out of her bottomless purse, turned around to face Sean and Aidan, and said, "Gentlemen, if y'all are through here? . . ."

Sean dragged his attention from Claire's hair and looked at the redheaded whirlwind who had effortlessly taken control of the situation.

Here's your hat, what's your hurry?

The message came across loud and clear. Olivia reminded him of a mama badger—small, surprisingly sturdy, and willing to fight to the death to protect her cub.

"Yes, ma'am," he said wryly, then turned to Claire. "We're going down to the station now, but here's my card. I've written my cell number and Aidan's on the back. Call us if you remember anything, no matter how unimportant, or if you just want to talk. I mean that."

Sean's piercing eyes stayed on Claire's down-turned head until she looked up. After hesitating a moment, she nodded and set the card within reach on the nightstand.

"We'll talk to you tomorrow," Sean said. "No big deal, just routine follow-up. Evening, ladies." He nodded to Claire and Olivia, then followed Aidan out the door.

Claire finished the gumbo under her friend's watchful eye. Then she pushed the empty bowl away and opened the bag of sweet beignets. The familiar taste of the soft, sugared bread filled her mouth as she chewed. There was nothing like a little comfort food to make the world better.

"I'm fine, Livvie. You don't need to hover like I'm going to fall apart."

"Sweetie, you're the strongest person I know. But it's been a shocking day, so please, let me fuss a little." Olivia began to tidy items on the bedside tray.

Claire chewed thoughtfully, then took another bite. "Yes, it has been a hell of a day. I'm sure it would be even worse if I could actually remember what happened."

Olivia picked up the brush and began to tame Claire's wild curls. "You can't remember anything?"

Claire frowned. "Nothing very helpful. Just some flashes and images. I remember being scared. Apparently I ran from the scene. My God, there was a woman murdered in front of me and I ran away!"

"And what would have happened if you'd stayed? You'd have been next, that's what," Olivia said sharply. "You did the right thing. You escaped and were able to alert the police about the murder and—"

"And haven't been able to give them a single thing since," Claire finished.

"*Chère*, you're being too hard on yourself. I know we all treat you like the Bionic Woman sometimes, but . . ." Olivia set the brush down. "Things happen for a reason. And you were somehow meant to get out of that horrible situation. Maybe your memory will come back and you'll be able to give the police some information that will help them catch the killer. But first you have to concentrate on getting better."

"I know. I just want to help so much. There's a young woman who's dead. And the man who killed her could know where I live."

"What?"

"My purse is missing. Sean thinks the killer picked it

up. My driver's license and keys were in there." Claire tried for a casual shrug.

Blowing out her breath audibly, Olivia began to arrange Claire's hair in a loose French braid. "Then you'll come stay with me until this is over. No arguments." Her tone was firm, as if she were dealing with one of her four younger brothers.

"All right." Claire's soft agreement sounded exhausted.

Olivia completed the braid and stepped back to examine the results. Claire's dark eyes had deep purple shadows under them, and her skin was paler than usual. Tomorrow or the next day her friend would bounce back, but right now she was too tired to fight.

Hoping to distract Claire, Olivia pulled up a chair and tapped Sean's card on the nightstand.

"So tell me all about your gorgeous policeman." She waggled her brows suggestively. "I suppose he spent the whole time at your bedside?"

"Please." Claire almost laughed. "He's just doing his job."

That's what she kept telling herself every time her thoughts came back to Sean and the look in his concerned blue eyes.

That look is called frustration. He wants something from me and right now I can't give it to him.

Claire glanced at his business card on her nightstand. She promised herself she'd get a good night's sleep so that she could do more to help the detectives tomorrow.

And she really hoped she didn't have any more nightmares about strange men with cruel smiles.

Chapter 10

"**D**o you have your car?" Sean asked Aidan as they walked out of the hospital.

"No. I left it at the station and caught a ride down here. I figured we could start going over the case on the way back."

"Roach Coach sound good for dinner?" Sean's question was absentminded as he walked out of the elevator and across the hospital lobby.

"Bring it on, baby."

Sean smiled. They'd both eaten worse—and been thankful for it—than the questionable offerings of the mobile catering van that usually parked near the police station.

Sean unlocked the police-issue sedan and folded his long legs under the wheel. His intellect was warring with his frustration as he tried to decide what to do next. He wasn't surprised that there had been another murder. What he couldn't believe was that they had an eyewitness who didn't remember enough to describe the scene of the crime, let alone the murder suspect.

He rubbed his neck tiredly. He hadn't managed more

than a couple of hours of sleep last night, and those had been sitting in a chair next to Claire's bed. Even worse, the last day had involved one disappointment after another. He was having a hard time coming up with a way to turn things around.

"It's a tough break," Aidan said.

"Stop reading my mind." Sean's voice held no heat. He and Aidan often depended on their uncanny ability to know what the other was thinking.

"Doesn't take a psychic, buddy. You've given these two cold cases a lot more than your others. You thought we had a big break and now it's gone—it shows, that's all."

"Yeah, I want to solve the cases. No one deserves to be gutted and left to die on the street, no matter what she does for a living. But am I losing my perspective here, imagining the connection?"

Aidan's response was immediate. "No. My instincts say the links are there. We just need to find a way to prove it and catch this guy."

"It would be hard to get a warrant citing 'instinct' for probable cause. We need something to break this open." Sean tapped an irritated beat on the steering wheel. "A week ago if we thought we'd have an eyewitness to a connected murder, we'd have been doing fucking back flips. Now we're just doing laps."

"Let's see what comes back from the forensics team before we decide whether we're wasting time or not." Aidan spoke carefully, sensing that Sean's legendary self-control was wearing thin.

"We should have a sketch out to the public—maybe one of the kids hanging around the crime scene during the investigation might have seen something," Sean said forcefully. "Or some old lady with insomnia who looked out her window at the right time. One corroborating witness, and we're onto this bastard!"

Aidan knew that Claire was at the heart of his partner's frustration. "She's trying her best," Aidan said.

"I know that. You think I blame her?"

"No. And I don't blame her either."

Sean sighed slowly. "Sorry. Guess I need some sleep." He sighed again and tried to remember the last time he'd seen his bed. "Hell, I know you're frustrated, too."

"Yeah, though probably not about the same thing you are."

"Huh?"

"I think we both know the real reason you're so tense has big dark eyes and is lying in a hospital bed down the street," Aidan said.

"What is that supposed to mean?"

"Exactly what you think it means. Even half-dazed in a hospital gown, that's a good-looking woman. And it's damn sure she's smarter than that houseplant you brought to last year's Christmas party."

"Claire is a witness on a case," Sean said. "Nothing more, and certainly nothing less."

"Oh, come off it. If you'd touched her hands or arms one more time *I* was going to start getting hot and bothered."

Sean was irritated. True, Aidan had an unnerving ability to understand what made most people tick, and he'd been practicing on his family for years. But Sean had worked very hard to suppress the attraction he felt for Claire. To have his nose rubbed in it pissed him off.

"She was scared and in pain, that's all," he said neutrally. "You know as well as I do that physical contact can be a powerful tool in the interview process, especially when the victim is feeling fragile."

Aidan snorted. "Fragile, my ass. Claire could probably go one on one with my boot camp drill sergeant and win."

"Look, I needed information and she needed some warmth and human contact. That's all there was to it."

That was all he would let it be. Claire was a witness on his case, and she was feeling vulnerable after having her life turned upside down. The last thing he needed was for her to pick up on the attraction he was feeling. He winced at the picture that formed in his mind—the lead investigator, sucked in by the false intimacy of an overnight vigil, hitting on a witness as she lay in her hospital bed. Christ, if he was reduced to trolling the ER for fresh prospects, it really had been too long since he'd been with a woman.

Sean ignored the voice in his head that said Claire would appeal to him even if he'd just come from a week-long stay in another woman's bed.

Aidan looked at his quiet partner. "Okay, so what's your plan?" he asked, settling back in the seat. Knowing Sean, he'd already figured a way to attack the case from a new angle.

"Assuming the captain lets us take a hot case," Sean began.

"He will. He's desperate for detectives after that double homicide in Adams Morgan."

"Anyway," Sean said, "if we get the case we'll go full-court on Mendes's life. If nothing comes of that, we'll interview Claire again. Maybe by then she'll remember something useful."

Sean didn't add that backing off Claire would also give him a welcome break from her presence, allowing him to be more objective about her.

"Hmmm," was all Aidan said.

"What?"

"I'm not sure how well Claire and the words 'back off' go together. Sure, she's quiet now, but she doesn't strike me as the type to quietly wait around until you're ready to play with her again. Hell, she'll probably be calling you for daily updates once she's feeling better." Aidan chuckled.

"She won't even get out of the hospital for a couple of days. She'll have plenty to keep her occupied, and so will we after the forensics team is done. Meantime we'll divide up and interview Mendes's fellow workers and boyfriends, ex-husbands, handymen, butchers, bakers, the whole lot, and see if anything pops."

Aidan asked without real hope, "You want Mendes's private or professional life?"

"Professional. It's your turn to soothe angry, grieving parents."

Aidan sighed but didn't argue. "In between all that we should get a list of men Claire might have seen coming or going from the Camelot office building last night."

Sean shrugged. "If there's time, or if everything else comes up empty, I'll contact the dating service Claire visited and see if we can get more details about her appointment. Maybe she saw someone who reminded her of the killer. Hell, it's remotely possible that she saw the real one."

"Makes me wonder," Aidan said.

"What?"

"If 'serial murder' is listed as a profession or a hobby in a dating catalogue."

"I'm betting on profession," Sean said. "And we're dealing with a guy who loves his job."

Chapter 11

Washington, D.C.
Saturday evening

" A *brutal murder has sent shock waves through a quiet D.C. neighborhood today. Good evening, I'm Mitzi Michele. On this hot July night, the grounds of Rock Creek Middle School should be empty, but instead they are teeming with D.C. police officers. Homicide investigators have set up a command post and cordoned off part of the schoolyard where a young Hispanic teacher was killed late Friday night."*

The man watched the Barbie doll reading from the teleprompter on the weekend edition of the 11 o'clock news. He'd been going over the online news all day, looking for details on the lead story in the nation's capital. But the Web stories, while titillating, lacked the punch of melodramatic presentation and video footage. He turned the volume up as the anchor switched to the reporter in the field.

"Thanks, Mitzi. Second-year teacher Renata Mendes was stabbed to death late last night or early this morning,

and police are still searching desperately for clues here at the scene."

He snorted. The police were fucking idiots. He was too smart and planned too carefully—he never left any clues behind.

"Mendes, pictured here in her graduation ceremony from Glenview Teacher's College, had apparently stayed late to plan a weekend retreat for a student government group she led. That retreat, sadly, has been canceled today."

The man tuned out the reporter's babble and studied the photo of the pretty young teacher with dark hair and eyes. She was perfect, really. The whole experience would have been perfect too, but for the stupid bitch who'd literally stumbled over them.

He bunched his hands into fists. Yes, he'd deliberately selected an area where there was a risk of discovery—that just added to the rush. But he was supposed to have controlled the situation and taken care of anyone who'd come along. How could he have known he'd be discovered by a woman who ran like an Olympic sprinter?

Anger boiled to the surface again as he remembered how the woman had slipped through his fingers. He'd never lost control of a moment like that before. He hadn't been able to think about anything else in the last twenty-four hours.

"We spoke to some of the victim's students, as well as her family, and as you can imagine they are absolutely devastated."

Good—his favorite part. The lamentations and tearful remembrances of the victim's family and friends. He waited for the familiar curl of arousal through his body, but it didn't come. He concentrated harder on the television report.

"We spoke with the victim's mother this afternoon in a Channel 6 exclusive. Here's what she had to say about her daughter's violent murder."

The camera view switched to a matronly woman in an old housedress. Her double chin trembled, and black tears ran down her heavily made-up face.

"My poor Renata. She was a good girl, she straighten her life around. She grew up in Southeast D.C. Maybe she had some trouble with boys and drugs in high school, but she get herself out of the neighborhood and go to college on a scholarship. The first person in the whole family to graduate from high school, but she never forget about where she come from. We were so proud of her." The woman stopped speaking and began to sob.

No, the teacher certainly hadn't forgotten about where she'd come from. That's how he'd found her in the first place. She'd been leaving the house of the woman now blubbering on the TV. He'd followed Mendes as she'd walked alone through an area where crack deals and five-minute "dates" were arranged on the corner of every street. Then he'd watched her home-to-school routine for days while he'd planned his next move.

In the end, she'd died just like any other whore from the streets where she grew up.

He waited again for the arousal that usually came when he remembered one of his knife games, but he felt nothing. All he could think about was the woman who had ruined everything. He opened his robe and began to masturbate, but his body refused to respond.

With an angry sound he threw the remote control onto the coffee table and paced around his apartment. The television droned on, more tear-jerking stories about how wonderful Renata Mendes was in life, how tragic her death.

Even the shocked faces of her sweet young students failed to arouse him. He turned to do another circuit of his large living room. It wasn't fair. This was the only pleasure he had in his controlled life, and it had been ruined. What good was slicing these women if he couldn't get off later thinking about it? If he couldn't get off remembering and fantasizing about every aching, hoarded detail of the acts?

He stopped next to an elegant cherry wood chest along the wall of the dining room. His hands trembled faintly as he opened the lid to examine the items inside. He took a pair of disposable gloves from the hospital supply box nestled in the chest, then pulled the top item out.

Turning it over in his hands, he studied the smooth grain of the black leather clutch purse. It was top quality, really fine stuff—unlike the teacher's cheap straw bag. This was the kind of purse a lady would carry. Of course, a lady wouldn't have blasted him in the face with pepper spray like he was a common thief.

She'd pay for that, just like she'd pay for ruining his game.

He caressed the smooth leather with a gloved hand. He reached inside, plucked out a matching black wallet, and set the purse aside. Opening the wallet, he studied the driver's license. His lips moved as he read what had already been committed to memory.

"Marie Claire Lambert. Five feet five inches and one hundred and twenty-five pounds. Black hair, brown eyes. No corrective lenses, organ donor."

He closed his eyes and tried to picture her as she'd been that night. But his blood lust had been running high when she'd come across him. He hadn't noticed any particular details about her appearance.

"You're right, Mitzi, the police really have very little to go on."

The man looked toward the television set again. Obviously the reporter was wrapping up his remote shot and was mouthing the rehearsed banter with the anchor back at the station.

"I did ask Captain Michaels about witnesses or investigative leads, but he told me he was not free to comment. Inside sources hint at an eyewitness or forensic evidence, but officially the police have no comment about this murder, the latest in a series of murders within the Hispanic community. Back to you in the studio."

So, there seemed to be an eyewitness? Then why weren't there any sketches or descriptions being released to the media? Maybe the bitch had been hurt in her fall down the stairs. Or maybe she just wasn't talking to the police.

Either way, he'd have to take care of her. Not too soon, because everything had to be perfect this time. He needed to plan carefully, a process that was often arousing in itself.

He felt the first hint of sexual tension in his body and eagerly looked down again at the driver's license. As he studied the Georgetown address, he knew he would make things right.

But this time he would do it with style.

Chapter 12

Washington, D.C.
Sunday morning

Olivia searched up and down Claire's street, looking for a place to park her car while she packed a few things from her friend's house.

"Jackass."

Olivia had to circle the block twice to find a parking spot because some jerk had illegally blocked the tiny driveway reserved for Claire's Georgetown home. She finally double-parked—blocking in the jerk's Lexus—because she would only be a few minutes.

She turned on the emergency flashers and locked the doors of her small sedan. As she straightened, she felt like she was being watched. She looked around casually, certain she would find one of the Police Department's parking enforcement units preparing to swoop in for the kill. Though it was only the beginning of the month, the police had revenue targets to be reached. She knew this from painful experience. Parking tickets in Georgetown were always a sure way to hit the monthly income targets.

She didn't see any squad cars, or even one of the golf

cart vehicles sometimes deployed in the narrow streets. Deciding it would be safe if she hurried, she ran up the steps and unlocked the front door. After making a quick circuit of the first floor of the house, an instinctive act for a female who lived alone in the city, she watered the lush houseplants scattered in the different rooms.

There were no fish, birds, cats, or dog to take care of. Claire often insisted she didn't have the time for the antics of either pets or roommates. She made enough in her job that she wasn't forced to share her living space to make ends meet.

While Olivia moved from room to room, she paid close attention to the locks on the windows and doors. Claire's elegant furniture and impressive electronics collection seemed intact.

Satisfied that at least one of her friend's fears could be put to rest, Olivia went upstairs to pack clothes and toiletries. Blessing Claire's innate neatness, as well as the detailed instructions she had given, Olivia packed everything in under ten minutes. Making a mental note to stop mail service and have Claire ask a neighbor to pick up the flyers that accumulated on the doorknob, Olivia locked the front door and turned to go down the steps to her car.

Pausing to shift the suitcase to her other hand, Olivia again had the feeling that she was being watched. The sensation was unpleasant, and she went down the stairs in a rush.

Given her new awareness of the dangers in the city, Olivia had worked herself into a major case of the willies by the time she got to her car. Glancing uneasily around the tree-shaded street, she opened the trunk and deposited the suitcase in record time. She didn't breathe easily until she was behind the wheel with the doors locked and the engine running.

Olivia stopped long enough to twist her hair into a careless knot, allowing air from the vents to move across her damp neck and shoulders. She chided herself for her jumpiness—she was just overreacting to Claire's recent attack. There was no one on the street, no other sounds but the occasional car driving by.

"Get a grip." She spoke aloud in the air-conditioned safety of the car. It didn't make her feel better.

Determined to push the uneasiness away, Olivia made plans to stop by the seafood market tomorrow morning before picking Claire up from the hospital. Some shrimp etouffée would do them both a world of good.

Chapter 13

The man sat behind the wheel of his two-door BMW, ignoring the trickles of sweat that slid down his face and neck. He'd been sitting in the car for over an hour with the tinted windows only partially opened. He would come back later, at night, and walk around the area again. He needed to get a feel for the place—neighbors, kids, dogs, lighting, and the flimsy fence around Marie Claire's house. But for now it was enough to sit and watch and think of his sweet prey almost within his reach.

Marie Claire.

The intimacy of knowing his victim's name during the planning stages of the game was a sexual thrill. He kept saying her name in his mind and whispering it in the car.

He'd been parked in several spots along Marie Claire's street all morning, waiting to catch a glimpse of her in one of the windows, or maybe even outside. There had been no movement at all. Judging by the junk papers and ad mailers that had piled up on the front stoop, she probably hadn't been home in several days.

The news hadn't mentioned her at all. Maybe she had a boyfriend. Or maybe she'd been injured badly enough to be in the hospital, but he didn't think so. It would have been all over the TV. Reporters loved a victim with a pretty face.

A small sedan passed his car for the third time in as many minutes, then slowed in front of Marie Claire's house. Under his intense gaze, the driver double-parked the car and got out, leaving the hazard lights flashing. He forced himself not to move as the petite woman looked up and down the street. He was sure she couldn't see him, over forty feet away and parked in the shadow of a huge tree. As she trotted up the steps and paused to unlock the front door, he noted her small size and vibrant red hair.

This wasn't Marie Claire. Maybe it was a roommate.

Over the next ten minutes, all the curtains were closed as the woman moved around both floors of the town home. He wondered what the hell she was doing. Maybe she didn't live there after all.

Less than fifteen minutes later the woman came out of the house again, this time carrying a small suitcase.

Excitement surged through him as he considered the possibilities. He was betting the little redhead had packed a suitcase for Marie Claire, which meant she was staying somewhere else. But where?

When the woman froze at the top of the steps, he deliberately looked away, sensing that she was somehow aware of his intense interest. He used his peripheral vision to watch her descend the stairs and put the suitcase in the trunk of the double-parked sedan. Then she got behind the wheel and started the engine. The sound carried through his open window on the muggy breeze.

He waited while she put the car in gear and headed

down the street away from him. It was easy to keep her in sight on the straight, meticulously planned blocks of the Georgetown neighborhood. He let another car go by before starting his own engine and pulling out to follow the redhead's sedan.

Within minutes she turned into the drive at an apartment building on Wisconsin Avenue. She ran in with the suitcase, apparently left it with the concierge, then came back out immediately to move her car out of the drive.

He parked illegally and waited to see what she would do next. Under his watchful eye, the redhead drove around the corner of the block and parked her car on a side street feeding into Wisconsin Avenue. When she locked the sedan and went back to the apartment building, he strained to see through the glass doors of the entry.

He could just make her out as she spoke to someone. Ignoring the No Parking signs, he turned off his engine and sat in his car across the street from the apartment building, hoping she would have one of the units that faced him. A few minutes later, she showed up on a fifth-floor balcony and began watering some plants.

The corners of the man's mouth twisted up in a smile.

Chapter 14

Washington, D.C.
Sunday afternoon

Captain Michaels hadn't been impressed with Sean's theory that the Mendes murder was tied into several cold cases, but he'd been happy to hand over what was becoming a political hot button—*"Murder in the Hispanic community and police don't care!"*—to two of his best investigators, at least on an interim basis.

After a few hours of sleep and a shower, Sean and Aidan had worked straight through the weekend. Aidan had already interviewed the Mendes family and found absolutely nothing that made him suspicious. Sean had been through interviews with Mendes's fellow teachers, nearly all of whom were female. There weren't any recently fired janitors, boyfriends, ex-lovers, other teachers, bus drivers or anything else out of the ordinary.

Renata Mendes was just what she seemed to be—a woman who walked down the wrong street one night and got herself killed by a stranger.

With a growing certainty that there wasn't going to be

anything in Mendes's life that would point to her killer, Sean and Aidan reviewed the Mendes file and forensic information, and traded off pestering the crime lab when the information didn't come quickly enough. Then Aidan went to work on Claire's file.

"This thing's heading for the 'unsolved' files," Sean said, throwing a file on his desk. "Not even a hint of anyone with a personal motive. If Mendes were any cleaner, I'd nominate her for sainthood."

"Anyone come up with something on the door-to-door of the murder neighborhood?"

"Does zilch count?" Sean asked.

"What about the hot line?"

"The usual number of whackos and earnest citizens who think that because their neighbor lets his dog shit on their lawn, the dude's also a murderer," Sean said.

Aidan snickered.

Sean pointed to a thin file labeled Marie Claire Lambert. "You get anywhere on that angle?"

"I talked to her boss and closest coworkers. She didn't interview any new male clients, and no new man was hired in her office recently. Did you get through to Camelot Dating Services?" Aidan asked.

"Owner is listed as Afton Gallagher of Washington, D.C. No personal number and no response at the business number. I'll try her Monday morning." Sean stretched and tried not to yawn. "How's the victim profile coming? I'd like to have more than a hunch the next time we go to the captain."

"Well, the three victims had similar physical descriptions. All of them were regulars in some of the ugliest parts of our fine city—though for different reasons in the case of Renata Mendes. She visited family in Southeast, but lived on the other side of town, near where she was killed. The crime scene is a high-traffic area with all kinds of fingerprints, hair, trash, and shit like that. It will take several days to get forensic analysis detailed enough to allow us to compare the three scenes."

"CSU isn't going to be able to pull anything useable from that scene and you know it," Sean said.

"Yeah, we need another angle. How about Claire's personal life?"

Sean flipped through Claire's file, telling himself he was only doing his job by checking on the veracity of their only witness. "No family, immediate or otherwise," he read, shaking his head. Family was a grounding force in his life; he couldn't imagine what it would be like to be completely alone in the world. "Her parents were both only children. They were killed in a car crash about eight years ago. No siblings. The only other relative was a grandmother who died a couple of years after the parents."

Aidan winced. "I know. That had to be tough."

"Yeah." Sean didn't like thinking about how tough. "Anyway, Claire is a well-liked and respected account manager for a D.C. software firm. Her colleagues describe her as smart, funny, and a workaholic. They also say she's a person who's honest to a fault." Sean read from his partner's notes.

"So this honest, smart, and dedicated woman is sure she knows the killer but just can't remember why or how," Aidan said. "Any obsessive boyfriends stalking her?"

"Can't tell. The security guard at Camelot's office

building remembers seeing Claire leave alone just before midnight. He offered to call her a cab, but she said she was going to walk to the bus stop. Idiot." Sean wasn't sure if he was referring to Claire or the guard who had let a woman go alone into a rainy night.

"I bet they've both learned a lesson," Aidan said.

Sean nodded and yawned so hard his jaw popped. He stood up and stretched the kinks out of his neck and back, then turned off his desk light. "I'm beat. I think we'll have more to go on once we speak to Afton Gallagher and look through her catalogue."

"Catalogue won't do much good if we can't place any of the guys at the scene of the crime."

"You have a better idea?"

Aidan shook his head. "Any activity on Claire's ATM or credit cards?"

"Nothing has turned up on the cards or the purse."

"I don't have a good feeling about that."

"Neither do I," Sean said. He couldn't describe the unease he felt whenever he thought about Claire's missing purse. If the killer had taken the bag from the scene, he had her address and keys. "I'm afraid he'll fixate on the one that got away."

"Jesus, I hate the whackos," Aidan said. "Speaking of which, I'm starting on a rough psych profile of our killer. Assuming the three cases are connected, there's enough in the forensics reports and victim descriptions to put something together. It's not going to be a solid profile, but at least we can take a stab at it. So to speak," Aidan said with a tired smile.

"Thanks for volunteering, partner. Nobody does the mind-fuck quite like you." Sean grabbed dark sunglasses and patted his pockets in search of keys.

"Flatterer. Heading home?" Aidan asked, burying his nose in the files on his desk.

"I'll probably grab something for dinner, or maybe go for a run to clear my head. You want anything?"

"No, go ahead. I'm starting on the profile while the information is fresh. I'll get something to eat later."

"I'll see you at Camelot tomorrow, then. Eight o'clock?" Sean asked.

"Not everyone likes to start their day at the crack of dawn. Ms. Gallagher might be a nine-to-five type." Aidan wasn't a morning person. He sympathized with those forced to drag their half-awake bodies into the office and be productive on someone else's timetable.

"Then we'll wait for her, maybe take a look around the place. Nice try, though." Sean departed without a backwards glance.

He stopped by his favorite Greek restaurant for take-out gyros, returned to his apartment, and wolfed down the dripping bits of meat and pita in record time. Afterward he still felt restless, unable to get the case out of his mind. He fought it for a few hours, then threw down the TV remote control and went to his car, resigned to the idea that he was going to work that night.

First he would go back to the hospital and talk to Claire's doctors. Maybe there had been some improvement in her condition. If not, maybe they could suggest some things to jog her memory—therapy, some type of mental exercises, drugs, anything.

It was beginning to look like a woman with amnesia was their best lead on a murderer. That was a good reason to keep in contact with her, see how she was doing, if she remembered anything at all. If she was awake, they could talk.

Shoving his hands in his pockets and whistling cheerfully, Sean chose not to examine too closely the reasons for his sudden good mood.

Chapter 15

The doctors Sean had hoped to talk to weren't available at nine on a Sunday night, but Claire Lambert was. He flashed his badge at the guard posted in the hallway and paused in the partially open door to Claire's hospital room. Knowing he was there after visiting hours, he did a brief check for roving nurses and began to close the door behind him. The security guard smiled and gave a thumbs-up sign.

Sean turned to the bed, half expecting to find Olivia in the chair, but Claire was alone. She was asleep. Her hair was pulled back, and she wore a deep purple robe that was bright against the white sheets. Someone had brought in a reading light and set it on the nightstand, where it threw soft light across her relaxed face. A paperback novel lay nearby.

The restlessness he'd felt earlier in the evening increased until tension once again filled his body. He hadn't seen Claire since yesterday afternoon, and he'd hoped his memory had exaggerated her appeal to him. It hadn't.

As he stared at Claire in her jewel-toned robe, illuminated from the side by soft light, he was forced to admit that he wanted her. Big time.

Down, boy. Didn't we already have a discussion about this?

He blew a breath up toward his dark bangs, trying to lift them from his suddenly damp forehead.

It's just because she looks like an angel, he told himself, *lying under the light with her dark hair and pale, smooth skin. All I have to do is turn the light off.*

He reached across her for the lamp switch. As the shadow of his arm fell over her face, she jolted awake. Eyes wide, she jerked away from Sean with a frightened sound.

"Hey, it's just me. You're all right." Sean's own heart was unsteady as he used his hand to soothe her.

When the light fell across Claire's face again, he looked down and saw that her eyes weren't completely black. In full light they were a deep, dark brown that drew him in like a spiral puzzle. He stood there, unable to say anything else, even when she recognized him and relaxed.

"Sorry, I've been a little jumpy," she said. She wondered how long he'd been watching her sleep. Silence stretched painfully as he just stood there, staring at her.

"Is anything wrong? Any news on the case? Helloooo?" She waved her hand in front of his face, causing him to pull his head back.

He blinked and moved the novel on Claire's bed. Then he sat on the edge, aiming for a casual note to cover his fascination.

"Ah, no. We've been working all weekend, but unfortunately don't have anything new. How about you? Have you been able to remember anything more?"

"Not really. The feelings I had earlier are stronger, but I don't have any real memories of the night of the murder. Sorry."

"What do you mean the feelings are stronger?"

"I told you, I've been really jumpy. Like just now." Her gesture took in the bed and Sean's presence.

"I think anyone would understand you being a little nervous—" he began.

"No, it's more than that. This morning I was standing at the window when a nurse came up behind me and touched my shoulder. I just about jumped out of my slippers." She gave a humorless laugh and started to speak again, then caught herself.

"What else?"

"It's so stupid, but . . . I've been having bad dreams. At first I thought this was a good sign, that maybe I'd remember something in my dreams. But the only thing I remember is what I feel when I wake up. I don't like it."

It was very difficult for her to talk about her vulnerability, but something in Sean's eyes said she could trust him.

"Ignoring these feelings won't make them go away," Sean said, choosing his words carefully. "When you're in an intense situation, when your life is at risk, the images burn themselves into your brain. You can either deal with them and hope to put the fear behind you, or you can suppress them."

"Guess which method my brain has chosen?"

"Suppression might work for a while, but eventually— on their own terms—the images will come to the surface. And then they own you," he said.

She shook her head. Even with Sean's comforting presence, she didn't want to remember the sickening flashes of her dreams.

"Claire." His voice and eyes were intense. "You can deal with the dreams now, or let them haunt you. It's your choice. And if you remember . . ." He shrugged. "If you remember, you can do something about stopping the bastard. Isn't that better than being eaten alive by nightmares?"

Claire was silent for a moment. When she finally spoke, it was in a half whisper. "I think the worst thing is feeling powerless. Feeling like prey. I was terrified—it was a mortal fear, knowing if I didn't get away I would *die*." She looked up at him. "I bet you've never been scared like that."

"You'd lose," he said, then stood up. "Before working with the DCPD, I was in the army. Special Forces. I saw action in some drug-infested sewers around the world, as well as the Gulf War. Believe me, even though CNN makes it all look like a freaking training video—a complete rout spliced nicely to fit into their sound bytes—the bullets were goddamn real to those of us on the ground."

"Oh." Somehow the knowledge that he'd once been afraid, that he really knew what she was going through, reassured her. "Were you ever injured?"

"Not seriously. Aidan was," Sean said, repressed emotion throbbing in his voice. "He was a Navy SEAL, but his career ended in a training accident after the Gulf War. Two men died, and they nearly lost Aidan as well. It took him almost a year to recover."

"It doesn't show."

"It's there. Before the accident, Aidan was a typical cocky SEAL. You know, the 'I'm invincible, and good looking, too' mentality. And he was all of those things." Sean gave a half smile. "But everyone's luck runs out eventually. Aidan changed after the accident. He dealt with all the survivor's guilt and grew up. He figured out what was important in his life."

"It must have been horrible."

"I'm not telling you this so that you feel sorry for him, but to make you realize that others have walked the path you're on right now. And they came out stronger on the other side."

Claire read through Sean's words to his unspoken love for Aidan. "You're very close to him, aren't you?"

"We were raised together—he's like my brother. He's also the reason I'm here, doing a job I love."

"It must be very nice to have someone who knows you so well." Though she felt a tug of envy, Claire's voice was even.

Sean hesitated. He knew that her childhood friend Olivia was the closest thing Claire had to family. It worried him. "When a person has an experience like yours, they should have someone to talk to. A family member, or someone who understands what they're feeling. You might want to consider seeing a therapist."

"A shrink? You've got to be kidding. How would he or she know what I was feeling?"

Something in Claire rebelled at the idea of seeking help, especially when she couldn't even say with certainty what was wrong with her. Basically, she'd witnessed a crime and bumped her head Friday night. Worse things happened to people every day without sending them to the psychiatrist's couch.

"But you need someone to talk to, and your friends certainly aren't qualified—has any of them ever been through an experience like yours? Why not see a doctor?" Sean persisted.

"I doubt I'd be able to find a shrink who had tripped over a modern day Jack the Ripper and then bashed his head on a stairway." She held up a hand to stop his next argument. "Besides, I have you."

"What?"

"You and Aidan, of course. You two, better than anyone, would know how I'm feeling. And you have a vested interest in me," she said, smiling.

Sean wondered if she was flirting with him. "I do?"

She gave him a strange look. "The case?"

"Oh, yeah. The case." He paused. "Of course you can call either one of us night or day to talk about the case, or to just—talk. You know how to reach us, right?"

"I have your card."

She continued to study him, curious. As she watched him, she sensed that he was deeply aware of her as a woman. God knew she was intensely aware of him. It was something she hadn't experienced in a long time.

Was he here late on a Sunday night for some reason other than just doing his job?

The phone on the nightstand rang, startling them both. While she talked, he looked at her face in profile, noting the clean line of her small nose, the delicate arch of her cheekbone, and the stubborn thrust of her chin. He wondered what it was about the combination of her features that made her so beautiful to him.

Sean didn't realize he was staring until Claire hung up the phone and tilted her head inquiringly at him.

"Who called?" he asked, hoping he didn't look as stupid as he felt.

"Olivia. She's going shopping tonight and wondered what I wanted. I'll be staying with her for a couple of days, until I can get a locksmith out to my place."

"Good. I don't like the idea of you being alone right now. Does Olivia have a security system?"

"She lives in a secured building. You don't think—"

"I don't think anything, except that it would be a good idea for you to stay quiet for a few days and avoid your previous routines. Don't make your life predictable. Stay with Olivia for as long as you can—it's just common sense. You can't always have a guard at your door."

"A *guard*?" Claire's voice rose.

He nodded toward the hall and then realized she hadn't noticed the hospital security guard outside her door. *Shit.*

"Since when?" she demanded. "And why?"

"There's a guard on this floor checking all IDs. It's probably just hospital policy."

"That's lame. Try again."

He rubbed his neck. "We're just being cautious, maybe overly so. We don't know for sure that you're in any danger." *Just a burning feeling in my gut whenever I think about it.*

Claire looked unconvinced.

Sean was angry with himself for scaring her. If he'd been thinking straight, rather than drooling over her, he might have handled the situation with a bit more finesse.

"Why don't you get some more sleep?" he said, backing toward the door before he stuck his foot in his mouth again. "Sorry I woke you. I didn't mean to."

"Sure. Run away. I'll sleep great tonight, thanks to you."

"Do you want me to stay for awhile?" He felt guilty enough to make the offer, though he hoped sincerely she wouldn't take him up on it.

"No. One guard is enough."

"Okay. I'll be in touch."

He slid out the door and shut it behind him.

"Jackass," Sean muttered to himself as he strode down the corridor. "You really screwed that up." He'd jumped out of airplanes during his years in the army. He'd faced down armed felons high on crystal meth when he was working the streets. And after twenty minutes with Claire Lambert he was tied up in knots like a horny teenager.

Distance, that's what he needed. A lot of distance.

Chapter 16

Sean dragged a grumpy Aidan through the revolving doors of the office building that housed Camelot Dating Services, Inc. They flashed their badges at the security guard and headed to the elevator.

"I told you there wouldn't be a problem," Sean said. "She's been here since seven. Some people appreciate the benefits of getting an early start on the day."

"Screw you. Some of us were at work until after eleven last night."

"Yeah, well, I didn't get to sleep much before one," Sean said, "so I don't want to hear any bitching."

"Why were you up that late? And don't tell me you had a date because I won't believe it."

"No date. I just couldn't turn my brain off and sleep. I went for a drive instead," Sean mumbled.

"How was Claire?"

Sean blew out an exasperated breath. God only knew how Aidan figured these things out, but he always did.

Aidan smiled. "Like I said, cousin, I know you. I figure

you were at the hospital within half an hour of leaving the station last night."

"Smart-ass. For your information, I didn't get there until after nine," Sean said.

"Sneaking in after visiting hours? How shocking. This gets better and better." Aidan heard Sean grinding his teeth and took pity on him. "Did she remember anything useful?"

"No. I think the memories are there, but she's having a tough time dealing with them. She talked about having nightmares, but can't remember anything when she wakes up. Maybe she doesn't want to." Sean shrugged and pressed the button for the eighth floor.

"The first few days after something like this are rough." Aidan narrowed his eyes as old memories of his own came to the surface. "She might need counseling or something."

"Jesus, don't say that to her. I suggested it and she almost took my head off. Says she'll be just fine without any shrink prying into her dreams." Sean stepped off the elevator and turned toward Camelot's offices.

"I told you, she's a tough one," Aidan said. "She'll work it out."

"How can you possibly know that?"

"Come on, you know I can read people. Besides, anyone can see Claire's got a backbone of steel inside that incredible body of hers."

"Even steel will bend or snap under the right kind of pressure," Sean said. Then he stopped dead as the rest of Aidan's words sank in. He grabbed his partner's arm. "You're not interested in her."

"Nah, I have a feeling she's already taken. Doesn't mean I can't admire a smart and pretty lady, though." Aidan's voice was cheerful.

"She's not taken. I told you, the preliminary investigation didn't turn up any boyfriend."

"How anyone as smart as you can be so thick about women is a complete mystery to me."

Aidan pushed past Sean and opened the door to Camelot's offices. He smiled in a friendly way at the young man behind the receptionist counter. "Detectives Burke and Richter here to see Afton Gallagher."

The kid's eyes widened as he carefully studied Aidan's badge.

"Afton is in her private office with her babies right now. I don't usually disturb her when she's there. You know—*breast-feeding*." The kid made a face.

"Right." Aidan leaned over the desk in a friendly way. "Maybe you could call her extension or something, see if the coast is clear."

"Sure thing."

Everyone seemed to open right up to his partner, Sean thought. Somehow, during interviews and in the field, Aidan always got to play good cop to Sean's bad cop. When he occasionally protested this arrangement, Aidan always pointed out that Sean did a lousy good cop when dealing with suspects. Something about his intensity put people off.

Within a few minutes the two detectives were being shown down a hall. A tall woman with short blonde hair was standing in an open doorway, looking toward them curiously.

"Hello, I'm Afton. I have no idea why you're here, but please come in." She stepped aside and showed them into the room.

Introducing themselves, Sean and Aidan walked past her. Though the sign on the door indicated that this was a "private office," the room looked more like a set from Sesame Street than a place of business. Fanciful pastel drawings of animals and fairy-tale characters decorated the yellow walls, and there were toys scattered on the floor. An oversize crib was pushed into the corner underneath a mobile of the solar system. A rocking chair sat nearby, next to a bookcase filled with oversized picture books.

Two infants lay in the middle of the floor, comfortably stretched out on a thick green blanket. As Sean and Aidan entered, the babies tracked the sounds and turned their heads to the newcomers.

"Twins!" Aidan said, taking the lead in putting Afton at ease. "You're a brave woman."

Sean made no comment, merely squatted down next to the babies and picked up a stuffed animal to get their attention. He knew exactly what to do. Over the years he'd been an honorary uncle to half a dozen of Aidan's sisters' kids.

"It's not like I had a choice, Detective." Afton smiled, charmed at how comfortable the men seemed to be with her babies. She supposed they must be married with kids of their own, but neither wore a wedding band. When she looked up, she discovered that Detective Burke was discreetly looking at her left hand, too.

Well, he won't find anything there, Afton thought.

"I'd offer you a seat, but there aren't any in here, unless one of you wants the rocking chair. I'm sorry, but my nanny doesn't get here until noon, so we'll have to stay with the boys."

"No problem." Aidan casually sprawled on the floor, drawing the attention of the nearest baby.

Sean settled himself comfortably as well, keeping a grip on the stuffed animal that was being earnestly gummed by the child at his side. He waited for Afton to decide what to do next.

She hesitated, then sat on the blanket as well. "These are my sons, Justin and Cameron. They'll be three months old next week."

Sean took in her slender figure and ringless hand. "Business owner and mother of two babies—that's a lot to handle. I hope their father helps out around the house."

"Their father is dead. What can I do for you gentlemen?" Afton's tone was flat.

Sean let Aidan jump into the hitch in the conversation while mentally filing away the information for Afton's file.

"I'm afraid we're here to investigate an incident involving at least one of your clients," Aidan said.

"Which client? What happened?"

"Claire Lambert was assaulted after she left here Friday night." Aidan studied her as he said the words, noting the way she sucked in her breath as her cheeks turned pale.

"Claire! Is she all right?"

"She's just fine, though she has a nasty bump on her head. I think she'll be leaving the hospital this morning," Sean said.

"Jesus. What's going on in this city? First there's a murder not ten minutes away, and now I find out that one of my friends was attacked after leaving here." Afton shook her head and reached out to stroke her hand over first one baby, then the other. "Is it this neighborhood? We just moved the business here four months ago, but maybe I need to find another office building."

"Crimes occur everywhere in the city," Sean said. "This building is as secure as most."

"What happened to Claire? Was she robbed, or . . ."

Afton forced herself to voice her greatest fear. "Was it a sexual assault?"

"We don't believe it was, and the doctor found no sign—"

"What did Claire say about it?" Afton interrupted. "I know cops are reluctant to believe the woman, but surely she told you what happened."

"Claire doesn't have any clear memories of the night she was attacked," Aidan said. "The doctor is hesitant to use the word *amnesia* just yet, but says it's not uncommon for a victim of head trauma to forget some or all of the events leading to the time of injury."

"That's where we need your help," Sean said. "There's a possibility that the man who attacked her may have some kind of connection to your dating service."

Guilt flooded Afton. "My God. I'm the one who talked her into this."

"How long have you known her?" Aidan asked.

"About six months. Claire's company hired Maura— my sister—to host several corporate events called Meet and Greet Mixers."

"Meet and what?" Aidan asked.

"You know, a sort of cocktail party after work where a firm's employees socialize with members of our dating service. Mostly the women members."

"Come again?" Sean asked.

"I'm sorry. I'm not being very clear, am I?" She ran a hand through her short blonde hair. "I just—I just feel so bad that I nagged Claire into this whole dating mess."

"Start from the beginning and take your time," Aidan said.

"Okay." She blew out a breath. "Most dating services have more female clients than male ones. My sister was always looking for creative ways around that problem. It turns out that lots of high-tech companies have many more male employees than female ones. Due to the technical nature of their jobs, many of these male employees are, um, introverted."

Aidan snorted, thinking of the geeks on the Police Department's IT staff. Sean glared at him.

Afton pressed on. "So Maura developed this plan to combine the two groups—she convinced some of the area firms that Camelot could host cocktail parties and invite only our female clients. The high-tech firms would invite their male programmers and technicians, and everyone could get acquainted in a casual environment. It was a brilliant plan, and the parties were lots of fun."

"But how did you meet Claire?" Sean asked.

"She's an account manager at her firm, and she leads a whole team of male programmers and technical experts. She sort of came along for moral support—you know, to act as an icebreaker. She was also the person who convinced her firm to sign up for the meet and greet parties in the first place. She told her management that the company had to offer unique and interesting benefits if they were going to hang on to their technical employees. After a while, we became friends."

"Do you still host these parties?" Aidan asked. The baby nearest him began to fuss, so he moved a toy within reach.

"No. With the bursting of the tech stocks bubble, many of our participating companies either went under, laid off their employees, or cut back dramatically on benefits and expenses. A lot has changed since my sister's time." Afton smiled sadly. "It's a whole new world out there."

"Did she sell you the business?" Sean asked.

"No, I inherited everything after she died two months ago. Leukemia."

"I'm sorry. To lose a husband and sister . . . this must be a very difficult time for you." Sean's sympathy was genuine.

"I've never been married, but it was still hard. As for my sister, she was sick and in pain for over a year. She was ready when the time came, even though we weren't." Afton's eyes filmed with tears, which she blinked back. "Anyway, Camelot is Maura's legacy, and I work very hard to keep things as she would have wanted them."

"We don't want to add to your burden," Sean said. "But we do need you to help us find out if Camelot is somehow involved with the attack on Claire."

The baby next to him began to fuss as well—Cameron, he thought. He picked up a rattle to distract him.

"It's almost feeding time," Afton murmured.

"We won't be much longer, just a couple more questions," Sean assured her. "If you could tell us what happened during Claire's appointment last Friday, that would be a big help."

"Claire's appointment started late, about seven. It was her first visit as a client, so we had a lot of paperwork to go through. She had to fill out several lengthy questionnaires on our computer system and provide detailed background information on herself."

"Can we see what she filled out?" Aidan asked.

"Member records are confidential, unless Claire is willing to release them. I can show you some blank questionnaires if you think that would help."

"Okay, so what did you do after the question-and-answer session?" Sean asked.

"My mother works with me. We both spent some time

helping Claire write a brief biography about herself. This will appear with her photo in our online catalogue. And yes," she added, before they could ask, "access to the catalogue is confidential and limited to members as well."

"And then?" Sean prompted.

"Then we spent several hours looking through our catalogue of male clients. We explained the system to Claire, then showed her how to search and sort candidates and their photos based on her preferences."

Sean came to attention. "Do you have the results of any of her searches? We can get a court order if necessary."

Afton looked unhappy at the thought of the police going through Camelot's files. "Claire, being Claire, decided not to use any sort criteria. She just started with the beginning of the alphabet and worked through to the last male candidate. She's very thorough. It took her until after eleven to finish the whole catalogue."

Sean thought quickly. If they could get a copy of everything they could cross match against the national criminal database and flag any Camelot members who had criminal records. "What format do you use for your files?"

"We use a database that was developed exclusively for Camelot. I can give you the name of our software consultant."

Afton picked up Cameron as the baby's fussing began to increase in volume. Justin also began to get restless, so Aidan jostled him gently, trying to distract him with strokes and pats.

Sean spoke over the sounds of unhappy babies. "What is the exact procedure you use to screen a new member?"

"Just as I explained to you. Claire's first visit was pretty typical. Once the new client leaves, we take their detailed background information and give it to a private investigator we have on retainer. They run a basic check for criminal records, credit history, that kind of thing."

Sean nodded. No help there.

"What does all this have to do with Claire being attacked?"

Sean hesitated, looked at his partner, then answered. "Claire remembers very little from last Friday night, but she did get a brief look at her attacker. She had a very strong impression that she'd seen the man before in a photograph—she's very certain about that. Camelot is the only place she can imagine having looked at photos recently, so we're checking it out."

Afton met his eyes for a long moment. "You think one of our male clients attacked Claire?"

"It's possible. The attack occurred only a couple of minutes from here," Sean pointed out.

"You're wrong. I'm sorry Claire was attacked—you have no idea how sorry—but our screening measures and security policy are excellent. Anyone with this type of behavior in their past would be discovered by our investigator. We'd cancel their membership and refund their money. My sister set the system up, and it's solid," Afton said.

The baby in her arms stopped fussing and began to wail.

"I'm sure it is," Sean said. "I hope you understand that we need to investigate every possibility."

"Of course. I just don't want you to spend your time scrutinizing Camelot when you could be exploring more productive leads."

With the crying baby in her arms, Afton made her way over to the phone. She spoke to someone and asked for two bottles of formula to be brought from the kitchen. As if on cue, the other baby began to cry as well, either from hunger or in sympathy.

"I need to, er, feed one of these guys while my mother gives the other a bottle," Afton said. "Then we switch. We'll probably be a while."

Both men shot to their feet. Aidan bent down, handed the second crying baby to Afton, and turned to leave.

"We need to talk with you again," Sean said quickly. "We'll leave our cards with the receptionist."

Almost before Afton could blink, the two men were out the door and moving down the hall at a good rate of speed. She smiled grimly to herself. Nothing like mentioning breast-feeding to send a grown man running for the hills. As she rocked the babies to calm them, she wondered if Claire blamed her for the attack, if that was why she hadn't called to tell her what had happened.

With her arms full of screaming babies and her heart full of guilt, Afton waited for her mother to bring in the reinforcements.

Chapter 17

Washington, D.C.
Wednesday evening

Sean grunted with the effort of blocking the basketball. He took an elbow shot to the gut from Aidan but refused to give way. Lunging forward, Sean swiped the ball from Aidan and jumped up to make a basket.

Using the back of his arm to wipe the sweat from his forehead, Sean passed the ball back to Aidan. "Fourteen to ten," Sean said, grinning.

"I'm just getting warmed up."

Aidan's bare torso, like Sean's, glistened with sweat. A sly wolf whistle from the left distracted Sean long enough for Aidan to get by him and score.

"Looking good, there, boys. Looking real good." A plump woman in her early forties gave them both a thumbs-up sign and lascivious smile on her way into the precinct's back entrance.

"Careful, Teresa, or I'll tell your husband you're window-shopping," Sean yelled as he tried to get by Aidan on the right, then lunged to the left.

"Boys, when the merchandise is really fine, there ain't

no crime in admiring it on the shelf." Teresa waved and headed inside to her job as a computer operator.

The two men continued to play, enjoying the rough game of one-on-one. The last few days had been an infuriating mix of bureaucratic roadblocks and dead ends. Both men were head-banging mad about their lack of progress on the case. Finally they had come outside to blow off steam at the basketball hoop someone had set up behind the station.

"Time out," Aidan panted.

He and Sean went over to their water bottles and towels. Even in the late evening the heat and humidity were intense.

After pouring cold water over his head, Sean took a long drink. "Any word on the court order to transfer Camelot's databases to our files?"

Aidan shook his head. "Attorney's office says we still don't have enough evidence to get a judge to issue the order. We'll have to talk Afton into just letting us have the records, or keep digging until we get something for the court. Maybe if we got a sworn statement from Claire saying she was positive the killer she saw was a client. . . ." He trailed off and shrugged.

"We've spent the last three days working on the dating service angle," Sean said, "and we've got squat to show for it. The forensics team has nothing from the scene—no fingerprints, hair, semen or skin samples that can be tied to the killer. Or to any of the other cases. The scene was just too contaminated." He set down his water and picked up the ball again, waiting for Aidan to finish gulping his drink.

Aidan wiped his mouth and headed for the blacktop beneath the hoop. "No one is this good, this careful. We have to be missing something."

"Well, we did get the medical examiner to agree that it's *possible* all three victims were killed with similar knives and, more importantly, knife strokes," Sean said, passing Aidan the ball. "None of the murdered women had incision marks or evidence of slicing. They all died from clean, deep wounds made by a six-inch blade that's at least an inch wide at the base."

Aidan grunted and made a jump shot over Sean's head. "I haven't had time to go over the preliminary forensics report. I've been too busy chasing court orders and trying to tie things up from the Camelot perspective."

"Me too. Maybe that's the problem. We've been running around trying to flesh out the dating service connection, going on the assumption that Claire really did see the killer in the catalogue. We've been trusting her instincts."

"That's nothing new. You and I go on instinct all the time," Aidan said, spinning around as Sean got by him.

"Yeah, but we always look to old-fashioned investigative work to back up our hunches. So far we haven't come up with anything. We've been working around the clock for close to five days," Sean said, slamming the ball through the hoop.

"What are you saying? You think Claire is imagining things?"

"It's possible. She took a helluva knock to the head." Sean's concentration faltered for a second, and his partner stole the ball. "Shit, I don't know. It seems like everything we follow turns to nothing. Mendes has nothing in her life to point to her killer. Nobody saw anything the night she was murdered but Claire."

"Slow progress is nothing new for murder investigations. Is Captain Michaels chewing on you?" Aidan asked, dunking the ball.

"Yeah. He's got this wild-ass idea to use Claire as bait to draw the killer out of hiding."

"She's all we have," Aidan said neutrally.

"Bullshit," Sean shot back. "We could go back and dig up everything that's been written in the files on the dead women over the years. And we need to go through unsolved stabbing murders for every precinct in the D.C. Metro area, maybe as far out as Baltimore. I have a feeling that this guy has been active for a while."

"No argument." Aidan caught the ball Sean fired at him after scoring and began a new charge toward the hoop. "The captain told me to dig into the Camelot angle."

"And Claire?"

"Yeah."

"He's really hot on the bait idea, isn't he?"

"Yeah." Aidan made a basket while Sean stood there. *"Shit."*

Sean grabbed the rebound and slammed it through hard enough to make the backboard vibrate.

Chapter 18

Claire was relieved when Olivia finally went back to
work on Friday morning. She felt guilty that her
friend had already missed so much work, guiltier still for
the fact that she had worried and fussed over Claire since
she'd left the hospital. But now Livvie was back to her job
at DC Child and Family Services, leaving Claire to enter-
tain herself in her friend's cozy two-bedroom apartment.

After locking the two dead bolts and chain behind
Livvie, Claire sat at Olivia's antique desk and opened the
laptop computer a coworker had dropped off. She barely
paid attention to the status update her team had sent.
Things were going well without her, and she was confident her accounts would be fine for a few more days.
When she heard her own thoughts, she paused. *Who
would have believed it?*

She was normally the type of person who took her computer and cell phone with her on vacation, half-convinced
that things would fall apart while she was away from the
office.

Funny how almost dying changed a person's perspective. She'd barely given work a second thought in the last week.

Giving herself a mental shake, Claire dealt with some e-mails needing replies and shut down her laptop. She wanted to keep Olivia's phone line free in case someone called. Specifically, in case Sean called with an update on the investigation. Since it had been days since they'd last spoken, Claire had to believe he would attempt to contact her soon.

The phone didn't ring, so she cooked a quick breakfast. While she ate it, she told herself Sean was busy following an investigative lead. That would explain why he hadn't called.

Later, as she surveyed the refrigerator for lunch prospects, she told herself she would give Sean one more hour. When the phone finally rang, Claire dropped the sandwich she'd been picking at and rushed to grab the receiver.

"Hi, Claire. It's Afton. When I couldn't find you at home, I called Olivia's number. I didn't want to disturb you before." Afton paused. "Anyway, I understand if you don't want to talk to me, since I'm the one who got you into this mess."

"Don't be ridiculous," Claire said. "No one got me into this. It just happened."

"And it wouldn't have if I hadn't nagged you into joining Camelot. The detectives seem sure the dating service is connected. I'm so sorry," she said miserably. "Is there anything I can do for you?"

"You spoke to Sean and Aidan? When?"

"The first time was Monday morning, but I've pretty much had daily contact since then. They're trying to get a court order to access Camelot's files. I'd like to just give them the information, but Mother contacted our lawyer and he says I could be liable if I turn over confidential details on clients. He's reviewing our membership contracts right now, to see what the liability is if we turn the database over to the police." Afton hesitated. "Are you all right?"

"Sure—I just knocked myself out when I fell down a set of steps. It really wasn't as dramatic as it sounds. Everything's fine."

"Is it really? The detectives are going to an awful lot of trouble just to catch an assault suspect."

Claire hesitated. Afton seemed to be under the impression that Sean and Aidan were treating the attack as an isolated incident, instead of one that was connected to the murder of Renata Mendes.

"What exactly did Sean tell you about last Friday night?" Claire asked cautiously.

"Just that you were assaulted while walking home from Camelot. He said you couldn't remember much, except for the impression you had seen the guy who attacked you in a photo. Possibly a photo from Camelot's catalogue. Although they don't seem to be pursuing that angle anymore."

"What do you mean?" Claire asked.

"It's just an impression. At first both detectives were involved in questioning me, and they really pushed for me to turn Camelot's catalogue over to their technical department. Recently, I've only been talking to Detective Burke. Frankly, he seems more interested in you, me, and Camelot as a business than he is in the catalogue. That's my take, anyway."

"Did they mention anything about the woman who was

murdered at the middle school near Camelot?" Claire asked, already knowing the answer.

"No. What's going on?"

Claire was reluctant to fill her in. Sean and Aidan had clearly withheld the information from Afton. On the other hand, no one had told her not to talk about that night.

Besides, if the police were going to play games, they could at least call her and tell her the rules. Since they hadn't, it didn't matter, did it?

With that, Claire told the entire story to Afton.

"My God. You witnessed the murder?" Afton was in shock. "And you think you might have seen the killer in Camelot's catalogues? I can't believe it!"

"Obviously, neither can the cops, since they've abandoned their efforts to get into your files and check out my story."

"If there is even a chance that murder is involved, I'll turn over the entire database with no questions asked—forget my mother and the lawyer. Jesus, all the police had to do was explain."

"That would be too easy," Claire said bitterly.

She told herself it was stupid to be hurt. She shouldn't take it personally that Sean had been holding back information—and his opinion—about Claire's version of the night of the murder. But she was hurt, and angry that she'd learned more about the status of the investigation from a chance phone call than from the detectives who were supposed to be her advocates.

She felt her temper rising and deliberately clamped down. Flying off the handle wouldn't help. Okay, so the police didn't believe her story. So they had been keeping her in the dark right along with Afton. And because the detectives didn't believe her, they'd blown off the dating service catalogues, which was the one thing Claire felt certain about in all the events of the last week.

"You're sure about seeing the man in a photo?" Afton asked.

"Do you have time to meet with me this afternoon?" Claire interrupted.

"I'll clear my schedule and be over in half an hour."

"No. I'll meet you at your office. I think we've let me fall behind on my membership obligations."

"What are you talking about?"

"I suddenly feel a great need to look through your catalogue again. I'm sure I must have overlooked suitable matches the last time around. When would you have time to go through the photos with me again?"

"How soon can you get here?"

"Give me twenty minutes." Claire hung up and got ready to leave for Camelot.

And to hell with a blue-eyed detective named Sean Richter.

Chapter 19

Claire stalked into the building that held Camelot's offices. She was still simmering over the fact that the police didn't believe her about having seen the killer's photo. Sean probably thought she'd just been hysterical. Maybe he thought she was wrapped up in some kind of dating neurosis and had subconsciously tied witnessing the murder with her visit to Camelot. After all, hadn't he almost lost it when she'd told him she'd gone to a dating service in the first place?

She stepped into the elevator and punched the button like it was a certain detective's face. Normally she wasn't one to simmer. When she got mad, she exploded, worked through things with the object of her frustration, and moved on with few hard feelings. But given Sean's annoying absence, that wasn't possible.

Coward. He knows I'm furious.

The fact that he could hardly know whether she was cheerful or killing mad didn't matter. It was much too satisfying to think of him hiding from her temper.

With a toss of her dark curls, she strode through the doors to the dating service. Afton was waiting there. She hugged Claire tightly, which surprised her. Afton was a good friend, but not normally a hugger. Claire returned the embrace, sensing that Afton needed to be reassured about something.

"I'm so glad you're all right," Afton said, leading her to the private office. She shut the door behind them. "I've been sitting here worrying about you, thinking what I would do if it turns out this guy is a Camelot client. It will destroy everything Maura worked so hard to build."

"Don't worry yet. I can't be certain I saw the guy in the catalogue."

"But how can we be sure?"

Claire took a deep breath. In some ways, she really didn't want to do this, but there wasn't any choice. "Since I have such a strong image in my head of a photograph of the killer, and since this is the only logical place I could have seen photos recently, I want to go through the catalogue pictures until something jogs my memory."

"You think you'd recognize the photo—or maybe have some kind of emotional reaction—even if you can't remember anything else about that night?"

"Exactly. If only you could see the photo in my mind. I don't really have an idea about his features, but his smile—" Claire stopped and shivered.

"Tell me about it. Maybe I'll recognize him and save us some time."

"It was a very unique smile, kind of tight and twisted up at the ends. Hell, it was twisted period. As if he were getting off, only there was real cruelty in the smile as well." Claire looked at Afton, needing to be believed. "I'm not doing a very good job of describing it, but I'm sure I'd recognize him if I ever saw that smile again."

"Okay, so we look through the catalogue for guys who have a twisted smile." Afton mentally reviewed the best way to approach this task. "Some of the clients aren't smiling in the pictures. Do you want to eliminate them?"

"No, I think we should go over every male client, in whatever way I did the night of the murder. I think that's very important. Maybe something will trigger a memory."

"Sounds good."

Claire looked at Afton, seeking any sign that she was being humored or patronized. There was nothing but determination in Afton's brown eyes.

"That night," Afton said thoughtfully, "you opted to view the catalogues alphabetically. You went through every photo and bio in the system. It took hours, but it should be easy to duplicate. Let me transfer my calls to voice mail and set the computer up, then you can pull a chair over here and start."

Claire dragged a chair over to the desk. "Have the police already been through the pictures?"

Afton shook her head. "I told you, my lawyer advised me against releasing the information until he could determine our liability. However, since you're a paying customer, I have no issues." She winked at Claire and gave the command to sort the database entries in alphabetical order.

Very quickly a photo popped up on the screen. Nice enough man, a little older than his bio stated, and smiling like a choirboy.

"Next," Claire said.

Another photo appeared. No smile.

"Next."

Claire settled in and concentrated on bringing up memories of having been here before, of seeing the parade of hopeful male faces. Something. Anything. Whenever she spent longer than a few moments on a photo, Afton wrote down the name for further research. She gave up asking Claire why she lingered over any photo. Her friend simply didn't know.

They had gotten to *F* when voices from the hall distracted the women.

"I think she's in her office, even though she's not answering." A pause, then a soft knock on the door. "Afton?"

"Come in."

The door opened a crack and Camelot's young receptionist popped his head in the opening. "Detectives Burke and Richter here to see you again."

Claire grimaced and muttered, "Busted."

Afton sighed. "Let them in."

The men came through the door, one after the other. Sean stopped abruptly on seeing Claire, and his partner smacked into him from behind.

"What the hell are you doing here?" Sean asked.

Claire's temper red-lined in a heartbeat, though she kept her expression calm. "Detective Richter, how nice to see you. I'm so pleased you remember me, because I was beginning to think you'd forgotten who I was. Certainly I haven't heard from you or Detective Burke in days, but I guess even common courtesy must be pushed aside during important police investigations." Claire's Louisiana accent was pronounced, the drawling tones doing nothing to hide the fire burning in her eyes.

Well, shit, Sean thought. *Who pissed in her chili?*

And when had he become *Detective Richter*, uttered in that nasty, syrupy voice? He knew she'd been raised in New Orleans, but her accent wasn't usually so pronounced. He exchanged a look with Aidan.

Afton stepped into the yawning silence to offer the men seats and some coffee. Claire continued to work one-handed on the computer. After giving a new command to the database program, she swiveled her chair, looked directly at Sean, and waited for him to make the next move.

Aidan tried to smooth over the tense silence. "You're looking great, Claire. How's the head doing?"

"It's just fine. You'd be amazed at what a few quiet days can do to clear up your thinking and put things in perspective. Especially when your office leaves you alone and all you have to do is think about your personal life."

"Have you remembered anything?" Sean asked.

"Nothing you would find useful, I'm sure." She turned back to the computer and began searching the next range of entries.

"What the hell is that supposed to mean?" Sean asked. It was better than asking what he really wanted to know, which was why she was mad at him. The composed, angry woman sitting before him had little resemblance to the one he'd last seen in the hospital, with wild curls and shadows in her vulnerable eyes.

"I think she's pissed about something," Aidan said.

"Now why would I be mad?" Claire asked, looking over her shoulder at Aidan. "Haven't you and your partner kept me up to date on what's happening with *my* investigation and when I can move back into *my* home? Haven't I had twice-daily calls letting me know what y'all are working on, and how things are going and if I could be any help?" Claire picked up Afton's letter opener and began to tap it on the blotter pad.

Sean's eyes narrowed.

Aidan started talking fast. If Sean lost his temper things would go to hell real fast. "That would be my fault," Aidan said. "I've been working on the part of the investigation involving you and Afton, while Sean has been buried in archived files for every precinct in the D.C. Metro area. We've both been so busy that some days we didn't remember to eat." He smiled his most winning smile.

Despite her annoyance Claire had to admit that what Aidan said made sense, if you didn't examine it too closely.

"Plus," Aidan added quickly, "your doctor told us to give you a couple of days to rest. Couldn't go against his orders, now, could we?" Aidan stretched the truth without hesitation. He *had* spoken to Claire's doctor as part of his background check, and the man *had* said the best chance for Claire to recover her memory would be through rest and recuperation.

Claire fiddled a bit more with the letter opener. From the corner of her eye she could see that Sean looked very tired, with deep circles under his blue eyes. His short, dark hair was carelessly combed, as if he had run a hand through it repeatedly.

Never one to hold a grudge, she decided to give the detectives a chance to redeem themselves by bringing her fully up to date on the status of the investigation.

"How have things been going on the Mendes case, then?" she asked.

Sean's expression became guarded. He resisted the

urge to glance at Afton and see her response to the question. They had planned to stop by Camelot today and explain to her in detail why they believed Claire's attack was related to a series of murders in the area.

"Don't worry," Claire said. "Afton knows the whole story about the night of the murder." She smiled defiantly at Sean. "You didn't tell me to keep things quiet, did you? Besides, Olivia already knew. I needed Afton's help, so I told her."

Sean sat back in his chair and told himself that losing his temper would be stupid. Obviously Claire had been doing quite a bit of thinking in the last few days. While he was pleased she was feeling well enough to be out of the hospital visiting friends, he was uncomfortable with the idea of her revealing information about an active case without consulting him in advance.

"You should have talked to me," Sean said.

"How? You didn't return my call. Twice."

"It's fine if Ms. Gallagher knows," Aidan said before his partner could put words to the anger narrowing his eyes. "We'd prefer if neither of you discussed it with anyone else, though."

Sean rubbed his neck and told himself to cool off. They should have known that Claire would talk with her friends. If they hadn't wanted her to, they should have told her so. He couldn't get mad at her for something that was their own fault.

"Sure, it's no problem," Sean said. "Saves us some explaining." He looked over the desk at Afton. "Now you understand why we want to go through your files."

"I certainly do. But since I hadn't heard anything more about the court order, I'd assumed you had, um, abandoned the idea that our files would be useful." She looked at Claire uncomfortably, seeking support as she became the focus of Sean's intense stare.

"Why would you think that? We've just been working other angles of the case," Sean said.

"What she means," Claire said, "is it seemed like the police didn't believe me about the potential connection between the killer and Camelot's catalogue. I can understand how she came to that conclusion."

"It's not that we don't believe you," Sean said. "And we haven't dismissed any possibilities. We're detectives, Claire. A lot of what we do would seem pointless to you, but it's all part of building an investigation."

"Puh-lease," Clare said, rolling her eyes. "Look, I understand that an eyewitness suffering from amnesia isn't exactly a slam dunk for a court order, much less a conviction. That's why I'm working on finding something more concrete than a *feeling* I've seen this guy's picture before."

"What are you up to?" Sean said.

"I'm not 'up to' anything. I'm merely pursuing something I believe is critical to regaining my memory."

Sean shot out of the chair and came around the desk. One glance at the computer screen was all he needed. "You're looking through the catalogue."

"Give the detective a cigar," she said.

Aidan started to say something, then shut up at a look from Sean.

"Do you really believe you're going to find the guy's picture here?" Sean said, ignoring her attitude.

"What I really believe is that if I don't do something to get my life back under control, I'll go nuts." With that, Claire lifted her chin and scrolled through the next entry.

Sean placed one hand palm down on the desk and the other on the back of Claire's chair, effectively making a cage out of his arms. "Were you going to let me know if you found anything in the database?"

She was smart enough not to answer a question asked in the deadly quiet tone Sean was using. She also understood body language enough to know that Sean was deliberately trying to intimidate her, so she resisted the urge to squirm in her chair.

Silence continued, punctuated by the occasional click of the mouse Claire used as she worked her way through the photos.

"Were you, Claire?" He leaned closer, frankly looming over her. He was angry and didn't mind letting it show. "Were you going to let us in on your little side investigation, tell us if you found a suspect? Or maybe you were just going to slip on your Wonder Woman costume and take the guy out yourself, huh?"

Claire leaped to her feet and tried to stare Sean down. It was a difficult task, given the fact that he was more than a head taller. "I'm not an idiot. How come if you look through the catalogues for a suspect you're just doing your job, but if I do it I'm some kind of nutcase with a Nancy Drew complex?"

"Because it's my job," he said.

She drew in a breath that was half sob. Until that instant she hadn't realized how stressed she was. "Your job. But it's my *life*. You go to the office, work on the case, then close your files and go home. I don't have any place to leave this locked up. Someone else is calling the shots, but *I* have to live with the results twenty-four hours a day."

Sean's anger faded as he tried to imagine what it would

be like to have his life turned upside down, then have strangers controlling his attempts to get things back to normal again. He'd be mad as hell.

"I have no idea what progress, if any," she said, "has been made on a case that has me afraid to stay in my own home. Worse, I feel like I'm being treated as a suspect, when in reality I've done nothing except be in the wrong place at the wrong time."

Sean clasped her rigid arms gently. "I'm sorry you felt that way." He waited until she looked up and met his eyes. "But until we're certain that the murderer was a stranger to Renata Mendes, we have to give that avenue all our resources and attention. Stranger murders—murders where the killer isn't known to the victim—are damned uncommon. The dead woman is, and has to be, our first concern. But I'm sorry if we've made you feel like we didn't trust you."

Claire looked intently into Sean's eyes and sighed. She couldn't stay angry in the face of his sincerity.

"Don't be nice to me," she said. "I'm still mad at both of you."

Sean let out the breath he'd been unconsciously holding. "No one can stay mad at Aidan for long," he said with a small smile.

"How about you?" Claire asked, still looking at Sean.

Aidan answered. "He lacks my charm and doesn't grovel worth a damn. There are probably some outstanding contracts on his life as we speak."

She smiled faintly at the image of either man groveling.

"So what's the plan then?" she asked to break the tension. "Afton and I have been through the catalogue entries up to *F*, and we've made a list of some names we think should be investigated. I know you're not convinced that looking through the database will help any, but how much can it hurt?"

"Can you give us one day before we pursue that?" Sean asked. "We'll get to the catalogues, I promise. Can you trust me, just for one more day?"

Trust me.

In her experience, those were famous last words coming from a man, but she told herself it was just temporary. Twenty-four hours wouldn't seem like much to most people. But he was asking her not to get involved in an investigation that was now her life. She wondered if he had any idea what he was asking and how deeply it went against her nature. Then she looked at him and realized he did understand, yet asked for her trust anyway.

She reminded herself it was only for a day. "Will you keep me updated on your progress?"

Sean recognized it as the compromise it was. "We'll tell you whatever we can, especially if it has to do with you."

Claire gave him a long look. She'd never been around anyone who could be so composed and yet angry at the same time. It was his strength of will more than anything else that angered and intrigued her. She'd never met anyone who could stand up to her when she was really mad. He'd not only done that but he'd also gotten her to agree to a compromise—a word not normally found in her vocabulary.

"All right. But I want regular reports," she added.

There was the steel that lay underneath the curls and sexy body, Sean thought with a smile. He was getting used to both. "Agreed. Now, why don't you take the doctor's advice and go home and rest for a few more days."

Claire shot him a "get real" look. "Like you, I have a job. Dr. Springer said to let pain be my guide, and I feel just fine. I'm working from Olivia's home, not sleeping around the clock. I'll talk to you soon." She left the room, followed by Afton.

As soon as the door closed behind the women, Aidan turned and raised an eyebrow at Sean. "Wonder Woman uniform?"

"Fuck you," Sean said with a half smile.

Aidan laughed and tried to remember the last time he'd seen someone get to Sean as fast as Wonder Woman had. "Is that what you're going to tell Captain Michaels?"

Sean stopped smiling. With every hour he and Aidan didn't make any progress on the case, the captain got more impatient about not using Claire. And putting Claire in the line of fire was something Sean was not ready to do.

Chapter 20

"We're so relieved that you weren't seriously hurt, Claire. What happened, exactly?" Tiffani Kensit's voice dropped, inviting Claire to share the juicy details of the night she was injured. "The only thing Mr. Webster said was that you had been attacked near Dupont Circle."

Claire wished that Tiffani had chosen another day to pile up overtime. Tiffani with an *i* was a crucial link in the network of office gossip. While the young woman was pleasant and even friendly, she couldn't wait to tell whoever cared to listen over the wall of the bathroom stalls all about the intimate details of Claire's life.

That's what had happened the one and only time Claire had dated someone she worked with. The office rumor mill had gotten hold of the details from Claire's scorned ex. She hadn't forgotten the humiliation of having her failed relationship discussed in rest rooms and over the water cooler in the employee lounge.

"Sorry, the police asked me not to talk about it. But I

appreciate your concern." Claire somehow managed to say the words without choking.

After closing her office door so she wouldn't be disturbed by other people playing weekend catch-up, she made her way steadily through the voice mails, messages, and faxes she hadn't been able to clear out yesterday. She tried very hard to focus on her clients and accounts, but in the back of her mind a timer slowly counted down, ticking off the minutes in the twenty-four hours she had promised Sean.

At exactly one minute after eleven, Claire still hadn't heard from the police. No missed calls were listed on her cell phone. She dialed Olivia's number.

"Hi, Livvie. Any messages for me?"

"No. Don't forget—late brunch with Afton today. Be ready to do decadent girly stuff. We all need a little break."

"I won't forget."

Annoyance gave a snap to Claire's stride as she walked to the metro station. She was just in time to catch the train that would drop her close to Sean's office. The cars were full of tourists and kids, who ranged from excited to whiny without warning.

Coming to the top of the long escalator exit from the metro, she saw that the skies were threatening rain. She still hadn't replaced the umbrella she'd lost the night of the murder, so she hurried to beat the storm. She just made it through the door as the rain let loose. Inside the police station, an older man sat behind a desk, chatting with a woman leaning on the counter.

"I'd like to speak with Detective Richter," Claire said.

The woman turned and gave her an assessing look. "I'll

take her, Frank. Follow me." The woman turned down a long corridor. "I'm Teresa—are you a salesperson or something?"

"No, I'm Claire Lambert. Detective Richter and his partner are working on my case."

"Right. Well, this is where Sean and Aidan should be."

Claire looked at the empty chairs.

"Wait here and I'll go drag them out of the kitchen," Teresa said with a wink. She headed for the doors at the other end of the room. "They're probably mainlining caffeine."

Claire looked around the men's work area, trying to guess which desk belonged to whom. She was pretty sure the desk closest to her was Aidan's, given its cheerfully cluttered appearance. Leaning closer to confirm her suspicion, she saw a file. The tab on the orange folder was labeled Marie Claire Lambert and had a number, presumably a case identification code.

She looked around quickly and reached for the file. As she read, a chill went through her body. Her jaw tensed as she flipped to the next page, and then the next. Settling into the chair with the file in front of her, she decided someone had a lot of explaining to do. She couldn't wait to hear it.

Trust me.

From where she sat, that looked like another way to say *Screw you.*

Chapter 21

The man sat outside the gourmet coffee shop on Wisconsin Avenue, sipping his iced latte. Despite the heat, humidity, and scattered rain, he wasn't alone at the chic metal tables with their canvas umbrellas. He'd been playing with the latte for half an hour. In that time he'd seen Marie Claire's redheaded friend enter the building with bags from a local grocery store. Little Olivia.

He'd traced her name through the license plate on her car last week, which had also given him her full address. The fifth-floor apartment facing the street was hers. Right now she was going through the room opening blinds. No sign of his target yet, but he was confident Marie Claire would appear soon.

He thought about his little surprise and wished he could be there to see how she reacted. Impossible, really, so he'd just have to imagine what she would do. That was almost as good.

He was prepared to sit outside for the rest of the day if necessary, camouflaged with his massive book on the history of Western civilization and his Georgetown University baseball cap. Just another grad student nursing a latte and eating biscotti while he crammed for summer finals.

He smiled at the thought.

Chapter 22

Sean and Aidan sat at a scarred table in the precinct coffee room, their chairs tipped back as each topped off on scalding coffee despite the sultry heat of the day and the room.

"The more we dig into Mendes, the less we find," Sean said.

"Everything we've found out about Claire indicates that she's a law-abiding citizen from New Orleans, working as a white-collar professional in D.C. for the last eight years. She's trustworthy, mentally stable, financially solvent, and an all-around good citizen who would be happy to work with the police to lure—"

"No," Sean said stubbornly. "I found four more murders within a two-hundred-and-fifty-mile radius that remain unsolved, all involving Hispanic prostitutes or semi-pros stabbed with a large blade. The cases span the last ten years, with the most recent murder committed two years ago."

"If they really are connected to our guy, he's been at

this for some time. I'm surprised the FBI hasn't picked up on the case yet."

Sean shook his head. "Different jurisdictions, large geographical area, and a long break between murders. Plus the victims were all turning tricks—not the type of victim who's going to inspire shock and outrage in the community. It's not surprising that no one has put the pieces together."

"But now the killer is escalating," Aidan said.

"Yeah. At first there were years between the killings. Now we're talking six months between Renata Mendes and Cristina Herrera," Sean said grimly.

Aidan shook his head. "Not good." And it would just make Captain Michaels more determined to solve the case before another agency could step in, which Aidan didn't need to point out.

"What did you come up with on Afton and Camelot?" Sean asked.

"Camelot is a legitimate operation, running at a decent profit. No outstanding debts, no lawsuits. Seems solid. Afton was registered as the owner just under three months ago, shortly before her sister's death."

"What about Afton herself?"

"Up until about ten months ago she lived outside of Boulder, Colorado. She taught theater and literature at a fancy boarding school for gifted teenagers. I guess she moved here when her sister was diagnosed with leukemia."

"What about the father of her kids?" Sean asked.

"They were never married. Apparently the guy was murdered on a business trip to South America. Neither her coworkers nor her neighbors had ever met the man, though the neighbor across the street had seen him a couple of times."

"Murdered? What happened?"

"I don't have any details. Afton's former colleagues reported that she missed a month of school just over a year ago. All the principal could tell me was that Afton's boyfriend had been murdered on a trip to Ecuador or something, and she took some personal time afterward. She moved to D.C. to be near her sister within a couple months of that, selling everything she had in Boulder."

"Poor kid." Sean shook his head, wishing he could shield Afton from a homicide case that would doubtless bring up bad memories. He liked her straightforward approach and admired anyone who took on family responsibilities without complaint.

"Yeah. She's been through a lot already. The last thing she needs is to be involved in a murder investigation."

The door swung open and Teresa leaned in. "I knew I'd find you hiding in here," she said to Sean. "Claire Lambert is here to see you."

The front legs of his chair came down with a bang. "She out front?"

"No, I showed her where you and Burke sit. She's waiting for you."

"Thanks. We'll be right there," Sean said.

"Think she's still mad at you for kicking her out of Camelot yesterday?" Aidan asked slyly as they walked to their desks.

"She wasn't really mad, she's just one of those people who needs to understand the why of any situation. I think now she realizes what we're trying to do and will leave the job to us."

Laughing, Aidan shook his head. "Put down the crack pipe, buddy."

Aidan was still smiling when he walked through the

doorway and saw Claire with an open file folder in front of her.

"Tell me that file isn't what I think it is," Sean said softly.

"Shit," was all Aidan said.

"This is why you asked me for one more day?" Claire asked calmly, without looking up from the file. "So you could have me investigated?"

"You want me to explain?" Aidan asked softly.

"I'll take care of it," Sean said. "Give us a minute."

Aidan grabbed his keys and left without a word.

"Investigating you wasn't my choice," Sean said to Claire. "Captain Michaels insisted that we have a full profile of you as a way of judging your reliability as a witness."

When Claire raised her eyes from the folder and looked directly at him, he was jolted by the emotions he saw in her black gaze.

"You asked for my trust, and then you investigated me. God, you talked to my neighbors and coworkers about my sex life."

Or lack thereof.

The thought of Sean reading the contents of the file made her want to curl up and die of humiliation. Instead, she drew on years of hard-won poise and got to her feet.

Sean had expected temper, even a shouting match, but she had just shut down. It made him nervous.

"Where are you going?" Sean asked.

"To Livvie's place." Claire gathered her purse and raincoat.

"Why did you stop by to see me? Did you have something new?"

"I wanted a report on what you've been doing for my

case. I got it." She closed the folder with her name on it and handed it to Sean. "Trust me."

"Goddamn it." He looked around the room, which was scattered with cops who made their living shoving their nose in other people's business. "We can't talk here. I'll drive you to Olivia's."

"That's too kind of you, Detective. I couldn't put you to so much trouble." She headed for the door.

He wrapped his hand around her upper arm and said in a low, angry tone, "Lose the attitude. I'll be damned if you're going to make me feel guilty for doing my job."

Without waiting for an answer he steered her down the hall toward the back parking lot. When he stopped at the passenger side of a police-issue unmarked sedan, she pulled away.

"I don't think it would be a good idea for me to get in a car with you right now, Detective. Too many weapons within reach."

"The weapons are locked up."

"The radio cord isn't."

"Keep it up and I'll put you in back behind the cage," he said.

"This is called kidnapping."

"This is called getting you to listen long enough to calm down." He crowded her into the passenger side, locked the door, and closed it hard.

When he got behind the wheel, she didn't look at him. He leaned over and fastened her seat belt, telling himself that it wasn't another excuse to touch her.

Claire hung onto her temper because it made her feel less like a victim. The rational part of her mind knew that she wasn't being reasonable, but nothing about the last few days had been reasonable.

She noticed that Sean turned onto the route that would lead straight to Olivia's apartment. Undoubtedly it was just one more fact he'd dug up in his investigation of Claire Lambert, victim.

"Are you going to talk to me?" Sean asked after several minutes of silence.

She turned toward him. "Maybe I can understand why you did this, but it's the way you did it that pisses me off. You said 'Trust me' and then you violated my privacy. Next time you want to investigate my money situation, or old boyfriends and lovers, you come to me. Don't go talking about my private life to anyone who ever looked out their living room window and thought they saw a car parked in front of my place for the night!"

"There's no need to make this personal."

"It's pretty damned personal to me."

"All right, but don't ask us to conduct an investigation with our hands tied. Look at it this way—if you were being stalked, we'd be talking to everyone who ever knew you, because you wouldn't be able to give us objective answers. You might not see an ex-boyfriend or date as a threat, but with our experience we can catch things you'd miss."

"As I'm sure your little file shows, there's no one in my past who cares enough to stalk me. I don't affect men like that."

"And that's a fine example of why we don't ask *you* about your life," Sean said.

"What does that mean?"

"Jesus," he muttered. "Don't you have any mirrors? Of course you affect men like that. You're fucking gorgeous."

Claire stared out the windshield and didn't say a word. She was too busy trying to see herself as gorgeous, much less fucking gorgeous. Unconsciously she shook her head. She couldn't see it.

Sean tried a different tack. "When you prepare a bid for a client, don't you thoroughly research a number of different alternatives, then present all the options, along with your recommendation for the best approach?" He didn't wait for an answer. "It's the same thing in police work, only it's more important for us to be thorough because if we screw up someone could die."

"Then why are you ignoring the dating service connection? It could be a big lead and you're just blowing it off! For all we know Renata Mendes could have been a member."

"Are you saying that the dating service fields sex workers?" Sean asked. "That's what the other victims were— Hispanic prostitutes. Mendes wasn't a hooker, but she was Hispanic and in the wrong place at the wrong time. As for being a client of Camelot, that was one of the first things we checked after we talked with you. She wasn't."

"You could have told me sooner."

"The fewer people who know, the better chance there is to keep it out of the headlines." Sean turned into the driveway of Olivia's apartment building, released Claire's door lock, and faced her. "This asshole cuts up women for fun. I want to catch him so bad I can taste it."

So much for fucking gorgeous, Claire thought as she undid her seat belt. When Sean looked at her, what he really saw was a case to be solved.

"I believe you, Detective. Thank you for the ride." She opened the door and bolted.

Sean opened his own door and shot out to follow her.

"Hey, buddy," yelled the doorman as Claire trotted by him. "Move the car before I call the cops!"

Claire quickly crossed the lobby and pushed into a

loaded elevator just as the doors were closing. The elevator stopped at every floor to exchange passengers. When the doors finally slid open on the fifth floor, she stepped out into the hall and kept walking while she looked through her purse for the key Olivia had loaned her.

Head down, she ran smack into a large male body. She knew without looking up that it would be Sean.

"Most people would be out of breath after running up five flights of stairs," she said, stepping around him.

"Guess I'm not most people," Sean replied, falling in step with her.

Claire rolled her eyes. "What do you want?"

Progress, he thought cautiously. She was no longer calling him "Detective" in that cuttingly polite voice. "I wanted to make sure you're okay. You haven't been out of the hospital all that long."

Claire stopped by Livvie's door. He was right, which only made the headache that was always lingering in the back of her brain worse. "I'm thirty years old—but then, you know that, don't you?—and I've been taking care of myself for a long time, which you also know from reading my file. I'm just fine, thank you."

"You've never been the potential target of a serial killer before." Sean felt an angry tic begin in his left cheek.

Claire saw the telltale tic and the fact that his icy blue eyes had turned silver with temper. "*Cher*, I've survived Mardi Gras in New Orleans every year of my life. This is a piece of cake."

"Mardi Gras? *Jesus Christ.*"

She clucked her tongue and tapped his left cheek. "You're going to rupture something if you don't calm down." She smiled slightly, feeling much better for his loss of control. She turned and slid the key in the door. "If

I'm that frustrating, why don't you stop fighting and work with me instead?"

It was her smile that did it. His hand shot out, captured hers, and pulled it toward his mouth.

"This is why," he said, pressing a hot kiss into her palm. He didn't take his eyes off hers as he parted his lips and gently stroked her flesh with his tongue.

Her eyes widened and her mouth opened in a soft sound of comprehension. With her heart pounding, she felt his warm tongue make a second leisurely slide across the suddenly hypersensitive skin of her palm. She moved closer, instinctively pressing her body against his as she came up on her tiptoes. Without conscious thought, she slid her free hand around his neck.

She only had to tug once before he bent his head down to her, stopping with his mouth a breath away from her parted lips.

"Hell," he said softly, and kissed her.

Claire shut her eyes and savored Sean. As he captured her closed lips in a teasing nip, she decided he tasted like spearmint and coffee. When he stroked the line between her lips with his tongue, her toes curled inside her shoes and she opened her mouth to let him in. A flash of heat shot through her body, bringing with it a restlessness she tried to soothe by pressing against him. She struggled to get closer, but he was too tall to reach the way she wanted to.

Sean felt her arching against him and stopped thinking at all. He wrapped his arms around her back and straightened, lifting Claire off her feet. Unable to believe she was actually kissing him back, he stroked repeatedly into her mouth with his tongue. Her responding moan made him tighten. He shifted his hold, trying to lift one of her legs around him so he could get as close as they both wanted, but he was frustrated by her knee-length skirt. He wrapped his hand around her hip instead, squeezing and releasing the supple flesh.

When he heard a small thump echo in the hallway, he thought it might be one of her shoes falling off, but was too far gone to care. He pressed her into the wall and continued the drugging kisses, concentrating on her taste, on the feel of her breasts pressed against his chest and her hips arching against his erection.

The sound of a door opening and closing down the hall finally got through to him. He couldn't believe he had lost his head so quickly. Breathing unsteadily, he stepped back and lowered her feet to the floor. He held her shoulders when she stumbled, thrown off balance by the missing shoe.

The change from being kissed senseless to being set aside was like a shock of cold water. Claire took several deep breaths and grabbed for composure. Rather than look at Sean, she glanced around for her missing shoe, giving herself some time to steady. He took an arm to offer support while she slipped her foot into the pump.

"Thanks," she murmured, and wondered if she looked as shell-shocked as she felt. What do you say after your world has been tilted on its axis with a single kiss?

"That was really stupid," Sean said, straightening his shirt and studying the top of her bent head. "I'm sorry."

Okay, those weren't the words she was looking for. Annoyed, she gave him a sideways look and spoke without thinking. "Never apologize for kissing a woman like that, *cher.* It makes her look foolish and you look like a pig." She heard the cutting words and winced. "Damn. I didn't mean the pig part. I guess I'm sorry, too. I, ah, got a little carried away." She fiddled with the gold hoop in her right ear.

"You didn't do anything. I'm the one who practically nailed you against your best friend's front door." He rubbed his neck in frustration. He'd never felt so out of control in his life. "Look, we've been taking shots at each other for the last two days, it's only natural that there would be some built-up tension between us. But I never should have kissed you," he said roughly. "It won't happen again."

Claire narrowed her eyes at his tone. "Did I just stand there like an inflatable doll while your tongue was in my mouth? You didn't force me to do anything I didn't want to."

"Claire, the last week has been very stressful for you. Your emotions are all over the place. I shouldn't have taken advantage of you."

The look she gave Sean made him shift uncomfortably. "Protecting me again, Detective? Or are you protecting yourself?" She shrugged as if she didn't care. "Thanks anyway, but I'm a big believer in free will. You didn't take advantage of anything."

"I don't normally lose control like that."

She looked him over from head to toe. "Now that's truly a pity."

The key was still in the lock. Claire had the apartment door opened and closed in Sean's face before he could think of anything to say. Automatically he tugged the light jacket he wore into place. It covered his holster just fine, but did nothing to conceal his hard-on.

He walked uncomfortably down the hall, hoping he didn't meet any little old ladies taking their trash out.

Chapter 23

As soon as Claire closed the door in Sean's face, she walked straight to the kitchen for some cold water, spotted the open wine, and poured herself a huge glass instead. Gulping half of the rich Merlot in one desperate swallow, she followed Olivia and Afton's idle chatter as they prepared brunch. Claire hoped they would be too busy to notice her own appearance. She was sure her cheeks were on fire, and her lips felt both chapped and swollen.

When she licked them, she swore she tasted spearmint. Groaning, she took another gulp of the red wine.

"Fettuccine Alfredo with garlic bread and Caesar salad coming right up. Not the usual brunch, but that's what I get for going shopping when I'm starved," Olivia said.

"How was work?" Afton asked.

"Fine," Claire said. "I caught up on some things."

At least she thought she had. Right now she was having a hard time remembering her own name, let alone what she'd done at the office before her world had tilted on its axis.

"Good," Olivia said. "Oh, the concierge downstairs received a package for you today. I put it on the buffet in the dining room."

Claire wandered in that direction, her mind still focused on kissing Sean. He'd acted like it was wrong. But all she could think was that thirty years was a long time to go without ever being kissed in a way that made her toes curl.

She sighed and set her wine down on the buffet next to the white box wrapped with red ribbon. A foil balloon bearing the message "Thinking of YOU" was attached to the bow. Claire undid the ribbon and looked inside while the helium balloon drifted slowly toward the ceiling. A folded card sat on top of white tissue paper, which hid the gift.

Wondering if a client had sent the box, Claire picked up her wine and drank as she flipped open the card.

> *Marie Claire,*
> *I so enjoyed our last meeting.*
> *I look forward to seeing you again soon.*

She frowned as she tried to think which of her clients would send her a package without identifying himself. She set aside the card, then pulled out the wadded tissue paper to see what was inside the box. A black leather clutch purse lay at the bottom of the cardboard container, wrapped in what looked to be a rust-colored piece of cloth.

Claire leaned closer. Her breath came in hard when she recognized her own purse, lost since the night of the murder. Breath froze in her chest as she saw that the cloth wrapped around her purse wasn't really rust-colored, but had once been a white floral sash that was now stained with dried blood.

The wineglass slipped from Claire's nerveless fingers, shattering on the hardwood floor and splashing crimson streaks on her pale legs. Her eyes darted to the card, open on the smooth wood surface of the buffet. The once-innocent words became a malevolent threat.

Olivia came out of the kitchen. "Was that breaking glass? Are you all right?"

Dark eyes huge in her ashen face, Claire looked at Olivia but couldn't force any words past her paralyzed vocal cords.

Olivia rushed toward her, ignoring the shards of glass and wine on the floor. "What is it, honey?"

"Claire, do you feel faint?" Afton asked.

"The gift," was all Claire could manage.

Olivia reached toward the box.

"Don't touch it!" Claire said quickly. "It's from him."

"Who?" Olivia and Afton asked.

"The killer."

"What do you mean?" Olivia asked.

Afton grasped Claire's hand in silent support.

"It's my purse," Claire said. "The one I lost the night of the murder. And there's some kind of fabric wrapped around it with . . . God, I think they're bloodstains. And the note. Read the note."

Silence grew as both women read the note without touching it.

"I'm not imagining things, right?" Claire said. "That's a threat."

"Come away from here," Afton urged, tugging Claire toward the living room.

Claire looked down at the floor as broken glass gritted under her feet. "I should clean that up," she said automatically.

"Later." Afton tugged again at her hand. "Come sit down. You've had a bad shock."

"I'm calling the police," Olivia said. "Do you still have Sean's card?"

"In the pocket of my raincoat," Claire responded numbly. "Use the cell number."

Within moments Olivia was dialing. She waited impatiently while it rang three times. He answered on the fourth, sounding like his mouth was full.

"Yeah?" he said.

"This is Olivia Goodhue. Something's happened. How fast can you get here?"

"I'm at a deli just down the street. What's wrong?"

"Someone sent Claire a package. Inside is the purse she lost the night of the murder, along with a pale piece of cloth that looks like it's been splashed with blood. And there's a note saying how he can't wait to see her again."

"Christ. Listen, don't touch anything! That's very important. Lock all the doors. I'll be right there."

"Hurry," Olivia said.

Sean didn't answer. She was talking to dead air.

Chapter 24

S ean made it in three minutes flat because he didn't wait for the elevator. Half-eaten deli sandwich in hand, he ran up five flights of stairs and hammered on the door.

"It's Detective Richter. Let me in."

The sound of locks opening pleased Sean—good locks and lots of them—even as it irritated him. *Come on, come on, open the damn door.*

When a crack of light showed, he didn't wait for an invitation.

"Where is she?" he demanded as he pushed past Olivia.

"In the living room."

"Dump this somewhere," he said, shoving the sandwich in her hands. "And lock the door."

"Please, thank you, you're welcome," Olivia muttered. Again, she was talking to herself. Sean was already gone.

Claire was sitting stiffly next to Afton on an overstuffed couch. Squatting on his heels, Sean took Claire's icy hands in his. Her pale skin and rigidly composed expression made him realize how vibrant she had been earlier in the hallway, when she'd kissed him like she'd just discovered sex.

"Claire? You okay?" he asked roughly.

"Fine." She noted his rapid breathing. "You took the stairs again. There was no need to come storming up here."

"Just doing my job, ma'am." He said it in his best cop voice in an attempt at humor.

She smiled briefly, then looked in the direction of the dining room. "It's in there."

Sean studied her for a moment longer, seeing the effort she was making to remain calm. *Good girl*, he thought admiringly.

With a gentle squeeze he released her hands and went over to the white box on the waist-high wood buffet. He saw the spilled wine and broken glass Olivia had started to clean up, and stepped around as much of the mess as he could.

Looking down into the box, his jaw clenched when he recognized the bloodstained fabric wrapped around the purse. It matched the dress Renata Mendes had been wearing the night she was murdered. He'd been right—the killer had taken a trophy to remember his latest victim.

Sean carefully examined the black purse. Pulling a pen from his pocket, he used it to shift the fabric aside and open the purse's leather flap. A cursory glance showed a wallet and compact, but no keys. Next to the box was an open white note card. After Sean read the short message, he began cursing viciously.

When he took a breath, he smelled Claire's delicate floral perfume. She was standing very close.

"Now would be a really good time to tell me I'm getting paranoid and letting my imagination run wild," she said without much hope.

He turned and met her dark gaze, wishing he could give her that reassurance. He couldn't. All he could do was offer a comforting squeeze of her shoulder before he pulled out his cell phone and called Aidan. When his partner answered, Sean could hear loud conversation and music in the background. Claire wasn't the only one who liked midday parties.

"Sorry to crash the fun," Sean said, "but I need you and a crime scene unit at Olivia Goodhue's apartment ASAP."

"What—are they all right?"

"Yeah. Looks like the killer sent Claire a little present."

"Shit. Not good."

"Tell me about it." Sean hung up and steered Claire back over to the couch. "When and how did the package come?" he asked her.

Olivia answered. "The building concierge said it was delivered for her during the morning." She glanced at the clock. "Their office closes at noon on Saturday. It won't open until eight on Monday morning."

"They'll open for me," Sean said.

"How did the killer know Claire was here?" Afton asked from her seat on the couch.

"I suppose he could have followed me from work or something," Claire said unhappily. "My business cards have my work address, and I always carry some in my wallet."

The thought that she had put her friend at risk chilled Claire. She shot to her feet. "That's it. I'm going home. I won't have Livvie in danger."

"You're not going anywhere!" Olivia said loudly, hands on hips.

"I'm leaving and that's all there—"

"No way in hell you're going home." Sean's deep voice cut through the argument.

Claire turned on him. "Somehow I've led a killer right to Olivia. I've got to get out of here."

"Think," Sean shot back. "He's still got your keys, and he knows where you live. But you're right about leaving here. You'll have to stay at a hotel. Staking out a public place like that will take a lot of manpower, but . . ." He shrugged. "Has to be done."

"She can stay at my place," Afton said. "I have a house in Georgetown, which would be much more comfortable than a hotel. There's an alarm and new locks."

"No. I won't put anyone else at risk," Claire said.

Sean ignored Claire and spoke to Afton. "That would be better than a hotel. Much easier to secure." He turned to Claire. "Can you arrange for time off?"

"They owe me three weeks of comp time and three weeks of vacation, but—"

"Good. Take care of it with your boss."

"You really think that's how he found me? He followed me from work?"

"Did you have business cards in your purse?" Sean cut in.

Claire shuddered. "All right. I'll arrange to work from home for a while, wherever 'home' is." She looked at Olivia. "I'm so sorry to drag you into this." She glanced back at Sean's grim features. This icy, analytical man wasn't anything like the one who had pressed her up against the front door and kissed her until her toes curled.

Dangerous territory. Hormones kill brain cells. She

took a deep breath and tried to be as analytical as he was. "What about Afton and her babies? It's too big a risk."

"We'll stay with my mother," Afton said quickly. "She'll be thrilled. She never wanted me to buy my own house in the first place."

"I can't let you—" Claire began.

"Hush," Afton said. "You wouldn't even be here if it weren't for me."

Sean turned to Olivia. "I don't know how long you'll be out of this apartment, but it will be at least a week."

Olivia was already making lists in her head. "I'll start packing."

Claire's objection was lost as the doorbell chimed and Aidan's voice called out. "Detective Burke. Let me in."

Sean went through the locks faster than Olivia had.

"Forensics team is right behind me," Aidan said, breathing more deeply than usual. "They took the elevator with all their stuff."

"The box is in the dining room if you want to take a fast look." Sean shut the door behind Aidan. "And watch out for the broken glass."

Aidan raised an eyebrow but said nothing. He went into the apartment, talked briefly with everyone, and walked to the dining room to study the package.

With a sense of unreality, Claire watched as Sean opened the door again for several evidence technicians, each carrying cases of equipment. Very quickly the apartment was a hive of activity. She started when she realized that Sean was calling her name in a patient voice.

"What?" she asked.

"We'll take a formal statement from you later. For now, pack your things. An officer will be here in half an hour to take all of you to Afton's house." He didn't add that an unmarked car would make sure no one followed, and that he really hoped the killer was stupid enough to try it.

"An escort," Claire repeated. "Great. Just great. What's happening to my life?"

Sean opened his mouth, only to be cut off.

"Oh, never mind," she said. "That's what I get for letting my toes curl."

She stalked off to pack her suitcase.

Chapter 25

Aidan locked the door as the last of the evidence technicians left Olivia's apartment. "Okay," he said to Sean. "Talk."

"About what?"

"Whatever is making you look so sour. The women are safe, nobody followed them, so what's chewing on you?"

"The fact that I was right about our killer fixating on Claire."

Aidan didn't buy it. "What else?"

Sean sat on Olivia's couch and scrubbed at his face with both hands. "I've screwed things up."

"How?"

"Claire. I drove her over here and we talked. Argued. Then I got kind of distracted."

"Distracted?"

"I stuck my tongue in her mouth."

Aidan managed not to laugh out loud. "So? Did she bite it off?"

"You're laughing, and I've fucked up the case."

"Sean," Aidan began.

"I never should have done it, never should have let my dick take over in a professional situation. She's a *witness*.

One who is now in need of police protection." Sean stood up and started pacing. "Did you see how upset she was at finding that box? If I'd stayed, if I hadn't run out of here like my ass was on fire after kissing her, I might have been able to spare her some of that."

"Anyone with half a brain," Aidan said patiently, ignoring everything but the main point, "could look at the two of you and see a hell of a lot more than a kiss in your future."

Sean glared at Aidan. "No way I'm that obvious."

Aidan just shook his head. "Hopeless."

"Shit. Maybe I should just take out a full page ad in the *Washington Post* about how I come on to witnesses."

"You don't."

"I did."

"Did she mind?"

Sean stopped pacing and almost smiled.

This time Aidan laughed. "Lighten up, cousin, and thank the gods for a break in the case."

"What break—the techs were muttering about not finding anything worth their trip out here."

"We know who the guy's intended victim is. We have her under twenty-four/seven guard. She knows what he looks like—or probably will if she sees him again. So let her go looking."

"No." Sean's voice was hard. "Too dangerous."

"Have you asked her?"

"No."

"Then how can—"

"No! Weren't you listening? I can't think like a cop when I'm near her and if I'm not thinking like a cop I could get her killed! This whack job is playing with her, with all of us. That's a change in his pattern. We need to get a real psychologist in on this ASAP, instead of tinkering with a profile ourselves."

Aidan rubbed a hand over his stubbly jaw. "You're right about that part. I'll secure the apartment and follow up with the management company. You jack up the shrink and check out the security arrangements at Afton's house."

"Security is your specialty," Sean shot back as he headed toward the door. It slammed behind him as he left.

Aidan sighed. It had been worth a try.

Chapter 26

"I still don't think this is a good idea." Olivia's voice echoed in the deserted lobby of the office building.

Claire ignored her friend, showed her passport as ID to the security guard, and continued to the elevator.

"Shouldn't we wait for the police?" Olivia asked.

"I left a message on Sean's voice mail. If he wants to join us here, he's welcome to." She didn't mention the fact that she'd deliberately called his office number and left the message there, instead of on his cell phone.

Olivia's silence was almost accusatory as they rode up to Camelot's floor in the elevator.

"Besides, all I am doing is reactivating my dating service membership after a brief lapse. This has nothing to do with the investigation," Claire said.

"Bullshit. If you're going to come up with excuses to stick your nose into police business, at least make them good ones."

Olivia marched out of the elevator and went to the door of Camelot Dating Services, Inc.

Claire followed and knocked on the door. "Afton? You in there?"

"Hang on."

The door opened, and Afton appeared. She looked stylish and carefree, dressed in a pretty summer outfit on a hot Sunday afternoon. But as soon as she locked the door behind her friends, she started in on Claire.

"Are you sure you should be doing this?" Afton demanded. "What about the police?"

"I'm not really doing this for the investigation," Claire said, speaking fast. "I'm just going through the catalogue looking for men who have common interests. A date possibility. That's what I paid for, right? If I *happen* to come across a picture that reminds me of the killer in any way, I will of course involve the police right away. But at this moment, I'm here looking for love."

Afton stared at her in disbelief.

Claire didn't try again. Everything she said sounded lame even to her. She sat down at Afton's desk and looked at her. "You're the expert at this. What's next?"

Afton looked at Olivia as if expecting her to reason with Claire.

Olivia shrugged. "When she gets an idea like this, forget reason." She turned and glared at Claire. "But you will be very, very careful, do you hear?"

"I promise, Mom."

"I'm still not comfortable with this," Afton said in a worried voice.

"Why?" Claire asked blandly. "All the men in your catalogue have been checked out, right?"

"We could have missed something. We must have."

"The police sure don't think so, or they'd have me staked out in front of the photos. As they put it, I could have seen the killer's photo in a lot of places."

"But—" Afton began.

"Let's all be realistic here," Claire cut in. "What are the chances that I'd stumble across a serial killer and actually know him from a club where I'm a member? Those are really pitiful odds."

"Yes, but what are the chances of stumbling across a serial killer at all, let alone one who is in the act of committing a murder?" Olivia asked. "Besides, the school is close. It's not inconceivable that the guy would have become familiar with the area after visiting Camelot a few times, then maybe decided to stalk his next victim here."

Claire ignored the icy feeling she got in her stomach whenever she considered the killer and the crime scene. She wondered how long it would take for the terror to fade. Or if it would fade.

"I appreciate your concern," she said to Afton and Olivia. "But right now, I need your support. I need to *do* something, and this is the only thing I can think of that might help."

"Of course you have our support," Afton said, sitting at her computer. "I just don't think it's safe for you to be going out with anyone right now. At least not until the police have done their own background checks on the candidates."

"That's good," Olivia said quickly. "Attacking a problem head-on like you normally do might not work this time."

Claire considered the idea. It might be a workable compromise, something she could discuss with Sean later. "I'll talk to Sean about it."

Afton held up a hand suddenly to quiet the other

women as she heard the muted ding of the elevator. There shouldn't be anyone with access to the building on a Sunday afternoon, at least not on this floor. Claire and Olivia had gotten in because Afton had cleared it with security first. But none of her employees had that authority, or after-hours badge access. The only one who did was her mother—and she was home with her grandchildren.

All three women paused at the sound of footsteps in the hall.

"Security?" Olivia asked. Afton shook her head.

Adrenaline kicked into Claire's blood. "Did you lock the outside door?" she asked very softly.

Afton nodded, then listened with a sense of disbelief to the distinct sound of Camelot's front door opening. Eyes wide, she jumped up and shut the door to her office as quietly as she could, turning the flimsy lock set into the doorknob. Then she backed up toward the other women as she heard the squeak of shoes on the smooth wooden floor of the hall.

Claire had unconsciously grabbed a letter opener off the desk, and she watched with wide eyes as Olivia picked up a pair of scissors lying on Afton's desk. Afton looked around for something that she could use as a weapon.

The doorknob turned. Once. Twice.

The tiny lock held.

After a brief pause and a scraping noise, the knob turned again. The door opened.

Claire's heart was pounding so loudly that she was sure everyone could hear it. She flashed on the night of the murder, the only other time in her life she'd felt this type of adrenaline rush and terror.

Sean walked in. He smiled grimly when he saw their

tense faces and the makeshift weapons they carried.

"They're here," he said.

"Thank God," Aidan said, crowding in. One look told him that everything was all right, except that his cousin was going to kick some well-shaped butt. A smart man, Aidan took a seat at the back of the office and waited for the fireworks.

"At least the three of you had enough sense to be afraid," Sean said.

"How did you get in?" Afton said. "The door was locked."

He held up the credit card he'd used to pop the flimsy locks. Olivia was closer, so he disarmed her first.

"*Jesus!* You scared the hell out of us," Claire said, waving the letter opener.

Sean plucked it out of her clenched fingers and examined its shiny length with interest. "You could do some damage with this, but you'd have to get pretty close."

"Oh, yeah? Why don't you let me try on you?" Claire smiled at Sean, showing more teeth than humor. Her pulse was still pounding, and she could feel the nauseating emptiness adrenaline had left in her stomach.

"Some other time, when you aren't mad enough to stick it in me." As he spoke, he slipped the letter opener into the back pocket of his jeans, well out of her reach. "Now, why don't you tell me what you're doing here alone on a Sunday afternoon when you know very well that you're being stalked by a serial killer?"

His voice was calm, patient, reasonable. It made Claire nervous as hell because she sensed he wasn't any of those things. She cleared her throat. "I, ah, guess you got my message."

"What message?"

"The one I left on your voice mail at the office," Claire said.

Sean shook his head.

"Then how did you know where we were?" she asked.

"Why did you call my work number instead of my cell phone?"

"I asked you first," she shot back.

Sean reminded himself that he was a professional. Calm, patient, and reasonable. "We have an unmarked police car parked outside Afton's house at all times, watching over you and Olivia. When you both left today, they followed you here, then called me. On my cell phone," he added pointedly.

Claire flushed. She was embarrassed that she'd been caught taking the coward's way out and leaving a message on his work phone.

"What are you up to?" he said. "And don't tell me it's nothing. It ain't gonna fly," he drawled in a fair imitation of her accent.

Unable to lie while making direct eye contact, she didn't even bother to try. Instead, she began drawing aimless designs on Afton's desk. "It's pretty simple, Detective. I paid for a bunch of dates and I'm going to go through the catalogue until I get them."

Aidan laughed out loud.

She glared at him.

"So we're back to the catalogue," Sean said.

"That's why I came here in the first place, remember?"

"You actually think I'd let you go out with anyone from Camelot's catalogue?"

It was the calm patience and reason in his voice that pushed her over the edge. She looked him right in the eye and drawled, "I actually think that you don't have any say in the matter, *cher*. I'm single, over the age of consent, and pay my taxes on time. Last time I checked the local laws, I don't need police permission to date."

"You're going to stand there and tell me this has nothing to do with the investigation?" Sean asked.

Claire shrugged. "No. But I defy you to prove otherwise."

Despite the anger in his gut, Sean kept his voice level. Every time he lost his temper with Claire, she got around him. Besides, there was a possibility—admittedly not much of one—that if he kept a lid on his temper, he wouldn't end up kissing her until he didn't have a single brain cell left above his belt.

"Are you such a control freak that you can't trust the police to do work you're not competent to?"

"It doesn't have anything to do with trust," Claire said.

Sean stared at her. She didn't look away. She was telling him the truth, no matter how ridiculous it sounded to him.

"Sean, let me feel like I'm more than a victim," she said. "I have an idea, something to get to the information locked away in my memories. I want to help—I need to. Can you understand that?"

"Why don't you tell us your idea?" Aidan asked from the back of the room.

Claire gave him a grateful look before meeting Sean's icy eyes again. "It seems pretty clear to me that the killer has, for whatever reason, decided to communicate with me. So I thought I'd go through the dating catalogue and make contact with all the candidates I react to, even if I don't know why."

"Assuming you're right," Sean said evenly, "there are

hundreds of pictures in the catalogue. How can you pick the right one?"

"I just know if I see the killer's face again I'll recognize it in some way, even if only subconsciously. Once I pick out the prospects, I can set up a date or something. Then he'll have to come out of hiding."

"Fuck me," Sean said. "I knew you were up to something crazy."

Claire gave up on convincing him. She turned to Aidan. "You know he won't be able to resist if I contact him directly. Then you can catch him before he hurts anyone else."

Aidan met Claire's pleading gaze and mentally weighed Sean's sanity against the importance of getting a predator off the streets. As a cop, his choice was obvious. But as Sean's family, he braced for the fight he knew his words would trigger.

"She's right," he said to Sean. "It's the best chance we have to draw the killer out into the open before he cuts up another woman."

"Claire's a civilian," Sean shot back. "We can't use her as bait. Besides, what's to keep the guy from guessing he's being set up as soon as he sees that his next date is one Marie Claire Lambert?"

"Yeah, he might guess," Aidan said. "But he's a risk-taker. An adrenaline freak. He'd get off thinking he could outsmart us."

"I don't believe this. She hit her head recently. What's your excuse—congenital stupidity?"

Claire opened her mouth, but Aidan was quicker.

"It's okay," he said to her, but it was Sean he looked at. "He's just pissed off because he knows I'm right, and he's too good a cop to ignore it any longer. He knows we don't have any choice. Not if we want to keep this bastard from killing again."

In silence Sean measured his options against his waning hold on self-control. "Yeah, well, it's an interesting idea. I'll kick it around with Aidan, sleep on it, and let you know."

Claire knew Sean was going to reject her idea, pat her on the head, and push her aside. She didn't like this calm, emotionless, screamingly reasonable Sean. She much preferred it when his mouth got tight, his cheek began to twitch, and he went nose to nose with her.

And then kissed her.

"There's a plainclothes officer waiting in the lobby downstairs," Sean said. "He'll take you back to Afton's place."

Claire opened her mouth to speak again.

"I said I'd think about it," he said softly.

She looked into his cool blue eyes for a long time, her heart sinking at the lack of expression. He wasn't really there, not emotionally. He was shut down and nailed tight, and there was nothing she could do to reach him.

Claire picked up her purse and walked out of the office without a backwards glance.

Chapter 27

Sean walked through the doors to the police station late on Monday afternoon in a bad mood. He'd been working in the field all day, doing follow-up interviews with the investigating officers of several murders that might be related to the current case. The work had given him the excuse to avoid Aidan. The two men hadn't exchanged more than a few words since they had left Camelot's offices yesterday.

The object of Sean's anger was hunched over a pad of paper on his desktop, making notes and rubbing his jaw. He looked up when Sean went to his own desk.

"How did your interviews go?" Aidan asked.

"Nothing new. The cases go so far back the lead officers couldn't remember much more than they had written in their notes."

"What about redoing some of the forensics?" Technological advance was one of the most powerful tools of the Cold Cases Division. Many outstanding investigations had been solved simply by applying new tools to old evidence.

"Already in the works."

Aidan nodded, then went back to his paper.

The silence finally got to Sean. It was one thing for him to be mad at Aidan, who had damn well earned it. It was another for Aidan to ignore him.

"What have you been working on all day?" Sean asked.

"Ways to use Claire and the Camelot catalogue without undue risk to her safety," Aidan said casually.

"There's no way to use her without putting her at risk. End of discussion." Sean jerked off his light jacket and hung it over the back of his chair. Sweat outlined the shoulder harness.

"I said minimal risk, not no risk. It's our best hope of nailing the killer. We have her full and eager cooperation."

"She isn't a cop. She doesn't have any special training." Sean paced, arguing with himself as much as Aidan. "We can't just throw her to the wolves because it *might* help us solve the case."

"Shit. I've met S.W.A.T. guys who weren't as tough as Claire. With some prep work we can turn her into a valuable asset. And what's more, it will let us keep a closer eye on her. She can do this, Sean. Or have you been so dazzled by the flesh that you haven't seen that cold-rolled steel backbone of hers?"

"Hell yes, I've seen it." Sean's voice was low, raw. He'd kept waking up in a cold sweat last night, imagining Claire alone, at the mercy of a killer who gutted his helpless victims. "How do you protect someone who won't admit she's in danger? If we use her, I'm afraid we won't be able to pull her out before she's hurt. Or dead. It scares the hell out of me."

Aidan stayed silent.

Sean sat down and leaned forward in his chair, elbows

braced on his knees while he scrubbed his face with his hands.

"There's only one way to make sure she's safe," Aidan said, "and that's to yank the bastard off the streets. If we work with Claire we can monitor her every move. That's a lot better than wondering what the hell she's up to, isn't it?"

"I don't like it," Sean said. "My gut says this is a one-way ticket to hell for Claire. Get her out of Washington. Hell, ship her to Bora Bora."

"She wouldn't go. It's not in her to back down from a fight. And it's not in you, either," Aidan said pointedly.

Sean slumped in the chair. "This is one fight where I'm completely outgunned. I've never been attracted to a witness or a team member before. The only thing keeping me from jumping her is distance."

"Yeah, that complicates things, but you're a professional. You can handle it. And when it's all over, well, it's about time you saw a woman you liked well enough to get tied in knots about. Whatever, I'll back you to the wall."

"Hell, I know that. It's just—" Sean stopped as he saw his captain walk in and head straight toward them. "Captain Michaels."

"Didn't Burke tell you I'd be by?" the captain asked, pulling up a chair and straddling it.

"I was just getting to that," Aidan said. His eyes told Sean to brace himself. "The captain wants to make sure we're looking at *all* our options."

"Use the witness," Michaels said bluntly. "She's willing, we're willing, and the press is getting restless. If we don't get somewhere soon, this case will bite us on the ass."

"Why?" Sean asked.

"Politics," Aidan said.

"Fuck politics."

The captain just looked at Sean.

"Beautiful," Sean muttered. "Think of the nifty head-lines if we use our witness and get her killed."

"Your concern is noted," Michaels said to Sean. "We'll follow every precaution—keep her wired, have you two ride along ahead and behind, run full background checks on all of the men she dates, only meet in public places we have secured. You know the drill."

"She's a civilian. Why can't we use a policewoman?" Sean asked.

"He's seen her driver's license photo, remember?" Aidan said.

"Hell, my own mother couldn't ID me from my driver's license photo," Sean retorted.

"Your mother needs glasses," the captain said. "Even if you're right about it, we can't afford to detail any more bodies to this case. You and Burke are the best investigators I've got in this division. I'm counting on you to make the dating sting work before the press makes sure our next budget is even smaller than the one we have now."

Captain Michaels stood up, returned the chair to its original position, and straightened his suit coat. "I'll expect to see your detailed plan within twenty-four hours, along with some requisition forms."

Chapter 28

Claire made a sound of annoyance as she set her cup down on the table next to Afton's comfortable couch. It was after eleven and she couldn't sleep. Didn't want to sleep, actually. When she did, her dreams were dark and disjointed, and she was no closer to remembering anything than she had been the night she was injured.

After going to bed early with a headache and jerking awake in a cold sweat, she'd decided that sleep was not going to happen again for a while. She took a warm bath with scented oil to help her relax. When that didn't work, she quietly went downstairs for a cup of herbal tea and some mindless channel surfing. That didn't do anything either. All she could think about was the killer, and how he might have been following her—watching her—before he sent his frightening "gift."

She jolted at the sudden knock on the door, then realized one of the officers watching the house from the outside must need something. Tightening the belt on her short robe, she walked barefoot to the door.

"Who is it?" Claire called softly, aware of Olivia sleeping upstairs.

"Sean. We need to talk."

Claire looked down at her outfit, then shrugged. Sean had seen her in less at the hospital. She opened the door.

He came into the entry and looked down at her. Her face was scrubbed clean of makeup, and her hair was pulled back into some kind of knot. She looked pale and tired, but still beautiful. He swept his eyes lower, running them over the short, jewel-toned robe she wore belted around her waist, then taking in her pale legs and bare feet. Abruptly he realized how late it was.

He checked his watch and cursed. After eleven. He'd been driving around for several hours, planning for the new path the investigation was going to take and telling himself that he could keep his hands off his witness. When he'd pulled up at the house, he hadn't even thought about the time. All the downstairs lights had been on, which was enough to have him out of his car and banging on the door without a second thought.

"Sorry to disturb you at this hour. The light was on, so . . . anyway, we can talk tomorrow." He turned away.

"I can't sleep. You can't sleep." She shrugged. "You might as well come in. Olivia's out cold, so don't yell at me and wake her up." Claire led Sean into the kitchen and closed the swinging door behind them. "You want anything to eat or drink?"

He looked at her loosely closed robe and knew he should never have come here. She wasn't wearing anything underneath—he'd bet his life on it.

"No, thanks," Sean managed to say.

Instead of fidgeting or cleaning something, as she desperately wanted to do, she folded her arms underneath her breasts and leaned against the butcher block that formed an island in the kitchen.

"What did you want to talk to me about?"

Sean faced her with his hands in the front pockets of his jeans. "There's been a change of plans—you're in on the investigation. We'll be using you to try and draw the killer out of hiding. Of course, that's assuming he really is a member of Camelot Dating Services in the first place."

Claire felt a brief surge of triumph, like when she found out she'd been awarded a sales contract or a particularly challenging project. Then she realized Sean was angry.

"You don't sound very pleased," she said.

"I'm not. If I had my way, you'd be in protective custody right now, instead of staked out like a sacrificial lamb."

"So why did you agree to the plan?"

"I didn't. The political heat is burning my captain's ass, he outranks me, and here I am." Sean began pacing the length of the kitchen, ticking off an imaginary list of items. "So this is the drill. We'll bring you in for a crash course in self-defense—nothing major, just some close quarters stuff. We need to explain how the audio and visual surveillance is going to work, because you'll be wired for sound and will have visual contact with two officers at all times. There will also be some basic ground rules for 'dates' which Aidan and I have to draft and go over with you." He stopped with his back to her. "Questions?"

She sensed his rapid-fire summary of details was meant to overwhelm and intimidate her. And it was working. "Why don't you want me involved? Do you think I can't pull it off?"

Sean sighed and ran a hand through his hair, but he didn't turn around and face her. "If sheer will and determination were all it took, I have no doubt you'd succeed. But this guy is good. He's been active for a long time, probably close to a decade. You don't get away with that many murders by being stupid."

"Then catching him however you can should be your number one priority."

Sean turned around and came back to stand in front of her as she leaned against the butcher block. She caught her breath at the look in his eyes.

"Not if it means risking you," he said.

She swallowed hard before answering. "I'm at risk whether I'm an active team member or not."

"I know. But I have a really bad feeling about this whole setup. If I could, I'd take you away somewhere and—" Sean broke off.

"And what?" God, was that really her voice? Somehow the question had come out husky and suggestive.

He stepped closer to her, his nostrils flaring slightly as he caught the light scent of orange that clung to her skin. He looked into her eyes, which were pure black in the dimly lit kitchen, and saw a mirror image of the simmering tension he was feeling. His heart began to beat faster. He lifted a hand that was none too steady to her face, gently brushing aside a dark curl that had settled on her forehead.

"I think we both know what I'd like to do," Sean said. Then his breath came in hard when she leaned closer to him, more an emotional closing of the distance than physical. "Help me out here. One of us has got to be reasonable."

"Let me know when it's my turn," Claire said.

She turned her face up to his, stood on her tiptoes, and brushed her lips softly against his mouth. He withstood the temptation for one brush of her lips, then another. By the third delicate pass he was gone. Kissing her back, he made a rough sound in his throat, then slid both hands around her waist and boosted her up onto the butcher block. Before she could murmur her approval, her knees were spread and he'd stepped into the space between, using one hand on her bottom to pull her closer to him.

The combination of Sean's tongue stroking into her mouth and his hand pressing her into his body was almost too much for Claire to handle. She cried out softly, the sound muffled by his lips. She moaned again and pressed herself against him instinctively, rubbing against his suddenly taut lower body in search of the sweet contact that would satisfy needs suddenly screaming through her system.

At the repeated pressure of her hips against his, Sean broke off the kiss to groan quietly against her throat.

"God, Claire, don't. I can't take it."

He stayed there, with his head buried in the curve where neck met shoulder, and breathed in the exotic scent of orange oil trapped there. Her neck arched gently against his mouth, so he began to delicately kiss and nibble her soft skin. He felt her legs wrap tightly around him, thighs hugging his hips, while her hands reached inside his lightweight jacket to pull his shirt out of the waistband of his jeans.

Sean knew things were sliding out of control, and he didn't care. Claire's hands were under his shirt, reaching as far up his bare back as she could with his weapon harness on. At the gentle scrape of her nails, his body tensed, and he abandoned her neck to press his mouth to hers again.

"More," she murmured between kisses, "more."

The word repeated itself again and again in Claire's mind, but she didn't realize she'd spoken aloud.

Sean did, and responded. Pulling himself away from her, ignoring her muted protest at the loss of contact, he stripped off his jacket and shoulder holster, put them on the counter, and reached for the belt of her silk robe. Within seconds he had the knot undone and was pushing fabric aside to reveal the bare flesh underneath. He studied her full breasts hungrily, feeling her eyes on his face. Looking up, he met her gaze and watched her cheeks flush a dusky red, even as she arched her back slightly to offer herself to him.

Her deep rose nipples were already hard. They tightened further when he ran the back of one knuckle along the delicate underside of first one breast, then the other.

"Don't tease," she gasped.

She gripped a double handful of his shirt, then smoothed her hands over his chest and began to undo the buttons running down to his waist.

"That's half the fun, Claire," he said, repeating her name as she ran her hands across his bare chest.

Bending over, he coasted his lips over the tops of her breasts, then turned and dragged his open mouth across a taut nipple. With one hand he arched her up against his lips and caressed her until she was flushed and tingling. With his other hand he stroked the gentle curve of her belly, edging toward the aching place between her thighs.

He paused to circle her navel, and her breath came in on a gasp. When he speared a thumb into the dark hair below and dragged across the tender flesh hidden there, her breath left in a soft cry. He kissed her lips gently, then used the arm around her hips to drag her to the very edge of the butcher block. Bending to take one nipple into his mouth and suckle in earnest, he began to run his thumb around and around the slick nub he had drawn forth.

Claire's head dropped back as her body responded to his skilled teasing. She no longer explored his chest, but instead dug her nails repeatedly into the firm pads of muscle she found there. When she felt his hand press against one knee, then the other, she relaxed her thighs to allow him further access.

Her eyes snapped open and met his when she felt a long finger circling the moist entrance to her body. Sean's pupils were dilated with passion, and the moment became almost unbearably intimate as he maintained eye contact and gently pushed his finger inside her.

She made a soft noise, part pleasure and part protest, when he began to caress her with thumb and forefinger. Her thighs were shaking against his hips, and her breath came in gentle pants, but she didn't pull away from him or his intent gaze.

When she felt a second finger join the first inside her slick body, then pause to find and stroke an unbelievably sensitive spot, Claire jerked in Sean's arms. Finally, her eyes closed under the rush of pleasure, and her head once again dropped backwards, baring her neck to his hungry lips.

The motion of his hand between her legs continued, first probing deeply then retreating to stab teasingly with his thumb. Claire quickly reached the point of no return. She was taut in his arms, a rosy flush rising from her breasts up her neck.

"Stop," she whispered, blindly fumbling for his belt.

Sean didn't respond, just continued the stroking and probing caresses with his hand. His eyes were fixed on her face as he watched the changes pleasure brought.

The pressure built higher than it ever had for her. Before she realized it was going to happen, the tension inside her snapped. She cried out sharply as she came, a sound he belatedly tried to stifle by pressing his mouth over hers and kissing her deeply. She moaned and moved against him as the waves of completion rolled through her.

The kiss gentled as Claire's breathing gradually slowed. Sean lifted both hands to frame her face, his eyes slightly open as he looked at her. He continued the kisses, moving his head one way, then the other, gentling her and preparing for the next level of sensation.

He laughed softly against her lips when she began to pull at his belt again. This time he helped her. Soon his belt and button fly were opened, and Claire was running a hand through the slit in his boxers to brush against the hard flesh beneath. He murmured something encouraging but kept his lips pressed to hers.

The contact between their mouths wasn't broken until they heard the kitchen door swing open. Sean jerked away from Claire's mouth and looked over her head as Olivia walked into the room.

"Claire? I thought I heard something—oops!" Olivia's face turned as red as her hair.

Claire remained frozen in horror for a moment before jerking her hand out of Sean's jeans. With her back to Olivia, she hoped that she shielded all of the important parts of Sean's body, though there was no way to pretend they hadn't been doing what it looked like they were doing. Feeling a scorching blush work its way up her body, she dropped her face against him.

Sean and Olivia stared at each other across the kitchen, she in her light floral robe and he with his shirt and jeans undone, standing between Claire's bare legs and cradling her head to his chest. He opened his mouth, but his brain shorted out. He couldn't think of anything to say, so instead he pulled Claire's robe up from her elbows to around her shoulders. He could actually feel the heat of her blush against his skin.

Olivia finally broke the moment of shared embarrassment. With a mumbled apology, she turned around and fled the kitchen.

Jolted by the *whap-slap* of the door as it swung open and closed in Olivia's wake, Sean finally stepped back from Claire and started to fasten his jeans. He winced at having to force his still aroused flesh past the rough denim of his fly, then he buttoned his shirt and reached for his shoulder harness.

With her face still painfully scarlet, Claire snapped her knees together and fumbled to belt the robe around her waist. She remained seated on the kitchen island, however, because she didn't trust her legs to hold her up. Pulling the hem of her robe as far down her thighs as it would go, she broke the awkward silence.

"That's got to be on the top ten list of reasons why I don't have a roommate," she said.

Sean laughed almost unwillingly as he pulled his lightweight jacket back on. His eyes were unhappy as he looked down at her. "I'm sorry. About this." He gestured toward her position on the wood block. "I shouldn't have done it."

"Done what?" she asked, deliberately misunderstanding. "Laughed? I think you should do it more often."

She tried for nonchalance, but it wasn't easy, considering the fact that she was sitting half naked in someone else's kitchen, thighs trembling as she tried to recover from the most erotic experience of her entire life.

And there was Sean standing in front of her, composure and clothing restored, talking about regrets.

"I'm serious," he said. "We can't let this happen again if we're going to be working together. It's just too dangerous—look how distracted we got tonight."

Claire nodded numbly and felt the warm sensation inside begin to fade. She had never forgotten so completely about her surroundings before, never been at the mercy of her physical side. Sex, when she chose to have it, was a relatively civilized affair carried out in the privacy of a bedroom.

And sex was always preceded by some kind of relationship based on mutual respect and affection. Those relationships had been few and far between, which probably explained why she had gone off like a rocket as soon as Sean had touched her. This was clearly just a case of rampaging hormones and mutual attraction.

It was also a vivid demonstration about the dangers of still waters. She had previously chipped away at Sean's control in an effort to see what was beneath. Now she knew. Next time she'd think twice before she tried to get a rise out of him.

So to speak.

Claire winced at the image and tried to focus on how to get out of the current situation. Given Sean's mood, the best approach would be to go along with whatever he said. And she should do what she could to defuse the sexual tension that was still sizzling between them.

All that would be a great deal easier if she could get off the damned butcher block and gather up what remained of her dignity. She started easing to the edge, only to have Sean lift her and set her gently on her feet.

"Say something," he said, watching her through narrowed eyes. "Give me an idea of what's running through that brain of yours."

"I agree with you completely," she said, leaning back on the wood to counter her wobbly legs. "We need to focus on the investigation, which is the only reason we ever met." There, that was the right approach. Unique circumstances had thrown them together, but they shouldn't read too much into the situation. Perfect.

"I'm glad you understand that, because if we screw this situation up, someone could get hurt." Sean wasn't sure if he meant physically or emotionally. He wasn't even sure which situation he was referring to, the investigation or their mutual attraction.

Stupid, sex-starved, moronic, goddamned idiot asshole!

Sean gritted his teeth. He had to guard her and keep things on a professional level. *OK, so how about you actually keep your hands off her, instead of just talking about it?*

Sean told the voice inside his head to fuck off and waited for Claire to speak.

She nodded vigorously. "Absolutely. You're right. We don't want anyone getting hurt," she said, looking like the picture of reason.

"I'll, ah, let you get some sleep." He knew his discomfort had to be as obvious as the bulge in his jeans. "We're going to have a long couple of days while we get things in place and everything under control that we can." Damned if he wasn't babbling.

"Sounds good. I'll just throw, um, *show* you out." She bit her tongue so she wouldn't say anything else incredibly stupid.

Afraid if he opened his mouth he would start blathering again, Sean didn't trust himself to say anything but "Good night."

Claire shut the door behind him, threw the dead bolt,

and pressed her burning cheek to the cool wood panel. How could things be so painful, so awkward, when not ten minutes earlier she'd been about to have sex with the man?

It's hormones, stupid.

She'd always been dismissive when she'd heard people claiming to be swept away by passion. Clearly she just hadn't met the right man yet.

Right man.

She jerked away from the door. Sean wasn't the "right man." He was someone she had great chemistry with, but that wasn't the basis of a solid relationship. Especially with someone who was fighting his attraction every step of the way, alternately kissing her and keeping her at arm's length. Maybe he was right and they should stay away from each other.

Or at least try to.

Chapter 29

The man settled more comfortably into his folding chair and took a sip of cold coffee. He was sitting in front of a curtained window overlooking the narrow street, which allowed him to watch Marie Claire and her friend as they came and went throughout the day. He could also easily keep tabs on the two police officers assigned to watch over the house.

His lips turned up in a crooked smile as he considered the officers. They were clearly assigned to watch Marie Claire, so when she left, they followed. They didn't pay much attention to the other homes along the street, no doubt assuming the upper-middle-class residents of the stylish neighborhood would pose no threat.

They probably thought the house he was in was vacant, given the tattered For Sale sign that had been leaning to the side in the overgrown front yard. It had been a simple enough matter to get in through the back of the house. He could park in the alley, come through the gate, and enter the house at will, just as the majority of the other residents entered their own homes every evening.

Not that anyone noticed him. The neighborhood was home to up-and-coming young professionals who worked in downtown office buildings all day long. They paid no attention to yet another resident in a business suit, casually parking his nondescript rental sedan and confidently striding through the backyard to the house.

Given the inflated asking price for the home, he was sure that realtors and prospective homebuyers wouldn't be a problem.

He knew it was risky to stake himself out so close to Marie Claire. But that was part of the rush. It gave him a satisfaction that he couldn't get taking a more cautious approach to stalking his prey.

Sweet prey.

That's how he thought of Marie Claire. She was the prize in an ongoing game between him and the police. He didn't have any doubt as to how the game would end. The police were so stupid.

He grinned as he considered how easily he'd found her new location. All he'd had to do was track down her little redheaded friend and follow her. He already had her license plate number, which in turn gave her name and address. From there, it had been a simple matter to search the Internet and determine that she was a city employee with the Social Services department. He'd staked out her building downtown and followed her from work to the place she now stayed in each night with Marie Claire.

The house across the street.

It had been luck, pure and simple, that the town home he currently occupied was vacant and up for sale—and had all its lights on a timer with a functioning A/C—but he'd learned to take whatever luck came his way. It was how he'd picked out his first prey ten years ago, and every victim since then. He'd told himself he would take the first dark-haired whore he saw, and he had. The rush had been incredible.

He wondered who owned the home Marie Claire had moved into. From a distance he'd seen a blonde woman with short hair, but he hadn't been able to get her license plate number. He would look into pulling property records, but there wasn't any hurry. For now it was laughably easy to watch over his beautiful prey.

Soon he would make his next move, but for now, he was enjoying the anticipation. The sexual jolt that came when he considered his options was too pleasurable. He wouldn't rush through the planning phase of his operation, no matter how eager he was to finally have her under his knife.

Chapter 30

The tension in Afton's office at Camelot was so obvious that Aidan felt like he could reach out and touch
it. Clearly something had happened between Sean and
Claire, and they were both desperately trying to act as if it
hadn't.

Claire slid a sideways glance at Sean's profile, then
looked quickly away. She felt as awkward as a teenager
on a blind date. Though it had been two days since they
had practically jumped each other in Afton's kitchen, they
had yet to speak in person. In fact, Sean had yet to speak
to anyone in the room. He seemed to be absorbed in whatever was written in his notebook.

Aidan cleared his throat. "Just so we're all on the same
page," he said to Afton, "could you explain again how the
dating service works and what the background checks involve? We don't need the sales pitch. We're interested in
what goes on after the clients are gone."

"It's very simple," Afton said. "The members fill out a
detailed questionnaire, which gives us insight into their

preferences. These are then fed into the computer. The questionnaire also forms the basis of the background checks, which are carried out by a private investigation firm."

"What about the matchmaking process, or whatever you call it?" Aidan asked.

"It's really up to the individual. The clients are invited to review the catalogue and pick out members who share similar interests, or they can let the computer cross-reference based on the questionnaire responses. We can then initiate e-mail or phone contact with the prospective date, and see where the couple wants to take it from there."

"So if they're interested, clients can have everything brokered through Camelot?" Aidan asked.

"Yes. They can also do things completely on their own. We want to offer as much flexibility as possible."

"How do clients hear about Camelot? Do you advertise?" Sean asked abruptly, startling Claire.

"Not in the conventional sense. We do place some personal ads and use a direct mail marketing firm. But the majority of our clients come from recruiting drives, open houses, or 'meet and greet' corporate cocktail parties. That's how Claire heard about us when my sister was running the service," Afton added.

Claire shifted in her seat as all eyes turned briefly to her.

"You said before that these corporate parties have tapered off due to changes in the local high-tech business sector," Aidan said.

"Yes. The last one was hosted by my sister before she got really ill, so it was at least five months ago."

Sean was silent as he wrote in his notebook. When he finished, he looked over at Aidan. "I think our only option is to do an initial screen on every male listed in the catalogue, regardless of how he came to be a client."

"I agree. At this point there's no reason to exclude any able-bodied men between the age of twenty and fifty." Aidan looked at Afton. "How many male clients do you have in your database?"

"Let me check," she said, typing rapidly. "Three hundred sixty-one male clients as of today who fit your description."

"Beautiful," Aidan said in disgust. "Do you have any idea how long it would take to run checks on all those guys?"

"I thought you said getting male clients was a problem. How come you have so many?" Sean asked, ignoring his partner's outburst.

"We just completed a huge membership drive, specifically targeting men because the ratio was skewed. My sales staff was out for the last two weekends in a row, recruiting new clients in bars, restaurants, clubs, and malls. Then they came in on the following Mondays and entered all the new members into the database at once."

"How many men were added to the catalogue on the last two Mondays?" Sean asked.

Afton squinted at the screen as she typed in the query. "Over one hundred and fifty male candidates have been added in the last ten days. It's been a good sales drive."

"So based on the assumption that Claire saw the guy's picture in the dating catalogue, we can eliminate these new additions and focus on the two hundred or so males who were clients prior to the murder," Aidan said.

Sean nodded. "Two hundred is still a huge number to work with, but it's better than every guy in the catalogue."

Afton typed some more, then scowled at the computer screen. "I'm not sure about the best way to run that type of search. Let me go talk to our database consultant. I'll have him run the query and save the results in a file we can use for the remainder of the investigation." She left the room, closing the door behind her.

Aidan turned to Claire. "While we're waiting for that file, there's one more thing to go over. Sean and I have been working on a preliminary psychological profile of our killer—it's pretty basic, but there's one thing you can clarify to help us."

"What?" she asked eagerly.

"We need to understand what motivates the killer, what makes him do the things he does the way he does them. We'll look at his choice of victims, the way they were killed, how the bodies were displayed, and what the crime scenes have in common. I'm sure you've heard about criminal profiling, which was first used by the FBI. This is basically the same type of stuff they'd be doing if they were involved."

"Why aren't they involved?" Claire asked.

"Because the case hasn't been solved for them yet," Sean muttered under his breath.

Aidan coughed. "Unless their assistance is specifically requested, it's up to the Bureau when and where they get involved with cases. Often they choose to get involved at the 'um, tail end of the investigation."

This time Sean was the one who coughed at the understatement. Aidan continued, "At this point we don't have any evidence of crimes occurring in multiple states, just a theory. That's not enough for our department to ask for help from the Feds yet. Besides, the FBI has limited resources just like we do, and right now those agents are assigned to high-profile national security cases and terrorism task forces."

"What my partner is trying to say is that dead prostitutes don't even make a blip on the FBI radar screen, even though it's not politically correct to point that fact out," Sean said.

"Sounds like politics is politics, regardless of whether those involved work with law enforcement or computer programs. Anyway, how can I help? I'm not one of your forensic technicians," Claire said.

Aidan hoped he didn't look uncomfortable. He'd never had to question a woman his cousin was involved with—and whether or not Sean admitted it, he was involved.

"Well," Aidan said, "one thing we don't have any insight into is why the killer would join a dating service. In fact, the whole dating angle doesn't fit your standard profile of a serial killer. They often don't have steady relationships with partners, either male or female."

"But wouldn't that be why he joined the dating service?" Claire asked. "To find a relationship?"

"Many serial killers don't want any type of normal relationship, sexual or otherwise," Sean said. "They live in a self-created fantasy world. It's hard to maintain that world if there are significant others constantly intruding into the alternate reality in which the killer lives."

Aidan nodded. "Many of these killers escape into fantasy to make up for whatever is lacking in their own world. Or to compensate for clinical mental illness. The degree to which the killer's fantasy is different from reality helps determine whether we're talking about a total social misfit, like Jeffrey Dahmer, or someone who can get around in society quite well, like Ted Bundy."

Claire considered for a moment. "If you want my opinion, I'd lean more toward the Ted Bundy angle on this killer."

"Why?" Aidan asked, intrigued.

"The way Camelot is set up, people have to be photographed as part of their profile. The clients then review the other profiles, including—let's be honest—the photos and bios. No one is going to sign up to date a troll, or a complete whack job like Jeffrey Dahmer."

"You think our killer must be at least passably attractive and successful in his career, otherwise he would have chosen another dating service with a more anonymous screening method?" Sean asked.

"Exactly. I mean, if the guy was a complete troglodyte with no social or professional life, he wouldn't have the nerve to put his picture in the catalogue. If you look through it, you'll see that all of the men and women in there are decent-looking professionals who have lots of normal hobbies and interests."

"What the hell is a troglodyte?" Aidan asked.

"Your last girlfriend," Sean replied instantly.

Claire giggled.

"Didn't she date you first?" Aidan asked.

Claire laughed out loud, then pressed her lips together as Sean slanted her a look.

He glanced at what he'd written in his notebook while he fought a smile at her infectious laugh. "I think it's an interesting theory, one we can run with for now. We'll need more, though."

"And you think understanding why people join a dating service will help you fill out this blank you have in the killer's profile?" Claire asked.

"It's worth a try," Aidan said.

She looked at the two detectives as they sat attentively, waiting for her answer. She tried to think of a way to explain to them what she had trouble explaining to herself.

How on earth had she reached the point where she needed to sign up for a dating service, and what did that say about her?

Too personal, she thought. *Generalize it.*

"I suppose there are lots of reasons to join a dating service," she said, choosing her words with care. "People these days spend long hours at demanding jobs. It's difficult to meet members of the opposite sex while working eighty-hour weeks, or traveling a great deal."

"Yes, that's exactly the kind of insights we need," Aidan said. "Go on."

"I imagine many people pay more attention to their careers than their personal lives," she said. "They always assume that a relationship will find them when the time is right. But when these people hit their thirties or forties, they realize their time is running out."

"So you hit thirty and the biological clock starts the countdown?" Sean asked.

"It doesn't work that way with males," she said, wincing inside at what she had revealed. "Anyway, male or female, it's hard to find safe places to meet strangers in the city, especially if one isn't into smoky bars or teeny-bopper clubs."

Sean paused in his writing to study her intently, blue eyes serious. "You've described all sorts of reasons not to be dating, but why did you actually join Camelot? Did you *want* to be dating?"

Claire narrowed her eyes at Sean's repeated references to her own life. She'd carefully phrased all her responses, trying to create a generic profile of a Camelot customer. The last thing she wanted to do was focus on her own rationale, her emotional state when she'd enrolled. She was afraid that would chip away at the tenuous wall of professionalism she was trying to build. Worse, she was afraid Sean would think she was completely desperate for a man, so much so that she would throw herself at him. Again.

"I suppose the desire for a partner becomes more pressing as people get older," Claire said neutrally. "As you mentioned, there are children to consider. Or maybe people are just lonely, and get tired of feeling that way."

"So you were lonely?" Sean asked, focused on her.

She stared into his eyes, caught for a moment in his intensity. He saw right through her supposedly generic explanations to the very core of her feelings—loneliness. With a few words he'd stripped away the protective layers she'd created.

"I believe we've already had a discussion about the importance of professionalism," she said to Sean. "I'd appreciate it if the questioning took on a less personal tone."

"What are you talking about?" he asked, confused. "I'm being one hundred percent professional here."

She saw that he was telling the truth. He was focused on the investigation right now, completely detached from her.

Oh, God. Is it possible to be any more humiliated and still survive?

Struggling for her dignity, she said, "I just mean that I'm beginning to feel like a bug under a microscope. You guys need to focus on the *killer's* motivations, not mine."

"That's what we're trying to do," Sean pointed out.

"Don't tell me you can extrapolate from my motivations to his," she said. "He's a man, and God knows I'll never understand what makes men tick."

"Regardless of your inability to understand the male of the species," Sean shot back, "there might be a common thread between your thought processes and the killer's that can help us in developing his profile."

"Bullshit. I'm not out there stabbing people."

"You don't need a knife. That sharp tongue of yours is enough to—"

"In the interest of world peace," Aidan cut in, "I'm going to declare this match a draw. Sean, why don't we take what we've gotten from Claire and put it together with additional insights from Afton. Who better than the owner of Camelot to explain why our killer might join a dating service?"

Claire sat back and wished he'd had that brilliant insight earlier, before she'd made a complete fool out of herself in front of Sean. Again.

Chapter 31

Safely hidden behind the darkened glass of a café window, the man watched Marie Claire leave the building, get into a cab, and drive off. With her police escort right behind. Satisfied he knew his prey's destination, he turned his attention to the three people who remained standing at the curb, talking.

One of them was the blonde woman he'd seen with Marie Claire at the place she was now staying. The two others he instantly pegged as cops. He didn't know the one with lighter hair, but he assumed he was working on the case. The cop with darker hair had driven Marie Claire to the redhead's apartment building a couple of days ago, the afternoon he'd sent his surprise.

He watched the blonde woman walk down the street, then enter a convenience store. The two men got into a tan sedan with city license plates. There would be no tracing them through the Motor Vehicle Division. He wanted a name for these cops, and for the other woman. He didn't like not knowing who all the players were.

He also needed to figure out what they'd been doing all day at the office building. It wasn't anything obvious. He knew the neighborhood because his father's company had offices two doors down. He searched his memory for any unusual business in the building he'd been watching but came up blank. He'd have to keep an eye on the situation, and get even closer to Marie Claire.

He wasn't worried about being caught. He was smarter than they were and had been proving it for years. He was setting up to prove it all over again with Marie Claire, his beautiful prey.

Chapter 32

"It's about time," Captain Michaels said when Sean and Aidan showed up at his office. "Sit down and give me an update."

Sean reached into the folder he carried and handed over a list. "We have a file covering approximately two hundred male clients of the dating service. These names are being run through the computers right now for prior offenses, known aliases, and so forth."

"How long will that take?" the captain asked.

"At least two weeks. We've monopolized the computer techs, but they still can't run more than a dozen a day between them, if we want to be really thorough."

"Shit, we don't have time for this," Michaels muttered.

Aidan nodded. "That's why we've decided to go through the two hundred candidates with our witness and see if we can't fine-tune the list. At least then we could come up with some prioritization for the background checks."

"Does she remember any more about the night of the murder?"

"Not as far as I know," Aidan said. "Even when I took her over the basic self-defense moves yesterday, which had to be pretty scary considering she was recently attacked, nothing came back to her. But she's confident she'll be able to help us narrow the field."

Michaels said nothing as he skimmed the column of names. "Detective Richter?"

"Burke has finished a preliminary psych profile," Sean said, using the name most of the department associated with his cousin. "It's a good start, but we both feel there are gaps. We've also been putting together a plan for the dating sting, based on the possibility that the killer is actually a member. We need to proceed very cautiously if we're going to draw this guy out of hiding with such an obvious operation. Of course, that's assuming that we're not wasting our time altogether with this idea."

Captain Michaels heard the veiled criticism. "I realize you're still not comfortable with the plan, Richter, but dragging your feet won't help. The chief is tired of dodging media bullets about the murder."

"He's weathered worse storms before," Sean said.

"Yeah, but that was before Shelly Whitcombe started doing nightly updates on the news."

Sean's eyes narrowed. The woman was an ambitious menace who had lied, cheated, and screwed her way to minor fame in the D.C. journalism world.

"She's sniffing around here after every press briefing," the captain said. "She gets someone to leak her information and we'll all be in deep shit."

Aidan muttered something about size six scum-sucking parasites.

Sean leaned forward in his chair. "All right, we'll pick up the pace. But I want a full background check on anyone Claire Lambert gets into a car with."

"Fine," the captain said. "Even though Burke took the precaution of giving her a short course in self-defense, if anything went wrong with one of her dates, and he had a rap sheet we'd overlooked, the press would crucify us."

"A bad date wouldn't do much for Ms. Lambert either."

Aidan started talking fast, before Sean got in more trouble. "It would be a big help if we could get some time with an FBI profiler. We have to plug the holes in our psych analysis of the killer. It could help Ms. Lambert and us look for behavioral traits or red flags."

Captain Michaels pulled on his lower lip as he thought about the request. "Talk to the department shrink. He's been able to give us some insights before. If we don't get anywhere with our own staff, then we'll consider bringing in the FBI."

"Sir, I think we should have a better idea of what kind of personality we're looking for before we start letting our witness spend the evening with strange men," Sean said, trying to be diplomatic in his response. "I'm very *uncomfortable* not taking every precaution in a case where we're using a civilian as bait."

"So noted. But do you have any idea what the press would do if they caught wind of the fact we were consulting with an FBI criminalist? It's too early to bring in the Feds." Captain Michaels stood up to indicate that the meeting was over. "Talk to the department shrink first, see what he has to say."

Sean was halfway down the corridor before he trusted himself to say a word to his partner. "Michaels doesn't give a shit about her. We might as well send her out with a big red target painted on her."

"He's a politician. He's looking at the big picture."

"Fuck the big picture."

"That's why he's the politician, not you. And not me," Aidan said.

"You're a better diplomat than I am."

"So is a rabid grizzly." Aidan looked at his partner's tight face and knew trouble was coming. "Ease up. Claire has us to watch over her, and the captain knows it. We won't let anything happen to her."

"Yeah? Are we going to stay over at her place, follow her to the store, stand outside the bathroom while she showers?" Sean demanded, knowing how easy it would be for a determined person to get to Claire.

"If that's what it takes."

"If I'm living in her back pocket, how the hell am I supposed to focus on the investigation?"

"Good question," Aidan said. "You've got two hours to find an answer."

"What?"

"We're meeting Claire and Afton at Camelot before lunch."

Chapter 33

Claire looked impatiently out the window of the cab. The Friday morning traffic was heavy, as people had taken cars and taxis due to the steady rain that fell. She checked her watch again—late. She should have taken the metro and walked from the Dupont Circle station to Camelot. It certainly would have been faster.

But she hadn't been ready to face the memories of what had happened the last time she'd taken that exact same route.

Claire jolted when the cabbie turned around and asked for the fare. She realized that they'd arrived while she'd been daydreaming. She paid the driver and hurried upstairs.

Sean and Aidan were already at work with Afton when Claire rushed into the office. "Sorry I'm late. One of my accounts went nuclear and I had to stop by the office for an emergency meeting. You find anything on my first five choices?"

"Where's Olivia? I thought for sure she'd want to be involved in the action," Aidan said.

"She had a court appearance this morning or she'd be here. And believe me, she was pissed I wouldn't push this meeting until later in the afternoon. She's been a bit concerned about me recently," Claire added, rolling her eyes at the understatement.

"Family has that prerogative," Aidan said, eyeing his partner.

"Can we get on with it?" Sean asked, straightening the stack of papers in front of him. He didn't look at Claire.

Afton said quickly, "Our security firm rechecked their data on the five men Claire chose. Nothing of interest showed up."

"We're still running the names through the law enforcement computers," Sean said. "The first two came back clean this morning, so we can go ahead and set something up with them."

"I'll contact them today and see if we can arrange a dinner meeting with each of them this weekend," Afton said. "I'm sure there won't be any problems, especially once they see Claire's picture," she added, smiling across the desk.

No doubt, Sean thought sourly. *The two losers will be slobbering at the thought of going out with someone like Claire. Then they'll try to slobber all over her.*

"We'll arrange for her dates to do the pickup and drop-off at Camelot," Afton continued. "They'll take a taxi to the restaurant, which is a pretty standard security measure."

"What about after the date?" Claire asked.

"Our couples usually come back here. The presence of

our uniformed security guard generally acts as a deterrent to, ah, questionable behavior at the end of the evening."

"Sounds good," said Aidan. "Once Claire gets in a taxi with the guy, either Sean or I will take up a position right behind. The other one will go ahead and be in place at the restaurant."

Sean flipped to the next page of his notes. "We've arranged to use Très Chic on M Street as our location. The management has agreed to reserve certain tables so we can keep an eye on Claire, and we've set up some of our surveillance equipment there. The facility has a restaurant, bar, and small dance floor, so there really shouldn't be a need to go anywhere else in a first date situation." Sean pinned Claire with a look. "If he does suggest another place, you're going to develop a sudden headache and give us the signal to end the evening."

"Unless, of course, I want to go with him." She gave Sean a brittle smile.

"Not on the department's nickel. You want to get cozy with someone, you'll have to wait until the investigation is over," Sean said, hoping his voice was calm and professional. "Otherwise, the only male you're alone with had better be wearing a badge."

Aidan gave his cousin a sideways glance.

Claire didn't push it. She didn't see much possibility of wanting to be alone with any of the dates she had selected for their potential to be a serial killer. She'd just wanted to yank Sean's chain. Something about his cool, professional attitude brought out the devil in her.

"Let's review the five candidates Claire picked out of the catalogue," Aidan said. He stood up and spread the photos and brief descriptions across the desk where everyone could see them. "Okay, we've got Taylor North, stockbroker, and Luis Cardinale, technical support supervisor. These two have been fully screened," he said, tapping one picture and then the other.

"What about the other three?" Claire asked.

"We're still waiting to hear back on Billy Green, congressional staffer. Also on Dr. Leonard Petrov, podiatrist, and Randy Klein, ad sales executive," Sean said. "Any particular reason why you picked out these five?"

Claire shook her head. "I was flipping through the pictures and paused on these ones. I just blew by the others."

"Maybe we have something here," Aidan said thoughtfully.

Sean stared at his partner. "We have nothing!"

"Look at their physical descriptions," Aidan said. "All of them are at least six feet tall. They have dark hair, medium complexion, and all but one have light-colored eyes."

"You think it's a hint about the killer's physical characteristics? Maybe a subconscious reaction?" Claire asked hopefully.

"Either that or you just happen to like tall guys with dark hair and light eyes," Sean said absently, studying the photos again. Then he realized what he'd said and made a big deal out of writing something in his notebook.

Sure her cheeks were flaming, Claire looked at the pictures. Thankfully, none of the bachelors she'd chosen had more than a superficial resemblance to Sean.

"When will you finish the background checks on the other three?" she asked.

"Sometime tomorrow," Sean said, grateful for the change in subject.

"Well, you'd better get moving. I'm going on a dating marathon. Five dates in five nights. I tried to think of a way to do more than one a night, but I was afraid it would end like a French farce with men hiding in the closet and under the bed."

Aidan laughed, but not Sean.

"I think of it as the New and Improved Dating Game." She smiled with true humor for the first time that day. "It's so nice of the taxpayers to foot the bill."

"I don't want to rain on your parade, but this is serious business," Aidan said.

"What my partner means is that your life could be at risk on any one of these dates," Sean cut in.

"Welcome to dating in the modern world."

"I'm serious."

She widened her eyes and drawled to both men, "Y'all sure about the danger? It never occurred to silly ol' me."

"This may be a joke to you," Sean began.

Aidan kicked him under the table. "You're going to be wearing a microphone so we can track your conversation," Aidan said quickly. "You'll be in visual contact with at least one of us at all times in the restaurant. Even when you're in the car with your date we'll be no more than fifty feet behind."

Claire winced. *This is supposed to make me feel better? Christ, Sean and his bad attitude are going to be following me like my own private thundercloud.*

"Wonderful," Claire grumbled. "You guys going to hand me toilet paper under the stall as well?"

"It won't be quite that bad," Aidan said. "But if you sneeze, several cops will be saying '*Gesundheit.*'"

She laughed ruefully. "Well, I wanted to be involved in

the investigation, so I'll try not to complain about the downstream effects."

Such as having to live within reach of the one man she was determined not to reach for.

Chapter 34

"So tonight's the big date, huh?" Olivia asked. She was watching Claire get ready in Afton's small guest bathroom.

"I'd hardly call it a date. The police are going to be listening to every word we say. It'll be more like an evening of 'Voyeur TV' or something." She winced as she reached up to fix her hair. "That tape bites."

"What tape?"

"The stuff plastered over me to hold the microphone in place."

Olivia studied her friend. "Doesn't show."

"It better not. I'd have a hard time explaining about the mike and the earphones Aidan and Sean are wearing and the machinery recording everything we say."

"Hey, if you let the stockbroker get into your dress, he won't be thinking about anything but your boobs."

"Ha, ha." Claire carefully blotted her lipstick. "I'm not looking for anything like that right now."

"What are you talking about? You joined a dating service not two weeks ago, plunking down God knows how much money to be set up with dates like this one."

"That was then. This is now. I'm not looking for Mr. Right."

"Why, because you've already found him?" Olivia said. "And don't look at me like that. Somehow I think you were cooking more than gumbo that night I walked into the kitchen."

Claire blushed and pointed at her hidden microphone, even though she wasn't in transmission range. "I told you that I'm not about to get involved with anyone when my life is in chaos."

"We can't always pick the time and place, sweetie."

Claire rolled her eyes and touched up the dark liner underneath one of them.

Olivia sighed. "Keep an open mind on your dates. You could have something in common with one of them."

"Ever the optimist." Claire dabbed on perfume.

"Listen, you don't need to find the love of your life in the next few weeks. Just be open to finding someone who's good company and who shares some of your interests. What's to prevent you from having fun?"

"Oh, I don't know. A serial killer, perhaps?" Or maybe a certain police officer who would be watching her every step of the way. And listening.

Olivia's blue eyes darkened with worry.

"Hey, it was just a joke." Claire touched Olivia's arm, then reached out to adjust a lock of her friend's upswept hair. "You look all dressed up yourself. Headed out?"

"Ah, yes. Some coworkers and I are going to get together for drinks and dinner. In fact, I should leave soon."

"Where are you guys going?" Claire asked.

"We haven't decided yet. Probably some place in Georgetown," Olivia said vaguely.

"Have fun. I'm off to Camelot to meet my Prince, or catch a frog. Something like that," Claire said with a wry smile. A horn blew outside, telling her that the taxi had arrived. "Wish me luck."

Chapter 35

Sean had won the coin toss, meaning he would follow Claire and her date to the restaurant. Aidan was there already, staked out at a table with an excellent view of the area where Claire would be sitting.

Sitting behind the wheel of his beige sedan, Sean watched Claire leave the taxi and listened while she introduced herself to Taylor North, stockbroker.

Taylor—what the hell kind of name is that, anyway?

Sean ran his eyes over Claire, taking in every bit of her appearance. Just so he'd be able to keep tabs on her throughout the evening, of course. Her hair was up in a twist, leaving her neck bare. She wore a cocktail-length dress in dark blue, with a matching short-sleeved jacket. Her legs looked long and lean in the strappy heels she was wearing.

Reading body language, Sean could tell the guy was very interested. Taylor North did a really thorough once-over of Claire while they introduced themselves. Sean watched as the guy directed her toward the cab, hand lingering on her lower back. *Creep.*

Claire was thinking pretty much the same thing as the warm hand settled above her butt. Barely above it. Gritting her teeth, she told herself that Taylor was simply being a gentleman. He didn't know—and certainly hadn't guessed—that she hated absolute strangers intruding in her personal space.

She got into the taxi and slid all the way to the opposite side. Desperately she tried to remember his biography. Nothing came to her. So she concentrated on making small talk—weather, sports, headlines, anything to find a common ground.

"Looks like it might storm later tonight," she said.

"Uh-huh. Excuse me for a minute. I have to check on something. I wasn't really expecting to be out tonight . . ."

In disbelief, then amusement, she watched while he downloaded e-mail and flicked through it on a PDA. "E-mail, huh?" she asked for Sean's benefit.

"Yeah."

She studied Taylor in the dim light. He was handsome enough, with straight features, dark brown hair, and blue eyes. He just didn't do it for her. Besides, he didn't need a date, he needed a data port.

She looked at his mouth and tried to find signs of the killer's distinctive smile, the cruel twist that she remembered so well. But Taylor wasn't a smiler. Settling back, she decided she would have her work cut out getting a humorous reaction from him.

Two cars behind them, Sean was grinning. *What a putz. He gets alone with her and the first thing he does is check in with the office.*

Nothing in Sean's opinion changed during the next hour as he watched—and listened—while Claire tried to interest Taylor in something besides the stock market updates that came in on his PDA. If it hadn't been for the guy's eyes glued to Claire's breasts every time he looked up, Sean would have sworn he didn't have anything but a spreadsheet between his legs.

Locking her jaw against a yawn, Claire pushed salad around on the plate in front of her and hoped the waiter would bring the main course soon. Maybe then Taylor would be forced to change the subject from the *importance, the absolutely vital importance of good tax shelters*. Apparently it was so important that it was some kind of crime to smile, much less laugh, about anything else.

If there was any humor in Taylor's soul, she hadn't found it. As a sense of humor was one of her top three requirements in a date, she was glad this wasn't a real Camelot match—she would have raised hell and gotten her money back. She wondered if another stiff drink would make Taylor's company more appealing. Unfortunately, she suspected there wasn't enough alcohol in the bar to make an evening of discussing Taylor's stock portfolio and financial planning strategies entertaining. The only real amusement in the date so far was looking at her butter knife and wondering if it was sharp enough to slit his throat. Or her wrists.

She realized he'd asked her a question, and she tried to cover her inattention with an inquiring sound.

"I'll tell you why I didn't lose my shirt when the market tanked. Diversification," he said emphatically. "It's the key to any successful portfolio. You don't want to be too heavily invested in any particular sector, though of course you want to focus on the profitable ones."

God, we're back to the portfolio again. I suppose that's an improvement over tax shelters.

At this point she was about one hundred percent certain that Taylor wasn't the killer—unless the other women had died of boredom.

Claire looked up and smiled brilliantly when the waiter took her salad plate away and said their entrees were coming out shortly. She let her eyes wander to where Aidan was seated alone at a table for two about fifteen feet away from her. She continued to glance around, scanning the bar and getting a jolt as she collided with Sean's intense blue gaze.

She knew she wasn't supposed to look directly at him, but she could feel his eyes practically burning into her. It was impossible not to glance over at him occasionally. Every time it happened, she grew more tense.

Deliberately pulling her attention from the bar area, she continued to casually look over the rest of the diners. A large party of women was just being seated at a corner table. Claire smiled when she recognized Olivia with some of her coworkers. Apparently Très Chic was a popular location for weekend nights out. Claire hoped her friend was having a better time than she was.

When their meals arrived, she made another valiant attempt to pay attention to Taylor. Hopefully, he had finally exhausted the topic of his two-, five-, and ten-year plans for diversified investing and financial security.

She forked in a mouthful of tender chicken and decided that the evening wasn't a total loss.

"Tell me about your portfolio," Taylor said.

Now he remembers me, when my mouth is full. Claire swallowed hard. "I have stock options in the company where I work."

"One company? That's it?" Her date looked horrified at the thought and set aside his fork and knife. "That's foolish. You would be wiped out financially if anything happens to them."

"I also have a modest number of shares I inherited from my father. You know, blue-chip stocks in companies that have survived for generations and will be around when I need them."

"Old-fashioned and outdated. You need to dump those and invest in more progressive companies, ones that will determine the future of their respective industries." He leaned forward, placing his elbows on the table. "I'd be happy to give you some pointers."

"Actually, the portfolio as a whole is doing well. I'm very comfortable with things as they stand. But thank you for the offer."

Taylor made an understanding sound and smiled. "I know the stock market can seem very intimidating to women. Their urge is to buy conservative stocks they know and understand. Particularly in a volatile market."

Claire narrowed her eyes. *Very intimidating to women my ass.* "My portfolio has consistently outperformed the leading funds and the market as a whole. I invested my father's life insurance settlement, and in a few years was able to buy a house here in Georgetown. Daddy always told me if it ain't broke, don't fix it," she drawled.

"Yes, well, that's a nice Beaver Cleaver approach to investing, and if you're happy with it—" he began.

"I am," she interrupted, setting her drink down hard.

"Well, that's just so yesterday," he said. He started writing on the back of the linen napkin. "Look, if you just take some of that stock and transfer it into one of these high-yield funds, in five, ten, or twenty years you'll . . ."

Claire tuned out, because if he kept on patronizing her, she was going to come across the table and commit murder under the interested eyes of two homicide detectives. Death by forced ingestion of PDA and cell phone. She would plead justifiable homicide.

From the amused look on Sean's face, he would back her.

Hoping to be able to eat her meal in peace, Claire interrupted, "So tell me, do stockbrokers have 401(k) plans?"

"Usually. Of course, it depends on whether they're working as independents or with a large firm, like I am. The 401(k) is a core element of my ten-year plan for personal financial freedom."

She smiled and made encouraging noises as she ate the excellent dinner. Her date had managed to numb her mind, but her taste buds were doing fine. If he noticed her lack of attention, it didn't bother him. He lectured over the steak going cold on his plate. The only good news was that he didn't talk with his mouth full.

As soon as Claire finished eating, she cut Taylor off in full flight on the difference between a 401(k) and something whose rank and serial number escaped her.

"Sorry, I have to . . ." She gestured toward the rest rooms.

"Huh? Oh. Sure." He looked at his plate like he'd just noticed it. "Guess I should eat something. I get carried away when I talk about my work."

"Really? I hadn't noticed."

Laughter came from the direction of the bar.

As she passed Aidan's table, she dropped her small cocktail purse in a prearranged signal that she was going to end the evening as soon as she got back from the ladies' room. When Aidan handed her the purse, she gave him a polite social smile and walked on.

Aidan signaled the waiter for his check. He had to get back to Camelot to be in position before Claire and her date arrived.

Sean told himself it was petty to feel so good about what had obviously been a lousy evening for Claire. Even without the small earpiece he would have known that the date was a dud. Her body language screamed *I'd rather be home watching a Discovery Channel special about hyena population growth in Kenya than here!*

If this guy was the serial killer, Sean would eat Taylor's stock portfolio—assuming Claire didn't feed it to him before the date was over. *One down, four to go.*

Sean's good humor evaporated. The thought of sitting through four more nights of guys ogling Claire made the mineral water in his glass taste like horse piss.

I love my job, he thought grimly, signaling the bartender to prepare his check.

When Taylor and Claire stood up to leave, Sean was ready to follow Claire and her date back to Camelot's building. Aidan would already be in position near the entrance, overseeing the good-night chitchat and waiting to take Claire home. At this point neither detective planned to jump in the cab after Claire went inside and strike up a conversation with the date about what deceitful bitches women were—almost always a hot-button topic for men who murdered prostitutes.

No small talk came through the mike as Sean followed the taxi to Camelot's building. When the cab stopped at the curb to let out its passengers, Sean went on one block, circled around, and parked across the street from Camelot.

Claire was already out of the taxi and going up the steps to the entrance. Just inside the revolving door, Aidan was leaning casually against a wall, seemingly absorbed in a newspaper.

"Thanks, Taylor," she said, stopping outside the building door.

She hoped he'd read in her the universal signals of a woman who wasn't interested and wasn't going to be. But somehow, she didn't think so.

"I had a great time, Claire," he said, standing between her and the door. "Here, let me give you my card. Just in case you're interested in updating your portfolio or . . . anything."

Claire murmured a response and slipped the card into her evening bag.

Taylor just stood there. "Evening is kind of warm, isn't it? Hope it rains before morning and cools things off a bit."

Oh, God. Now he wants small talk. Claire sighed. "That would be nice."

Another moment of awkward silence passed.

"Well, I'd best go in and get my things," Claire said, smiling brightly. "I left my laptop inside." She hadn't, but she didn't want him to offer her a cab ride home.

"Sure. Well, I had a great time." Taylor made no move to get out of the doorway.

Claire knew that he was trying to get up the courage to kiss her. She stuck her hand out firmly to discourage his big move and said, "Good night."

He took her hand and gave it a quick squeeze. Before she could avoid it, he swooped down and landed an open-mouthed kiss on her lips. Her head jerked back in shock.

"I'll call you, okay?" Taylor said.

Jesus, talk about not getting it. Claire slid past him. "Sure. Bye."

"Don Juan had better look out," Aidan said without looking up from his newspaper.

"Yeah, Taylor's a real charmer," she replied, moving briskly toward the ladies' room off the lobby. "Give me a minute and we can go home."

"Take your time," Aidan said, turning the page of his paper.

The first thing she did after locking the bathroom stall was to unbutton her dress. "Good night, sweet prince," she muttered and jerked off the microphone taped to her chest. She winced at losing several layers of skin in the process, then went to work on the remainder of the equipment taped to her waist.

In the car outside, Sean watched Taylor North get into a taxi. Then the sound of rustling in his earpiece distracted him, followed by something sarcastic he didn't quite catch. The abrupt silence that followed told him Claire had removed her microphone. The date was over. He got out of the car and jogged across the street to the building.

Aidan met him at the top of the steps. "Somehow, I don't think Taylor North is our smooth operator."

Sean leaned against the railing. "Don't think he's the killer, either."

"Agreed. The most we could charge him with is being a boring and self-absorbed asshole."

Sean snickered, then straightened as Claire came through the doors and began to descend the stairs. "Any impressions on the stockbroker?"

"Yeah. He kisses like a fourth-grader," she shot back.

Aidan laughed out loud.

Sean was smarter. He knew that Claire would turn her temper on him if he so much as smiled.

"Ah, I meant more along the lines of whether you recognized him," Sean said. "You know, whether he might be our killer?"

"I didn't feel any kind of reaction to him but terminal boredom. I managed to get a smile out of him. It wasn't like the one I remember from the night of the murder." She sighed and adjusted her purse. Just because the two detectives had witnessed the whole miserable farce of a date was no reason to be mad at them. "Sorry the evening was a bust."

"Part of the investigative process is to eliminate suspects," Sean said cheerfully. "Taylor is off our list. No point in even sharing a cab ride with him to talk about how awful women are in an effort to get him riled."

The smile red lined her temper. "I'm glad it was good for someone." She turned and stalked toward an unmarked police car. "Ready when you are, Aidan."

"Whew," Sean said when Claire couldn't hear. "Somebody's pissed."

"Yeah. I think I'll kiss her good night. Someone should do it right."

"Fuck me." Sean's head whipped around.

Aidan grinned. "That wiped the smug look off your face."

Sean wasn't laughing. "I'm following you back to Afton's house."

"No need."

"Like hell."

Aidan was still laughing when he caught up with Claire.

Chapter 36

Less than twenty-four hours after her last date, Claire found herself once again seated at a table for two in Très Chic, suffering the tortures of the damned. Luis Cardinale, technical support supervisor for a major local software firm, had spent the entire evening so far—from introductions at Camelot to appetizers at the restaurant—talking about his ex-girlfriend.

Claire took a healthy swallow of her vodka on the rocks and decided that she would rather hear about Roth IRAs and municipal bonds as tax shelters than listen to one more word about how Lydia Cockburn had screwed over poor, innocent Luis. If she hadn't known that Sean and Aidan would roll off their chairs laughing, she would go to the rest room, climb out the window, and run for it.

"That's how I knew you and I were going to hit it off right away," Luis told her.

"Huh?" Claire blinked at her date.

"Because you weren't wearing provocative clothing. Lydia always wore strapless tops and tight pants, or teensy little dresses whenever we went out. She wanted other men to look at her, be aroused by her body. She loved how upset that made me."

"I believe I'll have another drink."

"But you still have half of yours left," Luis said.

"Not for long." Claire picked up her drink and chugged the remainder. She set the glass down and flagged someone over to their table. "Vodka rocks," she said to him.

"You know, Lydia used to drink too much when we went out," Luis began.

Gee, I wonder why. "Make it a double." She smiled brilliantly at the waiter.

"Yes, ma'am."

Claire bit her tongue and wondered when she'd become *ma'am* instead of *miss*. Maybe it was the vodka. It wasn't her normal drink, but this wasn't her normal evening. She'd first ordered an icy margarita, only to have Luis point out sadly that it was Lydia's favorite drink. Claire had told the waiter to bring something with vodka instead.

"The last time Lydia drank too much in a club, she hit on one of the bouncers like I wasn't even there."

Smart lady. "What a shame. Do you suppose she just forgot?"

Luis blinked. "I didn't like it when she drank."

"Really? Why?" Claire looked at the butter knife. No help there. It was as dull as it had been last night.

As the waiter set Claire's new drink down in front of her, she caught Sean's warning look from a nearby table. She'd forgotten he and Aidan were listening to everything she said, because for this date the police technician had found smaller, lighter equipment. She hardly realized she was wearing anything extra under her little black dress.

Meeting Sean's gaze directly, she lifted her glass in a

subtle mock toast, took a delicate sip, and set the drink back down. She hadn't forgotten why she was on a date with the lousy Luis. Unfortunately she was almost certain he was not the man they were looking for. He'd smiled several times—usually on relating some memory of Lydia—and it looked nothing like the cruel smile Claire remembered from the night of the murder.

Even so, she was beginning to think her date needed psychological help getting over his ex-girlfriend. His obsessive, possessive personality would probably be of interest to the police.

With a mental sigh, Claire decided to keep the date going on the slim possibility that Luis might fit at least some aspects of the killer's profile.

"So, how long have you been working in tech support?" Claire asked.

At that same moment, the song playing over the speakers changed to a slow, quiet number. Couples gradually moved from tables to the tiny dance floor set to one side of the restaurant, and began swaying gently to the soft music.

"Me and Lydia used to love this song. It was, like, our song," he said, staring forlornly at the dance floor. His eyes shimmered suspiciously.

Claire briefly pinched the bridge of her nose before looking over to Aidan and Sean for assistance. She simply couldn't go through a whole evening of the ex-girlfriend blues, especially if Luis started sniveling.

Aidan studiously avoided her gaze and stayed in his position at the bar. She turned to Sean, who seemed to be staring intently at her. After several moments she realized he was looking behind her. She turned her head discreetly but didn't see anything worth his attention.

She did, however, catch sight of a table with three women ogling Sean. If he noticed their attention, it didn't show. He just gave the room a casual scan and went back to his mineral water. From the whispers, giggles, and rib pokes, Claire could tell the women were well into their drinks and working up the courage for a more direct approach to the lone man.

She didn't blame them. Sean was a handsome male seated alone in a known "meet market." He was just the type of prize some women would love to take home for the night. Pushing aside the disturbing thought, Claire looked back at her date.

"We went on a cruise and this song was always playing on the ship, so it kind of became our song, you know?" Luis said. "Those were the good times, before I found out she wanted to see other guys. That's why I now insist on exclusivity when I go out with a woman."

"Ummm," Claire said.

"So you're not, like, seeing anybody else, right?"

She couldn't quite believe what she was hearing. "Excuse me?"

"I told you, I have to have an exclusive relationship when I go out with a woman now. Because of what happened with Lydia. I just want to make sure we're both very clear on that," he said, studying her reaction carefully.

"Luis, we are exactly"—Claire checked her watch—"sixty-six minutes into our first date. I hardly think this is the time to bring up exclusivity."

"So there is someone else!" Luis jabbed at her with his fork to punctuate his statement.

"I paid to join a *dating service*. The whole point is to get out and date people. If you can't handle that, let's call it a night."

"No! I'm sorry, I guess I go a little crazy sometimes. Lydia left me with lots of emotional baggage, you know?"

Personally, Claire was starting to sympathize with Lydia. "Maybe it would be best if we didn't talk about her anymore, hmm?"

"Sure," he said, watching as the waiter set their dinners down. "So, have you ever been married?"

"No."

"Engaged, living together, anything?"

"No."

"I can't believe that. Someone like you must have gone out with lots of guys. How come you never married any of them?"

Excellent question. Claire finished chewing before answering, choosing her words carefully. "I came close to being engaged once, but things just didn't work out."

"Yeah? Did he cheat on you, too?"

"No, he just had different expectations. We worked together and initially kept quiet about our relationship because he wanted to. I guess that should have been a clue right away," she said, swirling more pasta around on her fork.

"What happened?"

"When things got more serious, he started pressuring me to get a job with another company. He wanted to be more open about us, even assumed we would get married someday—but because he was a manager at our firm he thought it would look bad for him to be involved with a coworker. He said it might affect his climb up the corporate ladder, and he expected me to make the big change in careers to avoid that. I disagreed. Things started to fall apart after that."

"I hear you. It's sort of strange when it all unravels,

isn't it? I couldn't believe things were over with Lydia for months."

"It wasn't that way for me. Now that I think about it, I really didn't have that much invested in the relationship except time." She'd been more embarrassed than anything else, because her private life had become fodder for office gossip.

Glancing over toward Sean's table, she caught him looking intently at her. Flustered, she glanced away and again saw the table of women giggling over Sean. One of the women beckoned the waiter over, whispered in his ear, and sent him off to the bar. Within a few moments, he appeared at Sean's table with a draft beer on his tray.

When the waiter was sent away with the beer untouched, Claire breathed a small sigh of relief.

"What's going on?" Luis asked her, looking around to see what she had been watching.

"Oh, nothing much. The table of women over there sent a drink to some guy, but he sent it back."

"That's how I met Lydia." He stared into the bottom of his glass as he swirled the ice around. "She sent me a Kamikaze at a club. We got drunk and danced all night, and then I went home with her and . . . well."

And you were surprised that things didn't work out when your relationship was based on Kamikazes and sex with a stranger? Claire resisted the urge to roll her eyes. "I hate Kamikazes," she said flatly. "They lead straight to bad choices."

At the bar, Aidan snickered over his soft drink. He felt sorry for Claire, but he'd just about sprained a rib trying not to laugh out loud. As a date, the evening was a disaster, personally and professionally. Luis Cardinale seemed to be a mild-mannered guy hung up on his apparently hot ex-girlfriend, but Aidan didn't think he was a serial killer. Still, they'd keep an eye on him to make sure he didn't have any more dangerous personality quirks.

Confident that Claire would be safe for the evening, Aidan turned his attention to a table in the corner behind her. About an hour ago, it had been empty, with a little Reserved card sitting on its surface. Now Afton and Olivia sat consuming an enormous tray of appetizers and a large bottle of mineral water. They had come through the kitchen to be seated without drawing attention, but he'd picked up on their presence right away, as had Sean. Both women had carefully avoided making eye contact with the detectives.

It was time to let them both know they'd been busted. Aidan lifted a hand to signal a waiter. Several minutes later, the waiter brought a nice bottle of cabernet over to the women, followed by a busboy bearing two enormous chocolate mousse cheesecake desserts. When Olivia looked inquiringly at the waiter, he turned and pointed out Aidan at the bar, glass raised in their direction.

Olivia made a face, gestured to the waiter that it was okay, and watched warily as Aidan approached.

"I'll take care of pouring the wine," Aidan said to the waiter, giving him a tip.

"How's it going?" Aidan asked, pulling up a chair and popping a spring roll into his mouth. Grabbing the two glasses, he poured wine to the rim in both of them.

"I can't drink that much," Olivia protested. "We're kind of working, you know?"

"No, you're not. It's a good thing I like you two, or I'd haul you in for interfering with a police investigation." Aidan set the wine down in front of them and smiled.

"We were just worried about Claire," Afton said.

"She's being watched at all times. She's in a crowded public place," Aidan pointed out.

"You don't know her like I do," Olivia said. "I can read what she's thinking, or tell when she's feeling uncomfortable or threatened."

"So can I," he replied, tapping his earpiece.

"We just wanted to help." Afton looked uncomfortable for a moment, then took a sip of the wine. She eyed the luscious chocolate dessert that had been placed in front of her and reached for a fork.

"We, my ass. *You*," Aidan said, pointing at Olivia. "You're the instigator here. Don't try to argue, just drink your wine and eat your dessert."

"What's up with all this stuff anyway?" Olivia asked, irritated at being ordered around, but not terribly surprised.

"The wine says you don't need to worry about keeping a clear head. The dessert says your evening is over and it's time to go home. Soon." Aidan stood up and headed back to the bar.

"Cocky bastard," Olivia muttered as she sipped from the brimming wineglass.

"Yes, but he's got excellent taste. Try the chocolate." Afton took another bite and all but purred.

Across the room, Sean watched the exchange and realized Aidan had gotten rid of their amateur sleuths for the evening. Warily eyeing the table of increasingly rowdy women who had sent several drinks over to him, Sean wondered if they would be so easily dismissed. Luckily, he could tell by the stiff way Claire smiled and the subtle shifting of her body that she was no more than two minutes away from flushing this date.

He could also tell when she was uncomfortable, like when she caught him looking at her. If someone were watching her closely, the whole dating sting would be over. Claire just wasn't used to hiding her feelings. She was too open and honest.

That was one of the reasons he was finding it so difficult to work with her. When she looked at him, he could see the conflicting emotions going through her. Above all, he could see the attraction she still felt. And since he was finding it damn near impossible to ignore his own feelings, he was always on edge, certain that they were constantly on the brink of another disastrous encounter.

Sean's earpiece suddenly echoed with Claire's gusty sigh. He heard Luis relating another Lydia story, this time about a trip to Hawaii he had paid for. Apparently his ex-girlfriend had spent half the nights in someone else's hotel room, so now Luis only went Dutch on shared vacations and dates.

Claire reached into her purse, dropped three twenties on the table, and said, "Excuse me."

As she headed for the rest room, she said quietly, "Fun's over."

Sean flagged down the waiter to settle his bill. This time he would be the one waiting at Camelot when Claire and loser Luis came back. Then Aidan would find a way to get in the cab and strike up a conversation with Luis about life in general and women in particular.

It wasn't likely that the man was dangerous, but no one was betting Claire's life on it.

Chapter 37

Claire stepped out into the muggy night air and turned to say good night to Luis. Before she could say anything else, Aidan trotted up, grabbed the open door, and asked, "Mind if I share the ride?"

He didn't wait for an answer, just got in as though he hadn't noticed Luis crying quietly in the corner. He'd finally been overwhelmed by the ghost of Lydia. Claire was relieved that he'd waited until she was getting out of the cab to start the maudlin tears.

"Bye, Luis," Claire said, closing the door behind Aidan. "Good luck getting over Lydia."

She felt like wishing Aidan luck, too, but was afraid she'd laugh out loud at the thought of what he'd have to go through during his ride. It only seemed fair that someone should suffer along with her. She waved after the cab as it pulled away from the curb, then turned to face Sean. He stood with his hands in the pockets of his jeans watching her. She could tell by the angelic look on his face that he was dying to make some kind of nasty comment about her date.

"Not one word," she said. "Where are you parked? I'm not waiting for Aidan to take me home, because he could be hours. Somehow I don't think Luis has gone through all of his Lydia stories yet."

Sean snickered. "Even if he has, Aidan will just get to hear the good ones again."

Claire laughed and got into the front of Sean's truck. She eased her aching feet out of the tiny sandals she'd worn and leaned against the seat. "Thank God I won't be seeing him again." She tilted her head to look at Sean as she drove. "I'm surprised you didn't bring one of your friends with you."

"Huh?" Sean said, distracted by the smell of Claire's perfume.

"You know, the women who sent you drinks all evening."

"Oh, them." He shrugged. "They were just having a night out, sucking up too much tequila and egging each other on. I don't take it personally."

Claire stared. He actually meant it. "How do you take it?"

"They were just goofing around. I was the only single guy in the dining area."

"Aidan was there, and he didn't get hit on."

"Yeah, but he was over at the bar. Besides, he was watching Olivia and Afton most of the evening. The other women could probably tell he was otherwise engaged."

Claire just shook her head. Unbelievable. He didn't have a clue as to how attractive he was. "Whatever. Where do we meet tomorrow night?"

"Afton's office. You have a date with the congressional staffer tomorrow, right?"

"Yeah. Can't tell you how much I'm looking forward to it."

"You knew the job was dangerous when you took it," Sean reminded her, grinning.

"I didn't think I'd be having dinner with the ghosts of girl-friends past. Luis needs an exorcist, not a dating service."

Sean laughed as he pulled up to the curb at Afton's house. Smiling slightly, Claire watched him. Somehow, she couldn't see him in Luis's position—more involved emotionally than the other party in the relationship. She didn't see Sean Richter mooning over anyone.

However, she might find herself in those shoes in the near future if she wasn't able to get a handle on her thoughts and stop comparing all her dates to Sean. Of course, it was kind of hard to stop comparing when he was no more than twenty feet away from her throughout the night, staring right at her.

Sean walked her to the door. She didn't invite him in because there was no official reason to prolong the contact. Olivia was inside, and the house had already been checked by one of the surveillance officers.

"Lock the door behind you," Sean said, and left without a backwards glance.

Watching Sean's taillights disappear through the window, Claire decided that she'd better grow thicker skin if she was going to continue with this dating game under the cool, watchful blue eyes of Detective Richter.

With her thoughts focused on Sean, Claire didn't notice the nondescript sedan that hesitated slightly, then drove past Afton's house.

Chapter 38

Washington, D.C.
Saturday night

The man braked at a dimly lit stop sign and ran his hands around the steering wheel, thinking about Marie Claire. She was going out to dinner with different men, but she had a police escort during and after each date. His lips twisted up at the corners. She must have really been rattled by his gift.

He'd enjoyed watching her, but would have to leave his sweet prey to her cops and boyfriends for a few days. Just when he'd decided he couldn't wait any longer for Marie Claire, fate had presented him with an outlet for his needs. All he had to do was a little groundwork before he could feel that lovely blade plunging into his next convenient victim. Then, refreshed and patient again, he'd return to stalking his beautiful prey.

"Good night, Marie Claire. Sleep well. I want you strong when we meet again."

Chapter 39

Claire walked into Afton's office Sunday evening and was greeted by a long whistle from Aidan. Smiling at him, she turned around, showing off the itsy-bitsy red dress she was wearing for her third date.

Sean lost all cognitive function as he looked at the crimson sheath that hugged Claire's soft curves, leaving her arms and shoulders completely bare. The heart-stopping sway of her rounded hips was accentuated by the black heels she was wearing, which matched the tiny leather evening bag she carried. When her back was to him, he saw that the dress hugged her butt so lovingly he actually clenched his hands at the memory of how it had felt to hold that same flesh.

"Wow," Aidan said.

Claire grinned. "Livvie picked it out for me today. She said that if this dress didn't have my date drooling on the floor and confessing his sins to the police, nothing would."

"She was right," Sean muttered.

"Your hair looks great, too," Afton said. "I've never seen it down before." She admired the cloud of curls that Olivia and Claire had spent the better part of an hour taming into a loose style around her bare shoulders.

"Thanks. Livvie's idea again."

Livvie is going to be the death of me. Sean took what felt like his first breath since Claire had walked in the room. When all heads turned toward him, he realized he must have sounded like someone surfacing after a deep dive. Claire tilted her head inquiringly at him.

"You look nice," Sean said, his voice sounding rusty.

She felt a little tug of annoyance at the lukewarm compliment. Then she remembered her determination to ignore him this evening and focus on charming her date. She'd been looking forward to this all day, and she wouldn't let Sean ruin things before the night had even started.

"You're too kind." With an irritated shimmy, she settled her dress in place.

All the blood in Sean's head went to his crotch. He forced himself to look away from her breasts, which were as lovingly cupped by the dress as her butt was. Then he risked another look at her. Jesus. "Where in hell are the microphone and transmitter?"

"The microphone is here," Claire said, running her index finger lightly over the shadow between her breasts. "And the transmitter is—"

"Forget I asked," Sean cut in, heading for the door. "I'll get your damned table at the restaurant."

Chapter 40

B illy Green, a congressional staffer from Dubuque, Iowa, was the most entertaining dinner companion Claire had had in years. He was smart, funny, well-read, and a genuinely nice human being. He shared several of her interests, including cardio kickboxing and abstract modern art.

It's too bad he's gay. And it's really too bad that he hasn't figured it out yet.

Claire took a sip of the excellent Chardonnay her date had recommended. She focused on him again as he finished telling about his disastrous first day on the Hill, when he'd lost his congressman's speech and then accidentally deleted the database of constituents who had made donations during a fund-raising dinner.

"Then I was in a meeting and asked someone I didn't recognize where the bathroom was. Turns out he was a very senior member of the Senate, and here I was telling him I had to pee like a racehorse."

Claire laughed and wished she had better luck with

men. Unlike some women she'd known, she simply wasn't attracted to gay men. She only wished she could meet some equally entertaining and charming male who liked women *and* wanted to have sex with them.

Oh, well. Win some, lose some, never had a chance with the rest. At least he's keeping my mind off the case and work, which is more than I can say of my last two dates.

Out of the corner of her eye, she saw Sean turn around on his barstool after ordering another mineral water. Now there was someone who generated great chemistry with her. Unfortunately, he was as unavailable to her as Billy, though for dramatically different reasons. Life really was a bitch sometimes. Still, she was having her best evening out in months. It would be stupid to ruin things by whining over what she couldn't have.

From the corner of her eye she caught a movement at one of the tables. Aidan met her eyes and raised an eyebrow at her, asking for a signal of some kind regarding her impressions of Billy. She studied her date for a moment, reviewing his broad, open features, blue eyes, and thick black hair. He grinned at her, and she knew this was not the cold-blooded killer they were looking for.

He's too young.

Claire frowned and wondered where that thought had come from. Before she could track that idea down, she sensed Sean staring at her, waiting for a signal of some kind.

The natives are getting restless.

She excused herself to go to the rest room. Once inside, she spoke to the microphone discreetly clipped to her bra.

"He's not the one. I don't know why, but I think he's too young. And his smile is open and real, nothing like the image I've had in my head all this time."

Ignoring a woman who gave her a strange look for talking to her boobs, Claire stopped to touch up her lipstick before she returned to her date.

"I ordered the appetizer platter for us both. It should be out in a minute," Billy said. "Do you want to dance while we're waiting?"

Claire looked out at the dance floor, where a dozen couples were moving to a fast-paced song with a pounding beat. Since this was the first night she didn't have a headache, she grinned at Billy. "Let's go."

He took her hand, and they squeezed themselves onto the tiny floor. She laughed when Billy swung her into a spin, then proceeded to jump around her in an energetic, if slightly graceless, circle.

Ten minutes later, flushed and breathless, Claire and her date returned to the table. She'd completely lost herself in the driving rhythm of the music and the throng of other dancers. In fact she'd forgotten why she was there. While Billy ordered her a frozen margarita, she glanced idly around.

As her eyes moved past Sean, she wondered why he shot her such an irritated look. When he turned his head and made no further contact, she mentally shrugged and glanced to the next table.

Aidan had moved. Now he was sitting next to someone at a table in the middle of the room. When the waiter moved, Claire smiled as she recognized Olivia. Livvie just wasn't the sort to sit back and let others do the work of watching out for her friend. Aidan didn't look happy at having to do damage control, or whatever the police called it when they dealt with people who didn't salute smartly and say "Yes, sir."

"This is a great place," Billy said. "I've heard of it, but never been. Do you come here a lot?"

"I've been here a few times. It was recommended to me by a friend," she said, refusing to let her eyes slide toward Sean again.

"I feel like I've been to every restaurant in the city since joining Camelot. This has to be one of the best places yet."

"You've been out on lots of dates through Camelot?" she asked, conscious of the need to gather information on Billy, if only to eliminate him from the list of suspects.

"Dozens. I just can't seem to find the right girl. Maybe . . . I don't know, maybe I'm trying too hard. Sometimes I'm not sure I even want to be dating at all." He picked at a piece of bruschetta from the appetizer tray.

"Why do it then? If you're not interested in a relationship, why force things with a dating service?" Claire asked carefully. She doubted that Billy understood the real reason behind his inability to "find the right girl."

"My mother is pressuring me to settle down and get married. I'm from a rural community outside of Dubuque, where guys get married out of high school and then go into whatever blue-collar occupation their father is in. They certainly don't go to college, or move to the nation's capital to live in roach-infested apartments and work for practically nothing."

Claire smiled. "I'm a long way from the Garden District of New Orleans, myself. All my friends from school, except my best friend Olivia, have been married for years and have at least one child."

"Tell me about it. I'm the oldest of three, and yet both my brothers have wives and kids already."

"There's nothing wrong with choosing to focus on your career. The wife and family will come later, if that's what you really want."

"That's what I keep telling my mom, but she's got this

idea of the perfect life for me. I just don't think it's the same as my idea." Suddenly he looked older, uneasy. "Hey, have you seen the new modern art exhibit at the Weir Gallery?"

Claire didn't blink at the change of subject. "The one with live tropical fish built into each sculpture? No, but I've heard of it. I wondered what was eventually going to happen to the fish, since they're sealed into the artwork."

"They're going to die in there. It's Fitz's commentary on the futility of modern life. He's saying that no matter how beautiful the prison, we are all trapped and dying by degrees. I think he's also highlighting the death of beauty in postmodern art. You know, that there seem to be pockets of color and splendor, but in reality they're fleeting and unsustainable."

"That's fascinating. Not many people understand and appreciate modern art. I can never find anyone to go to new exhibits with me. I tell my friend Olivia that she has to look beyond the shock value to see the statement beneath, but she doesn't buy it."

"I'd be happy to go with you to any exhibit you want. We don't have anything like it in Iowa, so I'm trying to soak up as much as I can."

"I'm trying to picture what people in Dubuque would say to a series of paintings featuring a blue dog," Claire said.

"My granny Ruth would probably say, 'What, did the artist run out of brown paint?'" Billy imitated a crotchety old woman's voice, making Claire laugh out loud.

Several tables away, Sean heard the delighted laugh. Gritting his teeth, he looked toward her table, where she and her date were leaning forward and talking animatedly about modern art.

Sean hated the stuff. If he wanted to see a painting of a soup can or a tennis shoe sculpture, he'd make one himself at home and save the ten-dollar admission ticket.

Checking his watch, he saw that more than an hour and a half had passed since Claire's arrival at Très Chic. Surely she'd figured out by now that Billy Green was gay and clueless. Being gay absolutely didn't fit the profile of their suspect. Unless Claire was attracted to sexually conflicted Iowa farm boys, Sean couldn't see any point in continuing with the evening's operation.

Sean's mood got worse as the evening went on. Claire and Billy made multiple trips to the dance floor to jump around with the other diners, though he noticed they returned to their seats during the slow numbers. After their meals arrived, the two swapped plates around like old friends. Sean was forced to listen when they engaged in a long and lively discussion of the selections on the dessert tray. He practically ripped his earpiece out in annoyance as Billy described the blueberry crème brûlée as "orgasmic."

Sean looked at Aidan, who was talking to Olivia while eating pasta and keeping Claire in sight at all times. When Claire and Billy headed out to the dance floor again, Sean decided the hell with it and ordered a bunch of appetizers to eat. Maybe he should join Aidan and the little redhaired mama tiger. Not that he minded Olivia being there as long as she stayed out of the way. She provided some cover for Aidan as he sat observing the other diners, and she didn't cost the operation nearly as much as a police officer would have.

Sometime before eleven Claire gave the signal that she and her date were headed back to Camelot. Since Sean was alone, he would follow Claire's taxi, which left Aidan and Olivia to go ahead and get into position. Sean easily kept the cab in sight as it drove through the empty streets. He listened to the casual conversation Claire and Billy were having, this time about Billy's longtime desire to learn how to scuba dive.

To Sean's disbelief, Claire let Billy dismiss the cab once they had reached Camelot's building. Instead of leaving, Billy led her over to take a seat on the low wall surrounding a fountain next to the lobby entrance. They continued their conversation about scuba diving, with Claire relating some of the experiences she'd had in the Caribbean.

When the discussion turned to great vacation destinations and the geopolitical considerations behind selecting a safe yet exotic location, Sean slowly banged his head on the steering wheel of his sedan.

After midnight, Claire began to yawn, even though she wasn't the least bit bored. Billy took the hint and said he had to be up early in the morning, but asked if he could see Claire again.

"I'd be happy to see you again—as a friend," she said.

"But I thought we were getting along great." Billy watched his shoes as he spoke, but in all he seemed to be more relieved than upset at her choice.

"We are. I had a great time tonight." Claire felt ten years older than her date as she tipped his chin up to look in his eyes. "But I don't get the feeling that you're attracted to me as a woman, just a friend. There's nothing wrong with that."

"I want to be attracted to you," he said desperately. "My mother would really like you."

Claire winced. *Talk about damned by faint praise.* "That's very sweet of you to say. But maybe you should worry about pleasing yourself in your choice of dates, not your mother."

"What do you mean?"

"You'll never be happy unless you live your own life. I think you know it. I think that's why you defied your family and local traditions to make a new start in Washington, D.C. Don't chicken out now, Billy. You're doing the right thing."

He stared at her for a long moment. "You're right. I just . . . I'm not ready to break all those ties yet." He smiled sadly. "I guess I'll say good night, then. Are you sure I can't drop you somewhere?"

"No, thanks. My stuff is inside, and there's a security guard at the desk. I'll be fine."

"Okay. I'll see if I can get tickets to the Fitz exhibit, and maybe we can go together. As friends."

"I'd like that. Good night, Billy."

She gave him a warm hug, friend to friend. He returned it the same way. She stood at the entrance to the Camelot building and waved as he got into a cab and drove away.

Poor kid. He's so messed up inside he doesn't know which way to go. I hope he finds a good man who understands where he is and helps him get somewhere happier.

"What the hell was that all about?"

Claire started at the angry voice behind her. Turning, she saw Sean standing with his arms crossed over his chest.

"It's called a date," she said. "Dinner, dancing, conversation. It's something the civilized members of society engage in on a fairly regular basis."

"Date, my ass. The guy's queer. Can't you see that?"

"Thank you for your Neanderthal summary of Billy's confused sexuality. It's because of people like you he's spent his whole life in the closet."

"Oh, bullshit. I work with gay officers all the time, and

some of them are damn good cops." He rubbed his neck un-comfortably. "I just didn't know if *you* knew Billy was—what's the latest psychobabble—sexually conflicted?"

"I'm not an idiot. Of course I could see he was gay."

"Okay. Some women can't, that's all."

"I'm not one of them. My gay-dar is highly functional."

Some of the tension seeped out of Sean's shoulders. "Then why didn't you end the date when you figured it out?"

"That would have meant turning the cab around on the way to the restaurant. I thought you wanted me to get more of an impression of him as a potential suspect."

"Is that why you were bumping and grinding on the dance floor all night with him?"

"No, I *danced* with him because I liked the music and was having fun. You know, you should come out of your cave more often. Then maybe you'd understand the con-cept of showing a lady a good time."

He slanted her an icy look. "We both know that I'm more than capable of showing you a good time."

Claire sucked in a breath. It was the first direct refer-ence either one had made to the night they'd almost made love. His words literally had her reeling. Then she re-membered the microphone stashed in her bra, recording every word of their conversation and relaying it to Aidan and anyone else who cared to listen to the surveillance tape.

Pointing to her chest, she silently tried to communicate the situation to Sean.

Sean stared at her in complete disbelief. He reached a tentative hand out to her breast, only to have her smack it away. She pressed her own hand over her chest in an at-tempt to muffle her words.

"The microphone is still on," she said between clenched teeth.

"Fuck."

Sean had taken off his earpiece once the cab had pulled away from the curb. But he'd be willing to bet that Aidan still had his receiver activated, which meant that he'd gotten an earful.

Claire and Sean shared a pained look. She rubbed her head like she suddenly had a headache.

"Turn it off," Sean said quietly. "I'll erase the end of the tape before we turn it in to Evidence."

Claire disconnected the microphone, reaching deep between her breasts in order to disengage the recording device. "I'm sorry. I can't get used to living under a spotlight. I have to forget about the microphone or I'd go crazy. Are you sure you won't get in trouble erasing some tape?"

"The information isn't relevant to the investigation," was all he said. He'd have some explaining to do with Aidan, but it wouldn't be a problem.

"I'll go get my things," she said. "Olivia can give me a ride home."

"We'll follow you."

Without another word Claire turned and went up the stairs to the lobby. She passed Aidan, who told her Olivia was waiting inside. She knew by looking at his face that he'd heard every word.

Aidan continued past her down the stairs and crossed to Sean. "Do you know what you're doing?" Aidan asked bluntly.

Sean tucked his hands into his front pockets. "I'm not doing anything. Things got a little out of hand one night. It won't happen again."

I wouldn't bet the farm on that one, Aidan thought. "Olivia's worried about her."

"Why?"

"She said Claire is a very private person and it's not easy for her to be under constant surveillance. I agree. She sure as hell doesn't need the additional stress of fighting with you."

"I know." Sean sighed. "I try, but sometimes I can't stop the words in time. Watching her being pawed by losers. . . ." He shrugged.

Aidan studied his cousin. "You're the most disciplined person I've ever known. Work with her instead of bickering. Hell, if you're nice to her, at least you might get it out of your system."

"And then what? I get removed from the case for sleeping with a witness? Or worse, I get her hurt—even killed—because my mind isn't on the investigation?" Sean shook his head. "Won't happen. Besides, neither one of us is looking for that kind of entanglement right now. It's under control."

"The kind of red-hot chemistry you two have isn't known to be convenient and timely and tame," Aidan cut in. "That's why it's called an 'entanglement.'"

"I said it was under control. Look, can we drop this?" Sean asked, gesturing to the women coming down the stairs.

Aidan shrugged and got into the car, preparing to escort Claire and Olivia home for the night. Sean didn't speak again.

Chapter 41

Claire sat next to Afton in the offices of Camelot. Sean and Aidan would soon be there, but Claire was too annoyed to wait for them. Besides, their damn earphones had told them everything she was going to tell Afton.

"Date number four was an absolute, total, and complete disaster," Claire said.

"Come on, surely last night wasn't that bad."

"It was worse." She began to describe it but stopped when Afton's assistant showed Sean and Aidan into the office and shut the door behind them.

"Hey, Afton, Claire. How's it going?" Sean asked cheerfully.

Approaching the desk, he set down a high-heeled shoe sealed in a zipper bag in front of Claire. "You can have your shoe back. We aren't going to be pressing any charges, so we won't need it as evidence."

Claire practically snarled at him as she snatched her

shoe off the desk. Sean pressed his lips together to suppress the laughter dancing in his eyes.

Mouth open, Afton looked at both Aidan and Sean. "Shoes? Charges? What's going on?"

"Nothing, at least as far as the investigation is concerned. You might want to take Dr. Petrov out of your catalogue, though," Aidan said carefully, rubbing a hand around his mouth to hide the smile there. He took a seat between Claire and Sean and carefully avoided eye contact with his partner as they both struggled not to laugh out loud.

"Why?" Afton asked.

Both men snickered.

"Because Leonard Petrov is a pervert," Claire said flatly.

"Now, Claire," Sean said, praying he wouldn't lose it. "We investigated him thoroughly and found nothing to support any evidence of a crime. He just has, um, unusual tastes."

"Very unusual." Aidan chuckled, but he straightened in his chair when Claire turned angry black eyes on him.

"What on earth happened last night?" Afton asked.

"Leonard attacked me at the end of the date," Claire said, "and these examples of Washington D.C.'s Finest almost wet their pants laughing."

"He didn't actually attack you," Sean pointed out, chuckling in spite of himself.

"That creep licked my foot!" Claire brandished the shoe as evidence.

Both men doubled over and howled. They laughed until they cried and still kept on laughing. Claire took the shoe and whacked Aidan with it, because he was the only one she could reach.

"It isn't funny," she said.

"Oh, God, yes it is! If you'd only—seen the expression—on your face," Sean managed between gasping laughs.

"I've had it with you two clowns," Claire said. "You're supposed to be protecting me, not laughing yourself into a coma at my expense."

"I consider it a fringe benefit," Aidan said, wiping his eyes.

She gave him another smack with her shoe.

Safely out of reach, Sean kept chuckling. As she glared at him, she realized she'd rarely seen this side of Sean before. Aidan was usually the mischievous one, but right now Sean's dancing blue eyes and infectious laughter were delightful, taking years off his age. Normally her own sense of humor would have been charmed by the entire situation, and she'd be laughing as hard as both men put together.

But she wasn't feeling like herself. She'd spent the last four nights living like a bug under a microscope, wired for sound and having every moment studied and catalogued for the police files. Death-row inmates had more privacy than she did. It was fraying her nerves and temper.

"Now I'm dying of curiosity," Afton said carefully. "What happened on your date?"

Claire took a deep breath. "I should have known it would get weird when the guy introduced himself. He was short, blonde, and had a very slight build. I'm sure I outweighed him by at least . . . by quite a bit."

"Wait a minute." Afton pulled up Petrov's file on

her computer. "That doesn't match his photo or description."

"He said he'd had someone else come in for the initial consultation and photo. He claimed he'd joined another service using his own picture and had very few replies, so he asked a more attractive friend to stand in for him."

Afton made a *tsk*ing sound and typed something in the database.

"I was pretty sure right away that he wasn't the killer," Claire said. "Way too short and skinny and blonde. In fact, I thought he was completely harmless."

"And you said so into the microphone. We felt confident you were safe," Aidan pointed out.

"You're cops. You're supposed to know a pervert when you see one." She stuffed her shoe into her purse so that she wouldn't be tempted to hit him with it again. "Anyway, we had a quick dinner. I cut the evening short because it was a dead end."

"Dead end from an investigative standpoint or a romantic one?" Afton asked with a grin.

"Both," Sean and Claire answered together.

She turned her head around to look at him. "How do you know I wasn't attracted to him?"

"Come on," Sean said. "I've been watching your every move for the last four evenings. I can read body language well enough to know when there's no chemistry between two people."

Not to mention the fact that he'd engaged in enough verbal and physical foreplay with her to recognize when she was interested in a man. She hadn't been even remotely attracted to the harmless podiatrist, which had allowed Sean to relax enough to see the humor in the entire situation.

"Great," she said. "Just one more piece of my private life ripped out into the open for public commentary and entertainment."

"That's not what I meant," Sean said, no longer laughing.

"That's what they all say." She wanted desperately to rub away the unhappy ache building behind her forehead, but she figured he would probably read and understand that gesture as well.

"So you cut the evening short and? . . ." Afton asked.

"We took a cab back here and he started to get kind of pushy," Claire said. "He wanted to go somewhere for a drink or drop me at my place or whatever. I wasn't worried, but I made sure I said good-bye on the steps outside the building."

"She stood on the step above his to emphasize his lack of height," Sean said. "Nice move."

"Christ, am I that easy to read?" Claire asked.

"Don't answer," Aidan said quickly to Sean. "It's one of those trick female questions."

"You're killing me," Afton said. "Finish it."

"I said good night and pulled my keys out," Claire said, "but he jostled me and I dropped them on the stairs."

"Allow me to point out," Aidan said, "I was in position less than fifteen feet away and Sean was across the street in his car."

"Yeah, yeah, I was never in any danger. We got that part, Detective," Claire said. "Anyway, Leonard bends down to pick up my keys, but then stays there at my feet, staring at my sandals. He says I shouldn't wear high heels, they cause all kinds of problems, blah, blah."

"Sounds like good medical advice to me. He is a podiatrist, after all," Afton said.

"Yeah, well then he starts to undo the straps on my right shoe, saying how they cut off the circulation when they're tight. He looks at my feet and says how beautiful they are, how I should take better care of them and not subject them to such stress."

Sean began to snicker again. "You should have seen Claire's face. Total deer-caught-in-headlights look."

"So he starts rubbing at the marks the strap left on my foot," Claire said, ignoring Sean. "He tells me he has just the trick to make things feel better. Then he *licks* my foot from toes to ankle."

"Omigod," Afton said. "What did you do?"

"She executed one of the more interesting gymnastic moves I've ever seen," Aidan said. "She went straight up in the air and backwards at the same time. I took the guy down about a second later. When I looked up, the revolving door was going around and Claire was *gone.*"

"And there's poor Leonard getting cuffed, her shoe still clutched in his hand, wondering what the hell is going on," Sean said, grinning.

"Poor Leonard? How about poor Claire? Do you have any idea how revolting that was for me?" she said angrily. "And the whole thing gets recorded and logged into the evidence file for this case. It's humiliating."

"I think you're overreacting," Sean said. "Leonard insisted he was very sorry if he offended you and wanted to offer you a free foot exam to show he's got no hard feelings."

This time Afton joined in the explosion of laughter that echoed around the room. Claire waited until it was quiet before turning to Afton.

"*Et tu Brute?*" she asked.

"You have to admit it's kind of funny."

"Really? This pervert is running around dating clients from your company and it's funny?"

"That reminds me," Afton said, turning to type a notation on the computer.

"Are you removing him from your database?" Claire asked.

"No, we'll just see if we can find a foot fetishist to hook him up with," Afton said.

Everyone but Claire laughed.

Afton sighed as she looked at Claire's angry face. "Of course we'll remove him."

"I'm starting to wonder about this service of yours. Look at my last two dates—gay and weird, in that order. Washouts, along with the other dates I've had so far." Claire felt mean for being hard on Billy, but facts were facts.

"I know the last few days have been difficult," Sean said, "but remember what we're trying to achieve here."

Afton added, "You're not the average customer looking for a dream date."

"That's how I started out," Claire said stubbornly.

"But now we're trying to help the police catch a killer. How can you say the dates were a disaster if through them we've managed to eliminate some suspects?" Afton asked gently.

"Because I wanted to find . . ." . . . *someone like Sean.* Claire forced herself not to look at him. "Oh, forget it. I just feel all this tension building, like something is going to happen and I can't do anything about it. I feel like the butt of some huge cosmic joke right now. Usually I'd be laughing, too, but I can't."

"Sorry," Aidan said. "We didn't help with the Leonard thing."

"I thought for sure you'd see how funny it was," Sean said.

"Try my sense of humor after you've caught the killer," Claire said, turning on him. "Have you found anything yet?"

"We've run several dozen Camelot clients through police background checks," Aidan said.

"I assume you didn't find anything interesting, since these individuals have all been extensively screened by our own private security firm," Afton said, tapping her pen on the desk. She really hoped her sister's screening methodology would stand up to checks run by the police.

Sean and Aidan looked at each other.

"Our checks are a lot more thorough than those done by a private firm, although we missed the photo switch by the podiatrist," Sean said. "In the future, we'll check driver's license photos against Camelot's records."

"We have access to national criminal databases," Aidan added, "and we can see when there's evidence of things like sealed records or juvenile convictions. We're also less likely to take things at face value than a corporate security firm, which works on a very high volume of clients."

"What are you trying to say?" Afton asked.

"Among the approximately four dozen clients we've screened to date, we've found some pretty serious misdemeanor crimes. Not surprising, since I'm sure your private firm only did a check for felony offenses," Sean said.

"That's right. Maura decided to only flag felonies because they were getting so many hits for neighborhood noise complaints and violations of doggie leash laws."

"I understand the policy. But a lot of felonies get pleaded down to misdemeanors, so they're a red flag for us," Sean said.

Afton braced herself. "Go on."

"We found three clients who are legally married, although we can't confirm the de facto status of those unions."

"Did the files show that?"

"No. They just said single, no mention of divorce or separation."

Clenching her jaw, Afton picked up her pen again. "I'll need their names. Withholding that type of information is grounds for cancellation of the membership."

"And we've found evidence of at least four clients with sealed juvenile records. I'm assuming everyone is required to divulge any and all criminal activity in their past, and so we flagged these names as well," Sean said.

"What kind of juvenile records?"

"It could be anything from malicious mischief to drug charges to murder," Sean said. "When juvenile records are sealed, nobody has access to them. But we'll speak to the arresting officers and see if they remember the cases. Until then, we'll have to assume the worst."

"Why?" Claire said.

"Many serial killers become active in their teens," Sean said without looking away from Afton. "Things like interest in the occult, misdemeanor sex crimes, animal cruelty—these can all be precursors of true sociopathic behavior in adulthood."

"If the crimes are that serious, why can't you access the files now?" Claire asked.

"Our legal system believes anything that happens before the age of eighteen shouldn't be held against someone once he or she is an adult," Aidan said. "It takes a court order to unseal juvenile records, and we don't have enough evidence for that."

"Great. So if the police can't even get this information, how is Afton's private security firm supposed to do a thorough background check?" Claire demanded.

"Amen." Afton threw down her pen in disgust.

"You do the best you can," Sean said. "There's nothing wrong with Camelot's system. You have the same limitations that your competitors do."

"What I have is a personal responsibility to my clients, people like Claire," Afton shot back. "They believe we offer them a safe alternative to the singles scene. What a farce."

"Aren't you being a little hard on yourself?" Sean asked.

"A week ago," Afton said, "when you came to me and said Camelot might have a killer hidden among the clientele, I thought you were crazy, that there was no way a murderer could get through the screening process. I can't say that now. This could be the end of my sister's company, her dream."

"No one is going to close this place down for having some inherent risks in the business. Hell, look at airlines," Aidan said.

"I won't need to wait for anyone to shut Camelot down," Afton said grimly, thinking about what she had already been through. "If I find we've been hiding a killer in our databases I'll close the place myself. *I can't live with murder.*" She looked at the detectives. "Are you one hundred percent certain you can protect Claire?"

"Nothing is one hundred percent certain," Claire said.

Neither detective disagreed.

Chapter 42

Washington, D.C.
Wednesday morning

"Thanks for coming in on such short notice," Sean said, holding the door open for Claire.

"No big deal." She glanced at him, wondering if his heart was beating as fast as hers. Probably not. "Since I'm burning vacation time at work, and all my accounts have been divided up among the other managers, my time is pretty much my own. What's up?"

"We were lucky to get some time with the department's psychiatrist. It's not quite like working with an FBI criminal profiler, but hopefully we can come up with a sketch of our killer that has a stronger scientific base than the one Aidan and I threw together."

"What does the shrink want from me?"

"He'll ask about your memories on the night of the murder, and any impressions you've formed since then. Maybe he can help jog your memory. Ever been hypnotized?"

"No, and I'm not about to start."

"Just a joke. Hypnosis isn't that reliable anyway, and

it's not admissible in court." Sean steered her down another hallway. "We'll meet with him back here."

"We?"

"You and me."

"I'd rather talk to the doctor alone," Claire said.

Sean stopped outside a door that said Conference. "Why?"

"Because that's the way I feel."

"But you know I'll be reading the notes from your session."

She winced and reached for the door. *Great.* "Read whatever you want, but one person poking into my brain at a time is all I can handle."

She shut the door, closing him out. Soon he reappeared at the window overlooking the room, crossed his arms, and leaned against the wall. She yanked out a chair facing the window, sat, and stared right through him.

A middle-aged, balding man stepped into the conference room through a side door. "Hi, Marie. I'm Dr. Morton."

"Actually, it's Claire."

"Right, sorry." After offering her a soft handshake, he pulled out the chair directly opposite her.

Sean hovered over his head like an impatient ghost.

"You're working on a profile of the killer with the police?" Claire asked, looking away from the glass.

"Yes. This is actually the first time I've worked with Detectives Richter and Burke, but the department has me on retainer to provide a number of services related to psychiatry and counseling. This is actually the fun part of my job."

The hinges on the swivel chair squeaked noisily as Dr. Morton leaned way back. The position caused his powder blue golf shirt to strain across the spare tire around his middle.

"I've reviewed the known case files on the victims and other crime scenes, and feel I've gotten all I can from them," he said. "I'd like to start with what you remember from the night of the murder."

"I don't really remember anything. Didn't Sean tell you?" Claire asked, glancing at the detective through the glass.

"Sean? Oh, Detective Sean Richter. No, he didn't say anything. Why don't you tell me?"

"I fell down a flight of steps and hit my head on the night of the murder, apparently running away from the killer. People at the scene reported that I talked about seeing a murder, and I mentioned a school. The police checked out the area nearby and found the victim."

"And you can't remember any part of the night?"

"No. I don't remember anything after leaving work that Friday afternoon, even though I'm told I went to Camelot Dating Services and spent hours there. I know I'd planned to walk to the bus at Dupont Circle after my appointment. That path would have taken me directly through the school's property. Sean and Aidan have pretty much pieced together everything since then, but I can't confirm any of it."

"Interesting." The hinges squeaked as Dr. Morton adjusted his position. "Your diagnosis at the hospital was a concussion, but they released you after a few days, even though you hadn't recovered your memory."

"I wasn't seriously injured. My doctor said the memories might come back slowly over time, or maybe not at all. So far, I haven't remembered anything except for some impressions and images, mostly in dreams or nightmares."

Dr. Morton leaned forward and picked up her file from the desk, scanning through the first page. "Hmmm. It says you have a memory of seeing a photograph that reminded you of the killer." He continued to read, occasionally repeating phrases from the document.

Claire waited impatiently while he went through her entire case file. If one of her assistants had come to a meeting so ill prepared, she would have scorched the person for wasting her time. When Dr. Morton leaned back again with a thunderous squeak and studied her as if a spaceship had just dropped her off, she wondered what was up with him. Her eyes strayed once again to the hallway. Sean was still there, still watching.

"If you can't remember what the killer looks like, how did you decide which clients to choose in the dating service catalogue?" Dr. Morton asked.

"We're hoping that subconsciously I picked out men who resemble him in some way, or that I may even have selected the killer himself."

"Subconsciously. I see." He looked thoughtful for a moment. "Did your doctor ever mention the term *hysterical amnesia* to you?"

"No. He used the term *traumatic*. He said that many victims of head injuries have no memory of the time leading up to the trauma."

"Yes, but we often see this in other types of injuries as well. There's some debate on whether there are physical or psychological factors involved. However, I'm of the opinion that since amnesia is found in patients with vastly different injuries, the roots of the condition are probably psychological. It's certainly not surprising that the brain would want to edit portions of a shocking event," he said, looking at her in an understanding way.

"Interesting. But I'm of the opinion I took a blow to the head that interrupted a few synaptic functions. I've been through horrible events before and never had any trouble remembering things in painful detail."

"Have you ever witnessed a murder before?" The question was accompanied by an eyebrow lift.

"Of course not. I didn't get knocked on the head, either. In spite of the trauma, I'm doing everything I can to help the police. I've been working with Sean and Aidan for over two weeks on this, to the exclusion of everything else in my life." She glanced out the window. He was still there. "I *want* to remember that night. I've tried thinking about it until my head feels like it's going to explode. I've tried to remember my dreams. But there's nothing there."

"You keep looking out the window. Why?"

"Sean is pacing out there, waiting for us to finish. He said he'd be eager to look over the notes from our discussion." She looked pointedly at the blank yellow notebook in front of the doctor.

"You seem to be on friendly terms with Detective Richter."

Claire stopped fidgeting and focused on the doctor. She'd have to tread very carefully here. "He and Aidan have been very kind to me. They have an excellent bedside manner with victims."

She thought about how Sean had been in the hospital before tension had developed between them, and told herself that she wasn't really lying.

The doctor flipped through a couple more pages in the file. "I see you've been working very closely with Detective Richter. He's detailed multiple meetings, interviews, and strategy sessions with you."

"Yes," Claire said, even though it wasn't a question. "He and Aidan have—"

"It would be easy, in a situation like this, for someone

to become emotionally attached," Dr. Morton continued, ignoring her words. "Especially someone who is vulnerable and needs help."

"I suppose someone who only looked on the surface might see things that way," Claire said neutrally.

"But you don't?"

"No. I see people working together to stop a killer. It's no different from one of my office projects, except the stakes are much higher."

"It's perfectly understandable that you would develop feelings for Detective Richter. His job places him in the role of protector, and in this case he's protecting you. That can lead to powerful emotional bonding, especially for someone like you."

"Someone like me?" she asked through clenched teeth.

"You've been through a traumatic event and are probably feeling a little fragile. Plus . . ." Dr. Morton pursed his lips thoughtfully.

"Go on. I assure you I won't break into pieces."

"You seem to have a need to be rescued. Call it a 'White Knight' fantasy."

She stared at him. "Excuse me?"

"It all fits quite neatly. Detective Richter—who you've repeatedly looked at through the window since I arrived—is responsible for guarding you. Your participation in the investigation reinforces the role of protector, because he watches over you every day during the operation. Furthermore, you need him to solve the case so that you can be freed from the role of victim, or in other words, rescued. It's pretty classic."

"So is bullshit," Claire said, trying to shock him.

"Look at what you did the night of the murder. You joined a dating service. Essentially, what that says to me is you're looking for a man to solve your problems. Even the name of the dating service, Camelot, underscores the White Knight fantasy. Why do you think you chose that company over the many others out there? You were attracted to the symbolism."

"The name had nothing to do with it. My friend recently took over the management there. My company had a contract with Camelot last year, so I knew the previous owner. It was only logical that I would go back to them."

"I'm sure you can rationalize it that way. But subtle clues like this only underscore my initial opinion."

She thought carefully before responding. Losing her temper would not improve her position with the doctor. "But you're not here to give an opinion about me. You're here to develop a profile of the killer."

"Which you're unwilling to assist me in doing," Dr. Morton replied. "Yet you're still working quite happily with the team of investigators, including Detective Richter."

"I'm sure you have an opinion about that, as well."

He nodded. "I do. As long as you keep working with the investigation, you get to be rescued. It's no wonder you haven't had any success 'recovering' your memory. Once you do, your role as damsel in distress will be over."

"Fascinating opinion, but I'm afraid it only underscores the fact that you don't understand me, or this investigation, at all."

The doctor looked her over. "Defensive posture, dismissive language, flushed cheeks. I'd say I scored a direct hit."

Claire had had enough, but she would be professional if it killed her. An emotional outburst at this point would only make Dr. Morton more smug. She stood up and straightened her skirt. Pretending he was a difficult, important client, she smiled warmly and held out her hand.

"Well, then I think we're done," she said. "Thank you so much for your time today, Dr. Morton. I'm sure you're a very busy man, and I appreciate being able to get some of your insights."

He stared at her switch from defensive victim to polished diplomat. "I don't think we're finished here."

"It's gracious of you to offer more time, but I'm afraid I have another appointment. If there's anything further you need from me, my number is in the case file."

Claire rounded the table, opened the door, and closed it softly behind her. Leaning back against it, she saw that Aidan had joined Sean in the hallway. They both turned inquiring looks in her direction.

"How did it go?" Sean asked.

"You'd have better luck consulting chicken entrails than relying on Dr. Psychobabble in there." She brushed past the detectives and walked quickly down the hall.

"Claire?" Sean called after her. "What happened?"

"Ask the shrink. If he's still capable, I'm sure he's panting to talk to you. He'll throw in an analysis of your relationship with your mother at no extra charge."

Claire went through the doorway without looking back.

Aidan glanced over at Sean. "What the hell . . . ?"

Sean headed into the conference room to find out.

Chapter 43

Aidan and Sean left the conference room and Dr. Morton behind, feeling like they'd been to a bad movie. The two detectives gave each other sideways glances, not knowing whether to laugh or bang their heads on the wall.

"What a putz," Aidan muttered.

"On his best day, he'd have to stretch to be a putz." Sean headed toward their desks. "I don't think we can use anything he told us."

"How did he describe Claire again?"

"I'm not sure. My mind had kind of numbed by then." Sean skimmed the single page of quickly scribbled notes Dr. Morton had pressed on them during the brief meeting. "Here it is. 'Ms. Lambert is an emotionally fragile witness whose potential contribution to the case is questionable given her tenuous mental state.'"

"Shit," Aidan said in disgust.

"And don't forget about the part where she wants to be the center of attention in an ongoing police psychodrama,"

Sean said. "He can't decide whether her amnesia is hysterical or feigned."

"If he can't see Claire, who's sitting right in front of him, how can he give us a useable psych profile on the killer?"

"He can't. I'm going to stick this crap under the 'related documents' tab at the end of the file." Sean went over to his desk and sat down with a tired sigh. "Christ, I'm surprised she didn't go for his throat."

"Nah, she's too refined." Aidan tossed back the last of a cup of coffee that had been poured hours ago, grimacing at the bitter taste.

"Bullshit. If she'd thought it would suit her needs, she'd have ripped Morton's throat out in a heartbeat," Sean said, for once having a deeper insight into someone than his cousin. "She must have had some other reason for walking out of there and leaving him intact."

"Well it sure wasn't his brains. Anyone who can look at you and Claire and babble about White Knights and Damsels in Distress deserves to have his jugular ripped out."

Sean moved uncomfortably. He didn't like thinking that Claire's attraction to him was less than it seemed. "Since Dr. Morton's a washout, I'm going to talk to Keeley in Vice. Her brother works for the FBI out of Quantico and has had some specialized training in criminal profiling. He even teaches a course. Maybe he can do an informal assessment, just to give us a jump start in weeding through our list of suspects," Sean said, standing.

"Good idea. Just don't let the brass hear anything about it. And cousin?"

"Yeah?"

"Morton was wrong about everything else—why

would he be right about what makes Claire hum like a race car whenever you're around?"

Sean kept walking because anything he could say would only dig himself into a deeper hole.

Chapter 44

"Why would three otherwise sane women pay outrageous prices to sit in a steam room in Washington, D.C. in July?" Claire asked, sweating.

Olivia wiped her face on a towel.

"It gives us the illusion of being in control of the climate," Afton said.

"Illusion," Claire muttered. "Great. Just what I need, another shrink."

Dr. Morton's analysis still burned. The thought that her actions and emotions might be interpreted in such an unflattering way was humiliating. She'd thought she was being cooperative, working with the police in order to catch a man who had made a very real threat against her life. Could it be that she had other reasons? Like the chance to be close to Sean?

Or worse, was she really waiting to be rescued?

"What did the police shrink say?" Olivia asked. "You've been in a terrible mood since you saw him."

Claire wiped her face. "The Cliffs Notes version is that

I'm a fragile personality. I have hysterical amnesia—if I have amnesia at all—but I continue to participate in the investigation because it feeds my need to be rescued. You see, I'm suffering from White Knight syndrome, meaning that I'm waiting for a man to rescue me from all that's wrong with my life."

"What? That is complete *crap*." Olivia's voice echoed loudly in the steamy room.

"He said that joining a dating service underlines my desire to be rescued."

"How on earth does joining Camelot indicate a psychological weakness?" Afton demanded.

"According to him, I'm searching for a man to fix my life." Claire hesitated. "I can't honestly say he's entirely wrong. I was unhappy and lonely, and looked to Camelot to help solve that."

"Joining a dating service doesn't mean you're waiting for someone to rescue you," Afton said, hands on towel-wrapped hips. "It shows that you're willing to go out there after something you want, something that's missing in your life. It's proactive behavior, not save-me passive," Afton said.

"Isn't that the same as wanting a man to solve my problems?"

"No! It means you're looking for a man to share everything that's right in your life," Afton said. "You're a smart, funny, successful, and beautiful woman who has a lot to offer a man."

Olivia looked at Claire's unhappy face. "You don't really buy into that passive and needy bull, do you?"

"I don't know what to think anymore. Look at me—I'm a wreck. I'm living in a fucking fishbowl and being analyzed by strangers. I'm being driven slowly insane by one man I can't date, and going out every night with a different reject from the gene pool."

"Forget the stupid shrink," Olivia said. "Focus on what's ahead of you."

"More dates? Kill me now."

"You can handle it. Repeat after me," Olivia said. " 'I am a modern, independent woman who can survive another evening of socializing with a perfect stranger.' "

Claire laughed and dutifully repeated the words. But even as she did, she wondered if she *could* survive another evening of socializing under the watchful eyes of a man who felt like anything but a stranger.

Even worse than that was the gut-deep feeling that a deadly stranger was never farther away from her than the darkness at the edge of light.

Chapter 45

Claire sipped her mineral water and decided that even modern, independent women shouldn't have to deal with the obnoxious, self-absorbed ad sales executive sitting across the table from her. Randy Klein, a beefy former college hockey player, liked martinis with pickled onions. He liked them a lot and he liked a lot of them. She looked with barely veiled disgust at the wrinkled onions bobbing on a toothpick in Randy's glass. He was finishing his third drink, and the appetizers had just arrived.

She'd already decided that mineral water would be her drink du jour. While she tried to decide if Randy's smile reminded her of anything more lethal than a used-car salesman, she kept up her end of the conversation. It wasn't hard. Randy was in love with Randy, which made her an unnecessary third wheel.

With each martini he'd grown more aggressive and loud, and she'd grown more quiet. He didn't notice. He picked the toothpick out of his glass, winked at her, and suggestively sucked a pickled onion into his mouth. To make sure she didn't miss the point, he stared at her breasts.

Obviously he thought he was going to get lucky tonight.

She focused on his mouth, looking for anything that reminded her of the night of the murder. *He's the right size.*

The thought startled her. Working to hold that thought, she tried to remember more. All she came up with was the fact that her date's mouth wasn't right. Sighing, she decided that while Randy Klein made her uncomfortable, he didn't make her fear for her life. He just had a remarkably coarse way of looking at her.

Claire caught a motion out of the corner of her eye. She turned to see Olivia getting up from the table she shared with Sean. When she headed toward the ladies' room, Claire excused herself and hurried to catch up.

After making sure the small bathroom was empty, Claire asked, "Did they just give in and deputize you?"

"No. I had my own table, but as soon as Sean came in and saw me, he pulled up a chair. I guess they figure I'm good cover or something."

"Well, you can relax. The only thing at risk tonight is my virtue, if there is such a thing in the twenty-first century. Have you seen this guy's moves?"

"Yeah, I can feel the slime all the way over at my table. Sean doesn't like the way Randy is acting."

"That makes two of us. I hate martinis, and I hate pickled onions. I can smell them every time he laughs." Claire made a face in the mirror.

"What do you want me to tell Sean?" Olivia asked.

"Save your breath. He's listening to every word we say, aren't you, Detective?" Claire asked the microphone clipped to her bra.

"I forgot about that," Olivia said. "They won't give me an earpiece."

"You don't need one and everyone else can relax. I've studied this guy's smile. While it's as sleazy as he is, it doesn't look anything like the killer's. Randy's not our suspect, so I'll be ready to go by the time the waiter brings coffee."

"Why not just end things now, at the restaurant?"

"Because I'm hungry and I haven't eaten." She grimaced. "Although if I get a few more whiffs of pickled onions, I'm going to lose my appetite."

"I don't like it," Olivia said. "He's twice your size."

"*Chère*, he'll be skunk drunk by the time we leave. I've handled much worse, and so have you."

"I still don't like it."

Neither did Claire, but she was damned if she would run to the cops for help with a situation all single women routinely handled. She sure as hell wasn't some whining damsel looking for excuses to be rescued.

By the time they finished dinner, Randy had downed seven martinis, pickled onions and all. *Thank God for taxis*, Claire thought. His speech was fine, but his reflexes weren't.

"Well, it's been great, but I'm working tomorrow," Claire said. "Time for me to call it a night."

Aidan signaled to the bartender to close his tab. Sean and Olivia began to get ready to leave, reminding Claire once again that she had an audience listening to her dinner conversation, and every cheesy line her date was pulling out as well. Sean and Aidan both looked tense. They were watching Randy like a snake.

Claire rolled her eyes. Great. Just what she needed—more testosterone. To prevent any type of confrontation, she hustled her date out the door. For once there was a cab waiting, and she all but shoved Randy into it.

When the cab stopped in front of Camelot, Claire said briskly as she slid out, "Keep the cab. Good night."

She was nearly to the top of the stairs when she felt a hand on her arm. For an instant terror swept her—it was too much like her dreams, the ones where she didn't escape and the killer reached out and caught her. After a few frantic seconds she realized it was her intoxicated date, not a serial murderer, who had grabbed her arm. With a shudder, she pulled her self-control into place.

"Wait a sec," Randy said, weaving slightly as he stood on the step next to her. "What kind of a good night is that?"

"The only kind you're going to get."

"C'mon, no need to be coy. We both know why we joined this dating service, so I'll still respect you in the morning."

He grabbed her before she could answer. Onion-laced martini fumes made her gag. She pushed, and he held on harder. Then he pawed her breast and slimed her mouth with his tongue.

To hell with this. She drove the spiky point of her heel right through soft Italian leather and into the most tender part of Randy's foot, just as Aidan had taught her during their brief lesson in self-defense. Randy yelped and let go. She shoved him hard. Off balance from a combination of surprise and alcohol, he went over like a felled tree, tumbled down the shallow stairs, and landed in a heap at the bottom.

Two seconds later Sean appeared out of nowhere, flipped Randy over on his face, and jammed a knee in his back. Once he was subdued, Sean searched him roughly.

"What the fuck? . . ." Randy asked, dazed.

"Is he all right?" she asked. "I didn't mean to—"

"Get back," Sean ordered.

Claire caught a glimpse of his furious blue eyes and instinctively took a step back. "It's all right. He's not the killer."

"Let me handle this." Sean didn't look up from Randy as he spoke. "Get back up the stairs."

"But—"

"Go." This time it was Aidan giving orders as he ran up to the scene. He took Randy's sports coat and turned it inside out, searching the pockets.

Claire turned and marched back to the top of the stairs, furious with everyone and everything, and most of all with herself for shaking inside and for being grateful that she wasn't alone. Dammit, she wasn't a damsel in distress sniveling for a knight. She'd slain the pickled dragon herself.

Arms crossed over her breasts, Claire watched as Sean called for a backup unit to take Randy to the hospital— and then to jail. Once Sean had finished his call, he turned and looked at her.

"Are you all right?" he asked roughly.

Unconsciously she rubbed her mouth. Ugh. Pickled onions. "Sure. He's hardly the first guy to make a grab at getting lucky on a date."

Sean came up the stairs to stand next to her, towering over the extra height her heeled sandals gave her. "Why the hell didn't you wait at the restaurant? You didn't give us time to get into place. You got out of range with the microphone. *I couldn't hear what was happening.*"

"I—I didn't realize you weren't behind me." She lifted her chin and faced his anger. "Contrary to Dr. Freud, I'm not whining for a man to save me. As you can see, I handled Randy just fine."

"It's not your job to handle him. You're supposed to let us do that. If you can't follow simple instructions, you're off the case." Sean's voice was like his eyes, coldly furious.

"What—"

"Is that clear?" Sean interrupted. "One word, yes or no."

She wanted to tell him to go to hell, but realized he was angry enough to pull her from the investigation. "Yes."

Sean saw that her eyes were dark and angry in the building's outdoor lights. "Don't glare at me like that. He may be a businessman now, but he's a former college hockey player who's used to violence and he's a hell of a lot stronger and meaner than you are."

"What the fuck is goin' on?" Randy mumbled from the bottom of the stairs.

Nobody answered.

Claire stared at Sean for a full minute without answering while the aftermath of fear, disgust, and adrenaline churned in her stomach. If she didn't leave right now, she was going to lose it, throw herself at him, and confirm every word that smug shrink had said.

"I take it we're through here, Detective?"

Without waiting for an answer, Claire went through the revolving door. She didn't look back.

"Well, *shit*." Sean went back to something that made sense—his job.

"What the fuck is goin' on?" Randy asked the pavement again.

Both cops ignored him. "When will the backup be here?" Sean asked Aidan.

"It's Saturday night, he's cuffed, and we're overworked. It will be a while. You think he's the killer?"

"My gut says no, but we'll run him again while he's locked up."

"So, ah, what exactly are you going to charge him with?"

Sean stared at his cousin. "Attempted assault."

Aidan hesitated. "Did Claire indicate in any way that she was in danger?"

"I saw him grab her and she nailed him with her high heel."

Aidan grinned. "I told you she was a fast learner."

"What the fuck is goin' on?" Randy asked. "I didn't do anything. Can't a guy kiss his date good night?"

Sean looked at Randy. "Shut up, fucko."

"Could it have been a misunderstanding?" Aidan asked. "The guy thinks he's going to score and his date lets him know otherwise?"

"He pawed her," Sean said tightly. "He grabbed her and pawed her like she was a ten-dollar whore. Drunken asshole."

Both of them heard the sound of running water transmitted through their earpieces, which were still activated. Then something glass shattered, followed by more sounds, running water, and something else.

"Is she sick?" Aidan asked. Maybe Sean was right. Maybe they should charge Randy.

"I'll go check. You stay here with the Hockey Puke. And keep a lid on Olivia," Sean added, nodding to the small car pulling up across the street.

More liquid sounds came through the earphones as Sean ran through the lobby. He hesitated outside the women's rest room. More gurgling sounds sent him inside.

"Claire? Are you all right?" He came around the corner just as she spat something green into the sink.

She jumped at the sound of his voice and dribbled some mouthwash down her chin in the process of spitting it out. "Dammit, this is the ladies' room. And I can assure you, you're not a lady," she said, wiping her chin.

"I thought you might be sick or something. I heard these sounds." Sean stopped at her furious look.

"You heard *sounds*?" She reached into her top, ripped the microphone out of the transmitter, tearing the delicate wires, and threw the mangled equipment at him.

Sean yelped at the feedback and wrenched his earpiece out with one hand. The other hand snatched the ruined mike out of the air before it hit him in the face.

Claire went back to the sink and started cleaning up the glass from the first bottle of mouthwash, which she'd broken because her hands were shaking. Sean watched her, seeing the roiling emotion beneath the surface calm she was desperately trying to maintain.

"What's with the mouthwash?" he finally asked.

"Randy ate pickled onions out of his martinis all night. When he shoved his tongue down my throat, I got to experience them as well. They're vile."

Sean felt his anger leap back at the image of Claire's date assaulting her in that way. "Goddammit, Claire. You should have waited for us at the restaurant. Then this never would have happened."

"How do you figure that? It happened so fast I didn't have time to duck, so I took care of it the old-fashioned way."

"What if he hadn't passed out at the bottom of the stairs? What if you'd just pissed him off, and he tried to rape you?"

"Then I would have handled him just like I've handled any other pushy guy I went out with before I met you,"

Claire said in a harsh voice. "Just like I'll handle them when you're no longer in my life."

He ground his teeth to keep from protesting at her statement. He didn't like thinking about her not being around every day. In a few short weeks Claire had made a place for herself in his life, and it wasn't just the investigation.

The silence in the bathroom grew heavy. Sean knew she was looking for a fight, and with his own adrenaline running high he'd be more than happy to give her one. But fighting wouldn't solve what was going on between them. Worse, it would undermine his self-control. Then he'd be tempted to do something stupid, like holding her and giving her something to taste besides mouthwash and pickled onions.

Shaking off the erotic images, Sean folded his arms across his chest and leaned his hip against the counter. "Until the killer is caught, I'm in your life and it's my job to protect you. Get used to it."

"Or you'll take me off the investigation?" she challenged.

"Yes. Any questions?"

"No," she said through her teeth.

"Then I'll let you freshen up."

After Sean closed the door behind him, Claire looked back toward the mirror and reminded herself she'd asked for this. She felt trapped, frantic, and a little crazy, but she could handle it. She had to.

"Claire?" It was Olivia's voice. "Honey, are you in there?"

"Hi, Livvie," Claire said with a faint sigh, feeling guilty that all she really wanted was to be left alone.

"Are you all right?" The door opened and Olivia walked in.

"I'm fine. I was definitely more disgusted than hurt."

"I'm glad. Randy's gone to the drunk tank, and the guys are waiting to take you home."

Claire thought about being alone with Aidan or Sean and knew she couldn't do it. "Can I borrow your car? You can catch a ride home with the guys."

"Where are you going?"

"I just need to go for a drive to clear my head. I haven't been alone in weeks. I have to—get out."

Olivia hesitated before giving her keys to Claire. "You be careful, hear? Keep the doors locked and take my cell phone."

Claire grabbed the phone and keys, then gave Olivia a quick hug. "Thanks."

Olivia watched while Claire gathered her things from the security guard and headed outside—the back way. Olivia had expected it. She went out and down the front steps in a rush to the detectives.

"I gave Claire my car keys and cell phone."

"What?" Sean asked. "You let her go off alone?"

"Of course, *cher.* Be careful when you follow her. She's close to . . . let's just say she needs some time out of the fishbowl."

Sean pulled his own keys out. "It's my fault she's mad. I'll follow her in my truck. You take Olivia home," he said to Aidan.

Olivia ducked her head to hide her satisfied smile.

Chapter 46

At the edge of Washington, D.C.
Saturday night

"It's called a turn signal, moron," Claire said aloud to the driver who had cut her off and then immediately slowed for an upcoming turn. "You might want to use it before somebody hauls a gun out of the glove compartment and shoots you."

With a jerk of the wheel, she whipped out and around the other car. She'd been on the road for over an hour, weaving in and out of light traffic and enjoying the luxury of driving with no particular destination or deadline. Every time her thoughts strayed to the past few weeks, she shoved them right out of her mind. At the moment she was free, and nothing was going to spoil that.

Claire rolled down the windows to enjoy the breeze. A thunderstorm was building in the distance, giving the night a hushed, tense quality that vibrated through the humid air. The smells and sounds brought back memories of summer nights in Louisiana with a clarity that was almost painful. Claire stared into the darkness and thought of her parents, dead for eight years. She needed them now more than ever, but took comfort in the fact that they were together. Wherever they were.

Biting her lip against the bittersweet pain, she watched lightning arc inside a distant cloud and thought how wonderful it would be to stand in a drenching rain and let it wash the last few weeks away.

The idea made her smile faintly and gave her a goal. Calculating the direction of the storm, she figured her best chance to hit the rain was to head toward Chesapeake Bay. She knew of several quiet coastal roads that led right to the water. She could park there and enjoy the storm in peace.

Peace. The thought of it was like a drug.

She reached down to tune the radio to an oldies station, one locally known for playing torch songs and blues. Humming along to Patsy Cline, she crossed the Chesapeake Bay bridge, turned off the main highway, and headed toward the water. After paralleling the coast for several miles, she chose another tiny road made of crushed shells and dirt. She was sure she wouldn't encounter anyone on this little track, because it didn't lead directly to the water. Instead, it ended at a wide turnaround separated from the high tide line by thick brush and scrub trees.

No one else was there ahead of her. She let out a long sigh, shut off the engine, and dropped her head back against the headrest. She closed her eyes and let her mind drift. The sound of water and the calls of night creatures came in the open window.

So did the sound of an approaching vehicle. Since she was at the end of a one-way road, the other car couldn't miss seeing her.

"Damn it!"

Headlights flared, and the outline of a large pickup pulled in directly behind her. Too late it occurred to her that she was alone on a deserted road on the Chesapeake with a large vehicle blocking her only avenue of escape.

Fumbling with the key, Claire turned the car on. She quickly raised the windows and hit the locks, while mentally calculating whether she would have enough space to get around the truck and not get stuck in the sand. Without taking her eyes off the rearview mirror, she felt around on the passenger seat for the cell phone.

She squinted in the darkness, trying to determine how many people were in the truck. She could only see the outline of one tall person behind the wheel. The driver's side door of the pickup opened, causing the dome light to come on and creating a silhouette of the seated man behind the wheel.

Sean.

"Son of a bitch!" Claire tossed the phone back onto the passenger seat and cut the engine. She shoved her door open and headed toward the truck. "What the hell are you doing here?" she yelled, marching unsteadily across the sand and shells in her high-heeled sandals.

Sean stayed in the truck and watched her approach through the open driver's window.

"Why did you follow me?" Claire demanded. "You scared the shit out of me until I recognized you."

"And here I was thinking you were too stupid to realize you should be afraid," Sean said, stripping out of his weapon harness. Lines of sweat showed everywhere the leather had been.

She stopped short a few feet away from him. "Did you just call me stupid?"

"I'll say," he muttered as he wrapped up the weapon and shoved it under the front seat. "What else do you call a woman who is under police protection but runs off all by herself and drives late at night to a deserted rural area?"

"I'd call her a woman who wanted to be alone! I still have rights, you know."

"You gave up those rights when you became the target of a serial killer. And when you agreed to take part in the investigation and play by my rules."

"Yeah? Well fuck your rules."

"Tired of playing detective?" Sean's voice was level, almost understanding.

"No, I'm tired of having my every move recorded and criticized. I'm tired of living my life on your microscope slide. You could understand that, if you had feelings. But you don't, do you? You just sit there behind your badge and watch."

Sean's jaw tightened. "Don't push that button. You don't want to pick a fight with me right now."

"Why not?" Claire asked, flinging her hands up in the air. "You're here. I'm here. I'd love to see if you have any normal human emotions under that badge, or if you've succeeded in completely eliminating them in order to *do your job*."

"That's it."

Claire took a step backward when Sean abruptly got out of the truck.

"What are you doing?" She took another step back as Sean began to come toward her.

"I don't want to fight with you, but I'm more than happy to give you everything else you're asking for."

She took another step backward, only to feel the ground give way beneath her heel. He grabbed her upper arms and finished the job of pulling her off balance. With a hungry sound he crushed her against his chest and brought their hips into full contact.

Before Claire could absorb the dual sensations, Sean's lips covered hers in a kiss that devoured. Tipping her head back, she let his tongue into her mouth. To her surprise, he began a gentle game of advance and retreat. She made a choked sound, then closed her eyes so she could drown herself in the taste of his desire.

This was what she'd been waiting for, and she was going to enjoy every second of it.

Sean also closed his eyes to better experience the sensation of kissing Claire after denying himself for days that seemed like years. He wrapped one arm more securely around her, pulling her closer. With his free hand he touched her hair, the side of her neck, and her gently sloping shoulder. Hungry for more, he ran his hand down the side of her breast, pausing to repeat the stroking caress when her breath caught.

With another deep kiss, he let his hand drop to her taut waist, then moved on to the curve of her hips. Repeatedly squeezing and releasing the supple flesh, he felt her body arch into his growing erection and knew that this time he wasn't going to let her go until they were *both* satisfied.

Without breaking the kiss, he released her and quickly unbuttoned his shirt. He jerked it free of his slacks, then caught his breath on a groan when her hands rubbed teasing strokes across his bare stomach and ribs. He tossed his shirt onto the hood of the truck and peeled off her short-sleeved cocktail jacket. In seconds it joined his shirt on the hood, and he was running his hands from her bare wrists to the sensitive skin where shoulder met neck.

A gust of salt-tinged air whipped around them. Chills roughened Claire's skin, though she wasn't cold. The temperature had to be at least eighty, and the humid night shimmered around them with the electricity of the coming storm. Still, she shivered again and pressed herself closer to Sean, wanting to crawl inside him and wrap him around her like a down blanket on a cold night.

The feel of her rubbing over him made his breath stop. He ran his hands down her sides to the soft skin of her thighs just beneath her hemline. It was as low as he could reach without breaking the contact of their lips. He let his hands slide around to the backs of her thighs, enjoying the sensation of slick nylon and warm flesh beneath. Pushing under the hem of her dress halfway to his elbows, he wrapped his hands around her bottom and shifted her until he had the dress up around her waist. He practically tore the nylons off her in his haste for skin-on-skin contact. Bunching the dress in one fist to keep it out of the way, he lifted her and wrapped her legs around him.

Twining her arms around his neck, Claire took advantage of being nearly his height. Sliding her fingers through the soft hair at his nape, she leaned forward and ran her tongue teasingly across Sean's lips. When his mouth opened, her tongue darted in repeatedly to find the soft flesh inside his lips and cheeks. He tried to deepen the kiss, but she pulled back to sip at his lips and flick them again and again with her tongue.

Two could play at the game of tease and retreat. She figured it was time for him to get a taste of his own medicine. The game lasted until Sean traced the sensitive base of her spine with his fingers, then sent his hand below the waistband of her panties and arched his erection against her. When she paused in her teasing to enjoy being caught between his hand in back and the hard thrust of his flesh in front, he captured her mouth in a deep kiss. He arched into her again, feeling her moist heat through the thin fabric that separated them.

When they came up for air, both were panting. Claire's unzipped dress sagged loosely around her breasts. Sean felt the first cool raindrops splatter his back. Still holding her wrapped around his waist, he turned around, ducked her head, and laid her out on the truck's oversized bench seat, a treasure he was about to devour.

Crouching down in the doorway, he looked into the black depths of her eyes and gently ran his hands up her bare legs.

"If this isn't what you want, you'd better say so now."

"What?" Claire was drowning in the erotic sensation of his hands caressing her thighs, slowly drifting closer to the center of her pleasure.

"Is this what you want?" Sean repeated, sliding his hands over her belly and up toward her breasts. The loosened material of her dress offered no protection from his wandering fingers, which stroked across nipples that were already hard and aching.

"Talk about stupid," Claire said. She caught Sean's belt buckle and tried to pull him onto the bench seat with her.

"Wait." He slid her hand off the buckle and undid his clothes. "I'm too tall to get undressed in the truck."

Moments later, he was naked. She reached a hand out to him, but he merely kissed her fingers and urged her to sit up so he could remove the rest of her clothing. He unzipped her dress completely and watched the fabric pool around her waist. Her breasts were bare underneath the silky blue material.

"Christ, woman. You're practically naked under this dress."

"Built-in bra," she said.

He rubbed his palms across her nipples while she wiggled the dress down over her hips. The shift and slide of her flesh made him groan. With one hand he drew her dress down her bare legs, and tossed it up onto the dashboard. He watched as she lay back across the seat and fiddled with the elastic waistband of her panties.

He reached for the scrap of dark fabric and slowly eased her out of it. Silently she lifted her hips to help him, then held a hand out to him when she was nude. In a heartbeat, he was stretched out across her. He groaned aloud at the pleasure of feeling her naked body against his for the first time.

Claire heard Sean's sound of pleasure and murmured a reply as she pulled his mouth back to hers. But they were too hungry to be content with kisses for long. Soon his mouth was traveling down her chest. He ran one hand up and down her ribs while he blew softly on the nipple closest to his mouth. She arched, and he ran his tongue across the taut crest, then blew on it again.

When she stiffened with pleasure, he lowered his head and took the nipple deeply into his mouth, tormenting it with teeth and tongue. Then he was distracted by her other breast, which seemed to demand the same treatment when she arched and rolled her head on the bench seat.

Claire closed her eyes and gave herself over to the sensation of Sean's mouth caressing her breasts. She moved her hands across his strong shoulders, stopping to dig her nails in when he teased her gently with his teeth. Smiling as he arched back against her, she continued down his back with her hands, stopping when she reached the firm flesh of his buttocks. She repeatedly clenched her fingers and released them in a rough caress that made him groan.

Suddenly fumbling, he reached to open the glove compartment. Pulling out one of the two condoms he had removed from his wallet, he tore open the foil packet and quickly sheathed himself. Settling on top of Claire once again, he pressed his erection against her damp flesh. He caught his breath at the sliding sensation and probed gently one more time.

When she felt the touch of his penis against the most sensitive part of her body, she moved against him in return. Breathing rapidly, she raised her head and found Sean's lips with hers. His tongue teased her mouth and his body teased hers, nudging her sensitive opening before retreating to rub his length against her. Finally, he stopped his teasing and pulled his mouth from hers.

"Look at me, Claire."

She lifted heavy lids and filled her nostrils with the musky scent of Sean and sex. His eyes were dark blue in the dome light of the truck, his pupils dilated with passion. She vaguely recognized the steady sound of raindrops outside the car, but was too focused on the storm inside to pay attention.

She kept her eyes on his as he nudged her legs even further apart and began to enter her. The incredible sensation of being invaded went on and on, until she felt sure she could take no more of him. Then he adjusted her thighs around his hips, and with a thrust seated himself completely inside her.

At Claire's shakily exhaled breath, he nuzzled her lips with his. "Everything okay?"

"Mmmmmm."

It was more purr than response, but Claire couldn't form a coherent reply. Instead, she tightened her legs and arched her body against his in a way he couldn't mistake. Sean took the hint and began to thrust slowly against her. When she began to meet his movements with her own, he quickened the pace, losing himself in her.

Claire felt the tension drawing her body tighter and tighter as he rocked against her. She realized her climax was fast approaching and protested softly, not wanting the experience to end so quickly. But she couldn't resist the temptation he offered and pulled him closer to her with a moan.

He also felt himself begin to lose control. It was too soon, so he levered himself up on his hands and tried to change the angle of penetration to slow things down. But she locked her legs around his hips and demanded everything he had to give.

He held back and kept stroking until he felt the shudders of completion begin to ripple through her body. Then he cried out hoarsely and buried his head in the curve of her neck. At the height of her orgasm, he locked his body into hers and stayed there, taut with his own climax.

When Sean collapsed against her, Claire wrapped her arms around his shoulders. She felt her heart pounding and heard her breath coming in rapidly, like his. Outside she could hear the rain falling harder, as the full force of the storm began to pass over the banks of the Chesapeake.

Little tremors continued through her body. She murmured and rocked her hips against him to prolong the delicious sensations. She stroked her hands across his damp back, feeling the taut muscles there begin to relax as he lay against her. Still the aftershocks continued, focused where he lay hard inside her.

Claire's breath caught and she moved her hips on the seat, trying to intensify the feelings.

"Am I too heavy? Do you want me to move?" Sean asked without lifting his head, drinking in the scent of her perfumed neck.

"Don't you dare move," she gasped, having just found the perfect angle.

He lifted his head to look at her. "Not even to do this?" He braced his feet and thrust into her.

Her only response was a choked cry as tension built inside her body once again. With a sense of disbelief, Sean felt his own heart begin to beat faster. He should have known that once would not be enough when it came to loving Claire. Leaning forward to kiss her reddened lips, he reached into the glove compartment for the last condom.

Though she protested when he pulled out of her, she murmured happily when he joined their bodies again moments later. This time there was no hesitation, no questioning advance of his body into hers. Suddenly greedy, Sean thrust into her until he could go no deeper, then withdrew and thrust again and again.

Claire felt as if every muscle in her body was tense, and

yet they grew tenser still as Sean continued to move against her. She clung to him tightly with her arms and legs, hearing his breath rasping in and out. She felt the sensations inside her build almost to the point of pain, then stay there.

Without realizing it, she dug her nails hard into his back as she tried to find a way to relieve the pressure growing and growing inside her. He pulled her legs higher up his body, until they wrapped around his waist. When he thrust again, she responded with a loud cry of pleasure. Soon every thrust was punctuated by a cry, and still the pressure built inside them both.

Sean levered himself up on his hands so he could watch Claire's face. Sweat burned his eyes, but he shook his head and continued to pound his body into hers, listening to the sounds of her pleasure while rain lashed the truck. He was breathing harshly, and groaned out loud as he felt her internal muscles squeeze him while her nails scored his back.

He didn't know where he found the strength, but he went harder and faster until her entire body went taut beneath him. The shudders that followed were his undoing. At the feel of her teeth on his shoulder, he dropped his head and buried himself as deeply in her as he could, then cried out as he came.

Several minutes later, Claire sighed as she was released from the last of the tension that had gripped her body. Relaxation flooded through her as completely as pleasure had. She cradled his head against her and wondered what she was going to say to him. Before she could think of anything clever, she fell asleep.

Sean felt her body go limp beneath him and decided he

was too exhausted to be offended. With his cheek cushioned against her breast, he allowed himself to doze with her, lulled by incredible satisfaction and the sound of rain.

Chapter 47

Sean woke when the rain stopped. The windows of his truck were completely steamed up from the heat of their bodies. The luminous dial of his watch told him it was after two in the morning. He knew they should leave, get back to Washington before Aidan and Olivia began to worry. But he was reluctant to let go of their time alone, away from the case and his obligations as a police officer. He certainly hadn't been thinking like a cop when he'd kissed Claire the first time this evening. And things had gone downhill from there.

He'd done some stupid things in his time, but this was in a class by itself. Not only had he become involved with a witness on a case but he'd also done it knowing she was emotionally vulnerable. This had to stop—this insanity that took him over so all he could think about was her. It could get people hurt, especially Claire. He didn't mind taking that kind of chance with his own safety, but he refused to put her life at risk any more than it already was.

Claire stirred beneath him. Instead of doing what he

should have, Sean stayed where he was and enjoyed the feel of her while she slowly stretched out her legs and rolled her head on the seat.

Claire's hands sifted gently through his hair, pushing it away from his forehead so that she could see his eyes. The combination of pleasure and guilt in them told her nothing had been solved. Well, nothing but the physical side, and that had been solved right down to the soles of her feet.

"My, my, my," she said in a husky voice. "Is that what the Brits mean when they say 'Fuck me senseless'?"

Despite his mood, Sean laughed at her hard language and soft drawl. No matter how low he was feeling, she could always make him laugh, which was dangerously appealing for a man who had little to laugh about in his line of work. He knew it was time to return to that unhappy reality, but instead he wrapped his arms tightly around her in a hard hug.

"Claire. A beautiful name for a beautiful woman. What in hell am I going to do with you?" Sean asked, running his thumb along her lower lip.

Determined to keep him smiling, she said, "Anything you want, *cher*. Anything at all."

Temptation streaked through him. With a muttered curse he began to separate himself from her.

"My wants are the problem." He sat up and ran both hands through his damp hair, disgusted with himself and the knowledge that he was going to kill the happy glow in Claire's face and eyes.

"Why?" She sat up and hugged her arms around herself, suddenly cold now that they were no longer touching.

"What I *want* is to take you home with me and not let you out of bed for a week." He turned to look at her and draped an arm along the steering wheel. "What I'm going to do is take you to Afton's home and not touch you again."

"But . . ." Claire trailed off, gesturing at the state of the truck cab, with clothes flung around the interior. Well, it had been good for her, anyway. Hell, it had been incredible.

"I'm sorry," Sean said. A lie, but not the first one he'd ever told in the line of duty. "It never should have happened." That was the bitter truth. He forced himself to keep going, to keep seeing the happiness drain out of her when all he wanted was to pull her into his lap and start all over again. "Chemistry is bad enough, but having an ongoing sexual relationship within an investigative team makes clear thinking impossible. If we're going to get through this operation without anyone else getting killed . . ." He shrugged.

"My thinking is pretty clear right now, for the first time in weeks."

"Maybe it's different for a guy," he said. "It's tough to stay in control of an explosive situation when all you can think about is getting your key witness flat on her back."

"Believe me, I've had similar thoughts about a certain detective."

He smiled slightly but didn't stop talking. "Claire, you told me yourself that these last few weeks are way off of normal for you. You were injured and now you're being stalked. You feel off-balance and, well, vulnerable. Anybody would. And I feel like dog shit for taking advantage."

"Hold it right there," she cut in. "I did everything but rip off your clothes, so forget about this taking advantage stuff."

He turned his head away, struggling for control. "Can't you see what's at stake? Don't you realize that if I'm reaching for you when I should be reaching for my gun, you could be dead? Are you hearing me?"

"Yes," she said, watching the muscle clenching in his cheek. What she was hearing was that the man she wanted didn't want her anymore. Too bad she had to find out when she was buck naked and trapped in the cab of a truck that still smelled of sex. "I hear you loud and clear."

He looked over at her and saw that she was hearing but she wasn't understanding. "Do you? Or do you think I'm feeding you some line now that we've had sex?"

She couldn't meet his eyes.

"Listen to me, Claire. I could be fucking you when I should be backing up Aidan and he could end up dead. Even if all of us get lucky and stay alive, I'm still jeopardizing my work. They'd fire my ass in a hot minute if they knew about this. I don't want to have to look Renata Mendes's mother in the eye and tell her that her daughter's case is in the toilet because the lead detective is bouncing on the only witness."

Claire winced and bit her lip. "I understand. Mrs. Mendes is lucky to have a cop who cares about his work enough to . . ." She searched desperately for a cliché. "To go that extra mile. Dedicated, I mean, and responsible."

Claire reached toward the dash and pulled her hopelessly crumpled dress over her lap.

"I'm sorry," Sean said, looking at her downturned face. "I wish like hell things could be different."

"It's what it is," she said, trying to smooth out her dress. He was worried about losing his job. She was worried about losing her heart.

This was unknown territory for her. Even in her most serious relationship, when she'd actually considered marrying the man, she'd been able to walk away without many regrets after his demands threatened her career and independence. But with Sean . . .

Her palms went clammy. She wondered when he'd become so important to her and how she was going to cope with losing him.

Her lower lip wobbled a bit at the thought. She bit down harder, refusing to give in to tears. She'd never once cried over a man. She wasn't about to start now, even when it was painfully clear that she was more involved at an emotional level than Sean was. She was determined to be as cool as he was, no matter how hard it was for her. She was a strong person who had been in the professional world for a long time. She could suck it up and continue working with Sean. From this moment forward her attitude would be that of a modern woman on the morning after the night she'd made a really big mistake.

"Maybe once this is all over we can—" he began.

"Don't," she interrupted roughly. "We're at a specific point in time, in a situation which will never be repeated. Given that, the whole thing was bound to turn out badly."

"That's not fair to either one of us. It was more than . . ." he looked around the cab of the truck.

"Steamy sex in the front seat?" she finished, then rushed on. "Whatever it was or wasn't, I'm not like you. I can't turn my feelings on and off like a switch. I'm either involved or I'm not. In our case it's not. It has to be."

Sean didn't like the sound of that. He didn't want to permanently let go of what was developing between them, he just wanted to put it on hold for a while, until things calmed down a little. "I don't want it to end like this," he said finally, frustrated.

"And I don't see an alternative. You've got your needs and I've got mine. They aren't compatible. I don't see either one of us changing—it's not in your makeup or mine to act like something we're not. It's one of the things we have in common."

"So where does this leave us?" Sean asked.

Naked in the front seat of your truck. Claire turned her dress right side out and shook it with a snap. "You're the expert in police investigations, you tell me."

"Hell, I don't know. This has never happened to me before." He pushed a hand roughly through his hair and thought about the mess he'd made of the situation.

"No sex would be a good start," she said. "No sniping would be a bonus. We need to maintain a professional distance."

Sean nodded.

"I don't suppose you've seen my underwear?" Hearing her own words, she cringed. *God, get me out of here before I do something else stupid.*

Silently Sean fished around on the dash for her panties, found them, and held them out to her. Then he took his clothes and slid out of the cab to give her room to dress.

Claire pulled her clothes on and congratulated herself for staying in control. While she could hardly pretend that making love in Sean's truck had meant nothing, it didn't have to mean *everything.*

Even if she knew it did.

Chapter 48

Claire awoke feeling tired, grumpy, and distinctly sore in certain portions of her anatomy. She crawled gingerly out of bed and into the shower. Despite the blistering July heat outside, she cranked the hot water on all the way. If she couldn't wash away the memories of making love with Sean on the bench seat of his truck, she could at least try to ease the stiffness that came from forcing her thirty-year-old body to do something that should only be attempted by oversexed teenagers. Or gymnasts.

Knowing she would be seeing Sean in Afton's office, Claire forced herself not to spend too much time getting ready. Instead, she pulled her hair back and put on a minimum of makeup. After throwing on casual shorts and a top, she headed out of the house. When she got to Afton's office, Aidan and Sean were just settling in. Claire jolted when she saw Sean's dark head, but she made herself continue into the room and take the only empty chair—next to him.

"So how did the date with Randy go?" Afton asked eagerly.

Claire felt her cheeks begin to burn at the prolonged, tense silence that filled the room.

"Ah, you'll probably want to cancel his membership with Camelot," Aidan finally said.

"Another one? What happened?" Afton thought at first he might be joking, but after looking at Sean's face, she decided otherwise.

"He got stinking drunk and then wouldn't take no for an answer," Sean said.

"He drank a bit too much and didn't seem to realize I wasn't interested in continuing the evening at his place," Claire said calmly, speaking over Sean's flat voice.

Afton looked from one to the other, then decided she wasn't feeling brave enough to probe further into a subject that had Sean narrowing his eyes and locking his jaw.

"Okay, we'll be sure Randy doesn't make any further dates through our service," she said. "But I take it we can also eliminate him as a suspect?"

"Yes. He's an ass, but I don't think he's a murderer," Aidan replied before Sean could speak.

"So that's five dates, and not much progress except for eliminating some potential suspects, right?" Afton asked.

"Not to mention flagging some real losers in your database," Sean added bluntly.

Afton bit her lip and looked at her friend.

Claire rubbed her hands together and tried for some enthusiasm. "Well, let's see who else we can pick out of the catalogue, hmmm?" Mentally pushing up her sleeves, she tilted Afton's monitor in her direction. "Where did we leave off?"

While Claire and Afton reviewed eligible bachelors to be investigated, Sean sat next to her and brooded. He didn't understand her comfortable—even cheerful—attitude. The Claire who had looked at him last night with dazed black eyes and wild dark hair was gone. In her place was a casually dressed, self-possessed woman who had barely glanced his way when she'd come into the room.

As she quickly scanned the photos and gave Aidan a running commentary on why she was choosing this or that candidate, Sean couldn't help but admire her efficiency and determination. She'd done exactly as he'd asked. She'd stopped reaching out to him emotionally and was treating him no differently than she treated his partner.

And it was driving him nuts.

He'd been sure he'd hurt her. Since his main goal all along had been to protect her, he'd tortured himself with recriminations all last night. Now it seemed that she was fine, while he was still reeling from the effects of the storm they had created together on the banks of the Chesapeake.

When he remembered how it had felt to finally be inside her, he felt sweat popping out on his forehead. He could feel control slipping out of his grasp, even though things should have been falling in place for the first time in weeks.

Quite a jolt to the ego, eh, pal?

Sean ignored the snide voice inside his head that implied he was having a hard time dealing with Claire's ease with the new boundaries of their relationship. He told himself to get over it, or remove himself from the case. But even as he was now, wrapped up in his unwilling attraction for his witness, Sean was convinced he and Aidan were the best team to catch the killer before he struck again.

Despite Sean's silence, Claire was intensely aware of him. Though he wasn't looking at her, he seemed to be focusing his attention on her. She could practically hear the gears turning in his head, and wondered what was making him so tense and quiet.

"Claire? Are you finished with the catalogue?" Afton asked.

Claire started. As she glanced away from Sean she caught Aidan looking at her speculatively.

"I'm done. Shall we call it a day?" Claire asked.

Aidan nodded. "We've got plenty of names to get started on for the second wave of background checks. You should be able to schedule some dates by late tomorrow."

"Great." Claire stood and gathered her things as Afton excused herself to take a call in another room. "Would you mind giving me a ride home, Aidan?"

Sean's head came up and he opened his mouth to object, then thought better of it.

Aidan looked between the two of them and shrugged. "Sure. Just let me check something first."

With his partner gone, Sean was alone with Claire for the first time. Before he could think better of it, he said exactly what was on his mind. "If you can't even stand to be in the car with me, how are we ever going to have a working relationship?"

"Just playing by your rules. You wanted us both to back off, and that's what I'm doing. That doesn't give you license to poke at me."

Sean shifted in his chair. "You're right. I'm sorry."

"It's already forgotten," she said with a professional smile. "I'm sure it will be a challenge for both of us to get used to the way things have to be from now on."

"Ready?" Aidan asked from the doorway.

The smile she gave him wasn't coolly professional. "Ready."

Watching them, Sean thought rather grimly that it didn't seem to be a challenge for Claire at all.

"So, do you feel better after your drive last night?" Aidan asked as they headed for the elevator.

She wondered if Sean had said anything. "Not really," she mumbled.

"Where did you go?"

"The Chesapeake."

Aidan rubbed his hand over his jaw and wondered if he should let it stand or try to pry more information out of her.

"You and Sean seemed kind of mad last night. Did you two work things out?" Aidan asked as he steered her across the lobby.

"He outlined how things will be from now on," she said, trying to keep the note of bitterness out of her voice. *Sure, he laid out the rules. But when I do exactly what he wants, he still pokes at me.* "And I agreed."

Aidan sighed and helped her into his car. As he walked around to the driver's side, he told himself to let the subject drop. He would be crazy to get between two strong-willed people who were desperately attracted to each other at the wrong time and place.

But despite his strong survival instincts, he found himself trying to explain Sean to Claire.

"Sean can seem kind of closed up sometimes, but he's the best friend and partner any cop could ask for. I consider myself doubly lucky that he's my family. Not everyone has relatives they like and respect, as well as love."

She nodded to show that she'd heard him but offered no other comment.

Aidan forged on. "He has very strict ideas of right and wrong, and sometimes that's a powerful advantage on a case. But it can make it difficult to deal with him if you happen to have an opposing viewpoint."

"Was he always like that?" she asked, curious despite herself.

"Always. We had a hard life growing up. It's not that we were abused or anything—far from it. We had a stable home, solid folks, and plenty of food on the table. My mother and Sean's are sisters. We all lived together on a family ranch in the most beautiful country you'll ever see."

"Where was that?"

"Wyoming. Mountains that reach toward the sky, streams with water pure and cold. And all around you was open space. It was like a kind of paradise, but we paid a price. Living on a cattle ranch in the high country wasn't easy, and we all worked from the time we woke to the time we slept. Even when I was four years old I had chores to do every day."

"Is Sean older than you?"

"Yes. He's the oldest of the five of us, including me and my three younger sisters. That placed an extra burden on him, but he never complained. My father split just after the last of my sisters was born, and my mom moved to the main house on the ranch after that. I guess I relied on Sean to be a role model from then on."

"What about Sean's dad? Wasn't he around to be a father figure?"

"He worked hard keeping the ranch together once his foreman—my father—left. Sean's daddy is a harsh man, one who never had time for 'coddling' children. He loves Sean and me, he just doesn't know how to show it. Nor does he particularly feel the need."

"That's sad," she said, thinking of her own loving parents.

"In a way. But Uncle Bob did teach Sean about responsibility, and about being a provider and protector for his family. Sean took those lessons to heart. They made him an incredible soldier and team leader when he was in the army. As a cop, he approaches things with a focus and determination that still blow my mind."

"I see."

"Do you? You have to understand that when Sean is given a task—or when he commits himself to a goal—nothing gets in his way. Especially when the job is an important one, like working murder cases that have been shelved without being solved. It's something he feels very strongly about. It's part of what he is."

"Oh, I understand," she said. "And I truly respect that. But sometimes I think he has trouble seeing that there might be more than one way to get a job done."

"You're right. He can get a powerful case of tunnel vision. But usually with perseverance and persuasion—and the occasional two-by-four applied to his thick skull—you can get through to him and change his mind. For the times you can't, it's been my experience that he's usually right."

She said nothing, not sure she wanted to consider where their relationship fell in that scenario.

"He's a good man, Claire. He just has trouble expressing himself sometimes. And he's a great cop. You couldn't be in better hands," Aidan said earnestly.

"Believe me, I know all about his hands," she muttered.

"Ahh . . ."

"Sorry. I know what you're trying to do, and I appreciate it. I understand that Sean is a good investigator, and I have absolute confidence the two of you will break the case." She turned toward him. "I mean that—it's the only reason I can sleep at night."

Aidan stopped in front of Afton's house and cut the engine. "You don't look like you slept much last night."

Claire turned away from his penetrating hazel eyes. "No, that was the last thing on my mind."

"Do you want to talk about it?" Aidan asked uncomfortably.

"No. You've explained a lot, really. I just—it's too fresh to talk about right now." Claire fumbled with the door handle but stopped when Aidan put his hand on her shoulder.

"I'm here when you're ready," he said.

"Thanks," she replied, smiling mistily at him.

Claire opened the door and stepped out. As she turned, she nearly bumped into Olivia, who had come out to see what was taking so long. With the excuse that she had to make a few phone calls, Claire hurried by her friend and into the house.

Olivia leaned down to speak through the open window. "What did you say to her?"

"Nothing. I was just trying to help with something."

"So what did Sean say to her, then?" Olivia asked.

"Damned if I know. But from the way they're both acting, I think the problem has more to do with what they *did* than what they said."

"Yeah, well you can't say we didn't see that one coming. If you'll pardon the pun," Olivia said.

Aidan snickered. "Well, they're two smart people. They'll either work it out or make all of us miserable for awhile. Regardless, it's no big deal—"

"It certainly is a big deal," Olivia cut in. "Claire doesn't sleep around. If she got involved with Sean then there's more to it than a one-night stand."

"Sean isn't my idea of a swinger, either. He's never done anything like this, especially not in the middle of an investigation. What I meant about it not being a big deal is that Sean's a pro. He won't let this get in the way of the case. And regardless of how things turn out between them, he'll protect Claire with his life."

Olivia winced. "Let's hope it doesn't come to that."

Chapter 49

Sean tried to put Claire out of his mind. It wasn't easy, even though he had a phone call scheduled with Jacob Keeley, a behavior profiler out of Quantico. Sean had sent a copy of the most pertinent case files to Quantico, along with the crime scene video from the Mendes murder. He hoped the FBI agent's experience with criminal profiling would help give them some direction in their investigation, which at this point was stalled.

The box with Claire's purse, the bloody sash, and the threatening note had been as clean as the evidence techs had feared. No one had been following Claire—or if he had been, he was too good to catch. And as for the Camelot dates, they were a joke. Too bad he didn't feel like laughing. He wanted to get this case settled and he wanted it to happen fast, before Claire's cheery professionalism made him grab her and find out how deep the I-don't-care act went.

Settling at his desk with pen and paper to take notes,

Sean dialed Keeley's number. He was put through immediately.

"Thanks for taking time to give an unofficial look at this case," Sean said.

"No problem. My sister said you and your partner could really use a break. The media coverage has even made it over here."

"Yeah. No doubt the weirdos and copycats will start on the prowl. That's why we need to move quickly."

Agent Keeley sighed. "I have to stress that I can't do a real profile without full access to the crime scenes, and a lot more detail than you've been able to give me. If you want something concrete, you're going to have to go through official channels—my boss meets your boss, and so forth."

"We're not looking to go to trial with this. I don't expect you to tell me we're looking for a middle-aged Caucasian janitor who happens to be a Sagittarius and likes French fries. We just need help making the killer stand out in our pool of almost two hundred suspects."

"So your witness can't remember anything and the killer has focused on the one that got away. Any more gifts?"

"No."

"Interesting," Agent Keeley said. "Maybe he's found a distraction."

"That would be good news for the witness and bad news for the investigation."

"Yeah. Okay, here are my general impressions, off the record of course."

"Absolutely. So far we have exactly nothing."

"I wouldn't say that. Anyway, I'm going to assume that

you're basically familiar with the different categories of serial killers, based on their motivations."

"Yes. I'm thinking we have a control freak or a thrill-seeker here," Sean said.

"So am I. At this point, I'd lean toward control-oriented over the hedonistic or thrill-seeking killer. Given the risky nature of these attacks, and the fact that he's never been caught or left so much as a fingerprint behind that we know of, I'm fairly sure he plans his killings in advance."

"Agreed. Although he may not have always been this good," Sean said. "I'm willing to bet he left some forensic evidence behind at his earlier crime scenes, but it somehow got overlooked. Maybe the investigators' techniques or tools weren't up to today's standards."

"That's possible. At this point in his 'career' the killer probably stalks his victims for several days to learn their routines and choose the perfect site—one that's risky, but not stupidly so."

Sean nodded as he wrote. "I figure it's like a game to him. He might get caught, so that adds to the thrill when he's selecting his location and victim."

"Yes. The stalking phase is a vital component in his fantasy life. I'm willing to bet he gets off on the process of planning the killing almost as much as the actual deed itself," Agent Keeley said.

"That's one thing that confuses me. It's almost like the killing is perfunctory. There's no sexual assault, no torture, no indication of restraints, no defensive wounds. He kills with a single stab wound, but then gives her three or four more postmortem. Then he leaves them where they're lying, possibly taking a small trophy with him."

"I'd say he has no respect for women. Once the operation has gone as planned and they're dead, he's essentially through with them. Then he walks away without looking back."

"And the postmortem stab wounds?" Sean asked.

"I imagine they're a crack in his self-discipline. He possibly doesn't even remember inflicting those additional wounds."

Sean closed his eyes, trying to visualize how the attacks had taken place. "So the first stab is done while the victim is upright. It's a fatal wound. Then she falls and he stands over her and stabs her again, probably in the heat of the moment."

"Yes, it's an angry act. He may not realize that it's rage against a slice of the female population that's driving him. He thinks it's the stalking and killing of his prey that motivates him—if he thinks about it at all. There's an underlying disdain for women you can see in his acts."

"Isn't that true in most cases?"

"Some, but not all. I imagine this guy had a very dominant father, and a mother who was either submissive or abandoned the family. But I don't think his mother was the defining female presence in his life. He definitely has rage toward a particular group of women, which the victims all represent."

"They've all been Hispanic females, similar in coloring and build. But I don't understand why most were prostitutes, while the last one was a teacher. The only thing the victims had in common was living on the wrong side of town, but for Renata Mendes that was in her past."

"It's not uncommon for this type of predator to change his victim selection and modus operandi as he perfects his craft. Sometimes, these guys hit on something they really like, and go back to repeat it and feel that gratification again," Keeley said.

"Is that what you think is happening here?"

"I see a couple of possibilities. First, prostitutes are often a target of opportunity because of the reality of their profession. They're always out there, always easy. But as the killer matures, he wants more of a challenge, which could explain the shift in victims."

"You sound like you think there might be something else."

"It's possible. Let's go back to the Herrera case," Agent Keeley said. "Cristina Herrera was a young mother of two, a reformed crack addict, and a former prostitute. She'd been living in a halfway house for a year and had just been cleared to get custody of her children again."

"In other words, she was a rehabilitation success story," Sean said thoughtfully.

"Exactly. When she was killed in her old neighborhood, just a couple of days before getting her children back, what was the local media reaction like?"

"They were all over it. She'd previously been profiled for a news story about a promising new rehabilitation technique. Her death was considered doubly tragic because she seemed to be on the verge of turning her life around," Sean said, remembering the newspaper coverage.

"You hit the nail on the head. The press was all over the story. I'm positive that fed the killer's need for more. He loved it—couldn't get enough, actually. That's why the next murder followed so closely after the first, at least compared to your estimates about his previous pace."

"That must be why he selected Renata Mendes," Sean said. "She was a poor kid from a bad neighborhood who had managed to make something of her life."

"And the media was sure to cover that angle of the story. It's one of the reasons she stayed in the headlines for more than one day. I'm sure he's still living off the thrill of that."

"Think of what would happen if the media got wind of the witness as his next potential victim," Sean said, feeling a cold sensation in his gut.

"Yes. I don't need to tell you she's in grave danger. This new victim he's stalking has raised the bar, so to speak. She's more challenging and alluring than any of the others, so he's probably willing to go to greater lengths to get at her. The payoff, in his mind, will be worth it."

"Jesus Christ."

"There's more. I see an element of ritual in the killer's MO, especially in the weapon selection, crime scene layout, and taking of the trophy. Ritual is very comforting to this type of killer, but in the case of Renata Mendes the routine was accidentally broken by your witness."

"She messed up his sick little game," Sean said. "She changed the rules."

"I'm afraid so. That may give him an even more powerful motivation, because he may feel the need to get things right this time. I think it's going to make his behavior even more risky, and certainly more difficult to predict."

Sean couldn't speak as rage and fear washed over him—even though he knew emotions wouldn't help him catch the guy who was threatening Claire.

But the killer's own escalating drive and need to take risks would.

Sean thought quickly. "If the killer is changing his patterns, taking more risks, wouldn't it stand to reason that he'd be more likely to make mistakes? After all, he hasn't perfected his new methods yet."

"That's a logical conclusion," Keeley said. "Many serial killers are caught when their thrill-seeking behavior and growing boldness take them out of their comfort zone. In essence, they become too caught up in the game."

"Like when you're playing chess and get so wrapped up in planning your strategy you forget to watch what your opponent is doing."

"Exactly," Keeley said. "I think that's how you'll eventually nail this bastard. The only question is when."

Chapter 50

Washington, D.C.
Friday evening

Claire stepped into her high heels and tiredly rolled her head, trying to ease some of the kinks out of her neck. It had been four weeks since she'd stumbled across a murder scene, and the police weren't any closer to the killer than they had been that night. Now she was heading out on yet another date from Camelot's catalogue.

While some of the men had gone out of their way to be charming and attentive, she couldn't say the same for herself. She did only what was required for the investigation—eating fine food, drinking sophisticated wines, playing a role to gather information, and then going home with a police escort.

And every night she went to bed alone, knowing that the investigation was mired in Camelot's endless catalogue and her own lack of memory—except in dreams. She didn't remember then either; she just woke up clammy and terrified. Awake and alone, she told herself that the murderer had lost interest in her, but she couldn't believe it. She sensed the lurking, malevolent threat as clearly as she had when she'd received her purse and a victim's bloody sash, a cruel gift from a sadistic mind. Added to the strain of being around Sean day after day, it was enough to make her jump at every strange sound.

Sean wasn't doing anything to lower her level of tension. Night after night he sat at the bar with his gaze fixed on Claire. Their eyes frequently clashed when she looked around the room during the evening, and each time was like a physical jolt. When she got up to leave the room, she could swear his eyes were burning into her back.

They had hardly spoken two words alone since the night they'd made love. He went out of his way to avoid her and communicate through others. The mixed messages she was getting from his piercing blue stare and his standoffish actions kept her awake long into each night.

She supposed it was better than obsessing about the killer stalking her.

With her mouth turned down at the thought, Claire fastened a set of dangling earrings in her lobes and picked up a light shawl from the chair in Afton's guest room. In the cab on the way to Camelot, she reviewed the file on her date for that evening. Just another normal guy, who worked a normal job and had no apparent fractures in his psyche.

"Seeking a true soul mate in a world of imposters." Claire smiled faintly as she read the line beneath his photo. *Who isn't, my friend?*

When the cab dropped her at Camelot, she was taken

to the nursery in the back. Afton was on the floor changing one of her babies, while the other howled loudly from
the crib.

"Am I interrupting anything?" Claire asked.

"No, come on in. The troops have just been fed, but
Justin seems to be a little annoyed at being put down for
his evening nap. My nanny is gone, so it's just me, and the
little monster will have to tough it out."

"Maybe he needs a little help to fall asleep, hmmm?"
Claire set aside her purse and shawl and stepped out of her
uncomfortable shoes.

Crossing to the crib, she looked down at the red-faced
baby crying in frantic gulps. She draped a cloth over her
shoulder and lifted Justin out of the crib. As soon as she
bounced him gently against her shoulder, he calmed
down. Trying to fit a clenched fist in his mouth, he surveyed Claire with owlish brown eyes.

"Someone's pretty tired," she said in a soothing
voice. "I bet a little time in the rocking chair will do the
trick."

She sat down in the rocker near the crib and gently adjusted the baby against her shoulder. He lay there, content to rest his head on her chest and look up at her shiny
earrings.

"You're going to spoil him," Afton said affectionately.

"It's not possible to spoil something this sweet." Claire
pressed her lips to Justin's forehead, then leaned her head
against the back of the chair and sighed tiredly. "Lord am
I beat. No offense, but when this is over I'm canceling my
membership with your company. If I never go on another
date it would be fine with me."

"Then how are you going to meet a man and have one
of your own screaming babies some day?"

"There has to be another way. Besides, I don't see you going out on a lot of dates, either."

Afton laughed. "I'm a single mother with twin babies. Plus I'm trying to run a business. Some days I don't even get around to brushing my hair, so where would I find time to date?"

"I know it's tough, but some companionship might balance out your life. Besides, you might meet someone and fall in love. Then you'd have a partner to help you raise the boys."

"I don't think so." Afton hesitated, then confided in Claire. "There's only one man for me—and he's dead."

"I'm so sorry. You never said anything, so I wasn't sure . . ." Claire trailed off.

"It's all right. It's been a year, so I should be getting used to the idea by now. But it still hurts. Even more when I think how he never even knew I was pregnant before he died."

Claire tried to imagine how Afton must feel, but couldn't. "You're very strong."

"That implies I had a choice. With two babies, I'm just doing what has to be done every day and nothing more. Believe me, I never thought I'd be doing it alone. But he had a dangerous job which took him all over the developing world, so I should have known that something . . . could happen."

"What did he do?"

"He was a geologist working for an international petrochemical company. He went on a surveying trip and was murdered in a robbery attempt at the compound where he was staying. I found out I was pregnant three days after I was told about his death. We were never married."

Claire bit her lip, unsure how to respond.

Afton looked up at her and smiled sadly. "It's okay. I'm learning to deal with it. And I can't regret the time we spent together, or the fact that I have two healthy boys to always remind me of their father. I don't want them to grow up without a male influence in their lives, but I'll never love another man the way I loved their father."

"Of course not, but that doesn't mean you can't love again, in a different way," Claire said.

"There isn't any point. I've known real love, so why would I settle for second best? As for finding another man, who would want to be my consolation prize, knowing my heart is already given to someone else?"

Claire felt her insides clench as the words hit dangerously close to home. Over the last week it had been almost impossible to work up enough energy to make small talk with her dates. Her thoughts were focused on Sean, and when she measured other men against him, they came up short.

Consolation prize. Is that what she would have to settle for once Sean was no longer in her life?

"Do you really think there's just one man out there for you?" Claire asked, cradling the sleepy weight of the baby against her shoulder. "One true love for everyone?"

"Yes. If you're really lucky, things work out. If not, you take what you can for as long as you can have it, and then you have your memories to get you by. I'm lucky to have Cameron and Justin."

Claire looked down at the child sleeping against her and envied Afton her certainty and her children. "They're wonderful boys, and you're a wonderful mother."

"You'll be a great mother, too. Look at how you settled him right down."

"First I need to meet the father," she said wryly.

"Which reminds me—it's time for your date." Afton stood up with her other son.

"Can I have just a few more minutes?" Claire asked, brushing her lips over the baby's incredibly soft hair.

"Would you watch them for a second then?" Afton said, putting Cameron in the crib. "I need to clean up in the kitchen."

"No problem." Claire closed her eyes. "We'll be right here."

And so would the question that she couldn't duck and couldn't answer. *Was Sean the one love of her life?*

She'd certainly never felt this way about anyone before. He was affecting her work, her sleep, her social life, and her peace of mind. Worse, he'd become her measuring stick for the male of the species.

And they could hardly bear to be in the same room together.

Shoving away the unanswerable questions, Claire continued to rock and cuddle the baby against her. Gradually the certainty of being watched made her eyes snap open.

Sean was staring at her.

"Sorry to wake you," he said. "Your date's here."

He didn't know how he'd managed to make a coherent sentence. He'd never really thought about having children, though he had always assumed it would happen someday—when he was ready. The sight of Claire, barefoot and dressed in a cocktail dress, gently rocking a sleeping baby in her arms, gave him an almost prescient feeling, a certainty that someday she would hold his child. It jerked the world out from under him.

He didn't say another word to her. He was having enough trouble breathing past the tightness in his chest without trying to talk.

Chapter 51

Washington, D.C.
Friday evening

The man frowned as Marie Claire's cab pulled away from the curb, quickly followed by an anonymous beige sedan. Watching, he clicked his thumbnail against his teeth in a nervous habit he wasn't even aware of.

This is ridiculous. Don't the police have anything better to do than follow her around?

At first he'd worried that she'd remembered something, perhaps even identified him, but after two weeks, he didn't think so. There was absolutely no sign that the police were interested in him. Even so, he decided that there wasn't any point in risking being noticed by following the cab as he had for the past three nights. Same time, same restaurant, different date, same cops.

My gift must have really shaken Marie Claire and the police if she has round-the-clock protection. He smiled at the thought and considered sending her something else just to watch the fuss and freshen up the story for the media.

It was a delicious idea, but he decided against it as he

had every other time it occurred to him. It wasn't that he was frightened by the police—they added spice to the game even as they made it more difficult—but the longer he watched Marie Claire and her escorts, the more he believed that the cops were using her as bait to get to him.

It wouldn't happen, of course. He was much too smart, far smarter than public servants driving tacky Chevy sedans. But that didn't mean he would be careless. As much as he wanted to feel his knife slicing into Marie Claire, he could be patient when the goal was worth it. His sweet prey was definitely worth whatever patience it took, even if he was getting more and more restless.

His thumbnail clicked more rapidly against his teeth as he tried to figure out why her dates picked her up and dropped her off at this building when she worked across town—not that she'd been at work lately. She spent her days in a house with cops parked outside and her nights coming and going from this building. The question was why. His own broker was based in the building, along with other trading offices and small businesses, but it wasn't likely that Marie Claire needed to check in with her broker on a nightly basis.

He needed to find out exactly where she spent her time in that office building, and if the police were really using her as bait. It would be risky, but at this point he decided there was greater risk if he didn't find out exactly what was going on. Besides, he was tired of just watching.

A movement across the street caught his eye. One of the building security guards was holding open the handicap-access door. A young woman with short blonde hair came out, pushing a double stroller in front of her.

The man smiled and licked his thumbnail as he recognized the woman. He'd seen her outside the Georgetown home where Marie Claire and her little friend were staying. He'd also seen her talking to the police. He sat patiently as she loaded her babies into car seats in the back of her minivan, then folded the huge stroller and stored it in the back.

After she pulled out into traffic, he waited for a few moments to be sure that no one followed her. Then he made a U-turn and caught up with her at a stoplight. He followed her as she drove past the town house that had been Marie Claire's home for the last two weeks. When she turned right, so did he, watching while the minivan turned into an alley that ran behind the row of houses. He paused for a minute, then pulled forward. He saw the blonde woman unloading her babies and their car seats and carrying them through a gate—right into the backyard of the house where Marie Claire was staying.

He drove further down the street until he found a parking spot, then doubled back to survey the entrance of the alley on foot. He was close enough to read and memorize the woman's license plate. After about twenty minutes, the woman came out alone with several duffel bags. She returned to the house and immediately brought the babies back to the car. Once they were secured in their seats, she stopped to close a padlock on the back gate.

As he watched the woman drive away, he smiled. Fate had been particularly generous with him lately. He now knew exactly how to make his sweet prey think of him, send the media and the police into a frenzy, feel another woman's terror just before she died, and be perfectly safe.

A sexual shudder built from the base of his spine. Tomorrow would be a very good night.

Chapter 52

Washington, D.C.
Saturday afternoon

Sean and Aidan sat at their desks reviewing the status of several leads on the Mendes murder investigation. They were developing a system to divide Camelot's male clients into several different categories of risk, a time-consuming procedure requiring daily updates to the database of suspects they were creating.

"All clients on our list who haven't been run through the law enforcement computers will be categorized as high risk," Sean said.

"Agreed. And once they've been through a preliminary check they'll get moved to medium risk, depending on the results. Only medium-risk clients will be allowed to go out with Claire for further assessment." Aidan made notes as he spoke. "After the dates, anyone who's been dismissed will be categorized as low risk, but we won't formally eliminate any suspect until we actually catch this bastard."

"We have to move faster. It's been a month since Renata Mendes was murdered. I don't think the killer will wait long before he strikes again. Keeley pretty much agreed with me that the guy was speeding up his pattern."

Sean looked up as their captain approached. He could tell it wasn't going to be a pleasant discussion when Captain Michaels remained standing, rather than taking a seat at one of the desks.

"What progress have you two made?" Michaels asked.

"We're putting together our weekly report—" Sean began.

"I need something right now," Captain Michaels interrupted.

Sensing their supervisor's foul mood, Aidan spoke cautiously. "The Crime Scene Unit in charge of the Mendes case hasn't come up with any conclusive forensic evidence for us to work with."

"We have details of the cause of death and the layout of the scene documented," Sean added. "There are similarities with several other unsolved stabbing deaths in the metro area, including Baltimore."

"But no hard evidence?"

"None. This guy is careful to carry out his attacks in heavily trafficked areas, so the odds of getting useable hair, fiber, or prints are pretty much zero," Sean said.

"What about the dating service thing? Any suspects there?"

"We've been able to classify every man the witness has seen as a low-level risk, which essentially eliminates them from further active investigation," Sean said. "Our witness continues to review the remaining members of the service. We have a nightly operation to get the witness and suspects in close proximity and see whether we can make an identification of the killer."

"At this rate, it could be months before you make it through every suspect, right?"

Both detectives nodded.

"That's not good enough." Michaels threw an advance copy of the Sunday paper on Sean's desk. "The shit will hit the fan tomorrow. Someone's been leaking tidbits to Whitcombe. She's written a story citing unnamed sources that could blow the lid off your witness."

Aidan stood up and looked over his partner's shoulder. In a small box on the front page was an article by Shelly Whitcombe slamming the D.C. police for not having any suspects or leads a month after Renata Mendes's murder. The story went on to question the capabilities of the investigative team, given the fact that they'd made so little progress despite the assistance of an eyewitness to the crime.

Sean clenched his fists around the sides of the paper as he flipped to page twelve and read the last of the story.

And in an ironic turn of events, an unnamed police department source has stated that on the night of the murder, the eyewitness in question, whose name has not been released, was returning home from an evening spent at Camelot Services Inc., a dating service located near the scene of the crime. The eyewitness was injured trying to escape from the killer, but the police source indicated that the individual has recovered and is resting at an undisclosed location. Is there no end to the perils of dating in the 21st century?

"Fucking gossipmongering leeches," Sean said. "Don't they have any idea how much danger this puts the witness in?"

"Why should Whitcombe care?" the captain said. "A dead witness makes a better story, especially if said witness is in protective custody when she dies."

"Very few people know who the witness is, and only her surveillance team knows where she's staying," Aidan said, more to reassure Sean than the captain.

"Move her anyway. I'll speak to the group doing the surveillance about some new rules. Unnamed source, my ass." The captain walked away without further comment.

"Shit. Any ideas on who the leak is?" Aidan asked.

"No, and he'd better hope I never find out. Dammit, this could drive the killer over the edge." Sean pushed back from his desk. "We'd better tell Claire and get her moved. Where is she now?"

"Her team said she returned to Afton's place about two hours ago. She's probably getting ready for her date tonight."

Sean made a sour face and headed for the door with Aidan right on his heels.

Chapter 53

Claire stood in front of the bathroom mirror and ran her fingers through her wet curls. She was preparing for date number whatever—she'd lost count, much less any sense of urgency. Olivia was out shopping and wouldn't be back until after Claire left. It had been a lovely, quiet afternoon, but it was time to put on her cocktail dress and perfume and pretend to be someone she wasn't for the evening.

She shrugged into a soft robe and wandered into the bedroom, looking out the window while she fastened the belt. She sighed and decided it looked like another storm was coming, bringing with it an early gloom. *Wonderful. I beat my hair into shape and the humidity makes it go sproing. Maybe I'll just let the curls do their curly thing.*

Since Claire's bedroom overlooked the back of the house, she couldn't see the surveillance team, but she knew they were around somewhere. They always were, like the humidity.

The gate in the backyard banged open and shut as a

burst of wind rustled the trees and shrubs. Claire frowned at the noise. The six-foot-tall gate was always closed and secured with a padlock. She was sure it had been closed when she had gone up to take her shower. Otherwise she would have heard it banging in the restless wind that preceded the thunderstorm.

From her second-story bedroom, nothing looked out of place in the backyard or alley. The patio furniture, glider swing, and barbeque set were all neatly arranged in the small yard. There weren't any strange cars in the alley.

The gate banged again, and her heart beat a little bit faster.

Tightening the knot on her robe, Claire padded down the stairs in her bare feet. Feeling foolish, she went through all the rooms to make sure she was alone. Only then did she go to the back door.

The gate banged again as the wind shifted direction. The hinges creaked and the gate opened after failing to latch properly.

Maybe Afton forgot to lock it yesterday?

A chill went through Claire's body. She blamed it on the fact that she was standing in an air-conditioned room with wet hair and nothing but a short robe for cover. She should really go secure the gate, but when she reached for the back door, something made her hesitate.

Don't be silly. It's still light outside, and you have two policemen within yelling distance. Just go out and close it.

With a deep breath, she opened the door and walked out onto the back step.

The wind gusted again, bringing the scent of rain and making her robe whip around her knees. She shivered and knew it was pure nerves. The air outside was heavy with humid heat. She slowly walked down the brick path, making her way between the chaise lounge and a patio table. As she passed the glider swing, she reached a hand out to stop its slow creaking motion. There was silence in the yard.

Holding her robe against another playful tug of sultry air, she continued toward the back gate, which was slowly swinging open again. As she passed the grill and oversized wooden barbeque counter, which were protected from the elements by a dark green tarp, she caught something out of the corner of her eye. Heart hammering, she turned and looked.

A woman lay curled on her side, facing the fence. She was slender and had a cap of blonde hair.

"Afton!"

Claire leaped forward and gently turned the woman over, then jerked back, instinctively recognizing the look and smell of death. The woman's brown eyes were open and vacant.

It wasn't Afton. It was a woman wearing a blonde wig.

Claire leaned closer in horrified fascination and looked at the woman's dark eyes and dusky skin. The wig had fallen off more than halfway when Claire turned her over. Underneath the wig, the dead woman's hair was thick and black and curly. She had been wrapped in a tattered, lightweight raincoat.

Claire held a hand to her mouth and began to shiver visibly. *He wanted me to think it was Afton. He's playing games again.*

She turned to get the police officers from the front of the house and found herself staring at a man holding the gate open. He wore a baseball hat and dark glasses, along with dark jogging clothes. She was opening her mouth to ask him for assistance when he smiled at her.

It was the smile from her nightmares.

"Marie Claire. Sweet prey, you're next." The man spoke in a harsh whisper, and then was gone. His running footsteps echoed down the alley.

Claire decided that the fastest way to get the cops was to scream. It felt so good that she did it again.

Thirty seconds later, a cop appeared on the back porch, weapon drawn. His partner came running through the alley and stopped in front of the gate when he saw Claire.

She motioned frantically at the open gate. "White male, blue jogging shorts, blue cap, dark glasses. Hurry, hurry! He's running away!"

The younger officer immediately turned and sprinted up the alley. The second cop took her arm and started hustling her back to the safety of the house.

"Wait—she—" Claire pointed with trembling fingers toward the woman lying on her back by the fence.

The officer briefly assessed the victim. "She's not going anywhere. Get inside until I get some backup here."

He dragged Claire through the yard and into the house. He locked the back door, pulled her into the kitchen, and shut the blinds. Claire dropped into a chair and put her head in her hands while the officer called in backup and checked with his partner on the radio.

"Any luck, Stokes?"

A few seconds later his partner responded. "Nothing," he panted. "I saw him running, but he headed up to the university and I lost him in the crowd. I'm doing another check of the area. Campus police are assisting."

"I'll get the CSU. We've got another murder victim here." The officer turned to her. "What happened?"

"I heard the gate banging and went out to lock it."

The cop said something under his breath.

"I saw her—the dead woman—and thought it was Afton. Then he—he—said 'Marie Claire.' He knew my name. He said I was next." Her voice broke as she finished, and the officer put a hand on her shoulder to steady her.

"It's all right now. You're safe. I'll ask CSU to bring a sketch artist. Is there anything more you can tell us about the guy?"

She took a shaking breath and then another, calming herself. "He's a tall white male, at least six feet, with a medium build. Between the hat and glasses, I really didn't see much. I got the impression he had dark hair, but didn't see it that well. A blue baseball cap and navy jogging shorts are about all I can remember," Claire said.

The policeman repeated her description into the radio.

Claire sat with her face in her hands again, her mind reeling. *He could have killed me. I'd be another case in Sean's files.*

Sean.

Claire covered her mouth with her hand and unconsciously rocked herself for comfort.

Chapter 54

S ean and Aidan were two blocks from Afton's house when they heard the call sign of Claire's surveillance team on the police scanner. Aidan was driving, so it was Sean who turned up the sound.

"Need medical examiner and CSU at backyard, this location. Female DOA, mid-twenties, brown eyes and dark curly hair."

Sean's stomach flipped. "Sweet Jesus Christ. It can't be." But he knew all too well that it could.

Aidan floored the accelerator for the last block, then hit the brakes for a squealing stop in front of the house. Sean bailed out before the car was fully stopped and ran up the steps. The front door wasn't locked, which saved him the trouble of kicking it in. He ran through the entry and saw a flash of purple from the corner of his eye.

Claire was in the kitchen, head in her hands, wearing her short purple robe. She looked up at him as the front door slammed into the hallway so hard that it punched through the drywall.

The relief Sean felt overwhelmed him. With a muffled sound that was her name, he rushed into the kitchen and swept Claire up in a bone-crunching hug.

"Are you all right?" Sean asked, his voice raw with emotion. He could feel the tremors shaking her body.

"Yes. Oh, Sean." She wrapped her arms around him and held on with all her strength. She felt her eyes start to sting with tears, but she was afraid to give in to the emotions that were tearing her apart. Instead, she buried her head in the curve of Sean's neck and blocked out everything but him.

Sean closed his eyes, letting his face drop into the damp warmth of her curls. He pressed desperate kisses everywhere he could reach—her hair, forehead, cheeks, eyes. He breathed in her scent repeatedly and willed his heart to start beating normally again. He was only distantly aware of Aidan pulling Officer Peterson out of the kitchen to request an update.

After several minutes, Sean gently set Claire back down on the floor. He cupped her cheeks with both hands and looked into her shadowed eyes before kissing her lingeringly on the lips. She tried to reassure him with a weak smile.

"I'm all right," she said. "Really."

He dropped his forehead onto hers. "Sweetheart, I thought you were dead. I thought Peterson was reporting that he'd found *your* body in the backyard."

"Oh." Her heart turned over at the look on his face.

"Yeah, 'Oh.' You took ten years off my life."

"To tell you the truth, I thought I was dead, too."

"What the hell happened here tonight?"

Her lips trembled as she remembered coming face-to-face with the killer in the backyard. "I saw him. He put a dead woman in the backyard. And he was standing not ten feet away from me. He looked at me and said my name."

"Jesus."

She shivered and whispered raggedly, "He said I was next."

She flinched at the vicious words that came out of Sean's mouth. He saw her reaction and pulled her to him again. "It's all right, sweetheart. We'll get him, I promise."

She nodded and held on hard to him. It was the only way she would be able to keep herself from falling apart completely, and that was the last thing anyone needed from her right now.

"Everything okay in here?" Aidan asked from the doorway.

"She's fine," Sean said, stepping back from Claire reluctantly.

"Then you don't mind if I do this," Aidan said, coming into the kitchen and catching Claire up in a bear hug of his own. He landed a smacking kiss on her lips before she could catch her breath.

"You scared the shit out of us, lady."

Claire hugged Aidan back. "I was pretty scared, too."

Feeling tears threaten again, she ended the hug and stepped back, struggling for her disappearing composure. She straightened her shoulders and tightened the belt on her robe, knowing she had to hold herself together for a little while longer.

"I appreciate your concern, both of you. But there's someone outside who needs you more right now."

"Claire—" Sean began, concerned by her visible effort to control herself.

"No. You need to go do your job. I'll be fine right here.

Believe me, I'm not going anywhere. But you need to do what—what you can for her. She looked so—so *small*."

Aidan went out the back door and out onto the porch.

Turning away from Sean, she went to a cupboard and began taking out the makings for coffee and tea. She measured scoops of ground coffee and poured them into the coffeemaker. Her hands barely shook.

Sean looked at the strong line of her back for a long moment, then brushed a hand over her wild curls and said, "Have I told you how great you are?"

He was in the backyard before she could answer.

Chapter 55

Sean went outside to where Aidan was making notes on the murder scene. They both stood over the body for several minutes, studying the details and mentally comparing them to previous cases. There was no blood or sign of a struggle in the yard.

"He stabbed her somewhere else and dumped the body here. No blood on the scene here—and probably not on him—because he wrapped her in the raincoat after she was dead," Sean said.

Aidan nodded. "He's changing his routine. He wants to make a statement. Look at the wig—he doesn't like blondes. He likes dark-haired women. But he wanted us to think it was Afton." He shook his head as he took in the blonde wig with its trendy pixie cut.

"Wrong," Sean said. "He wanted *Claire* to find the body and think it was Afton. He's playing with her emotions. He's building up to something big, and really getting off in the process. Keeley warned me about this."

"And the killer is improvising, too," Aidan pointed out.

"I think the actual encounter with Claire wasn't planned. But once he got here and the opportunity presented itself, he couldn't resist the temptation."

"He's taking bigger and bigger chances to get to her," Sean said grimly.

They looked back toward the house. Claire stood on the top step waiting for them to notice her.

"I've got coffee and tea for whoever wants it. Sodas as well," she said, as if she were offering refreshments at a backyard barbeque.

"Thanks. Is the sketch artist here?" Sean asked.

"In the kitchen drinking coffee."

"Work with her, okay? Then get some rest. It's going to be a long night."

She hesitated, then went back into the house. Sean turned as Peterson and Stokes walked through the back gate with frustration evident on their faces.

"We've done a thorough check of the alley and the roads all the way up to O Street and the university gates, and we've got nothing," Officer Peterson said in disgust. "It's all paved, so there are no footprints. No trash or papers left behind. No one saw anything or even heard a dog bark. What is this guy, a ghost?"

Sean said nothing, just examined the broken padlock and open gate. He turned his head and looked toward the house, realizing that Claire's room overlooked the backyard. With the drapes open, he could see right into the room. At the moment, she was standing in front of the closet. He watched her select some clothing from there before moving toward the bathroom.

"We've got to get both of them out of here," Sean said.

Aidan followed Sean's gaze. "The normal safe house is already being used by a witness from a drug trial. I don't think we want Claire or Olivia anywhere near that sleaze-bag. I guess we could use a hotel."

Sean shook his head and checked his watch. "I want them to go to separate locations anyway. There's a chance the killer has been tracking Claire through Olivia's move-ments. I want to make sure that doesn't happen again."

"Any idea when Olivia will be back?" Aidan asked.

"No. Peterson said she went shopping at one of those outlet malls, so it could be a while. Her cell phone is off."

Aidan shoved his hands in his pockets and waited, knowing what was coming next.

"I'm going to take Claire somewhere and lie low for about thirty-six hours," Sean said. "No one—not even the surveillance team—will know where we are. I'll take the sedan. Someone at the station can drop my truck off for you when you're ready to take Olivia to her new location."

"If that's the way you want to do things," Aidan said.

"It is. Once I'm sure the killer has been thrown off the scent, we'll find a safe location for both of them."

Aidan considered remaining silent, then thought better of it. "For someone who's trying to keep his distance from a witness, you're sure going about it in an odd way."

Sean gave his partner a hard look. "Someone needs to protect her. She knows and trusts me."

"And what about when we got here tonight?"

"What about it? I was glad to see she was alive. She needed to be held."

"But you needed it more," Aidan said. "I felt like I was intruding on a very intimate scene."

"Christ, you make it sound like we had sex right there in the kitchen," Sean said, ignoring the fact that he and Claire had once very nearly done just that.

"No, but sometimes emotional intimacy is more dangerous than sex," Aidan shot back. "And what's more, you know it, since you've spent your entire adult life avoiding it."

"Do you really want to get into my past history with women right now?" Sean asked between his teeth, aware of the fact they were not alone.

"I'm not attacking you. I just want to make sure you're thinking straight. I want you to ask yourself why you're breaking all the rules with Claire, and whether you're doing her any favors by acting this way in the middle of a homicide investigation."

They were both silent, aware that Sean's behavior today had edged over the line of professionalism—again. Only this time there were witnesses.

But the truth of the matter was, he wouldn't do things any differently if given the choice. Even now he felt an overwhelming need to find Claire, to hold her close to him and make sure she was going to be okay, mentally as well as physically. And he would do just that, once he got her out of here.

"She could have died today," Sean said. "Do you think I give a rat's ass about the rules right now?"

"No."

"I'm taking Claire with me. You can read into that whatever you want. I want her in a secure location for a day or two while we look for a more permanent arrangement. They're not coming back here."

Aidan sighed and gave in. "Johnston and his family are leaving for ten days. Caribbean cruise or something. Maybe we can use his house in Alexandria once they're gone."

"Good idea. Would you take care of that with Johnston and the captain?"

"Sure."

Aidan turned back to the dead woman, thinking how damn glad he was that it wasn't Claire. He couldn't imagine what Sean had felt before he'd found out that Claire was alive.

"I'll see if there are any missing persons matching her description—either blonde or brunette," Aidan said.

Sean nodded, but didn't feel optimistic. The victim, while having a superficial resemblance to Afton with the wig, was obviously a young woman used to hard living. Needle tracks scarred her dirty arms. She looked like she'd existed on the edge of civilized society—a woman who wouldn't be missed anytime soon. A quick and easy kill.

He told me I was next.

Sean's gut clenched, but he didn't say anything—he just studied the corpse as the Crime Scene Unit pulled up in the alley behind Afton's house. Aidan stepped aside as the team began to set up.

"Put a rush on all lab work, especially fingerprints," Sean said as he stepped back. "It looks like she was killed somewhere else, so we've got another crime scene somewhere in the city. Keep an eye out for anything that would help find it."

"We'll let you know as soon as we've got something, Detective," the supervisor promised. "Believe me, this case is getting top priority for labs and manpower."

For the next hour Sean and Aidan watched the crime scene team carefully gather evidence while early darkness descended. When the medical examiner's van came to pick up the body, the detectives went back into the house, knowing there was little else they could do that night. Peterson was gulping a cup of hot coffee in the kitchen.

"Where's Claire?" Sean asked.

"Upstairs."

Sean found Claire standing by the window in a dark room. He went to her and looked down. Someone was bringing a body bag through the back gate. He closed the drapes and flipped on a light before he turned to Claire.

"Don't torture yourself," he said. "There was nothing you could do about any of it."

Claire ran a listless hand through curls that were still damp. "All I can think of is that poor girl was murdered for no other reason than to terrify me. And it did. When I thought that body was Afton, I . . ." Her voice died.

Sean kept his hands in his pockets. It was either that or reach for her, and this wasn't a good time or place. "The killer gets off on power, on being in control."

"He—he seems unreal, like a ghost, not human." She tilted her head back and shook hair out of her eyes.

"He's human," Sean said, "even though we'd feel better about the human race if he wasn't. But he's a real person with real fingerprints and real mental problems. He can be analyzed, understood, and caught."

"Can he? This house is under police surveillance, and he killed her—"

"Not here," Sean cut in.

"—dumped the body," she continued without a pause, "had a chat with me and wasn't spotted by the police. Did any of the neighbors see him?"

"We've got a team out asking."

"Did they see him?" she insisted.

Sean sighed. "No. He's either really stupid or really willing to take risks."

"He isn't stupid. He knew just what buttons to push to terrify me. The blonde wig, the threat."

"Up to now we've been forced to play the game his way. That stops now. Pack up, Claire. You're leaving."

"What about Livvie?"

"Aidan will take care of her. I'm taking you someplace quiet for a day or two, until we find another house."

"All right, I'm ready." Claire pointed to her bags, which were neatly lined up by the door. "I knew I wouldn't be staying here."

Sean took Claire's large bag and let her lead the way downstairs. She went out the front door without a glance at the lights and activity at the rear of the house. The front yard was so normal it made her shiver.

He settled her into the front seat of the car. When she didn't pick up her seat belt, he reached across her to fasten it. He started the engine, worried by her silence. They drove without speaking for several minutes.

"Did tonight help you remember anything from the other murder?" Sean asked.

"No. Just that this guy is real and I can't forget for a moment he's out there."

"He's real, but he's not going to get another chance at you, so don't think about it."

"What about future dates with Camelot?" Claire said, thinking about her role in the investigation.

"Your dating days are history. From now on, you don't leave my sight. No one but me knows where you're staying. Neither you nor Olivia will be going back to work, or even calling in to the office. Hell, I don't even want you logging into the network remotely, okay? No grocery shopping, no day spas, nothing that has been part of your routine for the last month."

Claire was too numb to argue, and instead looked out the window. She was so emotionally spent that she could barely respond to what was happening around her. The only thing she could do was bounce between the blankness in the dead girl's eyes and Sean's urgent, protective embrace.

Finally Claire closed her eyes and put her head against the seat. She didn't move until Sean unfastened her seat belt and said, "We're here."

"Here" was a beautiful hotel with an excellent security system. Sean ignored the bellman, carried their bags, and showed Claire to the door of the suite. He put her bags in the bedroom and went straight to the lavish bathroom. Soon hot water was thundering from the elaborate faucet on the jetted tub. He added a few colorful bath bubbles for the hell of it.

"Go in and soak," he said. "If you don't relax your muscles, you'll never sleep tonight."

Automatically Claire looked over at the suite's only bed.

"When I'm ready to turn in, I'll take the foldout bed in the living room," he said, stuffing a plush hotel robe into her hands. "I'll order dinner and a bottle of wine from room service while you steam up the place. Any preferences?"

The thought of food made her wince. "I'm not really hungry."

"I didn't ask whether you were hungry, I asked whether you wanted to choose what you're going to eat or not."

She smiled faintly at his surly response. "Something light, I guess. Whatever. I trust you."

She went into the bathroom and closed the door, twisting her hair into a knot on top of her head. She took off her clothes and slipped into the hot, foamy water with a sigh. Five minutes later there was a knock on the door.

"Are you decent?" Sean asked.

"I'm wearing what people usually wear in the bath."

"Better dive into the suds. I'm bringing you something."

She sank to her chin in the bubbles, feeling ridiculously shy with a man who was—or had been—her lover.

Sean walked in carrying a brimming glass of red wine. "I found this in the liquor cabinet. I want you to drink the whole thing. It will help you to take the edge off your adrenaline high."

She eyed the huge glass. If she drank it she would lose some of the emotional control she'd been rebuilding shred by shred. On the other hand, she might also forget the sight of the dead girl's eyes and the killer's twisted smile.

"Medicine, huh?" she asked.

"Definitely."

Claire reached for the glass and took a healthy swallow. Raising her eyebrow at Sean as he continued to hover, she took another gulp to satisfy him.

"I'll call you when dinner gets here," he said, closing the door as he left the steamy bathroom.

Sighing, Claire idly rubbed her big toe around the spigot, catching the occasional drop of hot water that still fell into the bubbles surrounding her. She sipped and sipped again, deciding that the wine was the tastiest medicine she'd ever had. Between that and the bath, she was feeling warm for the first time since she'd heard Afton's back gate banging in the wind.

Suddenly she was seeing a corpse and vacant dark eyes. *No*, she told herself, *I'm not going there tonight. Tonight I'm going to concentrate on life and living.*

Sean.

It was time to quit fooling herself. Her last thoughts before going to sleep were about him, and first thoughts on waking. The day didn't really begin until she saw him. She'd never felt more alive than when she was with that impossible, infuriating, tender, and incredibly wonderful man.

I love him. It was that simple—independence and self-preservation be damned.

She felt shaky but better for having admitted her feelings to herself. Then she took a swallow of wine and wondered what to do next. Afton had been right. Claire should take whatever she could, for as long as she could, and be grateful for the opportunity to love a man like Sean. And maybe, just maybe, the maddening man could be persuaded to think the way she did.

From the suite came the sound of room service setting up dinner. Smiling, she drank the last of the wine for courage, grabbed a towel, and reached for her toiletries bag. She couldn't do anything about the future right now. She couldn't even be certain she would survive the next few days. But she had this moment, and she wasn't going to waste it.

She smiled as she caught her own reflection in the steamy mirror. Detective Sean Richter didn't know it yet, but he was in for the night of his life.

Chapter 56

Sean impatiently paced the suite's living room. He'd already told Claire their dinner had arrived, but she was still locked in the bathroom.

Easy. She had a hell of a scare tonight, so maybe she's earned some alone time. Everything here can wait until she's ready.

He thought about the box stashed in the room service cart and the whopping tip he'd given the bellman for rounding up some razor blades and such for Sean, who hadn't expected to be spending the night away from home.

He splashed a bit more wine in his own glass, though he wasn't planning on drinking any. Then he wiped a hand across his forehead. Even without his jacket and shoulder harness, his body felt hot, edgy. The dishes were all arranged and the wine was poured. He thought about the pale, distant expression on her face as they'd checked into the hotel and added another inch of wine to her glass. She needed to relax and not think about the man who could have killed her tonight.

Sean needed some reassurance, too, because he felt like he'd let her down. That son of a bitch never should have gotten within a Wyoming mile of her, but he had. Since Sean couldn't take the killer out at this point, the only way he could think to comfort everyone tonight was to wrap Claire in a cocoon of warmth and security. A hot bath, good food, wine, and then he'd tuck her into bed and sit in a chair guarding her, or sit up with her on the couch and hold her hand all night if need be. Whatever it took to reassure her that the sun would come up tomorrow and she would be there to see it.

As for any more than hand-holding, after the clumsy way he'd handled things the night they'd made love, he didn't blame her for watching him with wary black eyes. He'd really blown things by rushing her into sex, then pulling away afterward. He would have to be very careful not to place any demands on her physically at this point. If he was lucky and handled things right, maybe she would give him another chance when all this was over.

A cloud of steam and Claire's delicate perfume fogged his brain. She was walking across the bedroom toward him, wrapped in an oversize robe and looking good enough to eat. He smiled at her and held a chair out at the table.

"I feel silly eating off fine china when I'm only wearing a bathrobe," Claire said, picking at the plush collar and wondering if she should have changed into something more sexy. Well, outright seduction was new to her, and she would just have to learn it as she went along.

"It's pretty chilly in here with the air-conditioning," Sean said, looking away from her fingers touching the robe where it opened on flushed skin. "Dressing warm is a good idea."

Sean's prosaic answer set Claire back. She'd been fishing for a compliment, but he was more interested in serving baked chicken and rice than admiring the picture she made with her dark hair and eyes against the snowy white robe.

"This looks good. I guess I'm hungrier than I thought." She picked up her fork and smiled shyly at Sean.

He stared at her for a moment before returning her smile. "I'm glad. There's lots of good protein in that. Eat up."

"Why, am I going to need energy for something tonight?" She actually twirled a curl around her finger as she spoke, then bit her lip, wondering if she had gone too far. This seduction thing was tricky, and subtlety was against her nature.

"A full stomach is the best way I can think of to ensure a good night's sleep," Sean said with forced cheer, telling himself that there was no way she was coming on to him. She was just relaxed and vulnerable and trusted him. He'd live up to that trust if it killed him. He turned to set the serving dishes back on the tray.

Claire rolled her eyes at his back and ate silently for a few minutes. Then she tried again, this time ditching the subtlety. "Could you pour me some more water, please? I'm feeling awfully warm." She loosened the belt of her robe, allowing the fabric to gape at her neck and expose the top curves of her breasts. She fanned herself and looked at him with innocent black eyes.

Sean frowned at her. "How much wine have you had?"

"Just the one glass."

"The bathwater wasn't that hot. Maybe you're coming down with something." He reached across the table and felt her forehead like a nurse.

She slapped his hand away in exasperation. "Jesus, you

have to be the densest man on the planet. In case you haven't noticed, I'm throwing myself at you!"

Sean looked like he'd been hit with a two-by-four. Then his expression hardened and he pushed his chair back from the table. He went to stand by the window with his back to her.

"I thought, given your reaction to seeing me earlier tonight, you'd be a little more receptive," she said. "Is something wrong?"

"Oh, I don't know, let me think. Maybe the fact that you could have died today?" Sean asked. "How's that for wrong?"

"I realize that. It put a lot of things into perspective for me. It changed everything."

He sighed. "Nothing has changed. Your life is pretty much the definition of fucked up right now. You've been scared shitless and you aren't in any frame of mind to make decisions about anything. Your new 'perspective' is an adrenaline-induced hormonal rush."

"Bullshit."

He turned to face her. "There's too much going on in your life right now, all of it bad. When—"

"That's not true," she interrupted. "What I'm feeling right now, what we had together before, these are the good things in my life. Being here with you tonight feels *right*. What really scares me is the thought of never feeling this way again."

He didn't trust himself to say anything as she stood and walked over to him.

"That was the most terrifying part of looking at the killer," she said, "seeing my own death written in his face—knowing that I wouldn't see you again. You were what I was thinking about at that moment, just you."

"Sweetheart, don't." Sean touched her cheek, moved beyond words. "I'm trying to do the right thing here, but I want you so much and it's so wrong."

"Why? I'm alive, and I want to feel alive with you."

He stared down at her, drowning in the black depths of her eyes, torn by a temptation he'd never known.

She saw this, smiled sadly, and moved back from him. "But it has to be your choice. I'm going into this with my eyes open. I need to know that you are, too."

Sean thought about all the reasons he should take Claire to her room, tuck her in, and make his own bed alone on the couch.

For about a second and a half.

Then he pushed everything aside but the fact that she needed him as much as he needed her. He stepped forward, sank his fingers into her hair, and kissed her until the room began to spin around them both.

"My eyes are wide open, and all I can see is you, Claire."

The smile she gave him said he was the only man in the world. He kissed the smile gently, took her hand, and led her to the couch. She hesitated when he motioned for her to sit. Instead, she pushed against his shoulders to send him tumbling to the cushions. Or she tried, but he outweighed her by about a hundred pounds. When she pushed again, he took the hint and sprawled back on the couch.

Trembling with a combination of nerves and anticipation, she stood in front of him and loosened the belt on her robe. Two shrugs of her shoulders, and it was sliding to the floor to puddle at her feet.

His nostrils flared as he breathed in her perfume, and his hands clenched at his sides. He sat silently, running his eyes over her body as if it were their first time. It had been dark that night in his truck, and he was determined to glut himself on her beauty this time. He took in the paleness of her skin, the taut thrust of her breasts, the flare of her hips and the sleekly muscled line of her thighs.

Claire stood there, nipples erect and legs quivering, waiting for Sean to say something. Or do something. Anything.

"Um, I'm feeling a little self-conscious here. Could you give me some kind of sign?" She tried to joke, but her voice broke and a flush rose in her cheeks.

He leaned forward and wrapped his arms around her hips, burying his face against her belly and rubbing against its soft curve. He smelled the scent of her perfumed skin, then plunged his tongue into her navel while he shaped her buttocks gently with his hands.

"Oh!"

"Ask and ye shall receive," Sean said, nuzzling her again before lifting his head and pulling a breast into his mouth.

She slid her hands into his hair, letting the cool softness run through her fingers. Her eyes closed and her head tipped back as he wrapped her in sensation from front to back. She felt his fingers trail down to the sensitive under-curve of her buttocks, and drew a shaky breath when he lingered there.

She held that breath when those fingers slid to the insides of her thighs, trailing along the tender skin until they reached her knees. Before she knew it, he had nudged her legs apart and moved his knees between her own. She grew tense with anticipation as her most vulnerable flesh was laid bare before him.

He leaned forward and stopped an inch from her body,

drawing in the scent of her arousal, noting the way her thighs trembled and her belly had grown taut. Before she could say anything, he closed the distance and pressed his mouth between her legs. His tongue slid over her slick flesh.

She jumped at the lightning bolt of sensation. "Oh, God. Sean, no."

"Mmmmm," he said, licking her delicately. "Definitely yes."

He grasped her legs and widened them further, opening her up to the most intimate kind of loving a man could give a woman. As his tongue and lips and teeth caressed her, she dug her hands in his hair and held on until she couldn't stand up any longer.

"Let go, sweetheart. I've got you." Sean wrapped his hands around her hips to hold her, then pressed his tongue inside her body in a caress that nearly sent her over the edge.

As if it belonged to someone else, she listened to her voice cry and moan, begging him to stop, then begging him to go faster, harder. When he sucked her most tender flesh into his mouth and stroked it with the tip of his tongue, she went taut and climaxed while she called out his name.

When she came back to herself, he was leaning against the cushions, holding her in his arms as she straddled his lap. Her bare skin was pressed to his fully dressed body, and her face was buried against his neck. She could feel his pulse beating underneath her lips, and kissed the spot before running her tongue across it. His heart rate kicked up a notch.

When she gently sank her teeth into his neck, his body jerked under hers. She felt his hands in her hair, pulling her head back. She looked at him dreamily, then moved to kiss him. As their mouths pressed together and their tongues wrapped around each other, she could feel the tension vibrating through his body. She pulled away from his mouth, looked at him, and smiled at him in anticipation.

Sean felt his body grow even harder as he took in Claire's positively lustful grin. She licked her lips and began to unbutton his shirt. He knew he was in serious trouble.

Without a word she undid his shirt, stopping for a sultry kiss between each button. Once she had his shirt off and his jeans undone, he remembered what he'd forgotten up to now.

"Wait. Don't move a muscle," he said.

Kissing her, he gently set her aside, went to the bag on the room service cart, and fished out a box of condoms. He pulled off his jeans and underwear on the way back to the couch, sat down, and lifted her over his lap again.

"You can go back to what you were doing," he said, filling his hands with the curves of her hips.

She slanted a look at the box of condoms, then raised her eyebrow at him. "Pretty confident, huh?"

"More like resigned," he answered with a playful nip at her mouth. Then he leaned back to look her in the eye. "I got them just in case my willpower gave out. You know I'll always take care of you, sweetheart."

She nodded and felt her throat grow tight as she pushed the hair back from his forehead. "And you do a wonderful job of it. Now why don't you let me take care of you for a change?" She trailed her hand invitingly down the midline of his body as she spoke.

"I've never had any complaints," he said. "Not one. But if you insist . . ." Smiling wickedly, he placed his arms along the back of the couch. He lifted his head to receive her kiss, letting her explore his mouth with her tongue.

Within moments, he was no longer smiling. His face grew tense and sweat appeared on his forehead as Claire moved her mouth down to his chest, where she tested his strength with her teeth. Her hands trailed ahead of her lips, reaching to touch his erection with delicate butterfly strokes that concentrated on the throbbing tip.

He shook with the effort of enduring Claire's loving, when what he really wanted to do was grab her and bury himself in the moist flesh that was rubbing against his thighs with her every movement. But this was her time, and the torture was too sweet to end so soon.

She slid to the floor and made her way down from his chest to his belly, then became distracted by the tantalizing line of hair that ran from there to his groin. She teased that soft arrow of hair with her open mouth and slow strokes of her tongue, ignoring the thrust of flesh that silently demanded the same treatment.

When she slid around his erection without so much as touching it, Sean lost control and groaned his frustration out loud. She smiled angelically at him before moving to nip the taut lines of his thighs, which were clenched with the force of his passion.

"Claire, please—"

"Please what? Please this?" Claire reached for him and enveloped his erection with both of her hands, sliding up and down with firm strokes that had him rolling his head on the back of the couch in mindless need. When she leaned forward and slid her tongue across the tip, his hips moved toward her and his hands clenched into fists.

She felt a feminine power and joy in giving him such pleasure that was unlike anything she had ever experienced. She released him and blew across his wet flesh, calling his name softly.

His eyes slitted open and he groaned as he watched her take him into her mouth, laving every inch of him with her tongue and making his world spin with the suction of her mouth. He took her head in his hands and taught her the motion that gave him the most pleasure, and she soon had him spread before her with a vulnerability that belied his physical strength.

After a few minutes of sublime agony, he grabbed for the box of condoms and pried her mouth gently away from him.

"No more," he panted. "I need you too much."

She looked up at him with her wild black eyes, flushed cheeks, and wet red lips. He groaned and almost came right then and there.

She smiled as if she knew, then moved to help him with the condom. She climbed up into his lap again, then took his flesh and guided it home to her body. They both closed their eyes and sighed as she lowered herself until he filled her completely.

After pausing a moment to savor the sensation and catch her breath, she raised herself up until he almost slipped from her body. Then, acting on instinct, she lowered herself only partway down. She clenched her sheath around him, then raised and lowered herself again, never taking him completely into her.

As she repeated the motion again and again, Sean lost control of his senses. He panted and arched and dug his fingers into her hips until they left faint bruises as he tried to bury himself in her. But Claire's leg muscles were strong, and she resisted his attempts to complete their union. Shushing his groaned protests with her lips, Claire felt her own body shudder and wondered how much longer she would be able to resist plunging herself down and ending the delicious torture.

"Witch," Sean grated. "Stop teasing and let me love you."

Claire kissed him again. "A wise man once told me teasing is half the fun."

She lowered herself a little more, then clenched the muscles in her lower body as she raised up again. They both groaned at the sensation. Things continued at her slow pace until his hand slipped between their bodies and his fingers found the flesh that held the key to her pleasure. She paused in midstroke, shocked into arching and crying out as he worked his magic with the gentle tip of his thumb.

She arched again to take him all the way into her body, then held herself against him, shaking with need. "You win," she said breathlessly.

"I think this is a win-win situation," he said, and buried himself in her as they both began to climax.

Chapter 57

The man stepped out of his apartment to pick up the Sunday paper, eager to read about the latest murder in the city. He sat at the table where his breakfast waited, shook out the paper, and began scanning the headlines. He impatiently read about the discovery of a body in a house in Georgetown. The details were sketchy, as the paper had gone to press before the police were willing to release much information. So far there was no information about the connection of this murder to the others he'd committed.

His good mood began to dissolve.

He read on, looking for more information on the killing, but there was none. He flipped past the front page, feeling disappointment and anger build in equal amounts. His thumbnail clicked more quickly against his teeth as he fumed about stupid cops who couldn't recognize a serial murderer when he dumped bodies right in front of them.

He was so distracted that he almost missed the story that had been pushed to page three. Apparently some reporter had made following the murder cases her ticket to journalistic fame. He could feel excitement begin to flow through his body as he read her attempts to put the pieces of the story together. He stopped to read again the woman's blistering analysis of the police investigation to date. He closed his eyes and let the arousal build as he thought of the game he was playing with the police, and how he was clearly in the lead.

His hard-on shriveled pitifully when he read the last paragraph of the story, about the eyewitness and the appointment with Camelot Dating Service. A hollow feeling replaced his excitement as he realized this was one thing that could possibly lead back to him. He'd had no idea Camelot was located in that office building off Dupont Circle—the company must have moved from its previous location.

His mind raced as he considered how to deal with this new twist. At least now he knew why Marie Claire and the police were spending so much time at the office building near Dupont Circle—she'd been a member of the dating service. Now that the reporter had blown Marie Claire's cover, though, he doubted that she'd be going back to Camelot.

The man felt a flutter of concern. He might not be able to follow Marie Claire so easily without her predictable schedule between the office building near Dupont Circle and the house in Georgetown. Of course, he now had the information on the police officer who'd been practically glued to Marie Claire for the past few weeks. He comforted himself with the knowledge that he would still be able to keep tabs on her through Detective Sean Richter. It would be risky working so close to the cops, as he'd discovered to his chagrin last night, yet he'd been able to get away easily. He planned on doing it all again very soon.

But first he needed to find out where his sweet prey was hiding.

Chapter 58

Washington, D.C.
Early Sunday afternoon

Claire woke to a bright, sunny room and the unfamiliar weight of Sean's arm around her waist. He lay on his stomach with his eyes closed, so she decided to let him sleep. After last night, he'd certainly earned it.

Feeling smug, she crept out of bed and slipped into the shower, letting the hot water pummel her and massage away some of the aches in her body. She finished quickly and was just stepping out and wrapping a towel around herself when Sean appeared in the doorway.

"I missed the best part," he said, eyeing her towel. "You should have gotten me up."

She ran her eyes over his gorgeous, naked body. His eyes were a little puffy with sleep, his hair was standing on end in back, and he'd never looked better to her. She smiled at him, undid the knot on her towel, and stepped back into the shower. After she turned the water on, she looked over her shoulder, silently beckoning Sean to join her.

They washed each other more times than was necessary, reluctant to give up the pleasure of soapy hands on slick, wet skin. Sean insisted on washing her hair, marveling at its length when wet.

"I never would have guessed how long it is," he said, stroking his fingers down to the middle of her back to lather her hair.

"It's the damn curls. One day I swear I'm going to get them straightened."

"Over my dead body. I love these curls. They remind me of how wild you are."

Claire looked into his hungry blue eyes and shivered, thinking of how they had spent the night. "Enough of that talk, or I'm going to starve to death right in front of you."

His eyelids half lowered as he looked at her from dripping hair to wet feet. "I don't want you to lose an ounce. I'll call room service." He stepped out of the shower, wrapped himself in a towel, and left to place the call.

When Claire walked into the living room several minutes later, Sean was on the balcony, sprawled on an oversize chaise. He looked up and told her room service would be about half an hour, then held out a hand for her to join him on the lounge.

Claire nestled against his side and thought how little she knew about him. "So how did you decide to be a detective?" she asked, curious about the man who had become the center of her life.

"After ten years in the special forces, it wasn't exactly like I had a lot of career choices," he said. "I couldn't see myself selling life insurance or something. I was interested in police work, so I went to the academy and got my degree, then took an open position with Aidan's department. We both just gravitated to the Cold Cases Division because the work was challenging. We also get more freedom in how we handle cases. After pretty much being my own boss my whole life, that was appealing."

"You're very good at what you do."

He shrugged. "So many cases never get solved, and some of them haunt you."

She thought of her own case and wondered if it would be one of those that would haunt him.

"Yours isn't going to be like that," he promised, stroking his hand down her damp hair.

She leaned her head against his shoulder again, then noticed his cell phone sitting on the balcony table.

"I'm surprised Aidan hasn't called you yet," she said.

Sean looked away from her. "I'm not. I turned the phone off last night."

"Why? Don't you want to know what's happening with the investigation?"

"Sure." He looked at the phone like it was a snake. "But if I turn it on, then I'd get a call from my boss chewing out my ass for taking a witness into protective custody without authorization. Not to mention getting involved with her in the process."

"It's not like I'm going to turn you in for harassing me." She sat up with a frown. "I don't plan on saying anything. What happens between us is our business, no one else's."

"You won't need to say a word. It's written all over your expressive face." He smiled faintly and stroked a finger down her soft cheek. "Besides, there were plenty of officers around yesterday who saw how things are between us. The word is bound to have gotten back to my boss by now."

"Oh, God, I didn't even think of that. I never wanted you to get in trouble. I'm sorry, I shouldn't have . . ."

"Shouldn't have what? Shouldn't have been irresistible to me? Don't be ridiculous. I knew exactly what I was doing, and I have no regrets. Now it's time to see what the damages are."

Claire got up to pace while Sean turned on the phone and called Aidan.

"Where the hell are you? Is everything okay?" Aidan demanded without even bothering to say hello.

"We're in a safe place, and we're fine."

"As long as you're not at your place. Remember how I was supposed to have your truck brought over from the station?"

"Yeah," Sean said.

"I asked Teresa to bring it at the end of her shift. She stopped at the market on the way, and when she was going back to the truck there was a guy standing at the passenger side. She called out to him and he ran away, but when she got to the truck she saw that he'd broken in and gone through the glove box."

"And?" Sean knew there was more.

"Your registration is gone."

"Beautiful. Just fucking beautiful," Sean said, rubbing his neck.

The vehicle registration had his name, home address, and vehicle license plate printed on them. With that information, anyone would be able to easily track his movements.

"There's more," Aidan continued. "Teresa said she had a feeling she was being followed by a white car after this incident, so she took the long way to Afton's place to be sure. She figured she'd lead the guy right to all the cops parked at the crime scene, but the tail pulled off as she turned onto P Street—like he knew where she was going."

"He's after Claire again," Sean whispered harshly, not wanting her to overhear.

"I'm sure of it. When I left with Olivia in your truck late last night, I picked up a tail about four blocks from Afton's place. I played with him for a while, then pulled down an alley. I got out to confront the guy, but he took off in a white Taurus with no license plates. He was wearing a ball cap and sunglasses."

Sean sat pinching the bridge of his nose with his fingers, trying to think of a way to deal with this dangerous twist. He'd been worried last night that the killer was following Olivia to get to Claire, but now he realized he could have been the one endangering her all along. He'd used his truck several times to drive Claire to or from Camelot, or to follow her on a date. Clearly the killer had picked up on that.

"You thinking what I'm thinking?" Sean asked bitterly.

"Don't beat yourself up, cousin. We both missed it. We underestimated this guy."

"What about Michaels?" Sean asked.

"He admits he hadn't considered this angle, either. But he still wants your ass for taking off with Claire last night. Brace yourself—he'll probably yank you off the lead investigator role, though he's too good a cop to pull you from the case completely. He knows you're our best chance."

"He'd be right to fire me, and I know it. I knew it last night and I didn't care. I still don't care, if you want to know the truth."

"Yeah, well, that's not the approach I'd take with him if I were you. You might want to try for a little more groveling and contrition."

Sean grimaced and paced on the balcony, but it was too

small. He walked into the bedroom and did more circuits while Aidan talked.

"There's a press conference at five this afternoon," Aidan said. "Captain Michaels wants you here for it. I think he's going to throw you to the wolves as part of your punishment."

Sean looked at his watch. Only a few hours before he would be separated from Claire. He wasn't ready for that. But after Captain Michaels got through ripping him a new asshole, that was exactly what would happen.

"I'll be there for the conference."

"I'll have Olivia with me at the station," Aidan said. "We'll take good care of Claire for you."

Sean disconnected, sat on the bed, and stared into space.

He felt Claire sit next to him on the bed. She ran a hand down the soft cloth of the hotel robe he wore, trying to offer comfort without understanding why he was upset.

"Can you talk about it?" she asked.

"The shit is hitting the fan as we speak. We need to get you to the station and then Aidan will—" Sean broke off and dragged her into his arms, holding her against him and wondering how to explain that they had to be separated in order to keep her safe.

"It's all right, love." She returned his fierce hug and stroked her hands down his back. "Whatever it is, it's all right."

Sean pulled away and sat on an oversized chair between the bed and the window. He rested his elbows on his knees and hung his head down, rubbing his hands tiredly over his eyes. "It's not all right. I've really messed up, and you're in more danger because of it."

She came over to him. "I don't believe that. Whatever has happened, we'll deal with it together."

Sean lifted his head and looked at her, seeing the absolute trust in her eyes.

"We should leave," he said, "but I don't want to let go yet. I have a really bad feeling that if I do—" He broke off and shook his head, not wanting to frighten her further.

She didn't know what to say, so she offered comfort with her lips and her hands, bending to kiss Sean and stroke the sides of his face. He kissed her back tenderly, then with growing hunger. He pulled her down to him and held her close. His kisses grew more purposeful, and he all but tore her robe off in his sudden desperation to get closer. He undid his own robe, pressing their bodies together from knee to mouth, urgently trying to push aside his fears by loving her one more time.

She sensed his turmoil and kissed him harder as he leaned back in the chair and reached for the condoms on the bedside table. A moment later she shifted and took him deep into her body, arching her back at the feeling of his sheathed flesh sliding into her once again. She stopped in that position and he rested his forehead against her chin. When she tried to rock against him, his hands on her hips stilled the movement. She looked into his eyes and shivered at the blue fire she saw there.

"Let me move," she said softly.

"No. It would be over too soon. I want to stay like this." He pressed his forehead to hers and watched her wild black eyes.

They stayed that way, intimately joined, while their heart rates and breathing accelerated and their muscles trembled with the strain of holding still. She could feel the pulse of him inside her, and the muscles of her sheath reacted involuntarily. When they rippled around him, he groaned softly and grew harder still inside her.

She gasped and pulsed around him again, holding him tightly and invisibly straining to press her body even closer to his. The tension grew and grew, but they remained locked together, motionless, their only movements hidden away deep inside Claire's body.

They held on to each other as the sensations built and then overflowed, causing them to shudder and cry out. They rode the storm together, and eventually the sound of labored breathing and gasping moans was replaced by quiet sighs and soft kisses.

Then he held her, just held her, trying not to believe that he'd led a killer straight to the woman he would die to protect.

Chapter 59

Aidan was seated at his desk, but he jumped up when Sean and Claire walked in.

"Any problems?" Aidan asked.

"We're clean. No one even tried to follow us."

"Good. I'll take her and Olivia to Johnston's place in a sedan with tinted windows, and we'll have a couple of unmarked cars ride along behind."

"Where's Livvie?" Claire asked.

"I put her in the conference room. You should go to her before the captain—"

"Richter!"

Sean snapped to attention at the sound of his name being barked out by Captain Michaels. Like a man about to face a firing squad, he turned toward his supervisor.

"Sir."

"I don't know what the hell you think you're doing, but it stops right here. Do you understand me?" Michaels was red-faced as he came to a stop three feet away from Sean.

"Yes," Sean said. He'd broken just about every rule

there was and would take the fallout without complaint, if only because he'd ended up putting Claire at risk.

"You're a good investigator, one of the best I've known. But you've lost your objectivity on this case." The captain shot a look at Claire, who was sitting white-faced and miserable at Sean's desk.

Sean bit his tongue and remembered Aidan's advice about groveling. "Yes, sir."

"The only reason I'm not going to fire your ass is I know this isn't like you. You've never so much as looked sideways at anyone involved in one of your cases. But whatever is going on between you and the witness ends here."

Claire's head snapped up at this, but she stayed quiet when Aidan placed a warning hand on her shoulder.

"As of this moment, I'm pulling you from lead investigator role," Michaels said. "You are to have no further contact with Ms. Lambert until this case is closed. Is that clear?"

She visibly flinched as Sean said, "Yes, sir."

"That's a direct order. It's also for Ms. Lambert's own protection, given that the killer may be using you as a way to find her. I also feel that Ms. Lambert needs to be guarded by someone who is less emotionally involved in the case."

"I would never do anything to endanger her or anyone else on the case," Sean said angrily.

"Jesus, I know that," the captain said, disgusted. "It's the only reason I haven't kicked your ass off the force for being such a stupid son of a bitch. But that doesn't mean I'm not pulling you. I've already set up another team to take over guard duty. Burke asked to take the lead, and I agreed."

"Thank you, sir," Sean said, feeling his knees go weak with relief.

"I'm placing you in charge of forensic evidence and continued background checks of suspects. Burke has agreed to assist you, even if that means working remotely from the safe house," Captain Michaels said.

Sean looked over at his cousin, knowing that meant Aidan had basically agreed to work twenty-four hours a day until the case was solved. He swallowed hard and glanced briefly at Claire's down-turned head. At least she would be safe with Aidan watching over her.

"You and Burke will have two calls a day, once every twelve hours, to update each other and hand off the active parts of the investigation," Michaels said. "You'd better catch this guy, and soon. We can't afford a twenty-four seven operation for very long."

Sean let out a silent sigh of relief. He was getting off easy, probably because the captain knew Sean would be harder on himself than anyone else would be.

"Ms. Lambert and her friend will remain at Johnston's home in Virginia under protective custody," Michaels said. "Neither one will leave, nor will they discuss their location with anyone. Burke has the details on the rest of the operation and will fill you in." He turned away. "I've got a press conference to set up."

"Captain," Claire said.

He stopped and met her gaze for the first time.

"I want you to know that it was never my intention to place anyone in a difficult situation," she said. "I asked to be part of this team, and since then Detective Richter has been a model of professionalism—"

"Oh, yeah? Is that why you have a hickey on your neck?" Captain Michaels said.

She flushed to the roots of her hair. The captain looked at her with eyes that had seen everything, but even his cynicism couldn't overlook the tangible connection between Claire and Sean.

"Ms. Lambert," he said, and his voice softened. "I understand that my investigators are human. But they're also officers of the law, and their behavior is held to higher standards than yours. If it were anyone else but Sean, I'd have his badge, weapon, and balls—in that order."

"But it's not his fault!"

Michaels ignored her and looked at Sean. "Five minutes, Detective. You have the lead in the press conference. Don't fuck it up."

"Yes, sir."

Michaels stalked off.

"Sean, I'm so sorry," Claire said. "I never should have . . ." *Thrown myself at you.* She glanced sideways at Aidan and flushed even more.

"I have to stay," Aidan said unhappily. "You're my job, now."

But he stepped back to give them as much privacy as he could in the busy room.

"I shouldn't have made you an offer you couldn't refuse," Claire said miserably, looking down at her clenched hands. "You told me this would happen. You said you could lose your job, but I wasn't thinking about that. I was just thinking about me."

Sean sat on his heels in front of her and took her hands in his, waiting until she met his eyes. "Sweetheart, I wouldn't change a single thing about last night or the first night or any of it. When this is over, we're going to have a serious talk about your taste for red wine and seduction, but in the meantime I'm going to live on the memory in the lonely nights to come."

"How can you joke about this?" Claire asked.

"It's that or start busting furniture," Sean said, squeezing her hand.

"But I won't see you until this is over. Who knows how long that will be?"

"It should be very soon now that we know he's trying to follow me."

"But he's dangerous! You could be hurt or—God, Sean. Why don't you remove yourself from the case entirely? It scares me that the killer is focused on you."

"Better me than you."

She knew she couldn't change his mind. Nor should she continue to try. His job was hard enough without having to worry about her weeping and clinging to him.

Still, she tightened her grip around his hands, painfully aware that she didn't know when she would see him again. She tried to speak, to tell him about the emotions that were shaking her, but her throat closed with the tears she refused to shed in front of him.

"It's going to be all right," he said.

He released one of her hands to cradle her cheek and kiss her gently, sweetly. Her breath came in on a sob, so he kissed her again before forcing himself to stand up. He kept Claire's hand clutched tightly in his as he pulled her to her feet and turned to face his partner.

"Take good care of her," Sean said in a strained voice. He looked at Claire again. "You do what Aidan says. Be strong, and remember—no regrets."

She nodded. Sean brought her hand to his mouth and pressed a kiss into her palm, then turned and walked away.

She watched as he left, feeling lost, scared, and guilty as hell for seducing him.

"Hey," Aidan said, putting his arm around her and guiding her back to the conference room where Olivia waited.

"Show me some of that ass-kicking spirit all you Louisiana girls seem to have."

Claire reached deep inside her for a strength she wasn't sure she had, telling herself that she wouldn't—would *not*—cry. If Sean could crack jokes instead of breaking furniture, she could suck it up and make jokes with the best of them.

"So does this mean we're partners now?" she asked, her voice husky with the emotions she was suppressing.

"Why the hell not? I've never had a female partner before," Aidan said.

"Can I drive the squad car?"

Aidan laughed and pretended he didn't notice Claire's trembling lower lip.

Chapter 60

Washington, D.C.
Tuesday morning

The man sat in his apartment dining room and carefully arranged his breakfast and newspaper before him in what had become a daily ritual. Today he added the noise of the local morning news show. He was looking for updates on the murder investigation, and was sure there would be something in one of the lead stories of the broadcast.

His efficient kitchen was air-conditioned almost to the point of being cold, so the steamy morning outside had no impact on him as he sat in his business suit. His hand was steady as he flipped through the newspaper, looking for any article on the case. Nothing in the main section. He set it carefully aside and forced himself to cut a piece of cantaloupe and eat it before reaching for the metro news section. He turned the pages slowly, then faster, as he found nothing of interest. He finally pushed the newspaper aside with a controlled motion and switched his attention to the television.

It had been three days since he'd last seen Marie Claire.

He'd been close enough to touch her on Saturday evening but hadn't been able to find her since. Her disappearance was starting to make him very angry. He'd come to rely on the feeling of anticipation and pleasure that seeing her gave him. It was so enjoyable that he'd been driven to take the almost crazy risk of delivering a body to Claire underneath the nose of her police guard.

He'd almost gotten caught and knew he had only himself to blame for it. This is what happened when he broke the rules.

There had always been rules, and he'd always followed them. But lately his own rules had bored him, so he'd changed them. First there was that night with the pretty schoolteacher, when he'd chosen a location that was different from the others, more public. Because of that, he'd run into the complication of Marie Claire.

Marie Claire had ruined everything for him that night, and everything since then. He hadn't even enjoyed killing the whore and stuffing her hair into a blonde wig. It was all Marie Claire's fault. He spent too much time following her and figuring out how to get her attention without getting caught.

Dropping a body at her feet had been risky. Speaking directly to her afterward had been undisciplined. And following the cop's truck had been just plain stupid. But he'd been desperate to keep tabs on Marie Claire.

Nothing would be right until he killed her.

The longer she was out of his sight, the more panicked he felt. He had to find her before somebody noticed how long he'd been gone from his job. Even with his cushy figurehead position at his father's company, an unplanned "vacation" that stretched into five weeks would start people asking questions.

When he realized he'd begun to sweat, he used a napkin to wipe his forehead.

Think and plan. Logic and discipline are the only way to make things right.

First, he would assess any known threats, then take appropriate steps to neutralize them. Since there were no new stories in the paper, it didn't seem like the police were following any hot leads that might bring them to his door.

The man's attention shifted to the television, where the local news was finally broadcasting an update on the murder investigations. He listened as the morning anchor reported that the police had no new leads, nor had they made any official comments since a press conference on Sunday afternoon.

He sat up in his chair as the footage switched to tape, and he saw the familiar face of the dark-haired cop standing in front of a cluster of microphones. He smiled as the cop's identity was confirmed by the small type at the bottom of his television screen.

Detective Sean Richter.

The name matched the registration he'd stolen from the truck on Saturday night. He'd thought the cop would lead him straight to Marie Claire once more, but Detective Richter had changed the game. The bastard had actually hidden her away somewhere new.

That hardly seemed fair.

The man considered the problem for a while, running through a number of possibilities and evaluating them based on speed, risk, and magnitude of mess. He finally decided he'd have to take a chance on quick and messy, because he really was running out of time.

He looked at his watch and pushed back from the table decisively. He'd have to hurry to be on time for his appointment at Camelot this afternoon.

Chapter 61

Washington, D.C.
Tuesday afternoon

"Your noon appointment is here," Afton's receptionist said.

Afton glanced up from the work she was doing on the database and rubbed her forehead. "Isn't it Friday yet? Or at least time to go home?"

"Sorry, it's only Tuesday. Do you want me to have your appointment wait in the conference room?"

"No, show him back here." She stood and stretched her tight muscles. Since the newspaper had run the story about the murders and linked Camelot's name to the case, she'd been buried in calls. More new clients had come in during the last two days than in the previous month.

A tall, dark-haired man stepped into her office, and she walked around the desk to greet him. "Mr. Wilson, I'm Afton Gallagher, owner of Camelot."

"Please, call me John. I'm not much on formality." The man smiled at her briefly, then took the seat she indicated.

"How can I help you?" Afton asked.

"Well, it's a little embarrassing, but I've just moved

here and I've been having a lot of trouble meeting women. I thought about joining a matchmaking agency to jump-start the process. I'm an engineer, so of course I felt the need to research all the dating services in the area. I'm currently in the middle of interviewing their owners to find the one that best suits me, but I'm getting a little anxious for results."

"I'd be happy to answer any questions you might have about Camelot."

"How long have you owned the business?"

Afton hesitated. "I inherited it from my sister when she died a few months ago."

"Oh. Well, you seem very organized. What I'd really like to do is take a look through your list of eligible candidates," Wilson said. "I'd like to see the caliber of woman your service attracts before I commit myself to membership."

"I can certainly understand that. However, we've recently implemented new security policies, and only members are allowed to review the catalogues."

"None of the other agencies had any problems giving me a quick peek." The man raised an eyebrow. His blue eyes watched for any signs of flexibility.

"I'm sorry. With all the publicity the whole dating service industry has had in the city, I have no choice but to support the rules."

"Yes, I recall reading something in the paper the other day." John leaned forward, as if to invite her confidences. "Is Camelot under investigation or something?"

"Absolutely not. We've done everything we can to assist the police, even though it hasn't helped any that I can see. But the whole affair has underlined the importance of having firm security policies."

"Yes," he said, "I suppose you can never be too careful."

"We're a very thorough company," Afton said. "Your satisfaction is our goal. If you join the service and for any reason are not happy with the female clients in our catalogue, we'll gladly refund your money."

"All right, you've convinced me." He reached into his coat pocket for his billfold. "I'll pay for the membership right now."

"Wonderful. I just need to have you fill out this questionnaire, including some of your personal information. Once we get a routine background check done, you'll be able to go through our catalogue and contact any of the ladies listed there."

Wilson put his billfold back. "Questionnaire? Background check? How long does this whole process take?"

"Usually about three days."

"But I don't have that much time. I have a dinner party at my vice president's home tomorrow night. If I don't come with a date—" The man broke off and winced.

"I'm really sorry. We could possibly expedite the background check, but we couldn't get it back before tomorrow night."

He shrugged sheepishly. "I guess I put things off too long. Isn't there any way around this little glitch?"

"I don't see how," Afton said regretfully.

"Even if it means losing business?" The man's smile invited her to understand that a background check really wasn't necessary in his case.

"I'm afraid so. I wish there were some way I could help you."

"It's my fault for letting things go so late." Wilson stood and walked out of the office without letting his feelings show.

While he hadn't been able to verify that Marie Claire

was a member, at least he'd learned the dating service hadn't been able to provide the police with any concrete information for the investigation. Hopefully the attention would shift away from Afton Gallagher's company entirely. Even if it didn't, the only person who might have tipped off the police about his link to Camelot was dead.

Now, finally, it was time to find where his sweet prey was hiding.

Chapter 62

Aidan was in the kitchen of the safe house, reviewing his computer files of the three suspects Sean had culled from hundreds of possibilities in a three-day work marathon. Sean was interviewing one of them this morning. The other two were slated for the afternoon—assuming Sean stayed awake that long.

When the portable phone rang, Aidan picked it up quickly and looked at the caller ID. Sean's home number appeared in the display.

"I wanted to pass the updates along before I try to catch a few hours of sleep," Sean said, yawning.

"Did you just get home?"

"Yeah, I had an interview at the station with suspect number one. No go on him. He's got an airtight alibi for the night of Renata Mendes's murder. It was his birthday, and he was with a group of friends from work until after two in the morning."

"Several of the friends confirmed?" Aidan asked.

"Yes, dammit. Anyway, I've already scheduled interviews for suspects two and three this afternoon. Can you make it into the station to do those, or do you want me to go back?"

"I'll do it. You've been working straight through since you turned Claire over to me. You'll do something stupid if you don't get some sleep."

Sean had promised himself he wouldn't ask, but he couldn't stop himself. "How is she?" He hadn't talked to her, afraid that it would just upset her even more, and him as well.

Aidan smiled. "She's amazing. That's a very strong woman you've got, partner. I can see the strain is wearing on her, but she kicked my ass at Hearts until three this morning."

"That's my girl," Sean said.

"Yeah, well just don't ever play cards with her for money. I think I owe her my next three paychecks."

"Is she sleeping now?"

"Like an angel, which is a clear case of fraud in advertising."

Sean chuckled despite his exhaustion. "Who's doing inside surveillance while you're at the station?"

"I'll bring in the officer parked out on the street. During daylight hours we should be okay with one mobile guy securing a perimeter around the house."

"Sounds good, as long as there's plenty of activity in the neighborhood during the day."

"Kids, soccer moms, gardeners and dogs. They should be fine. Captain Michaels approved it rather than assign another body to the case."

"Okay, I'm going to catch a few hours of sleep. If one

of the interviews looks hot, wake me up. Otherwise I'll call you after you get back to the house tonight."

Sean disconnected and went facedown on his bed, sleeping for the first time since he'd been separated from Claire.

Chapter 63

The man walked confidently through the lobby of the shabby Adams Morgan apartment building. Quickly scanning the area, he noticed several people waiting in line for the elevator. He took the stairs instead. He didn't want to encounter anyone who could potentially identify him later. Not that he would stand out, with his Georgetown baseball cap and aviator sunglasses, but he wanted to be extra careful.

Two flights up, he opened the fire door and made sure no one was in the hallway. He tucked his cap into his waistband and headed for apartment 225, at the end of the hallway. His knock was answered after a few moments by a young man with painfully bad hair, and some serious fashion issues as well.

"Hey, Scott. How's it going?" The man spoke in a casual, friendly manner, as if they were old buddies. The fact that he'd barely spoken to Scott Lincoln before now was ignored by both.

"Fine, sir. I was surprised to get your call last night, but I'm happy to do what I can to help."

"Why don't you call me Rich, okay? All my friends do." He stepped into the apartment and shut the door.

"Um, sure, Rich. Let's go over to the computer room."

The man looked around and found the usual squalor of an apartment occupied by a single male in his mid-twenties. He knew Scott was paid a good salary for his computer consulting at Wilkes Brothers Software, but it was difficult to tell from the ratty furniture and lack of decorations.

As they entered a second bedroom, Rich saw where Scott's paychecks had been going. A huge sound system took up much of one wall, and the computer equipment that filled the remainder of the room required three separate desks to hold everything. He'd clearly picked exactly the right techno-geek to assist him.

"Listen, Scott. I want to thank you again for agreeing to miss work this morning to help me with my personal problem. You didn't tell anyone, did you?"

"No, you said you wanted it private," Scott replied. "You're the boss."

"Actually, my father is, but I appreciate your help. As I mentioned, the situation is extremely . . . delicate. I'm going to rely on both your technical skills and your discretion."

Scott puffed up a bit. "Sure. What do you need me to do?"

"Well, the whole thing is quite distasteful, really. But I'm pretty certain my girlfriend is cheating on me with a certain ex-boyfriend. She's always talking to someone on the phone, then she hangs up when I come in the room. She's tried to hide it, but a man just knows these things. I'm sure you understand."

Scott didn't understand any such thing, since the only relationship he'd ever had was with his computer. But he nodded manfully and tried to look knowledgeable and sympathetic.

"I have this guy's name and address," Rich continued. "What I'd like to do is have you, um, look into his phone records and see who he's been calling. I'm sure my girlfriend's number will be on the list. Then I'll have the proof I need to confront her."

"Phone records, huh? That's illegal, you know." Scott was eager to show off his hacking skills, but wanted to make sure his boss's son knew what was involved.

The man shrugged and tried to look sheepish. Beneath the sunglasses that he had yet to remove, his blue eyes were as cold as his voice was warmly understanding. "I know it's probably a little uncomfortable for you to do this, but I just don't know of anyone else with your technical abilities. I hate to ask, but I'm in a desperate situation here. And I'll be happy to pay for the inconvenience."

"No problem." Scott sat down at one of the computer screens. "Getting into phone records is a bit time-consuming, but not all that difficult. You just have to be careful not to leave any tracks behind, you know?"

"Yes, I know all about cleaning up after oneself. I assume you have the skills to do that?"

"Piece of cake. What's this guy's name and number?"

"His name is Sean Richter. I don't have his number, but I do have an address for him." The man read off the address and watched the nerd get to work.

The next quarter hour passed with Scott muttering to himself and typing furiously. Occasionally he would stop and jot down something on a yellow pad next to his computer.

"Hmmm. Unlisted number, but that shouldn't be a big problem," Scott said to himself and opened another window on his screen.

The man stood motionless during the whole process, his heart pounding. He was so close he could taste it.

"Got it! Here we are." Scott magnified the size of the type on the screen and turned around triumphantly.

The man stepped forward to read over the geek's shoulder. The screen showed a list of calls, including the phone number and duration of the calls that originated from Richter's home telephone number.

Starting last Sunday, the day after Marie Claire had disappeared, the cop made two calls a day to a number in Fairfax County, Virginia. Every day, like clockwork, morning and evening. It had to be connected to Marie Claire and her current location. He was close, *so close.*

Rich tried to disguise his eagerness, aware the geek was looking at him. He had to be really careful here. He reached out with a steady hand and pointed to the number in Fairfax County.

"That number there," he said. "It might belong to my girlfriend's best friend. It would be just like that bitch to cover for her. Can you get me a name and address to go with it?"

"Sure. You don't even need to hack for that. Lots of websites let you do reverse number searches." Scott pulled up a browser window and selected a website. He typed in the information and hit send, and a reply came back within thirty seconds.

"That number is registered to Mitchell Johnston at three twenty-three Crepe Myrtle Lane, Alexandria."

"Damn. I don't recognize that name. But my girlfriend's friend just got married—can we find out who this Mitchell is and see if he's connected somehow?"

"Sure, I'll just run a search on Johnston and see what kind of hits we come up with," Scott said, typing rapidly.

A few moments later, Scott shifted uncomfortably in his chair. "Seems Mitchell Johnston is a detective with the DCPD."

Rich smacked his forehead. "How could I have forgotten. The girlfriend married a cop a few months ago. She must not be on the phone listing yet." He spoke automatically, while his mind changed gears as he processed this new information.

"Is there anything else you need today?" Scott asked. "I'm in the middle of something online."

Wilkes had already memorized the address, so he stepped away from the screen. "Would you mind printing it out for me? I'm going to hire a private detective to see if my girlfriend has been using this house for her little affair."

"Sure thing." Scott typed in the command, and then waited as the printer began to warm up. He took the opportunity to check his own work e-mail. "I can send you the whole file if you want."

Wilkes thought about the rubber gloves in a pocket of his shorts, but he was afraid that even Scott would notice if his unexpected guest snapped on gloves. With a mental shrug, Wilkes pulled a gun out of his shorts and grabbed a cushion off the floor to muffle the shots and keep the gore off of him.

"That won't be necessary," he said and fired into the back of Scott's head. He set the cushion aside, put the gun back in his waistband, and pulled on the rubber gloves. He looked at the blood splattered over the computer monitor and keyboard, and decided to shut off the machine manually rather than power the system down properly and risk getting bloody.

Watching where he stepped, he saw that the printer still hadn't processed the earlier request. Impatient at the delay, he reached behind the unit and unplugged it from the wall. His memory was as good as, and certainly faster than, the printer. From there he went to the nerd's closet, frowned at the clothes, and pulled a wrinkled button-down shirt over his bloodstained T-shirt.

As he checked his appearance in a mirror, he hummed quietly. Tonight Marie Claire would be his.

Chapter 64

Sean stepped into the offices of Camelot and tried not to think of how many times he had seen Claire there, and how much he missed seeing her now. Nor was he likely to be seeing her soon—his three hot suspects hadn't worked out. One of them had been overseas. The other had a broken foot that was still in a cast.

"Thank you for letting me disrupt your work schedule and agreeing to stay late," Sean told Afton.

"No problem. Mom has the boys and she'll keep them all night if necessary." Afton tilted her head and studied the detective's tired features. "Things aren't going well."

"There has to be some clue here that we've over-looked," Sean said. "This is where it all started, so this is where I'm going to start all over again."

"Any particular place you want to begin?"

"Remember how we agreed to eliminate the male clients who had been entered in the database after the night of the murder?"

Afton nodded. "Yes, because Claire felt she'd seen the

killer's picture in our database the night the murder took place."

"We've been through all the names of men who were members before the murder, and we don't have anything useful. Now I want to go through the rest of the clients."

Afton looked doubtful. "All right."

"Aidan is at the station right now," Sean said, knowing how lame his idea sounded. Lame or not, he just *knew* they must have overlooked something, and this was the most obvious place to start. "He's waiting for us to fax him over a list of the remaining names in the catalogue. He'll run them through the computer. I'll compare photos with sketches the department artist drew based on Claire's description of the man she saw in the backyard of your house."

Afton went to her computer. "I'll print a list of names sorted by date of membership initiation. Do you want pictures, too?"

"Yes, but send Aidan the text list first and do the photos separately."

Within five minutes, she had a list of male clients who had signed up since the night of the murder. She handed the printout to Sean, who scanned it quickly.

"That's almost a hundred more than there were the last time we checked," he said. "Do you normally get this many new clients within a couple of weeks?"

"No. It's the publicity from that news story. Last week we were swamped with inquiries and new members. It's ghoulish if you ask me. Give me Aidan's fax number and I'll send the names. The photos are up on my computer."

Sean wrote Aidan's number across the top of the list and went to Afton's desk. He stacked the files he'd brought in alphabetical order across the desk. After a few minutes of flipping back and forth in his own files and on the screen, comparing faces with sketches, he made a frustrated sound. "Do you have a room with more table space and network access?"

"Let's go to the conference room down the hall. It seats about ten, and it has a computer that can run the catalogue database."

Sean gathered files, followed Afton down the hall, and set his papers in orderly piles on the big table. She went to the computer at the head of the table and turned it on.

"This will take a few minutes," Afton said.

Sean stifled his impatience and stuffed his hands in his pockets, then began to pace the room. Outside the window, the sun was setting in a blaze of summer color. He glanced back at Afton, who was still waiting for the database to come up. Cursing technology, he resumed his pacing of the room.

As he walked around, he noticed that there were framed photos hung on every wall in the room. He stepped closer to examine the nearest ones, then slowly made his way down the entire wall. Studying the photos of happy, smiling people hoisting drinks or making silly faces, he felt a sudden clenching in his gut.

He turned and went down the next wall. More pictures of people, sometimes alone, sometimes in groups. They were all dressed in professional clothes and seemed to be having a good time.

Afton watched while Sean walked purposefully around the room, staring intently at the pictures that were hung on the walls.

"Is something wrong?" she asked.

He whipped his head around, jolted out of his concentration. "Are these all Camelot members?" He pointed to the framed photos.

"Not necessarily. The pictures were taken at the corporate mixers my sister used to host."

"So, for example, the men in this group here," Sean pointed at a picture, "aren't necessarily in Camelot's catalogue?"

Afton came over to study the picture herself. "No. See the photo next to it? That's my sister, and the two men standing with her are executives at a high-tech company that folded a couple of months ago. The executives were never members, but they hosted singles parties for their employees. Some of the workers later joined Camelot, but not all of them."

"Was Claire ever in this room?" Sean asked.

"Yes. This is the room we generally use for the client's first visit and review of the catalogue. It's much easier to spread out here than in my office."

"When was she in here?"

"It must have been—" Afton gasped and looked at Sean, who had already put the pieces together. "Oh my God. It was on the night Renata Mendes was murdered. Claire spent several hours in this room with me, going over the questionnaire and photos."

"The killer was never in the catalogue," Sean said. "God *damn* it. We've been chasing our tails for weeks, and he's been here all along." He turned to Afton. "I need to identify the men in every picture hanging in this room, and any other place in the offices where Claire might have been."

"Most of the pictures have the names printed at the bottom, or they have labels taped to the back. You read them to me and I'll start a list right now," Afton said, sitting at the computer.

"Okay. At the same time, we'll cross-reference that list with the catalogue, and eliminate anyone who is a Camelot client and has already been investigated. After that, we'll get Aidan to expedite a background check on the remaining names of non-members."

Sean walked around the room, removing pictures and reading names to Afton, who typed them into the computer. Anyone who was a member had a flag placed on his file in case they needed to return to him in the future. When they came across a man who was not a client, his name was entered on the new short list of suspects. Then Sean placed the picture on the table and went to the next photo. It took almost half an hour to enter all the names into the computer.

"Okay, now we're sure this new suspect list includes only names that were not in the Camelot database?" Sean asked.

"Yes," Afton said. "We've got twenty-seven men who appear in photos in this room but were never investigated as Camelot clients."

"Let's get this list to Aidan and cross our fingers." Sean picked up his cell phone and called his partner.

Aidan answered on the fourth ring.

"It's Sean. We fucked up big time, buddy." He quickly explained about the photos in the conference room and the list of twenty-seven men they had compiled.

"Shit," Aidan said. "*Shit*. How did we miss that?"

"It doesn't matter. We caught it now. I just faxed the names over to you."

"I've got it," Aidan said as someone handed him a fax marked Urgent. "I'll drop everything and get right on the new list."

"How long do you think it will take?"

"I'll pull in some of the other guys, but it will be at least an hour for a prelim check. Sit tight, partner. We'll get the bastard."

"I'll be here with Afton, running through the rest of the names and double-checking."

Aidan hung up, then quickly dialed the number of the safe house. He started speaking as soon as the officer picked up.

"Diaz, it's Burke. I want you to stay with Claire and Olivia for a couple of hours. We've had a big break, and I'm needed here at the precinct to follow this lead."

"No problem. I'll let Brown know he's in charge of securing the perimeter alone until further notice."

"Right. If you need anything, you've got my cell. Don't tell the women yet. I don't want to get their hopes up," Aidan said, then hung up.

He rushed into the room that housed the computer investigators, or the techno-nerds, as they were more or less affectionately known. The four people on duty were already checking through the list of names Aidan had given them.

"Everybody, drop what you're doing and listen up. I've got a new list with twenty-seven names. These individuals have never been checked, and there's a strong possibility our killer is among them. We'll divide the names among you, then I'll take the extras and use the spare terminal over on the end."

There was some good-natured grumbling, but everyone closed files and waited to receive the new names. Aidan took the last names for himself, then sat down at a computer and began to run his searches. He wasn't nearly as fast as the others, but he was thorough.

Half an hour later, one of the technicians called him over.

"I've got a sealed juvenile record here. Thought you might want to take it and run. It was a DCPD arrest, so you should be able to dig around without too much trouble. The guy was even fingerprinted."

Aidan ripped the papers from the printer tray. "Richard Gerald Wilkes the Second. Fancy name. Any relation to Wilkes Brothers Software?"

The technician typed briefly, then grinned at Aidan. "He's a vice president and holds a seat on the board. His father, Richard Gerald Wilkes the First, is the president and CEO."

"A spoiled rich boy with a sealed juvenile record," Aidan said gleefully. "Would your wife mind if I kissed you, Cal?"

"Get away from me, Burke."

Aidan laughed and waved the papers triumphantly. "I'm going down to Latent to see if we can do anything with the fingerprints taken from Wilkes at the time of his arrest. Could you do some more digging and find out who the investigating officer was?"

"As long as you don't come near me," the technician yelled after Aidan's retreating back.

Chapter 65

Afton paced around the conference table, stopping occasionally to sift through the framed photos and criticize herself for not putting the pieces together sooner. "It's been so long since I even looked at these pictures. They were all taken before my sister died, before I was involved with Camelot. Still, I should have thought of it."

"It's okay," Sean said. "We all assumed Claire had seen the guy in the catalogue. And you know what they say about assumption."

"No, what?"

"It's the mother of all fuckups." He laid the police artist's sketch alongside the photos of several men. He moved down the table, comparing the drawing with the pictures, until he found one with a superficial resemblance.

Afton looked at the sketch, then at the photo, and frowned. "Other than the smile, I don't see much similarity."

Sean grunted.

She studied the picture Sean had selected. From the date, the photo had been taken at a corporate mixer a year ago. It featured a man in a business suit with a bored smile holding up his drink and wryly saluting the photographer.

"I think I've seen that man before," she muttered.

"You've been in the conference room a lot."

"No, I meant more recently." She flipped the picture over and read the caption, hoping it would jog her memory.

> *"Richard Wilkes II, Vice President of Marketing at Wilkes Brothers Software, comes along to offer moral support at his company's first meet and greet party."*

She frowned over the name, then turned the frame to look at the photo again. "I think he was in the office not long ago, but he didn't use the name Richard Wilkes the Second."

"Are you sure?" Sean asked.

"Absolutely. I would have remembered, because the Wilkeses—father and son—are executives with Wilkes Brothers Software. The company was one of my sister's biggest clients, so I would have paid special attention if I'd seen their name in my appointment book."

"Did you ever meet him or his father?"

"No. They ended the contract before I moved here. But I know I've met this man before. And his name wasn't Richard Wilkes the Second."

"Do you remember where you met him, and why?"

"We met here—recently. He wanted to join Camelot right away, but only if he could look through the catalogue first. Basically, he wanted to see if the women were worth paying to date."

Sean looked up. "Did you show him the catalogue?"

"No, it's strictly against our new policy. I told him he'd have to fill out a questionnaire and wait for a background check before he saw our female clients."

"Did he fill out a questionnaire?"

Afton shook her head. "He tried to pressure me to change the rules for him, but I wouldn't. So he put away his wallet and walked out."

"Did he say why he chose your dating service?"

"He must have read the name in the papers, because he asked about the police investigation."

Sean went still. "What name did this guy use?"

"I don't know, I'd have to check my calendar."

She hurried down the hall toward her office, with Sean following close behind. When she opened her computer calendar and ran through the appointments for the last week, he was leaning over her shoulder.

"There it is. Tuesday. Initial consultation with John Wilson," she said.

"Wilkes, Wilson. It could be he was trying to hide his identity. Did he act embarrassed to be signing up with a dating service?"

Afton shook her head. "Too arrogant. Too confident, as well."

"Okay. I'll have Aidan check out John Wilson and Richard Wilkes the Second as a priority." Sean shook his head in disgust at the work that would go into following up this new angle. "There have to be ten thousand John Wilsons in this country. We'll start with driver's license photos of the ones who are geographically close to D.C. and see what happens."

"I have a better idea," Afton said. "Follow me."

He hesitated, then went down the hall with her to a place that looked like some kind of equipment room.

"After the murder investigation started," Afton said, "and especially once a question had been raised about some clients, I had my IT manager set up a hidden digital camera in the reception area. We should have a photograph of everyone who stopped at the desk and signed in."

"You're shitting me."

She grinned. "No. My IT manager said it would be easy to store the photos short term, as long as we didn't accumulate too many of them. Didn't want to use up his precious disk space. I'll call him and ask where the files are saved."

Sean handed Afton his cell phone, then waited as she called her technician and got instructions on how to call up the files on the server.

"Okay," she said. "Here's last week, so it should be under the folder marked Tuesday."

They clicked through the photos in silence, pausing when they reached Afton's noon appointment. Sean held up the framed picture he had brought from the conference room and compared it with the grainy digital image on the screen in front of him. Then he compared it to the sketched image of the man who had threatened Claire in Afton's backyard.

Gotcha, you smug bastard. You took one risk too many, and now you're mine.

"I'll need a copy of this digital photo to send to the lab," Sean said, looking at the computer. "Then we'll just pick up Mr. Wilson and ask him a few questions."

Sean took back his cell phone and dialed his partner's number.

"Aidan, rush the background check on Richard Wilkes the Second. He had a meeting at Camelot last week, tried to look at the catalogue. He was using the alias John Wilson. I've compared photos of the two and they look good."

"Hell, Sean, are you reading minds now?" Aidan asked.

"What have you got?"

"Richard Wilkes the Second has a juvenile record. I just put in a call to the lead investigator on the case."

"Was it a violent offense?" Sean asked.

"Looks like it. Reading between the lines of the closed case file, aggravated assault charges were initially brought against him, but they were later bumped down after the victim and main witness boarded a plane and returned to Costa Rica. She'd been working as a maid and cook in the home of Richard Wilkes, the father."

"Hispanic female, mid-twenties," Sean said, thinking of the string of murder victims.

"Shit, I hadn't thought of that. We can verify with the lead investigator. I'm guessing that Richard's daddy managed to get the charges pleaded down to harassment, and got his son enrolled in court-ordered counseling. But not before the little bastard was booked and fingerprinted."

"You've got prints on file?" Sean asked sharply.

"I'm in the Latent Fingerprints lab right now. The technician is doing a quick search of prints from the crime scenes we've linked to the killer and comparing them to Richard Wilkes the Second. I've asked the technician to expedite manual verifications of any computer matches on the prints."

"We need to run a location check on Mr. Wilkes, as well," Sean said.

"I called both his legal addresses already. The first is his father's estate, where a housekeeper answered and said the son had been in Aruba for the last month or so. The second number is an upscale apartment complex in Alexandria. No answer." Aidan paused as the fingerprint technician came rushing over. "Hang on a sec, Sean. We might have something."

The technician waved the enlarged fingerprint she was holding. "I ran a second computer check of Wilkes's prints against all known fingerprints in the system, in addition to the ones from the crime scenes you requested," she said. "The computer showed a potential match between the old Wilkes prints and a partial that was recovered at a homicide in Northwest D.C. today. I've done a manual verification, and it looks solid to me."

"Nina, you're beautiful," Aidan said. "Who's the investigating detective on the D.C. homicide?"

"Ron Garvey."

Aidan picked up his cell phone again and raced down the hall. As he did, he explained to Sean about the potential match. "I'm going to hang up and call you on my desk phone, then conference in Garvey. I'd be very interested to see what Richard Wilkes the Second was doing at this dead guy's apartment."

"I'll be right here with Afton," Sean said. "Call me."

Sean hung up, looked over at Afton, and squeezed her hand reassuringly. "Stop beating yourself up. You did great."

"Really?"

"Really. Thanks to you, we'll nail the little shit."

Chapter 66

The man sat quietly behind a lilac bush, waiting for the police officer to make his six-minute circuit of the property where Marie Claire was staying. The officer constantly kept moving and checked in regularly via his radio. Presumably he was checking in with his partner in the house, or possibly one of the dispatchers.

It would make the timing of this operation critical, because he'd have to strike as soon as possible after one of these brief radio conversations. That would buy him the maximum amount of time to get into the house and get Marie Claire before the alarm went out.

He was confident he could get to her in the short time he would have. He'd spent most of the morning and all of the afternoon watching the house, and he already knew which room belonged to Marie Claire. Although the curtains had been closed, he'd seen her silhouette as she sat by the window. That curly hair of hers gave a very distinctive profile.

Things were running smoothly so far. The only possible glitch was the fact that the roving police officer was wearing body armor. That would make his usual method of attack impossible, because the knife wouldn't penetrate a bullet-proof vest. He wasn't eager to try to slit the officer's throat—even if he managed it, the result would be too messy. In addition he risked losing the element of surprise, because he wasn't sure he could get the job done on the first pass. He was used to being much stronger than his victims.

He supposed he could use his gun, but the noise would be unmistakable. He'd brought it along to ensure Marie Claire's cooperation, not to start shooting people—at least until he had her and both officers under control. Then he would use whatever he wanted, knife or gun or both together. The idea made him smile, even though it was another departure from the script he had laid out in his mind.

It's a good thing I react quickly under pressure and can improvise, Wilkes told himself.

The properties in this neighborhood were large and had dense vegetation, which would be to his advantage. And the ground was damp and covered with a layer of fallen leaves, which would muffle his approach. He picked up one of the large landscaping stones that formed a border around the bush where he was hiding.

Wilkes hefted the weight of the rock in his hands and ran through what he would do several times. Then he checked his watch and waited in the dark for his chance.

Forty seconds later, the cop walked by on his umpteenth circuit of the property. He didn't notice the additional shadow in the bushes. Wilkes rose up and smashed the rock into the back of the officer's head with both hands. The cop went down and stayed there, motionless.

Wilkes crushed the police radio under his foot and threw the officer's weapon deep into the bushes. Then he hit the man again several times for good measure.

With the first part of his mission accomplished, Wilkes crept slowly toward the house.

Chapter 67

Sean pounced on his cell phone when it rang. "Aidan?"

"Yeah. I've got Garvey on the line, and he was just about to tell me about the homicide case that came across his desk today. Go ahead, Ron."

"We had a call this afternoon after some computer consultant didn't make it in to work," Garvey said in a gravelly voice. "Seems our caller and the consultant were in the middle of some computer game and he was impatient to get on with it. Anyway, the guy went over to the consultant's apartment after lunch and found the body."

"And?" Sean asked impatiently.

"I'm getting there. The consultant—a kid, really—had been shot in the back of the head as he sat at his computer, so the place was a mess. But he did have a shitload of high-tech equipment, and his friend hinted the kid might have been a semi-pro hacker who pissed off a customer."

Sean told himself to be patient. Garvey was one of those people who told a story in his own way and at his own snail's pace. Pushing him just made him go slower.

"Who did he do his hacking for?" Sean asked.

"No idea. But he collected a paycheck from Wilkes Brothers Software."

"Bingo," Sean said softly.

"Told you I'd get there," Garvey retorted. "So imagine my surprise when Burke called me with a match for the partial print we got off a monitor in the victim's apartment, and it belonged to none other than a VP at Wilkes Brothers Software."

"It could be coincidence," Sean said. "Wilkes might have an explanation for being there. He was the kid's boss, after all." *And the guy who's after Claire uses a knife and only kills women.*

"I'd still like to talk to him," Garvey said. "I've had the computer technicians here going over the victim's equipment since we brought it in. I figure if the kid was a hacker, whatever he was last working on might have something to do with why he was killed."

"So what was he doing?" Aidan asked.

"The computer and printer had both been shut down improperly, so my guys are working on getting stuff from document recovery or some such thing. According to the browser history, the kid had been on a web page that enables reverse phone number searches—you know, getting the address and name when you only have a phone number?"

Sean didn't like that at all. "Any record of who he was looking up?"

"We couldn't tell until we powered up the printer. The techie here is a genius, and he managed to pull the last print job from the buffer memory thing, or whatever the hell it's called. Hang on, I've got a copy of it in the file."

Garvey made rustling sounds as he flipped through the

papers on his desk. "Here it is. The document isn't much—just an address. Three two three Crepe Myrtle Lane, in Alexandria."

"Jesus Christ. *That's our safe house.*" Sean's hand clenched tightly around the phone. He heard Aidan dropping Garvey off the conference with a promise to get back in touch soon.

"I'm less than ten minutes from there," Aidan said to Sean. "I'll go."

"Damn it, I—" Sean stopped, knowing his partner was right. Sean was half an hour away, and he didn't have a unit with lights and siren. "I'll call Diaz and have him put the women in a secure upstairs room until you arrive. Call me on my cell the instant you get there."

"I'm gone," Aidan said and hung up. He raced down the hall, shouting at people to get out of his way.

Sean wanted to keep his cell phone line open, so he ran back to Afton's office.

She took one look at his pale, grim face and said, "What's wrong? Is Claire all right?"

Sean held up a hand to keep Afton quiet while he dialed the safe house's number on Afton's desk phone. He got Officer Diaz on the line within one ring.

"Where are the women right now?" Sean asked.

"Upstairs playing cards."

"Secure the house and get up there with them. The killer has your location."

"What! How in—"

"It doesn't matter," Sean cut in. "Burke is on his way right now. I want you to move the women into the upstairs room with the best locks and most limited access."

"The master bathroom," Diaz said instantly. "There's only a small window and two doors to protect."

"Good. Get them in there. Tell Brown to be extra careful on his foot patrol."

"You got it."

Sean hung up the phone and looked at his watch, counting off the minutes, and willing his cousin to call.

Chapter 68

"Gin," Olivia said. She laid down her winning hand and grinned at Claire triumphantly.

"That's what, ten times in a row? We're going to have to handicap you." Claire tallied up the points on a notepad. "Wait until Aidan gets here, then I'll win some of my money back."

She looked up as the phone rang, then froze. A man was standing near the doorway behind Olivia, pointing a gun at her head.

Olivia paused as she shuffled the cards, wondering at Claire's sudden silence. She looked at her friend's ashen face and rigid posture, and realized something was very wrong. She jolted when a strange voice spoke from behind her.

"Hello, Marie Claire. You aren't going to do anything stupid, like call for help, are you? Because if you do, I'll blow your friend's pretty little head away. Do we understand each other?"

Claire nodded numbly.

"Don't move, Red," Wilkes said to Olivia. "Marie Claire, come over and stand next to me."

Claire stood and wiped her clammy hands down the front of her jeans. She moved slowly to stand next to the man who was holding a gun on her best friend. He was tall, probably just over six feet. He had short dark hair and navy blue eyes, but other than that she didn't notice anything outstanding about his features. Nor did he trigger any memories of the night she had run for her life.

Yet she *knew* this was the man who meant to kill her.

"Excellent," he said. "You're being very cooperative— this time."

He shifted the gun to his left hand and pulled a knife from inside his dark jacket. In a heartbeat he had his hand wrapped around Claire's neck and was holding the knife to the tender side of her throat. The gun stayed trained on Olivia.

"Okay, Red. Now it's your turn. You can help with the cop downstairs. Come stand over here, to my left, about six feet away from me. Don't make any sudden moves, or I'll cut Marie Claire's throat and kill you before she hits the floor."

Olivia stood slowly and did as she was instructed.

Downstairs Claire heard Diaz moving around the ground floor quickly. Windows closed noisily and the front door banged shut, followed by the sound of the dead bolt slamming into place. *A little late for that,* she thought bitterly.

Wilkes flinched when Officer Diaz called from downstairs.

"Claire! Olivia! Which room are you in?"

"Answer him, Red," Wilkes said. "Tell him where you are, nothing more."

Olivia spoke, but only a hoarse sound came out. She

closed her eyes, cleared her throat, and tried again. "We're up here, in Claire's bedroom."

"Stay there. I'll be right up," Diaz said, still locking everything downstairs.

"Now be quiet," Wilkes said to Olivia, tightening his grip on Claire. He had to think and think fast.

Olivia's eyes moved toward Claire's. Both women knew they had to get away somehow, and to do that they would have to work together. Thinking frantically, Claire looked around the room, then she motioned with a hand at her waist toward the open bathroom door behind Olivia. She prayed the man holding a gun on Olivia wouldn't be able to see the faint movement.

Olivia blinked her understanding without turning her head, thinking the same thing Claire was—escape.

The bathroom sat between the two smaller upstairs bedrooms, and it was connected to each by a heavy wooden door. While a gun and knife stood between them and the hall door, if the women could get to the bathroom, they would have another way out.

Both froze at the sound of footsteps on the back porch. Claire could hear Diaz calling out to his partner on the radio, then using his voice alone.

Claire motioned to Olivia with her hand again, this time pointing at herself. Then she pointed at the hallway. For emphasis, she once again pointed at Olivia and the bathroom door, willing her to understand that Claire would go for the hall door, while Olivia should go toward the bathroom, through it, and into the master bedroom, where there was a door to the hallway.

Olivia bit her lip, not liking the idea of splitting up. But it was their best chance of dividing the killer's attention, so she blinked again in agreement.

The man holding Claire tensed as he heard heavy foot-steps on the old wooden stairs of the house. Officer Diaz called out as he made his way up to them. She watched in horror as the man moved his gun away from Olivia's head and aimed instead at the doorway.

She realized that he was going to kill the officer, and probably Olivia as well. Their best chance for escape would be when the officer came through the doorway, dis-tracting the killer. She wanted to cry out a warning to Diaz, to tell him of the danger, but she was very aware of the knife resting against her throat and the fact that the killer's gun could be pointed back to Olivia before the first word of warning left Claire's mouth.

But then she thought of Sean, and knew what she would do if he were the one coming up the stairs. Officer Diaz had a wife and children and grandchildren, whose pictures he showed at the least excuse. She couldn't just stand by while he was murdered. Frantically she thought back to Aidan's brief self-defense instructions, and his advice on how to handle someone who grabbed her from behind.

The footsteps reached the top of the stairs. Claire met Olivia's wide-eyed gaze to let her know that now was their chance.

Without warning Claire yelled and raked backward with her hand, gouging at the killer's eyes. "He has a gun!"

Surprise loosened the killer's hold on her. She felt the sting of the knife on her neck as she jerked away from him.

Instead of running, Olivia hurled herself at the killer, knocking him off balance and breaking his hold on Claire. Only when Claire was free did Olivia turn and race toward the bathroom.

"Run!" Claire shouted as she threw herself toward the hall.

Claire heard the bathroom door slam behind Olivia just as she reached the hallway. She ran smack into Officer Diaz, who was advancing cautiously down the hall with his weapon drawn.

"Go back!" she yelled at Diaz.

He reached to pull her behind him when the sound of a gunshot rang out. Claire screamed as the officer crumpled at her feet, blood pouring from his head. Knowing there was nothing she could do for him now, she ran past his body, desperate to draw the killer away from Olivia.

A hand grabbed Claire from behind, yanking her to a stop. She stood there panting as she felt the killer slide his arm around her neck and lay the knife along the cut already bleeding sluggishly there.

"I really am going to enjoy hurting you, Marie Claire." Wilkes dragged her past the fallen officer and down the hall. "Now, where's that little friend of yours? We'll take care of her, then you can see what I have in store for you once we get to the special place I've chosen." His voice was rough with adrenaline and almost dreamy at the same time.

Knowing the bathroom was a dead end—literally—Olivia hadn't stayed there. As soon as the killer followed Claire into the hallway, Olivia had tiptoed across the attached bedroom to the open hall door. She could hear the man talking to Claire. They were coming back down the hall toward her, cutting off any escape. Olivia knew if the man found her, she would die—there would be no witnesses to Claire's kidnapping.

I've got to get out of here! I've got to call the police and help Claire, and I can't do that if I'm dead. And dead is what I'll be if I stay glued to the middle of the room like an idiot!

But she couldn't get out—the hallway was the only escape, and the killer was already there. With shaking hands, she closed and locked the bedroom door and thought frantically. The lock wouldn't keep the killer out for long. She had to hide somewhere in the room. That way she could follow the killer when he left with Claire, and somehow find a way to give her friend another chance to escape.

Briefly Olivia considered the window, but she already knew it was warped by age and wouldn't open easily. It was the old-fashioned type with multiple tiny panes that would take too long to break.

The killer began pounding on the locked door. "I'll kill Marie Claire if you don't open this door."

"He'll kill me anyway, Livvie! Don't open the door!"

Olivia knew her friend was right. She looked around the room one more time, then slowly looked up. There was a small trapdoor leading to the attic. She grabbed the chair from a nearby desk, stood on it, and slid back the bolt that held the trapdoor in place. She pulled on the release cord as hard as she could, then jumped back when she was almost knocked over by the folding ladder that tumbled down in response to her tugs. It came partway down and stopped.

She scrambled up the first few rungs to the attic, kicked the chair into a corner, and pulled herself up the rest of the way. Keeping a grip on the cord so that it wouldn't dangle from the ceiling, she strained to pull the staircase closed behind her. Just as she managed it, the bedroom door below crashed open.

"Come out right now or I'll kill your friend."

"Don't do it!" Claire called.

"Shut up!"

Olivia held her breath and didn't move. She prayed the man wouldn't look up. For a few seconds she thought she'd pulled it off. Then she heard him laugh.

"Come out of the attic, you stupid bitch."

"Don't listen, Livvie!" Claire cried out, then choked as the killer jerked his arm even tighter around her neck.

Bitches, Wilkes thought, fighting the panic that came whenever he wasn't in control of women. *Stupid bitches can't even follow simple orders.* Too much time had passed since he'd fired the gun. Some neighbor would have called the police by now. And even if he got lucky and no one called, the police were overdue for their radio check.

I have to get Marie Claire out of here now.

He didn't have time to chase her redheaded friend through the rafters—if that was where she had gone. She could have escaped through the window, and even now might be calling 911.

Swearing loudly, he pushed Marie Claire toward the chair lying on its side and pointed the gun at her head.

"Pull the chair over here, then get on it and throw the bolt. Quickly!"

Claire climbed up on the chair and slid the bolt closed. Anyone up there was now trapped. She fervently hoped that Olivia was long gone by now, yet she had a sick feeling her friend was on the other side of the trapdoor, waiting for a chance to make another break for help.

Wilkes yanked Claire off the chair, dragged her backward, and fired four shots around the outline of the trapdoor.

"Livvie!"

The blunt side of the killer's knife choked off Claire's scream. When she was silent, he turned the sharp side to her neck again.

"Come away with me, my sweet prey. I have something very special for you."

Chapter 69

Fairfax County, Virginia
Wednesday night

Olivia waited in a dark corner of the attic until she heard footsteps leaving the bedroom below her. The attic was hot, dusty, and she was trapped in it. A shaft of light came through a small window on the far side. Carefully she made her way over to it. She heard the killer on the stairs and knew she'd only have one chance to open the window.

It probably wouldn't go quietly.

Taking a breath, Olivia undid the latch on the window and pushed on it as hard as she could. She was astonished when it opened outward. The yard was about thirty feet below.

Feet first, Livvie, she told herself. *Dangle from your fingertips and then let go.*

Turning around, she wiggled out the small window frame. Once she was past her hips, she pushed the rest of her body through the narrow opening, then held herself for a moment by her fingers.

Claire's voice came from below and to the left, asking

the killer what he'd done with the other police officer. He didn't answer. Olivia held her breath and waited for them to pass. Once they were out of earshot, she closed her eyes, pushed herself back as far as she could, and let go. She tried to roll as she landed, but ended up taking the force of the fall on her left ankle. Biting her lip against the pain shooting through it, she lurched to her feet and headed after Claire.

When Olivia peeked around the large shrub at the end of the drive, she saw brake lights come on a block down the street. She had no chance of chasing after a car in her condition, but she might get close enough to see the license plate. Awkwardly she went down the shadowed side of the street as fast as she could, ignoring the pain, running her heart out and following the car for several blocks before it turned onto a main street.

The killer gunned the engine. A few seconds later, even the car's brake lights vanished.

Olivia stood in the middle of the street and screamed Claire's name.

Then she turned and ran unevenly back toward the house, repeating, "Maryland seven two three. Maryland seven two three."

Chapter 70

Fairfax County, Virginia
Wednesday night

Aidan drove recklessly down the narrow suburban streets—dispatch hadn't been able to raise either of the officers assigned to guard Claire for over five minutes. Backup units were on the way, but he would arrive before they did.

Without a pause he rolled through a stop sign and turned right onto Crepe Myrtle Lane. About half a block from the house he saw someone running awkwardly down the middle of the street. Ice congealed in his gut when he recognized the red hair and petite frame.

He stopped the car with a screech of the brakes, then bailed out and grabbed Olivia's arms. Her white face had dark smudges on it, and her pupils were so dilated that he could see no color in her eyes, even in the bright glare of the headlights.

"What happened? Where's Claire?"

"He took her in his car. Maryland seven two three."

"Easy, Livvie." Aidan slid an arm around her. "Slow down and tell me what happened."

"The killer got into the house," Olivia said in a flat voice. "Claire and I split up, and we almost got away. Then he shot Officer Diaz and took Claire. I managed to hide. I went out the window and tried to follow, but they were in a car and it was going too fast. Maryland seven two three."

"What does that mean?" Aidan asked over the sound of her shuddering breathing. "Livvie, look at me. You're okay. Slow down and breathe deeply. You're safe."

"But Claire isn't!" Olivia panted. "His license plate began seven two three—I didn't see the rest, but they looked like Maryland plates. Red car, American, like a rental. He took her, Aidan. He took her and I couldn't do anything."

Aidan reached through the open window to grab his radio and report the kidnapping of a witness from protective custody. He described Claire and the vehicle, including the partial plates. He paused to ask Olivia for a description of the suspect, then relayed that information as well. He finished by calling for multiple paramedic units and backup to the safe house.

As soon as the dispatcher put out the all points bulletin, Aidan threw the radio back in the car. "Lock yourself in my car," he said to Olivia. "I have to check on Diaz and Brown."

Olivia took a step, cried out, and then collapsed against Aidan.

"Your leg?" Aidan asked, supporting her.

Olivia nodded and breathed through her teeth against the nauseating pain. "I think I broke something."

Aidan lifted her off her feet and headed for the house, where med-techs would soon be arriving with lights and sirens. "How the hell did you do that?"

"I jumped out the attic window."

"Christ, woman. That's got to be a thirty-foot drop," Aidan said, eyeing the tiny window on the right side of the house.

"Tell me about it."

Aidan strode up the steps, put Olivia in a rocker on the porch, and unlocked the front door. Sirens screamed, coming closer to the house with every second.

"You'll be safe here while I check on Diaz," Aidan said. "Okay?"

Olivia nodded and wrapped her arms around herself for warmth while official vehicles pulled up from all directions and armed men leaped out. Very quickly Aidan was back. She looked up at him, afraid to ask how Diaz was.

"He's alive," Aidan said. "Looks like a bad furrow on the side of his head, but his pulse is good."

Olivia listened numbly while Aidan gave orders to the others to help Diaz and look for the missing officer. Then he sat next to Olivia and pulled out his cell phone. He took hold of her hand and squeezed it as he prepared to make the most difficult call of his life.

Chapter 71

Sean held the cell phone in his hands, trying not to worry as time passed and he still didn't hear anything about Claire. When the phone finally rang, he checked the caller ID—Aidan.

"Is she all right?" Sean demanded.

"God, Sean. I'm sorry. She was taken about five minutes ago. Diaz was shot, and Brown is missing. Olivia managed to get away, then followed the suspect as he dragged Claire to his car. The description sounds like Richard Wilkes."

"Sweet Jesus," Sean breathed. He literally felt his heart stop beating.

"I was just a few minutes too late. But Olivia got a partial plate, and we've got an APB out already. He's only a few minutes ahead of us. Olivia said he seemed to have some kind of destination in mind."

"We've got to find her before they get there," Sean said flatly, his mind racing through possibilities. "Send units to all of his known home addresses, as well as Afton's house, Claire's house, and Olivia's apartment."

"What do you think he's going to do?" Aidan asked.

"He had a plan, but things didn't go well when he tried to take Claire. He's probably flustered. He'll want to go back to something familiar, something comfortable."

"Right. I'll send someone to Wilkes Brothers Software, too. Can you think of anywhere else he'd go?" Aidan asked.

"I'm working on it."

"I'll try to get some information out of Diaz, and I'll have someone call the precinct. Maybe the tech guys there have dug something else up."

"Keep this line open so I know what's going on," Sean said.

"Okay. Right now I'm going to hand Olivia over to the paramedics."

Aidan stuck the cell phone in his front pocket, lifted Olivia, and started toward one of the ambulances that was pulling up on the street.

"No, I want to go with you," she said.

"You can't go anywhere on that ankle. We'll send an officer with you and give you regular updates, okay?"

"But maybe I can help," she protested.

"You've been an incredible help already. Without you, we'd have nothing to go on and no hope of finding Claire. Now let us do our job. We'll get her back."

"Promise?" Olivia asked. She grabbed at his hand as he set her on the stretcher.

"I promise you we'll bring her home safe," Aidan said.

Olivia wanted to ask how he could be sure, but the grim set of Aidan's features told her that was a question he didn't want to answer. She released his hand, letting the paramedics begin to work on her.

Aidan headed for his car and wondered how in hell he'd keep his word.

Chapter 72

Washington, D.C.
Wednesday night

Claire sat in the passenger seat of the killer's car with a gun pressing hard into her ribs. If she hadn't been so frightened, she would have laughed—she'd been working with police to identify the killer out of Camelot's catalogue, and she hadn't even recognized the man when he'd stood in front of her.

He looked so horribly *normal*. If she'd seen him walking by her on the street, she wouldn't have given him a second thought.

And he was going to kill her.

How is that for irony, Dr. Morton? Take your hysterical amnesia and shove it right up your ass.

Biting her lip, she told herself she wouldn't scream, wouldn't cry, wouldn't fly apart.

The killer saw her betraying gesture and smiled. "Nervous, Marie Claire? Don't be. It will be over before you know it. Just a case of tidying up loose ends, really, and that shouldn't take long at all."

She bit the inside of her lips to keep them from visibly

trembling. She'd be damned if she'd give this bastard any satisfaction.

"I just need to make sure we're not being followed, first," he continued in a normal tone of voice, as though he was talking about the weather. He checked the mirrors as he drove in seemingly random patterns, but never once did he reduce the pressure of the gun against Claire's ribs.

I'm going to have bruises there for sure, she thought, then had to force back a nervous laugh. It was stupid to worry about bruises when she was going to die.

She eased further into the corner of the seat, praying that Olivia was all right, that she'd somehow escaped. Other than involving Livvie in this mess, Claire had no regrets about the last month—except that she hadn't had the guts to tell Sean she loved him.

She wondered now if she'd ever have another chance.

Claire stopped herself in mid-thought. She wasn't going to die right now. The killer said he had a plan, and he needed her alive so he could implement it.

Think—what do you know about this man?

Claire stared out the window, keeping her features passive as her mind raced through the discussions the team had had on the personality of the killer.

He's a control freak. He gets off when he's planning things and will draw them out to continue getting off. He's cocky—he took you from under the noses of the police.

She strained to remember anything else she'd heard Aidan or Sean talk about when discussing the killer.

Like most control freaks, he's got his routine. He gets very upset when it's disturbed. Look at what happened to me the last time I got between him and his precious plan.

She could use that, all of it, against the killer. He was a control-oriented, overconfident, and routine-obsessed person. If she acted unpredictably, took bigger risks than he did, and was able to upset his plans for the evening, she might keep him off guard long enough to get away.

And she would definitely tell Sean she loved him the next time she saw him.

Chapter 73

"Where is Diaz? Is he able to answer any questions?" Sean asked Aidan when his partner picked up the cell phone again.

"They're bringing him out right now. After I talk to him, do you want me to pick you up or do you want to meet at the precinct?"

"Pick me up."

The sound became muffled as Aidan talked briefly with Diaz. Cell phone clenched in his hand, Sean waited impatiently, trying not to think of Claire and a killer who called her "sweet prey."

"He couldn't help much," Aidan said a few moments later. "He was out cold when the guy got away. He did say Claire was actively fighting the killer, and she almost managed to get away at least once. The only reason she got caught was she took the time to warn Diaz about the gun."

Sean pinched the bridge of his nose, using pain to help himself focus.

"Olivia said the same thing," Aidan continued, knowing what his partner was going through. "Claire was thinking and plotting from the moment they were captured. Olivia also said the guy was losing it at the end. He was screaming at her when she hid in the attic."

"Good," Sean said. "If Claire keeps her wits about her, it gives us an edge. Wilkes is shrewd, but he's been off balance since the night he met Claire and she ruined the Mendes girl for him. That's why he had to keep coming after her. She upset his sick little world."

"Keep going," Aidan said, getting into his car and starting it. "I like that line of thought."

"What line of thought?" Sean asked, pacing Afton's office.

"He's off balance, has been since he met Claire and she turned his life upside down. He's got to get back in control, and Claire is the key. Where would he take her to do that?"

"He loves his rituals, his routine. And with what we now know about his juvenile offense, I'm betting there has to be some symbolism in his choice of victims. Routine and symbols," Sean said again, thinking out loud.

"When you say routine, what does that mean? He always does things in a certain sequence, or is the routine in the planning, or is it covering his tracks?"

"Keeley said the routine in some cases is quite elaborate, involving days of ritualistic activities. With other killers, the routine could be something as simple as completing the act according to plan."

"Which Wilkes was unable to do in the Mendes case because of Claire," Aidan pointed out.

"So the ritual could be the act itself, and the symbolism . . ." Sean muttered. Suddenly he stilled. "You don't suppose he'd go back to the scene of one of the other crimes?"

Aidan considered it. "There's no evidence that he fixated on the location in the past."

"Wilkes was always successful in the past—until Claire stumbled over him at the wrong time. He never got closure with Mendes because he was interrupted. I think he might be taking Claire back to finish the job this time. He knows the location. He's comfortable there, it's his turf."

Aidan shot through a light just as it went red, grateful that weeknight traffic was light in D.C. "I'll pick you up in a few minutes."

"Go straight to the school," Sean said. "That's where I'll be."

"No! Don't go there without backup. He's armed with a gun and a knife, and he has a hostage."

"You want to back me up, get your ass over there."

"At least leave the phone line open," Aidan said quickly, "so I won't head in blind."

"It's open."

Sean shoved his phone on a belt clip and turned to Afton, who had been listening with wide eyes. "Go downstairs and sit with the security guard until a policeman comes for you." As he spoke, Sean checked his weapon with a few swift motions.

Afton surprised Sean by standing on tiptoe and kissing his cheek. "For luck. It's an Irish thing." She kissed his other cheek. "That's for Claire."

"Thanks. We'll both need it."

Sean left the office and headed for the stairs, but the elevator was waiting with doors open. Within two minutes, he was running down the path Claire had taken the night of the Mendes murder.

"Where are you, Aidan?" he said on the cell phone.

"Less than three miles away."

Sean acknowledged and kept running. With every step, he pushed back thoughts of what Claire must be going through and the anger he felt at himself for allowing it to happen in the first place.

I never should have let her out of my sight.

Once he had her back, he'd be damned sure she didn't leave his side again. He couldn't imagine his life without her, and he'd never even told her. He'd thought there would be plenty of opportunities once the case was closed. Now he was running out of time.

Hold on, Claire. Hold him off, fight, kick, bite, gouge—whatever you have to do. Just stay alive. Please, love. Stay alive.

Chapter 74

Washington, D.C.
Wednesday night

Wilkes looked in the rearview mirror, then in both side mirrors. Nobody was following him. He dug the gun into his prey's ribs until she flinched. "I knew it would work this time," he said, smiling. "Ah, Marie Claire, this will make up for everything."

We'll just have to see about that, you smug son of a bitch.

She turned toward him and spoke in the most casual voice she could manage. "So, do you have a name?"

He stared at her for an instant. She should be cringing and crying, but there she sat like he was her date instead of her killer. "Why should I tell you?"

"Okay, I'll just keep using all the lovely, nasty words that run through my mind when I look at you."

He laughed, his confidence unaffected by her insult. He knew her name and she didn't know his, and that made him smarter than she was.

"What do you think my name is?" His voice was taunting as he jammed the gun against her ribs again.

Claire pretended to take the question seriously. "I'd have to say you look like a Jim to me. I almost married a guy named Jim once, so I should know."

"Ah, so I remind you of an old flame, someone you loved."

"Not really. The guy turned out to be a retrograde ass-hole. And to be frank, he was lousy in bed, though I didn't realize it at the time." Claire looked the killer up and down as if assessing his potential. "Yeah, you're definitely a Jim."

"And you're a foulmouthed little whore, Marie Claire. I can see I've chosen well," the man said, tightening his hand on the steering wheel.

She sat back in her seat and shut her mouth, figuring the points for round one had gone to her. When she looked out the window, she recognized where they were. Her heart began to beat a little faster.

She said nothing as they drove around Dupont Circle, then turned and headed in the direction of the middle school where Renata Mendes had been murdered. Claire was surprised when he slowed down and parked the car several blocks away from the school.

"Now what, Jim?"

"Don't call me that."

"Then give me a better name," she said.

"I'd prefer that you don't address me at all." Angrily he shut off the car and unlocked the doors.

Round two goes to me, Claire thought with grim satisfaction.

Unfortunately, she didn't have long to savor her victory. Her captor reached across her, opened her door, and used the pressure of the gun against her ribs to force her out. She stood with the metal barrel digging into her as he got out of the car on her side, giving her no chance to get away.

She swallowed hard when he once again drew the knife from his pocket. It was stained with blood. Her stomach churned with the knowledge that the blood was hers. She held very still as he put his arm around her shoulders and rested the tip of the knife against her neck.

Then, to her utter astonishment, the killer leaned down and locked the pistol in the glove compartment of his car.

He met her blank look with a smirk. "Come along, sweet prey. The game wouldn't last very long if I had all the advantages."

The game.

She swallowed hard, feeling the knife shift with the motion. She reminded herself that for all her psychological digs at him, she was dealing with a dangerous man who had no conscience. Time for her to put phase two of her plan in action—get the hell away from him.

"Let's take a walk down memory lane," he said with an odd, cruel smile.

He kept his arm around her neck in an embrace that would probably look affectionate if it weren't for the knife in his hand. But no one was close enough to see that little detail. In fact, no one was around at all.

Claire walked slowly. She never stopped watching him out of the corner of her eye, waiting for any break in his concentration. She lagged slightly and gained some distance from the knife blade. He didn't seem to notice, apparently lost in his own thoughts.

Or his ugly little fantasies, she thought. She didn't like the glittery look in his eyes.

She stopped short when she saw they'd reached the place where Renata Mendes had been murdered. The killer bumped into Claire, and she cringed when she felt his hard-on against her hip. She didn't need a psychology degree to figure out that he got off on murder.

"It's time for me to make things right. You understand, don't you? Run, Marie Claire. Run!"

She stood, frozen by the certainty that once she started running, he would chase after her just as he had done before. But this time he could catch her. This time he would kill her.

That was why he'd brought her here, to kill her the way he hadn't done weeks ago. *Ah, Marie Claire, this time will make up for everything.*

"Is it the knife?" he asked when she remained motionless. "Here, I'll give you a head start, just like you had before." He lowered the knife from her neck and gave her a hard shove.

Claire realized he'd pushed her in the direction she'd run that night, toward the narrow path that ultimately led to Dupont Circle. *Not this time, asshole. We do things my way tonight.*

She shifted her weight and sprinted away from the direction he'd chosen for her.

"What are you doing? That isn't the right way, Marie Claire!" the man shouted after her. "Come back here, you're doing it all wrong!"

Claire didn't waste her breath taunting him. She just ran as hard as she could toward the main building of the middle school. Footsteps behind her warned that he was following.

"You can't cheat, you little whore! You're doing it wrong!"

The rising edge of hysteria in his voice made her run faster toward the school. She cried out when her path was suddenly blocked by a tall chain-link fence that encircled the school. She hadn't seen it in the darkness. She looked behind her and saw the killer approaching fast.

She jammed the toe of her shoes through the links and grabbed on with both hands. Panting, she climbed the fence like a ladder and heaved herself over the top. She staggered to her feet and began running again, glancing back only long enough to see the killer awkwardly making his way to the top of the fence. He hadn't let go of his knife, which forced him to climb one-handed.

That's an advantage, she told herself. *You can climb faster, so go up.*

Claire ran around the side of the old brick school, using her lead to briefly study the exterior of the building. An old metal fire escape went down the side of the three-story building and stopped just above the ground. She jumped but couldn't quite reach the ladder to pull it down.

Looking around, she found a large metal trashcan the students used during recess. She ignored the smell and flipped the can over, then hopped onto it and reached for the ladder. This time she was able to pull it toward her and start climbing.

She heard a shout behind her, and kicked the trashcan away, figuring that would buy her a few seconds. There was a scraping sound below her, but she was on the first level of the building and moving up before the killer even managed to grab the ladder. The man stopped shouting and instead poured all his energy into pursuing her.

She turned a corner on the iron platform and began climbing the fire escape to the third floor. She was high enough to have a good view, but she didn't see anyone who could help her.

"Fire!" Claire screamed, knowing better than to call for help in a city. "There's a fire at the school. *Fire!*"

"Shut up, you bitch," the man panted below her as he began to climb to the second story.

Claire made her way to the top floor, but didn't go on the roof. She might get trapped there. Instead, she decided to take her chances inside the school building itself. Maybe there would be a phone or an alarm she could trigger. But first she had to get through the window, which seemed to be securely locked.

She took one step back and drove her foot through the glass, ignoring the burning when glass cut through her skin. Hurriedly she reached through the jagged opening and released the simple metal slide that secured the window, cutting herself again in the process. She opened the window, swung her leg over the side, and found herself inside at the end of the hallway. She slammed the window shut and locked it again. Let him cut himself getting in. Maybe the bastard would hit a vein and bleed to death.

Below her, the killer grunted as he climbed the third flight of stairs. He was winded and had finally been forced to put his knife away in order to haul himself hand over hand up the fire escape. He couldn't believe Marie Claire was getting away from him again. His frustrated rage gave him the strength to surge up the last of the steps and break through the remnants of the window.

Claire heard the killer behind her as she frantically went down the hall.

Locked. All the doors are locked!

She ran from classroom to classroom, stopping only long enough to rattle the doorknobs before moving on.

The only route that wasn't locked from the inside was the interior stairwell, so she went through the metal door marked Exit and raced down to the second floor. The ventilation window between floors was open. She stuck her head out and screamed, "Fire! Fire at the school!"

She took a breath to scream again, but heard the metal door above her slam open, and bolted down the next flight of stairs instead.

Chapter 75

Sean forced himself to slow down as he neared the school where Renata Mendes had been murdered. It wouldn't do Claire any good if he went storming blindly into the scene Wilkes had set up. At least, Sean was betting the killer had set something up at this location—betting Claire's life, in fact.

He shut off his cell phone and crept forward. But when he approached the former crime scene, he didn't see anyone or any sign that anyone had been there.

He melted into the shadows along the edges of the school's parking lot, trying to calm his breathing enough to listen for signs of a struggle or some other indication Claire was nearby. Then he heard a car, didn't see any headlights, and drew his gun just in case he'd gotten lucky and beaten the killer to the school.

A car approached and cruised the parking lot with its lights off. The driver cut the engine and coasted into the shadows beneath a large tree. Aidan stepped cautiously out of the car, looking around for his partner. He heard a signal from his childhood and moved swiftly toward the sound.

"Patrol unit found a red rental car with the partial plates Olivia identified parked about four blocks away," Aidan reported in a nearly soundless whisper against his cousin's ear. "I told them to secure the area, and that you were on the scene and I soon would be."

Sean made a gesture with his hand to indicate understanding. He turned bleak eyes to his cousin in the shadows. "I've already been to the site of the Mendes murder. Nothing. Maybe he didn't—"

The distant sound of a woman's scream cut off Sean's words. Even before the word *fire* registered, he was running in the direction of the scream with Aidan half a step behind him.

"It's coming from the side of the building, probably one of the stairwells with a window," Aidan said, running and assessing their entry points.

"Fire! Fire at the school!"

"That's my girl," Sean said fiercely.

He and Aidan came around the corner of the building near the trash Dumpsters and assaulted the old door. It took a few good kicks before the lock gave way.

"Which—" Aidan began.

Sean held up a hand for silence. A moment later they both heard the distant sound of running feet on the far side of the building.

"Fire!" Claire screamed, but Sean could barely hear it through the corridors.

"Hang on, Claire!" Sean shouted as he took off in the direction of the footsteps.

Aidan ran right behind him, wanting to urge a more cautious approach and knowing it was useless. Sean wasn't going to stop until he had Claire back safely and the killer was either out cold or dead.

Chapter 76

Claire's brilliant idea to go into the school didn't seem quite so brilliant right now. She tugged on another knob, but all the doors she tried on the first floor were locked. As she ran from door to door, she tried to follow the faint arrows on the floor that appeared to be a secondary fire escape route. She figured regulations would prohibit the locking of any doors along such a path.

So far, that theory hadn't panned out. And in the dark, it was hard to see anything, let alone find her way along unfamiliar hallways. She hadn't even found a fire alarm to pull.

Claire paused for just a second to catch her breath, thinking at any minute she should hear the sirens from the fire department. But all she heard was the sound of pounding feet in the hallway behind her. She ran to the end of the hall and was faced with double doors that led into the gymnasium. Locked doors.

She squinted in the dim light and spotted a fire extinguisher on the wall nearby. She yanked down the metal canister and used its weight to break out the glass pane in one of the gym doors. She stuck her arm through and turned the lock. With one tug, she was inside the gymnasium, pulling the door shut behind her. She wrapped her hands around the long bar, leaned back to make a counterweight out of her body, and looked over her shoulder.

It was a nice old-fashioned high school gym, the kind with slippery wooden floors and bleachers lining both walls. Unfortunately, there was only one set of doors, and they were right in front of her.

She was trapped.

Claire jumped as she saw the killer's face through the broken glass pane. She leaned further back, trying to use her weight to keep him from getting in while she struggled to turn the lock.

It was a losing battle. Even if someone had heard her and the fire department arrived in the next few minutes, she wouldn't be able to hold the door for that long. The killer was much stronger than she was. When she got too tired to hold the door against him, he would shove inside and see what she had already seen—there was nowhere left to run.

Okay, Aidan said that if you can't run, grab anything that could be a weapon and bash your attacker with it. Nose, throat, balls, in that order.

Breathing rapidly, she braced her feet, leaned back to hold the door, and looked frantically over her shoulder for something that could be a weapon. The only thing she could see was an orderly row of hand weights and barbells laid out on a pale exercise mat to her left.

The door leaped, jerking her forward. If she didn't let go of the bar, she would be pulled along with the door and land right in his arms. She pushed away and pivoted toward the row of weights on the floor nearby.

The killer was quicker. He grabbed her, but her bloody, sweaty wrist slipped right through his hand. With an enraged sound, he slashed at her with the knife.

Claire instinctively held her arm in front of her face as she fell toward the exercise mat. Her retreat and the killer's momentum brought them both crashing to the floor. She lay on her back, facing the killer as he lunged to his feet above her. She scrambled away from him as he came at her, swinging the knife in vicious arcs that made the air whistle.

Again she held up her arm to protect herself, then screamed with rage and pain when she felt the knife connect with her flesh. The killer laughed and kept coming.

She cried out again, a primal sound of frustrated fury that echoed in the empty gymnasium. She flipped onto her stomach and pulled herself along the floor. The barbells were almost within reach. When her hand connected with the cold, heavy weight of a barbell, she grabbed it so tightly that her nails broke at the quick.

The killer was straddling her, knife raised, certain of his triumph. She threw herself over onto her back and hurled the heavy weight at his face. It struck him on the temple, forcing his head around and away from her, giving her the opening she needed. With a grunt of effort, she drew her knee back toward her chest, then sent her foot shooting heel-first into the killer's bulging crotch.

With a high-pitched scream of agony he flew backward.

Sean and Aidan burst through the broken door just as Claire's heel connected. With guns drawn, they ran over to where Wilkes writhed on the wood floor, making inhuman sounds of pain. Aidan kicked the knife away from where it had fallen on the mat. Sean's foot went straight for the killer's balls, landing a brutal blow despite the protective hands the killer was holding between his legs. Wilkes let out another keening sound and abruptly stilled.

Sean jammed his weapon back in the holster, then turned and threw himself down on the mat next to Claire. Her arm and one leg were bloody. "Are you all right?"

Claire launched herself at Sean and wrapped her arms around him. She was shaking uncontrollably now that the whole thing was over, and she didn't trust herself to speak. She tried to get closer and squeezed him until her arms were numb.

He decided that anyone with her grip couldn't be too badly hurt. He buried his face in her hair and rocked her against his own trembling body. "That was too close, love," he said roughly. "Too goddamned close."

"L-Livvie?" Claire asked, terrified for her friend.

"Aidan says she probably broke her ankle bailing out of the attic window, but otherwise she's fine."

"Thank God." Claire loosened her hold on Sean enough to lean back and look at him for a moment. Then she pressed her mouth to his.

He kissed her back, urgently at first, then more gently as he finally realized that she was alive and in his arms again. He shifted to his side, then sat up and pulled her into his lap. She kept her arms tightly entwined around him, trying to reassure herself that he was really here and she was alive. She could feel the tremors making their way through his body, echoed in the shudders that were making her own hands tremble as she held him.

Aidan stood over them and grinned at the picture they made. He couldn't tell which one was more relieved—or more white.

"You going to share some of that loving with me?" he asked.

She shifted to look at him. "I'll kiss you later."

"Promises, promises," Aidan said. "Are you all right?"

"Now I am. How did you guys find me, and what the hell took you so long?"

"It looks like you had everything under control," Aidan said.

"Yeah, but it sure is nice to have good backup. Thank you. Both of you," she added, but had eyes only for Sean.

Wilkes groaned and made gagging noises. Sean slanted him a feral glance. Knowing what his partner was thinking, Aidan shook his head. Sean turned back to Claire as she watched the man who had terrorized her for over a month.

"Right in the family jewels, lady," Aidan said, feeling involuntary male sympathy for Wilkes. "That's got to hurt like hell."

"Actually, it didn't hurt me at all," Claire said.

Sean laughed and pressed a kiss to her temple. "Remind me never to piss you off, sweetheart."

"Five years of cardio kickboxing," she said. "Builds excellent leg muscles."

Aidan put his hand dramatically over his heart. "Will you marry me, Claire?"

"No way," Sean said, before she could respond. "Find your own Amazon. This one is mine."

Aidan shrugged, then caught sight of Sean in back. "Jesus. Which one of you is bleeding?"

"What?" Sean and Claire said together.

"Good thing backup and a medic unit are on the way," Aidan said. "There's blood all over Sean's back. I thought you said you weren't hurt, Claire." Aidan leaned over to examine the fresh red streaks on his partner's shirt.

"I'm not. I have a little cut on my neck, but nothing else hurts."

Sean tilted her chin up and thoroughly inspected her neck. "That one doesn't look too bad. It's already scabbing over. You must be cut somewhere else."

"Really, I'm not," Claire said. "Oh, a few little ones here and there, but nothing hurts."

Aidan reached down to probe her forearm.

"Ouch!" She glared up at him.

"Nothing hurts, huh?" Sean carefully drew her arms from around him and pushed aside her light cotton shirt to check the deep gash on her forearm.

"It didn't before. Now it does," Claire said, as her arm suddenly began to throb.

"Adrenaline is a great painkiller," Aidan said, "but it wears off fast."

"You're going to need stitches," Sean said grimly. "Lots of them."

He took off his shirt and wrapped it around the wound on her arm. Despite her hiss of pain, he applied firm pressure. Then he put his arms around her again and held her, talking nonsense in her ear to distract her.

They stayed that way until the other police units arrived, followed by four paramedics with two stretchers.

Chapter 77

"I'm not normally a needle fan," Claire said to Sean, "but whatever the doctor shot into my arm was good stuff. It feels much better, see?" She wiggled her fingers at Sean, trying to wipe the tight, grim expression off his face.

He said nothing, just surveyed the neat line of stitches down her arm while a muscle in his cheek twitched. She was sitting up in a hospital bed dressed in a ridiculous institutional gown. The whole thing reminded him way too much of the first time he'd seen her, bruised, concussed, and so beautiful it had rocked him back on his heels.

"I'm all right," Claire said. "Quit beating up on yourself."

"You came too close to dying tonight! We barely put the pieces together in time, and it was sheer luck that Olivia managed to get out of the attic to tell us about the car. Just a minute either way and—" He clenched his jaw and wrapped his fingers around Claire's uninjured hand. He didn't like to think what might have happened, but he had a whole file of morgue photos to haunt him.

"Hey," she said, squeezing his hand back, "if I'd been a few minutes off that first night, I wouldn't have seen Renata Mendes get killed. Then I never would have met you. That's worth a few close calls."

He shook his head but lifted her hand and kissed her palm.

"And speaking of a few minutes off, and almosts," she said, "I'm not going to miss this chance. There's no pressure here on you, I just promised myself I would say it as soon as I saw you again."

"What?" he asked.

"I love you." She smiled up at him. "Wow, that felt really good. I love you, Sean."

She repeated the words again. Then again, until he leaned down and kissed her, undone by her softly spoken words and the glow in her dark eyes.

"I think you're breaking hospital rules. Especially if there's tongue involved." Aidan stood in the doorway to the suture room, arms crossed over his chest.

"Beat it. I'm busy here," Sean growled.

"So, I just got off the phone with the investigator who handled Richard Wilkes's arrest twelve years ago." Aidan came into the room and sat down, ignoring his partner's words.

Sean sighed and lifted his mouth from Claire's. "Hold the good thoughts, promise? What did the detective say?"

"Pretty much what we figured. Wilkes had fixated on a Costa Rican girl who worked as a maid and cook in his father's household. When he was sixteen, he approached the girl and declared his affections, but she laughed it off, figuring he was just a kid with a crush."

"But he wasn't," Sean said. "He was a disaster waiting to happen."

"Yeah, well it turns out the maid had plenty of boyfriends to keep her busy. So many, in fact, that the investigator thought she might have a job on the side."

"She was turning tricks?"

"He didn't go that far. She sent most of her salary home to family in Central America. So she dated lots of the guys who worked in the house and on the grounds, and if they gave her presents and money, she certainly didn't turn them down," Aidan said.

"Let me guess. Wilkes found out about this?" Sean asked.

"You got it. He flipped. Called her a whore and said his money was as good as the gardener's and chauffeur's. He assaulted the girl, pretty violently I guess. She went to the hospital afterward and was talked into pressing charges by the staff there."

"So how come he's walking around free today?" Claire asked.

"His daddy had money and a good lawyer. He paid the girl to go back to her own country and keep her mouth shut, then the lawyer got the charges reduced to harassment." Aidan shrugged. "Wilkes did court-ordered counseling until he turned eighteen, then was declared rehabilitated."

"Rehabilitated, my ass," Sean said. "If we're correct about the homicides we think Wilkes is linked to, the first one was committed within six months of his 'rehabilitation.'"

Sean looked at Claire and clenched his jaw at the thought that everything she had endured was the result of a rich father and a system that was too easy to manipulate in favor of violent juveniles.

"Yeah, he's a whack job, all right. He fit Keeley's profile pretty well—thank God. Otherwise, we never would have known where to look for you, Claire."

"How *did* you find me?"

"Sean figured it out," Aidan said. "He thought Wilkes would need closure on the killing that went wrong, so he went to the schoolyard."

"My hero," Claire said softly.

Sean shifted in his chair. "It was a team effort—you, Olivia, Aidan, the fingerprint lab, homicide team, Diaz."

"What about the whole Camelot connection?" Claire asked. "Was Wilkes a member?"

"No, but his company had been a corporate sponsor. His picture was on the wall in Afton's conference room. We realized tonight that you must have seen it there the night of the first murder."

"The conference room? That never occurred to me. I was thinking only of the catalogue."

"So were we," Sean said.

Claire hesitated, then asked the question that had been bothering her. "What if he pleads insanity and gets 'rehabilitated' again?"

"It won't fly," Sean said. "He shot a computer hacker this morning. We figure he used the guy's technical abilities to track down where you were."

"How could he do that?"

"He hacked into Sean's home phone records," Aidan said, "noted the new pattern of calls to Virginia, and traced the phone number to its address through another website. Once Wilkes had the address of the safe house, he was done with the guy. So he blew his head off."

"That's why you're anxious to test the gun Wilkes locked away in the glove compartment, right?" Claire asked.

"You bet," Sean said. "I'm no lawyer, but the chain of events we saw tonight proves premeditation, planning, and clear knowledge that Wilkes knew what he was doing was wrong. Otherwise, he wouldn't have tried so hard to cover his tracks with everything from Renata Mendes to now."

"That poor girl," Claire said. "I still don't remember that night. Is there any chance of linking Wilkes to her murder with physical evidence alone?"

"We'll do our best." Sean stroked Claire's cheek. "I'm glad you don't remember that night, love. You have enough horrible memories from tonight to last a lifetime." He pressed a kiss into the palm of her hand.

"They're not *all* horrible memories." She smiled and drew a finger across his lips.

A voice spoke from the hall. "Oh, so I get left alone in the frigid X-ray department," Olivia said, "and you're having a little slap and tickle with the love of your life. That's gratitude." She sat in a wheelchair with her splinted left leg sticking straight out and tried to look mad despite the grin that kept sneaking over her mouth.

"Livvie!" Claire tried to get up to hug her friend, but Sean held her back.

"You stay put until the doctor says otherwise," he said.

Aidan wheeled Olivia over to Claire so she could gently hug her friend. Both women had tears in their eyes as they held each other.

"I was so worried, honey," Olivia said. "I thought I'd done the wrong thing by hiding, and maybe I'd never see you again. I would never have forgiven myself." Two tears slipped down her cheeks.

"You did exactly right," Claire said, pulling back to look at her friend's pale face and smile at her reassuringly. "Sean and Aidan say you saved my life."

Sean leaned over and gave Olivia a hard kiss and a gentle hug. "Claire's right. Without your help—" He broke off and hugged Olivia again, his throat closing up as he thought about how close it had been.

Aidan looked up as the attending physician entered the suture room, which was by now crowded with people.

"I heard we had an escapee from the X-ray lab," the young doctor said with a grin, "and I suspected I knew where she might be hiding out. Ms. Goodhue, you're going to have to go back and get that leg properly splinted."

"But what about Claire?" Olivia asked. "Will she be all right?"

"She'll do just fine with some rest and tender loving care, which I see is already being taken care of," the doctor said, winking at Sean. "Back to X-ray with you."

Olivia protested, but a nurse came and took control of her wheelchair. *"Merde!"* Olivia said. "Claire gets to stay and snuggle with two handsome men and I'm left alone in an icebox with radioactive machinery."

"I'm on my way to rescue you," Aidan said. "And Afton will be here soon."

"Give us a few minutes first," the nurse said, then pushed Olivia down the hall.

"Where's Wilkes?" Sean asked.

"Oh, he's headed up to surgery right now," the doctor said.

"Surgery?" Claire asked.

"Yup. He'll probably lose at least one testicle. They're swollen up like grapefruit," the doctor cheerfully informed her.

Claire's jaw dropped. "I didn't think I kicked him that hard."

Sean smiled grimly and said not one word.

"I see no reason to keep you, Ms. Lambert," the doctor said. "Come back and have your stitches removed in seven to ten days. Unless you have any questions, I'm due in X-ray."

The doctor left before Claire could gather her wits enough to decide if she did have any questions.

"I'll go protect Olivia," Aidan said, heading out the door.

Sean looked over at Claire as she shifted on the bed, pulling up the gaping neckline of the hospital gown. He waited until she turned her face up to his. "How are you feeling? Still on an adrenaline rush?"

"No. I just feel a little tired."

Sean looked at her intently. "So your head is all clear right now? No medication, adrenaline, hormones, or anything else that might interfere with your judgment?"

Claire stilled. "Nothing is clouding my thinking right now."

"Good. I love you, Claire. I've never said that to a woman before."

"You know I love you, too."

"I hope you do. I hope it's not just adrenaline or something, because I'm not letting you take the words back."

"I don't want to."

"Good," Sean said, smiling at her. "God, I can't believe you're here right now. I wanted to kill Wilkes with my bare hands when I learned you'd been kidnapped. I wanted to die myself when I thought we might not make it in time."

"But you did make it," she said, laying her hand against his cheek.

He turned and kissed her fingers. "I know the last few weeks must seem like an out-of-body experience for you.

But I've been on adrenaline jags before, and I want you to know that what I feel is very real. I'd say I'll spend the rest of my life protecting you, but God knows you don't seem to need it. So I'll just say that I want to spend the rest of my life with you. Will you marry me, sweetheart?" Sean held his breath as he waited for her response.

Speechless with emotion, Claire stared at him while tears filled her eyes.

"I know it's too soon to get married right away," he said, rubbing the back of his neck and cursing himself for dumping it on her all at once. "I mean, we've only known each other a month and all. But that's where I'm going with this, and I wanted to know if that's where you want to go, too."

The tears in Claire's eyes spilled over, and she laughed with the sheer joy of being alive and being in love. "I can't believe this! I thought I was going to have to take you home tonight and throw myself at you again."

Sean grinned back at her. "You can throw yourself at me anytime you want. I'll always be there to catch you."

Claire tunneled her hands into his hair and pulled him down for a thorough kiss.

In the hallway outside the suture room, Aidan smiled and walked away, whistling silently. Olivia owed him five bucks.

Claire finally pulled back. "I love you, Sean Richter. And I do want to marry you. But I think we should have a long engagement."

"Whatever you want," he said, stroking butterfly kisses over her mouth and cheeks.

She laughed even as his lips brushed hers. "In fact, considering that we just met a couple of weeks ago, I think we should date for a while first," she said, smiling wickedly in anticipation of his reaction. "You know, holding hands and looking shyly at each other."

Sean's head whipped up. He took one look into her dancing black eyes, then groaned and kissed her again before she got any other brilliant ideas.